dark
talents

MAX TURNER

dark talents

TWO BOOKS IN ONE

night runner AND end of days

ST. MARTIN'S GRIFFIN
NEW YORK

DARK TALENTS: NIGHT RUNNER copyright © 2008 by Steven Maxwell Turner and END OF DAYS copyright © 2010 by Steven Maxwell Turner. All rights reserved. Printed in the United States of America. For information, address St. Martin's Press, 175 Fifth Avenue, New York, N.Y. 10010.

www.stmartins.com

ISBN 978-1-250-03862-3 (trade paperback)

St. Martin's Griffin books may be purchased for educational, business, or promotional use. For information on bulk purchases, please contact Macmillan Corporate and Premium Sales Department at 1-800-221-7945, extension 5442, or write specialmarkets@macmillan.com.

Night Runner was first published in Canada by Harper*Trophy*Canada™, an imprint of HarperCollins Publishers Ltd

First Edition: December 2013

10 9 8 7 6 5 4 3 2 1

Night Runner

For my mother
(gift of life and all that)

Chapter 1
The Visitor

My name is Daniel Zachariah Thomson. Everyone calls me Zack. I live in the Nicholls Ward of the Peterborough Civic Hospital, and this is the story of how I died, twice.

I know what you're thinking: *The Nicholls Ward—isn't that the loony bin? The nuthouse? Where they put people who torture squirrels or think they're Julius Caesar? That explains it. Only a loo-loo would think he could die two times and still be around to talk about it.* Well, the truth is a funny thing. It can be its clumsy self and it doesn't matter what anyone believes. I guess it's like way back in the Middle Ages when everyone and his dog thought the world was flat. That you could sail too far from home and your ship would drop right off into space. The whole planet was wrong on that one, and it didn't change the truth one pinch. My story is sort of like that. Read it and see for yourself. I'm not crazy. I'm here for different reasons.

The other people on the ward aren't all crazy, either. My neighbours all have mental disorders, that's true, but these are never as bad as you might think. Certainly not like the villains in Hollywood movies who turn their victims into wax dummies or serve them up for dinner. Most of the patients in the Nicholls Ward are older people. They need help just to eat. I don't expect to see them appearing in a horror movie anytime soon. They're all pretty harmless.

But I'm different. I stay up all night, for one thing. That's when my whole life happens—when the others have all taken their happy pills and are snoozing away. I do ordinary stuff, like read, or lift weights. And I run every night, usually outside, but I love movies, so if there's a good one on TV, I'll hop on the treadmill instead and watch it in the fitness room. I love video games, too. There's a big-screen TV in the common room. It takes up half a wall. When you wire up a game, the characters are almost as big as you are.

On good nights, my friend Charlie comes to visit. He's my major contact with the outside world, and because of this, and the fact that my schedule is a bit off, the hospital staff usually let him stay after visiting hours have ended, so long as the two of us aren't making too much trouble. Chaos is one of Charlie's specialties. I'm sure he could have a room of his own here. He'd fit right in.

Life in a mental ward is pretty routine. Meals, naps, TV time, medication and lights out—it all takes place according to a carefully crafted schedule. It helps keep everyone stable. I have a little more leeway than the others because I'm the only one awake after ten o'clock, but even my nights follow a regular pattern. You can't exactly set a clock by it, but it never changes very much, either—dinner, free time, exercise, breakfast, reading, sleeping. But all this changed the night a strange old man crashed his motorcycle through the front doors of the lobby and destroyed our big-screen television.

I was in the fitness room when it happened. It was about three in the morning. One of my all-time favourites, *Terminator*, had just ended, but my eyes were still glued to the small television hanging from the ceiling. A woman with hair so perfect it must have been made of plastic was telling me all about the wonders of Miracle Glow hair care products. The way she carried on, this stuff was our ticket to world peace. While she yammered away, interviewing other people whose lives were now fairy tales thanks to Miracle Glow, I pounded the treadmill. My shoes were practically melting. It was a night like any other. Until I heard a noise like an asteroid hitting the building. I felt it, too. A tremor that came right up through the floor. A second crash quickly followed, and the wail of a police siren.

In a flash I was out in the hall, past the reception counter and into the lobby. The whole time I was thinking, *He's really done it this time.* Charlie, that is. But when I saw the devastation, I knew right away it had to be somebody else. Not even Charlie could have managed this. The lobby was a total disaster. There was glass everywhere. The outside doors were blown right off their hinges.

The common room was even worse. The ping-pong table was tipped over and furniture was scattered all over. Actually, this was partly my fault. Well, *our* fault, Charlie's and mine. As soon as everyone had gone to bed we'd set it up that way so we could have a ping-pong fight. Charlie had wanted to celebrate the end of the school year, and so we'd spent a good hour pelting one another with ping-pong balls. Forts of overturned furniture were still set up all around the room. And we'd forgotten to put the ping-pong table back. I could see tire marks on the floor where the driver had swerved to miss it. The black streaks led straight to the wall where the TV used to hang. It was on the floor now in about a million pieces. I could tell right away that no amount of Krazy Glue was going to bring it back from the dead.

Right in the middle of the floor was the driver. He looked about seventy, with long black hair streaked with white and grey. It stuck out in all directions, as if he'd just been attacked by a tornado. He was on his hands and knees. His long overcoat looked too tight, and his mismatched gloves had the fingers cut out of them. Not the best for crawling across broken bits of TV. Sitting against the wall where the television used to be was his motorcycle, though I'm guessing it wasn't actually his since it said "Peterborough Police" on it. The siren was still wailing and the red and blue lights were flashing all over the white walls.

The old man looked up at me with milky blue eyes. He seemed dazed. Like he was trying to bring me into focus but couldn't quite manage it. He looked like a homeless person, or an undercover police officer dressed like a homeless person, in which case, his costume was perfect. On the ground in front of him was an old top hat smushed flat as a pancake, and it looked as though there were about ten layers of clothing sandwiched underneath his coat. That explained why he wasn't in pieces like the television. The padding must have saved him.

I glanced over my shoulder at the reception counter, where Nurse Ophelia, Nurse Roberta and the other overnight staff normally hung out. You could usually spot at least one security guard. Someone had to be there in case the police showed up with a new patient, which often happened just after the bars closed. No one was in sight now.

I made my way over to the old man as quickly as I could. I was worried he might try to get up and fall back into the sea of glass. Down the hall just ahead of me, a door opened and someone stuck his head out. It was Jacob, my red-haired neighbour. I waved for him to come over and give me a hand. He started up the corridor, then turned around. He did this a couple of times, turning back and then turning away again. His hands were over his ears and he was muttering something to himself, so I just let him pace in front of his room and turned my attention back to the old man. His head was shaking back and forth like he was dizzy, and he was mumbling to himself too, so I put my ear closer to his mouth.

"Hurry . . . hurry up . . ." he was saying. I couldn't tell if he was talking to me or to himself. I asked him if he was okay, but he didn't answer. He just shook his head one more time and grunted. Then he took hold of my arm. His grip was strong, which surprised me. I wondered for a second if his fingers were going to punch right through my scrubs. As he stood up, bits of glass fell from his overcoat. I noticed a small cut on his forehead and another across the bridge of his nose. Blood dribbled down his face and into the stubble on his chin, which was grey and black and white, just like his hair. He looked pretty gory, but I couldn't help myself. I just kept staring, I guess because I felt sorry for him. All the Miracle Glow in the world wasn't going to turn his life into a fairy tale. He smelled like the inside of a wine barrel. And, cuts or no cuts, unless he had a good explanation for all the remodelling he'd just done, when Nurse Roberta showed up, he was in for it.

The old man shook his head a few more times, then he looked me over again. It was like he was waking up or something. His eyes came into focus. He stared at my face for a second, then sort of nodded. A smile spread up one cheek. It made his eyes go wrinkly. He clenched his fists, leaned back and turned his head to the ceiling like he owed the man upstairs a miracle-sized favour.

"Thank heavens, boy!" he said. "Finally . . . I've found you."

Chapter 2
Breakout

The old man put a hand on my shoulder and gave it a firm squeeze. Then he glanced down the hall at Jacob, who was still rocking back and forth with his hands over his ears. A door opened beside him, then another farther down. A pair of curious heads poked their way into the corridor. I recognized the Chicago Man and Sad Stephen. With all the noise coming from the siren, we were going to have a lot of company before long.

As soon as the visitor saw the others, he shoved me towards the motorcycle. Now, I was only fifteen years old, but I was tall for my age, and strong, too. Still, I had trouble staying on my feet when he pushed me away. He had a lot of oomph in those arms. By the time I had my balance, he was right beside me again. His head was swivelling every which way. I couldn't imagine what he was looking for. Behind him, through the window, I could see the parking lot was empty. Hardly surprising. Most people wouldn't choose to visit a mental ward at three in the morning.

"Well, what are you waiting for, boy, the Apocalypse?" he said. "You're going to be worm food if you don't get a move on." He looked at me with his eyebrows high on his forehead and a weird expression on his face, like I was supposed to jump on the motorcycle and ride it to freedom or something.

"He's coming," he continued. "He could be here any second." The man put a hand on my shoulder and pushed me gently towards the motorcycle again. He looked back over his shoulder at the parking lot. I got the feeling Darth Vader was about to waltz in and lightsabre us both in half.

When he noticed I wasn't moving, his nostrils flared and an expression of annoyance came over his face. He reached down, grabbed the handlebars of the police cycle and picked it up himself. That was when he noticed the front forks were all mangled.

"Damn piece of garbage!" he shouted. "No wonder the police can't catch anybody." Then he tossed the bike aside as if it deserved a special place in the junkyard for letting us down. It smashed into the wall, and the fierce roar of the siren turned into something that sounded more like the mewing of a dying cat. "We're going to have to run for it," he said.

The wine smell on his breath was so strong I started to gag. He didn't give me time to recover. Instead, he just grabbed my scrubs near the collar and started to sprint. And just like that, I was practically airborne. And I had no control whatsoever over where I was going. The guy must have been bionic or something.

He hauled me through the lobby and out the gaping hole that had once been the main entrance. Our feet made crunching noises on the broken glass. I tried to work his hand free from my shirt, but it was as if he'd tied his fingers into knots. I couldn't budge them.

Then a bunch of things happened, all at the same time. I heard

Nurse Ophelia shouting my name. She was somewhere behind me. About six police cruisers pulled into the parking lot. Two security guards ran into the reception area on our left and started chasing us. And someone shouted, "DON'T MOVE!"

Well, maybe the old man was deaf. Maybe he was so used to hearing strange voices that he'd learned to ignore them. Or maybe he didn't understand English all that well and thought "DON'T MOVE!" meant slip it into overdrive, because that's what he did. And he was fast. Even hauling me alongside him, I bet he would have beaten half the Canadian Olympic team. We almost made it off the lot, but just as we were approaching the street, I heard a sound like a firecracker. The old man slowed a bit. Then a whole bunch of firecrackers went off, and he let go of me, stumbled and fell.

I couldn't keep my balance, so I fell down beside him. I scraped an elbow on the asphalt, and my hands hit something warm, wet and sticky. Then I rolled up onto my knees. The old man was lying right beside me. Blood was pooling underneath him. It was all over my hands and clothes. And it was all over him.

He'd been shot. Many times.

I felt the old man's hand digging into my arm again. He was struggling to speak.

"Run . . ." he said. Then he coughed several times. "Don't let the cops get you. He's coming. Run!"

Chapter 3
The Second Coming

As the blood spread across the asphalt, the old man's eyes went glassy and the strain on his face seemed to go away. A slow smile spread up one side of his mouth.

I didn't know what to do. Smile or no smile, this man was dying. And there was blood everywhere. I started to get dizzy. My eyes spun in quick circles, like they couldn't focus all of a sudden. Everything went red. My teeth started grinding. I was so confused and agitated that all I could do was put my hands against the sides of my head and groan. To be scared or sad would have made more sense, but all I could think was that this was wasteful. I should have been able to do something.

An instant later, police officers were everywhere. Hands took hold of my arms, helped me up and pulled me away. I didn't resist. I just turned my head so I could get one last look. The old man's milky eyes were glazed over. His breathing had stopped. His smile looked wooden now. Frozen on a dead face. Then, just before some-one stepped in the way, his head tipped sideways in my direction. One of his eyes twitched and closed. It made him look as if he was winking at me.

I don't remember if I said anything as the police took me inside. I kept trying to look over my shoulder to see what was happening, but a group of officers had formed a ring around him faster than you could say *shoot*, and the two escorting me didn't slow down until I was back inside the lobby.

Nurse Ophelia was waiting there.

"Oh, no . . ." she said when she saw me. I was still covered in the old man's blood.

"It's not mine," I said.

Nurse Ophelia stepped behind the nurse's station and came back a second later with a handful of tiny square packages. She started ripping them open. I noticed her hands were shaking.

"We'd better get that off," she said.

Inside the packages were folded wipes that smelled like medicine. She gave one to me and started wiping at my face. She was a bit more clumsy than normal. Or maybe it was just that I was still dizzy. All this commotion was probably making everyone a little jumpy.

I was just getting down to the business of cleaning my hands when I heard a loud screech. It was the kind of noise a car makes when it stops too quickly—tires skidding on asphalt.

I looked up. A train of police cruisers was pulling out of the lot, and right in the middle of them was an ambulance. It had stopped suddenly, halfway onto the road. It tilted a bit to one side, then the back doors flew open and someone jumped out. It was the crazy old man! He looked around, then his eyes settled on me and he started sprinting back to the ward. A police car was in the way, but he didn't even break stride. He actually stepped right on top of the hood, cleared the roof in a single leap, then jumped off the rear bumper.

The police in the lobby reached for their guns, but the old man obviously didn't care a pinch.

Then he saw Nurse Ophelia and stopped dead.

I couldn't blame the man for staring. Nurse Ophelia was probably the most beautiful woman on the face of the earth. When we were window shopping last Christmas, she caused three accidents just walking from Brock Street to Simcoe. Unless you were blind, she pretty much stopped you in your tracks.

Well, the old man looked at her and his face calmed, but then his brow wrinkled up again, as though he'd just remembered he was supposed to be annoyed. He pointed a finger at her. "Get him out of here," he said. Then he turned to go, and I don't know if it was because of all the police lights or what, but for just an instant, his watery blue eyes glowed red, just like a person in a photograph when the flash doesn't work right. I'm not even certain it really happened, because he sprinted off so fast that no one even had time to take aim and fire.

I looked at Nurse Ophelia and the officers nearby. Some still had their guns out. They looked stunned. I don't think if Santa Claus had flown down in a flying saucer you would have seen more mouths hanging open. One woman started talking into a radio that was clipped to her shoulder.

"Yeah, I think so. The same guy . . ." The way her voice sounded, it was like she didn't believe herself. I didn't hear the rest because Nurse Ophelia quickly took hold of my hand and started pulling me down the hall.

"Where are we going?" I asked.

One of the policemen interrupted before she could answer me. "We have to ask him some questions, ma'am," he said.

Nurse Ophelia barely slowed down. She just looked over her shoulder. "I'm going to get him cleaned up. I'll be right back."

When we got to my room she opened the door. It was dark inside. I like it that way, unless I'm reading.

"I want you to stay out of sight," she said. "Just for tonight."

I didn't really know what to say, so I nodded and took a bunch of the antiseptic wipes from her. I noticed her hands were still shaking.

"I'll get a hamper for your clothes," she said. "They're soaked. Try not to get the blood all over everything."

"What about that man?" I asked.

"Don't worry about him for now."

"Do you know him?"

Nurse Ophelia shook her head. "No. But he's gone. And I need you to focus on getting yourself tidied up. The police will have to talk to you soon." She pointed towards the house phone beside my desk. "You can buzz me after you've had a shower. And you might want to tidy up a little, just so no one gets lost in here trying to find you."

I looked at all the clothes on the floor. It wasn't that bad. There were at least two or three patches of tile that weren't covered.

"Do I have to talk to them?" I asked.

"The police? Yes. I would imagine so, given what's happened. Why?"

"The man on the motorcycle said someone was after me. And he warned me to stay away from the police."

Nurse Ophelia nodded slowly. "Right. Well, if you think this through carefully, Zachary, I'm sure you'll come up with a few reasons not to trust that man's advice."

She had a point. He was a little weird. But then again, so were the rest of us. And when a guy steals a motorcycle for you, tells you to scram, gets blasted full of holes and then comes back to life just to tell you the same thing all over again, well, maybe that guy is someone you should listen to.

Chapter 4
The Interview

I'd just finished kicking the last of my dirty clothes under the bed when I heard a knock at the door. An officer with a round head and big arms was standing in the hall. The badge on his chest said "Officer Cummings." His partner was a brown-haired woman with a pretty smile. Her name was Officer Philips. She asked if they could come in. I said yes and then had to answer a bunch of questions about what happened. I sat on my bed the whole time and pretty much told them everything. Officer Cummings sat at my desk and wrote it all down in a notepad.

"Isn't it a little late to be exercising?" he said when I finished.

"Sunlight gives me hives," I explained, "so I do everything at night."

I looked at him when I said this. I wanted to make sure that he believed me, but he wasn't looking at me. He was looking at Nurse Ophelia, who had arrived from down the hall and was now standing in the doorway.

"Is everything all right here?" she asked.

I thought for just a second that Officer Cummings's eyes were going to roll out of his head and onto the floor, but then he got it together and half stood. His face was a little pink. "Yes. Fine, ma'am. I was just asking a few, um . . ."

"Please sit down," she insisted.

"Isn't it a little unusual for a boy to be up at this time of night?"

"Zachary keeps a unique schedule. It's necessary. He requires very specialized medical attention. It's one of the reasons he's here and not in a foster home. Do you have any other questions for him? I'd like to get him his dinner. And he needs some rest."

"Of course. Just a few more." He sat back down and clicked his pen a few times. Then he cleared his throat. "This guy—did he say anything to you? Did he threaten you?"

"Not really," I said. "He only said what I told you already. That I should run. And that someone was after me." I almost added that he'd told me to avoid the police, but I didn't want to offend anybody.

Officer Cummings smiled. "You don't need to worry about anything. There'll be a car here twenty-four hours a day until we catch him."

I tried to look impressed, but the truth was, the old man had been shot so many times he should have looked like a cheese grater, and it had barely slowed him down. Unless they dropped a building on his head, they weren't ever going to stop him. I wasn't worried about him, anyway. He'd come to warn me. I wanted to know why.

"Was he armed?" Officer Cummings asked me. "Did he have a knife or a gun or anything?"

I shook my head. "Just a top hat."

"Did he offer you anything? Drugs, anything like that?"

"No." I said. "Well, he did offer me a ride."

"And it was just you and the other fellow who saw him? What's his name . . . ?" Officer Cummings leafed back through his pad. "Jacob?"

"Yeah. By the end, other people were in the hall too, but it was mostly just Jacob and me. I doubt he heard very much. He was pretty far away. And he had his hands over his ears."

"Is there anything else you can think of that might help us catch this guy?"

I glanced up at Officer Philips, who was leaning against the wall, then at Nurse Ophelia, who was still in the doorway. She moved her head just a little, like a mini nod, so I knew it was all right to answer.

"He smelled like he'd been drinking," I said.

"No doubt," said Officer Cummings. He flipped his pad closed. "Well, that does it for now. If we need anything else, we'll be in touch." He rose, tipped his head in a goodbye sort of way, then stepped out to wait in the hall.

Officer Philips lingered for a few seconds longer. "Are you going to be all right?" she asked.

I looked at Nurse Ophelia. She nodded and so I nodded.

"Is there anything we can do for you before we go?"

I did have some questions. "Is somebody after me?" I asked.

Officer Philips was about to answer when Nurse Ophelia cut in.

"No," she said quickly. "No one is after you, Zachary. You're perfectly safe here." Then she stepped aside so Officer Philips could leave.

I watched the two officers to see if they had anything to say about that subject, but apparently they didn't. I wasn't finished, though.

"How did he do it?" I asked.

Officer Philips looked confused. Her forehead wrinkled up. "What do you mean?"

"How did that man do all those things? He should have been a splat on the wall after that crash. Then he picked up the motorcycle and threw it. And he got up after being shot. He was supposed to be dead."

Officer Cummings was still waiting in the hallway. He perked up when he heard my question.

"Do you know what PCP is?" he asked.

I shook my head.

"Angel Dust?"

I didn't know that one either.

"Well, he was probably on drugs. I once arrested a guy who was so cranked up on speed, even with a bullet in his shoulder he just wouldn't quit. He had this cleaver—"

Officer Philips put her hand on his arm.

"Yeah. Well, the point is," he continued, "that old guy was probably on something potent. It's not hard to find if you know where to look. Makes you do all kinds of weird stuff. I wouldn't worry too much about it. He won't bother you again. Not with us here."

"So what was he warning me about?" I asked.

The officers looked at each other. They clearly didn't know. Nurse Ophelia answered for them.

"Nothing, Zachary. It was nothing."

Chapter 5
Family Resemblance

Once the officers were gone, Nurse Ophelia stepped into the hall and got the laundry hamper for my bloodied clothes. I still hadn't moved from the bed. She said something to me, but I wasn't really listening, not until she gave my shoulder a squeeze.

"Do you understand what I'm saying?" she asked.

I nodded and said yes.

"You aren't even listening," she said. Then she smiled. "You're going to be fine. I know you better than anyone, Zachary. There's nothing for you to worry about."

It was difficult to disagree with Nurse Ophelia when she smiled at you. And she *did* know me better than anyone. Unlike the other staff, she worked the night shift all the time. She looked out for me. Whenever a therapy session went bad, or if I got irritable with the other nurses, which sometimes happened if I got hungry before mealtime, she always smoothed things over.

"Would you like to go back to the fitness room and finish your run?" she asked.

I didn't know what to say. Running was usually a sure bet with me. And, like she said, she knew me better than anyone. But I knew her, too. And there was something she wasn't telling me.

"*Is* someone after me?" I asked.

Nurse Ophelia sighed. Her eyes suddenly looked very tired. I was hoping she might say something like, "No, of course no one is after you. Who would want to harm you? You're the greatest kid on earth. *Blah, blah, blah,*" but she didn't. Instead, she put her hand over her forehead like I was giving her a headache.

"I should get back to the desk," she said. "The cleanup crew will be here shortly. As soon as this mess is cleared away, I'll check in with you at dinner. We can talk then, okay?"

I nodded and watched while she backed out the door, pulling the hamper with my dirty scrubs behind her. I waited until the squeak of the wheels had faded down the hall, then I flicked on my reading light and picked up my copy of *The Hobbit*.

Of all the books ever written, *The Hobbit* is king. I've read it seven times. Captures, escapes, riddles, battles, magic swords and a magic ring, death and deception, goblins and elves and trolls and dragons, men who turn into bears, and giant eagles and wolves. It pretty much has it all. I think that's why I've always been a bit jealous of the main character, Bilbo. At the start, his life is pretty much the same thing, day after day, just like mine, until Gandalf the wizard knocks at his door. Then, in a snap, he's off on an adventure so grand it can hardly be packed between two book covers.

Well, that was exactly what I needed—a knock at the door and an adventure of my own. But I guess wizards were in short supply. Instead of Gandalf, I got a crazy old man on a stolen motorcycle who smelled like he'd had enough wine to drown a horse. And all he did was trash the lobby.

I opened the book and started reading. After a few minutes, I realized I was still staring at the same page. I started again, but the same thing kept happening. Instead of seeing Gandalf and Bilbo, I kept seeing the old man on the motorcycle. *"I've found you,"* he'd said. Like he'd recognized me. But from where? Nurse Ophelia took me bowling sometimes, and to movies. And, of course, window shopping at Christmas. But I couldn't remember ever seeing him before. How could he know me?

I read slowly for about another hour, my thoughts drifting from the book to the strange incident with the old man. Then I had to get up. I was starting to get hungry.

I'm sure you've had that hole-in-the-stomach feeling that everyone gets when they've missed a meal. For me, it was a lot worse. I'd get pain behind my eyeballs like someone was pinching them really hard, and my throat would get itchy. It might have been because I couldn't eat most foods, and so it was hard for my body to get all of the nutrients it needed. It might also have been related to my blood. I had a degenerative blood disease, so I needed to get transfusions a few times every year. Those were the worst. For days afterwards I felt like I'd been drinking gasoline. If I could have found the right foods or the right medications, my problems probably would have gone away, but that never happened. So I got hungry often. And it always made me irritable. I remember this one time when I was ten years old, the nurse on duty forgot to bring me my dinner. When she showed up just before sunrise to make sure I was safe in my room, I was so angry I tried to bite her. After that, Nurse Ophelia delivered all my meals. She was more dependable.

In the common room, a couple of guys in grey uniforms were sweeping up the glass. They both looked at me as I walked past them, like the mess was somehow my fault. Two policemen were leaning on the reception counter. They were chatting with Nurse Roberta. She was young, and I think most people found her quite attractive. I can't really separate how a person looks from how they treat me, so to me, she wasn't all that pretty. More like cranky and disappointed. I'm not saying she was a bad person, but once she yelled at me for not making my bed, and I was still sleeping in it.

As soon as I got closer to the counter, the two officers stopped talking. They both looked a bit embarrassed, as though they should have been hard at work doing something useful and not chatting up the hospital staff.

"Do you know where Nurse Ophelia is?" I asked.

Nurse Roberta pointed over her shoulder with a pen. "In the kitchen."

I found Nurse Ophelia making my dinner. I sat on one of the metal stools and watched her. She turned and slapped gently at my leg to get me to move out of the way. That was the closest she ever came to showing affection, when she hit people. I slid my stool over and she reached into the refrigerator behind me. She took out a small bag that was full of red syrup. I think it was strawberry.

"Stop scratching your throat," she said.

"I can't help it. It's itchy."

She squeezed the gooey flavouring into the blender with the rest of my dinner and fired it up. Once it was good and frothy, she poured it into a tall cup and stuck in a straw. I always drank my meals. Solid foods just didn't agree with me, so twice a day, it was bottoms up. My friend Charlie called these "brain cocktails." He said they looked like they could bring a zombie back to life. They were the only thing I ever ate. I think they must have had the same thing in them that coffee has, because I got a real jolt from them. And they were filling, too. Nurse Ophelia never made more than two in a night for me. Any more than that and I would have exploded.

My "brain cocktails" also had my meds in them. I wasn't sure exactly what I was taking, but I remember when I was younger having to swallow a lot of different stuff—pills and syrups—and

I got plenty of needles too, and lotions to put on my skin. They all had names that made them sound like they were made on the planet Mongo. Most of them made me sick. That might have been why the doctors kept changing their minds about what was wrong with me. Nothing really worked, and so they had to keep switching drugs all the time. After a while I stopped paying attention. It was too hard to keep track. To make things easier, Nurse Ophelia decided one day just to dump it all into my dinner. It was a pretty simple arrangement for me. She did all the work and I did all the drinking.

The two of us sat in the dining room with the lights dimmed. Nurse Ophelia was very quiet. There was something in her manner that was sort of off. She seemed irritated one minute and sad the next. Her eyes didn't seem comfortable unless they were fixed on the floor.

"What is it?" I asked. I was feeling a lot better with food in my stomach.

"You're looking more like Robert every day," she said.

Robert Douglas Thomson was my father. Just like me, he'd used his middle name, so everyone called him Doug, or Doc, or Dougal or Dr. Thomson. And some of his students used to call him Dr. T. But Nurse Ophelia was the only one who used his first name, Robert. I always wondered if she was right. Did I really look like him, or was she seeing a resemblance that wasn't really there? Since she was the only one on the ward who had known him before he died, I never got a second opinion. I sometimes thought she must have been in love with him, because whenever she mentioned his name, her tone of voice would soften just a bit and the words would come out a little slower, like they were heavy or something. And she would smile differently, too. Like it was nice to think about him, but it was sad at the same time. I guess that's why we rarely talked about him. I don't even know how they met. The most she ever told me was that he'd gotten her out of some trouble when I was just a baby, but I never got the details.

Tonight, she was wearing the same sad smile she always did when she talked about him. Her finger traced a little circle just in front of my mouth. "The nose and chin especially," she said. "Anyone who knew him would recognize you in an instant."

I smiled. As much as I missed my father, I liked it when Nurse Ophelia talked about him. But then she added something strange.

"You look just like him. That's one of our problems . . ." She took a deep breath and shook her head.

So I looked just like my father. She'd told me that before. Big whoop. Didn't most kids look like their parents?

"That must be how that man recognized you," she said. "He must have known your dad." She spoke slowly, as though she was trying to convince herself. Her eyes were staring past me into space.

"I don't understand what the problem is," I said.

Nurse Ophelia put her elbows on the armrests of her chair and started massaging her temples. "So many bizarre things have happened tonight. I just need a minute to clear my head and think things through, okay?"

After a few moments she looked up at me and continued talking. "Are you feeling all right?"

"I'm okay," I said.

"Are you getting better?"

"I feel fine. I feel *strong*. I *am* strong."

This was true. When you're alone most of the time, you need to have ways to keep your mind busy. Exercise is great for this. And reading, too. I never felt lonely when I was moving, or buried in a good book.

"I know you're strong. But do you think you're getting any better?"

I didn't know what she was getting at, so I just shrugged.

"How did things go with Charlie?" she asked.

"Fine," I answered. "He's always happy when the school year's over."

She smiled, but her eyes still had a far away look.

"What is it?" I asked her again.

She sat up in her chair and focused her eyes on me. I was surprised to see how tired she looked. Not haggard. Just deflated. And sad. She took a deep breath, as though she was gearing up to say something important, but before she could get started she was cut off by a quiet hum and a beep. She reached down to her waist and unclipped her pager.

"What now?" she muttered. She'd barely had a second to read the message when the phone beside us rang. It was the house phone, so the call was coming from somewhere inside the ward.

"That will be Roberta," she said, nodding towards the phone. She clipped the pager back to her belt. "I have to make a call. And I need to get back to work."

The disappointment on my face must have been pretty obvious because Nurse Ophelia reached out and put a hand on my shoulder. Then she gave it a gentle squeeze and got up to leave the room. When she reached the doorway she turned around.

"I'll check in with you as soon as I have a minute," she said. "We can talk then, and if not, I'll come in early tomorrow night. Okay?" She pressed her lips together in a flat smile. I did my best to smile back. Then she slipped into the hall.

I sat there by myself for a few minutes, just looking around the room at all the empty tables. It was strange to imagine that in a few hours everyone would be awake. The room would be packed, and full of the sounds of people eating and talking together. I stood up and started back to my room. It bothered me to be there, all of a sudden. I couldn't say why.

Just before dawn Nurse Ophelia knocked at my door. Four quick raps. She opened it a crack, and light from the hall made a yellow line across the floor. She slipped in quietly and set the rest of my brain cocktail on my desk. I must have left it behind.

"I have to go now," she said. Then she asked me again if I was all right. I'm not sure if I answered. I probably didn't, because she put a hand on my shoulder and gave it a gentle squeeze, just like she had earlier in the dining room. Sometimes you had to do that to get my attention. And it didn't always work.

I often got quiet. It seemed to upset everyone, but I didn't think it was that big a deal. I just had a lot on my mind, that's all. And I didn't always want to talk to other people about it. We all need downtime now and again. I was no different, except that for me it sometimes lasted a while, a few days even. It was one of the reasons everybody told me I needed counselling and psychiatric evaluations and anger management and group therapy and all that other stuff. But I never thought so. I was fine. Just as long as people didn't act like it was the end of the world when I wanted a few moments to myself. And that's how it was just then.

Nurse Ophelia must have known, because she walked over to the window, closed the blinds and pulled the curtain shut. She might have said something to me, but I wasn't listening. I was thinking about my father. He had been a professor of archaeology. I'm guessing he was good at it because he got invited to do lectures all over the world, and digs in places like Egypt and Libya and Turkey. But mostly I remember that he held me lots and read me stories about Jim Hawkins and Captain Ahab and Hawkeye, and he always smelled good and had just enough stubble on his chin that when I got too close it tickled my face.

I missed him. I missed my mother, too. That might sound strange because she died when I was two, and so I didn't really know her, but I somehow missed her anyway. Nurse Ophelia once said it was because I missed the idea of having a mother. I don't really know about that. But I do know that I should have said something to Nurse

Ophelia before she left. Something like "Thank you for dinner" or "I just need to think for a minute" or even just "Goodbye." I should have, but I didn't. I just lay there and stared at the ceiling. And so I missed my last chance to say goodbye. After that night, no one at the ward ever saw her again.

Chapter 6
Charlie

I woke up the next day when I heard the doorknob rattle. I checked my clock radio. It was almost four in the afternoon. Since no one was supposed to bother me when the sun was up, I guessed right away that something was wrong.

My guess was off. It was my best friend, Charlie.

Charlie was my only regular visitor. Dr. Shepherd used to visit me once a week, but that didn't last very long. He wasn't a real doctor, by the way, he was a shrink. Since none of the doctors knew what was really wrong with me or how to fix it, they brought in the brain mechanic to see what he could do. He said my problems were all psychosomatic, which is another way of saying that they were all in my head. Well, if being allergic to most foods and losing half my red blood cells every few months was in my head, Dr. Shepherd was a genius and ought to have won a Nobel Prize. When he gave us his assessment, Nurse Ophelia went off like a car bomb. So he never came back.

Charlie was one of the few outsiders Nurse Ophelia really liked. I think it was because he treated me like I was normal. Ever since we were little, we'd liked the same things. Just like our dads. They were best friends too, so I guess our friendship sort of ran in the family. He was a year older than me, sixteen, but when he let his stubble go he looked about twenty, which meant he could sometimes get into the beer store without being asked for ID. I didn't have any facial hair, so I figured I wouldn't even get into the beer store parking lot.

We often talked about how cool it would be if his family adopted me, but his parents were divorced, and Nurse Ophelia told me that they wouldn't be able to look after me properly, which was probably true. His mother drank more than most hockey teams, and with all my problems, I probably wouldn't have lasted a week with her. And Charlie's dad was a naval officer. He lived in Halifax and was out at sea a lot. He also moved every few years. I didn't think I'd like that. Charlie said he changed schools so much as a kid that he got held back a grade, but I think that was only part of the reason.

I was still a big groggy when he opened the door and burst in.

"Rise and shine, chowderhead!"

Sunlight flooded in and bounced off the floor. I jammed my eyes shut.

"Close the door. Close the door," I told him. I didn't open my eyes until I heard the knob click.

"I love what you've done in the lobby," Charlie said. "It really opens the place up."

He moved over to the window and peeked under the blind. He was more careful this time and didn't let too much light in.

"You're looking awful pasty, Zack," he told me. "What're they feeding you around this place, Elmer's Glue?"

If you ever had a teacher who said that there was no such thing as a stupid question, they'd obviously never had Charlie as a student.

Like chaos, stupid questions were one of his specialties. I turned and sat on the edge of the bed.

"You still wearing that necklace?" Charlie asked.

That might not sound like a stupid question, but my necklace was dangling right out in the open. It was a disc fashioned out of silver, etched and polished so that it made a perfect map of the moon. It even had the Lunar Seas on it. I tucked it back under my shirt. I never took it off, not even when I was sleeping, and so if I rolled onto my stomach it left a perfect circle on my chest. It was a gift from my dad. The last thing he gave me before he died. He told me there was another piece to it and that they fit together, but the other part belonged to my mother. She must have had it when she died, because I'd never seen it.

Charlie handed me the rest of my dinner. Nurse Ophelia had left it on the night table by my bed. I drank until the straw made sucking noises on the bottom of the cup.

Charlie shook his head. "I don't know how you can stomach that stuff. Just the sight of it makes me want to puke. What is it, a lung milkshake?"

"I don't know," I said. "Strawberry, I think."

"It doesn't smell like strawberries."

I shrugged.

"So, what happened?" Charlie asked. "You still upset about the whipping I gave you in our ping-pong fight? Looks like you tore the place apart."

"You mean in the lobby?"

"No, in the ladies' room, you dweeb. Of course in the lobby."

I told him about the old man and the motorcycle, how he annihilated the television, and how he'd gone on and on about me being in danger because someone was after me.

"Get out!" Charlie said. "You? In danger? In danger of dying from boredom, maybe. Why didn't you follow the guy's advice and jump on the motorcycle?"

"I wouldn't have gotten too far. It was mangled."

Charlie pulled out the chair and sat down. "We need to find him," he said.

I didn't think it would be so easy, with the police on his trail. Unless he was hiding under my bed, I wasn't likely to run into him anytime soon.

"Did Ophelia flip?" Charlie asked.

"No."

Charlie seemed surprised by this. No wonder. Weekends in the summertime, this place was a magnet for weirdos, especially after hours. Once, a bunch of high school kids showed up drunk at about four in the morning and tried to get into the building. Nurse Ophelia went out into the parking lot and politely asked them to leave. She was always like that. Polite. No matter what. But you had to be careful, because when she used her polite tone of voice, she expected you to do whatever she told you. Even if she asked you to grab a fistful of bees and jam them up your nose, I'm telling you, if you heard that polite tone, you'd better get on it. Well, one of the kids told her off. He used the *B* word. I almost felt sorry for him. She walked over to the boy, smiled, then picked him up by the scruff of his neck, carried him over to the Dumpster and tossed him in with the trash. *Whoosh.* Like he weighed as much as an empty pop can.

"She didn't toss the old geezer out on his butt?" Charlie asked.

"He was too fast. He ran right over a police car."

"Did they shoot him?"

"About twenty times."

"Wow. There must have been blood everywhere."

"Yup," I said. "It was all over me."

He shook his head like he couldn't believe my luck. "Well," he said, "if someone is after you, I guess we'd better get you outta here. We'll have to plan a breakout."

I laughed.

"I'm serious," he said.

He *was* serious. That's why it was so funny.

"I don't need to break out. I can go for a walk or a run whenever I feel like it."

"So maybe you should go for a long walk? Does three days sound good?"

I shook my head. With nowhere safe to hide from the sun and no way to feed myself, I wasn't going to last that long. But I sensed what he was getting at.

"Have you been up to the cottage yet?" I asked.

Charlie's father had a place on Stoney Lake. He spent most of his summers there, unless he was on a naval mission someplace. Now that school was out, I figured Charlie would be going to visit him there.

"I got a call from the Yacht Club this morning," he answered. "I got the job. There's a meeting early tomorrow, so I'm heading up tonight."

Charlie was a sailing guru. He usually spent his summers racing. I'd forgotten he was hoping to instruct this summer instead. He was saving up for a car. I guess that meant no more ping-pong fights for a while.

"Do you have to go tonight?"

He nodded. I guess that explained why he was here during the day. He didn't usually interrupt my sleep unless it was important. And I think he liked to come at night because Nurse Ophelia was always working. He sort of had a thing for her.

"I'm going to be up at the cottage for the next month or so," Charlie said. "They told me they had work for me in July, at least. August is a maybe. That's why I'm here. I wanted to see if you could come up for a while. My dad's still overseas, so we could pretty much do whatever we wanted until he gets back. It's a perfect getaway place if you're on the run. What do you think?"

Charlie was smiling. I knew exactly why. With his father gone, he was free to stay up as late as he wanted, free to sleep all weekend, free to eat Captain Crunch cereal for breakfast, lunch and dinner, and free to grow his stubble and try his luck at the beer store. Well, that sounded perfect to me. Unfortunately, leaving the Nicholls Ward for so long was probably out of the question. Especially after last night.

"I doubt I'll be allowed," I told him. "Especially if your dad's not there."

"Well, Dan will be up with his kids. He's stuffy enough to count as an adult."

Dan was one of Charlie's older brothers. Or half-brothers. He was from an earlier marriage. I think Charlie's father was working on number three right now.

"We'll pull some strings," Charlie said. "Even a weekend or a Saturday night would be better than nothing. Would you rather sit here all summer watching the paint peel?"

I shook my head.

"What about my allergies?" I asked. It wasn't easy to find food I could eat.

"Can't you take Lactaid or something?"

"What's that?"

Charlie looked at me with a weird expression, like even the dead frogs on Highway Seven knew what Lactaid was.

"It lets you drink milk and dairy products. How else do you get through dinner?"

"I don't know."

"Don't you even bother to ask?" he said.

"Not any more. I just take what they give me."

"Well, is it working? Are you getting any better?"

I shrugged. "I feel fine."

"When was your last transfusion?"

"Three months ago," I said. That meant I'd have another in a few weeks. I wasn't looking forward to it. Days of nausea. But there was no helping it. It was that or keel over.

"Let me see your scars," Charlie said.

I pulled up the right pant leg of my hospital scrubs, and revealed the two circles of scar tissue. It looked as if someone with red paint on their finger had daubed me twice just above the ankle.

"They look better," Charlie said.

"They get fainter every year."

Charlie seemed pleased with this. He'd heard the story of my scars long ago. I'd got them the day my father died. He was on a dig in Libya. Not everyone knows it, but there are a lot of ruins there. It was once part of the Roman Empire. Anyway, my father was working, and late in the day a temple he was examining collapsed on him. He was crushed instantly.

Thinking back, I suppose it was good that he didn't suffer, but at the time I wasn't thinking about that. I just wanted to find him. Since no one could show me his body, I didn't believe he was really gone. And so I took off from camp by myself. I shouldn't have, but it's not every day you become an orphan.

I never found him. I found an angry dog instead. It was hiding in the shadows of a building. Nurse Ophelia once told me that animals will do that when they know they're going to die. They crawl off by themselves and look for a dark hiding place. Well, that dog must have had more diseases than a vet hospital because when it bit me, it made me so sick no one even yelled at me for running away. Apparently I fell into a coma afterwards and stayed like that for a few weeks. I had a high fever too, and a bunch of convulsions.

Because all of my problems started the day my father died, Dr. Shepherd thought the trouble was all in my head. He thought it was just about sadness and loss. But what does a shrink know about Libyan dogs? Five-eighths of sweet diddly, as far as I could tell.

Charlie stayed for another half hour or so. He was a reader, like me, so we talked about books, and that led to movies, and that led to which actors we would want to play us in our life stories. Charlie picked Christian Bale because he was a good Batman. I picked Leonardo DiCaprio, but not because he looked like me, just because he was very good at playing complex characters. Not that I'd have been all that hard to play. I slept all day.

"He's too skinny to play you," said Charlie. "You need that guy . . . what's his name? He played Robin Hood in the old movie."

"Errol Flynn?"

"Yeah, he'd be perfect."

"He was totally skinny," I said. "Plus, he's dead."

Charlie laughed. "Yeah, but you need someone like that."

Then he told me how his classes had ended, and which couples in his grade were doomed to break up over the summer. I didn't know any of the people he was talking about, but I didn't mind. Then he said he had to go, but he'd call the next night and see if I could go with him.

"Try to find out what it takes to get a day pass," he added.

"A day pass? What's that?"

He shook his head. "A day pass out of this place, you numbskull. A 'get out of jail free' card. So you can come to the lake. Don't you want to show off your tan?"

He was backing out the door when he stopped.

"Man, I can't believe I almost forgot." He stepped back in and closed the door. "I met a girl last Saturday. Suki."

"That's her real name, Suki? It sounds like a motorcycle."

"Her real name is Suzanne. God, you are such a dork. Anyway, she has a younger sister, Luna. I told her about you and she wants to meet you. I said you were cool, so you'd better spend the next few days ungeekifying yourself. And you have to find some way out of here."

"How?" I asked.

"I don't know. Can't you chew through the wall or something?"

He opened the door again, then turned back and smiled. "It will be worth it."

Then he left. And although he'd visited me many times before, this time was different because it was the first time he had ever told a girl about me, and it was the first time I'd ever heard of Luna.

Chapter 7
Bad Dreams

It didn't take me long to fall asleep after Charlie was gone. I was good at that, falling asleep. It once happened while I was standing up in the shower. That's how it was with me. When my body needed rest, it was very insistent.

So, I fell asleep and had a dream about my father. This didn't surprise me. I once read that dreams occur because your mind has to reorganize itself when you're sleeping. So much happens during the day that you need to sort what is important from what is not. Some memories you keep close to the surface and others get buried. I think my mind was just trying to keep the memories of my father close to the top, where they belonged.

The dream started back at our old house on O'Carroll Avenue. It's right here in town. An old couple lives there now. They have a big RV in the driveway and the TV is always on. I could tell by the way the light changed in the room when I was running past. I thought about stopping to visit them one night so I could tell them I used to live there, and see what it was like to be inside again, but in the end, I just couldn't do it.

In my dream my dad was cutting the grass. He saw me and stopped.

"Hey, Zack," he said. His voice always had lots of energy in it. Like talking to me was the highlight of his day. And even though I was fifteen, and big for my age, my father was always a lot taller than me in my dreams. Like I was still a little kid. He reached down and mussed my hair.

"You getting better?" he asked.

"I feel better," I said. "I feel strong."

"You look strong," he said. Then he scooped me up in his arms and asked to see my scars.

I pulled up the right pant leg of my scrubs and revealed the two circles of scar tissue.

My father ran his fingers over them. "They look almost better!" he said.

"They get fainter every year."

He seemed pleased by this.

And then, just like that, we were inside the house. I was looking out the window at the snow on the tree branches. It must have been Christmas, because my grandparents were there, and so were Charlie and his dad. I called him Uncle Jake, even though he wasn't my real uncle.

I had lots of gifts to open, but I never got to because my father was suddenly missing. I looked around and caught a glimpse of his pant legs disappearing up the stairs. I ran after him and opened the door to his room, only when I got there it wasn't his room any more, it was an old Roman city. Right in the middle of it was his desk. He was writing in the journal he always kept. He looked at me for a few seconds. Then he closed his journal and stood.

36

"I have to go now," he said.

I didn't want him to leave. I started to shake my head.

"You don't have to be afraid," he said. "You're not alone."

He waved me over to give me a hug, but the instant I moved towards him he froze. Then he started shouting at me.

"Get away! Run! Run!"

He was gone a second later. Buried in dust and wood and old square stones. I moved closer and looked down into the shadows. Two red eyes were staring back at me. Even though I knew the danger, I couldn't help myself. I had to move closer. And I knew what was going to happen. The shadow darted out on four legs, swift as thought, and bit me hard above the ankle. The pain was very real. When I woke up it was still hurting. And my father's words were loud in my ears.

"Run!"

Maybe I should have. Because there was a man in my room staring at me.

Chapter 8
Family Matters

It took me a moment to figure out what was going on. I usually woke up if someone tried to come in my room, just as I had when Charlie came to visit.

The man was looking at me intently. He was wearing a suit that probably cost more money than an average person would want to spend on their car. It had pinstripes and a perfectly folded hanky in the pocket. His dark hair was perfect too, like a statue's, with just a little grey above each ear, and his face, which wasn't bad as faces go, looked strong enough to crush rock. He shifted so that his elbow was resting on the arm of the chair and his index finger and thumb supported the side of his face. He looked like the next president of planet Earth.

"Are you awake?" he asked.

I sat up and blinked and looked at the door.

"Would you like me to open that a crack? I didn't want anyone to disturb us."

I shook my head. The room smelled a bit funny. Like cigars. It would have been nice to open the door and window to let some fresh air in, but the sun was still up. I didn't want any light spilling in from the hallway.

"Who are you?" I asked.

"I am your uncle, Maximilian."

I looked at him carefully, and then I glanced over my shoulder at the reflection of him in the mirror on the door. He didn't look familiar. It made me wonder if he was lying. Maybe he was the person the old man on the motorcycle had warned me about.

"I don't have any uncles," I said.

"Hmmm," he said, rubbing the backs of his fingers over his chin. "I expected you might say as much."

He stared at me for a few seconds as though he expected me to respond. When I didn't, he reached into the inside pocket of his suit and pulled out a card-sized envelope. He folded it open, then handed it to me.

There were several photos inside. The first was of a young girl and boy sitting on an old fence made of split logs, the kind you might see on a farm. I flipped to the next one, quickly. It was a picture of my father. He must have been on a dig, because he looked dusty and exhausted. His arm was draped over the shoulder of another man, who was more or less holding him up. The photo was a bit blurry, but it was clear enough for me to recognize the other man as the person now sitting in my room. He looked tired in the photo too, but he had a smile on his face like he'd just conquered Everest.

The last one was a group shot. It was from a wedding. I recognized my mother and father, the bride and groom, and Charlie's dad. My grandparents, too. Others I didn't know, mostly women. And this man, smiling again, standing beside my father.

I flipped back to the first photo and looked at it more closely. I'd never seen a picture of my mother as a girl, but this had to be her.

She was wearing a summer dress and her hair was in pigtails. I tried to focus on her face, but my eyes were watering, so it was hard to see.

"My sister's name was Dorothy May. She married your father on our parents' farm, where the two of us grew up together."

I was still looking at the photo of my mother and the boy. It was him.

The man coughed gently several times, as though he was clearing his throat.

"You had no idea, did you?"

I shook my head.

"That means you don't have your father's journal."

"No."

"That's unfortunate. He would have wanted you to have it. And he would have wanted you to know about me. I haven't seen you since you were a baby, but I can see you are growing up to look much like him."

I turned back to the picture of my father in his dusty clothes. I still didn't see the resemblance between the two of us, but it pleased me that others could. In the photo he was standing beside something that looked like a well. There was desert behind him. And large mountains. Or maybe it was rock. I wondered what he had been doing to get so tired.

I tucked the photos into the envelope and reached out to hand them back.

"No, they're for you," he said. Then his eyes widened for a split second. He was looking at my necklace. It must have slipped from beneath my scrubs when I leaned forward.

"You're still wearing his necklace." He smiled. Then his jaw clenched and I saw the muscles there tense for just a second. His eyes looked very sad. "My sister, your mother, had the matching piece. Did you know that?"

I nodded.

"It was a golden crescent that snapped to the side of the one you're wearing. It might be the most beautiful piece of jewellery I've ever seen."

My father had said exactly the same thing.

"We have much to discuss, you and I."

I didn't exactly know what to say. Under other circumstances, I probably would have jumped for joy to discover that I had an uncle—someone who could answer questions about my father and mother. But when a deranged motorcycle thief destroys your television and warns you that trouble is on the way, it sort of puts you on your guard. And I was still stuck in my dream. "You're not alone," my father had said, but he'd also said, "Run." And where had this guy been all these years? The moon?

"Are you really my uncle?" I asked.

He smiled. "Yes," he said.

"Well . . . where have you been?"

He laughed, and I felt myself smile, too. The sound of laughter just does that sometimes.

"Where have I been? Why, I've been many places."

"But I've been here for eight years."

He looked at me and nodded. Then he covered his mouth and coughed quietly.

"I know. At least, I know that now. But I only discovered it recently. I was told eight years ago that you had died after lapsing into a coma. You can't imagine how shocked I was when I got the news you were still alive. Shocked, but very pleased."

I couldn't believe what I was hearing. And yet it made sense. I *had* been in a coma eight years ago. It explained why he hadn't come looking for me.

"How did you find me?" I asked.

"Good question, but the answer is complicated and probably not worth getting into right now because I can't stay long."

He glanced down at his watch. The red numbers on my clock radio told me it was 7:53. The sun would be setting soon.

"Not tonight, anyway," my uncle continued. "And we have more important things to talk about. Like your father, for instance."

He paused. I didn't know what to say. Since I didn't want him to stop talking I kept my mouth shut. Nurse Ophelia had once told me that some people will talk forever if you let them. In this case, I didn't think that would be such a bad thing.

"You were with your father the day he died, I know. I hope it isn't painful if I speak frankly."

It didn't bother me, and I told him so.

"Do you remember what happened?"

"Yes. He was crushed when a temple collapsed."

My uncle nodded almost imperceptibly. He was looking at me intently again.

"That was the official version," he said. "But that's not what really happened."

"No?"

"No."

He put his elbow back on the arm of the chair and propped the side of his face on his index finger and thumb again. This looked like his thinking pose.

"And you probably thought your father was an archaeologist."

"He was," I said. "I went with him on all his digs. After I was two, I did. After my mother died. And when he went to lecture at universities, I went with him then, too."

"Of course," my uncle said. "And the whole world would have agreed with you. Your father was an archaeologist. One of the very best. But he was much more than that. Much more."

Here he leaned forward in his chair. I was sitting on the bed with my back against the wall and I found myself leaning towards him. He looked at the door and paused to cough again, then he turned back to me and spoke in a whisper.

42

"He was a great believer in truth, your father. He used to say that it longed to be discovered by people like him, people willing to dig it up. He loved archaeology and he admired archaeologists, just as he admired historians and police detectives and other people who search for the truth. But archaeology was a front, of sorts. It was a disguise. It allowed him to conduct his *real* work, the work he did with me."

He looked at the door again and leaned in even closer. His eyes were intense now. Dark and focused.

"Your father was a vampire hunter," he said.

Chapter 9
The Crazy Truth

Well, this guy had certainly come to the right place. He was nuts. My uncle stared at me for a time. I guess he wanted me to take all of this in. My dad was a vampire hunter.

"That's crazy talk," I said.

He smiled, but then his face went flat and serious.

"Crazy talk? Perhaps." He looked around the room. "But here you are, living in this dreadful place, totally unaware of what is really wrong with you. Isolated and alone. If you ask me, this is crazy, but it is also the truth. The crazy truth of your life. So, who says the truth can't be crazy?"

He moved forward again, his elbows resting comfortably on his knees, his hands clasped together.

"I believe your father was right about the truth. It longs to be discovered. And some truths, once discovered, cannot be ignored. Your father and I hunted vampires. I understand this must come as a shock, but it was vital for your father to keep it a secret—for your protection, as well as ours. It is the reason you and I never met. Sadly, it is also the reason you never learned the truth about your father's death. Or, rather, about his murder. But let me assure you, the truth of this is very important, because the vampire who killed him is looking for you."

My uncle leaned back in his chair, his dark eyes watching me. I was beginning to feel uncomfortable. I almost asked him to leave right then and there, but I wanted to hear him out before I spoke to Nurse Ophelia. She had known my father well, but she had never hinted that there was anything unusual about what he did. And she had never mentioned my uncle. Or vampire hunting. Or murder. It all sounded like hooey. Then I remembered that she'd wanted to talk to me. That she'd been keeping secrets. Could this have been why?

"That doesn't make any sense," I said.

"And your condition, does it make sense?"

I shook my head. "No."

"Well, it makes perfect sense to me. But that is how life is. It makes sense. And if it doesn't, you haven't thought things through well enough. Or you don't have the right information. *That* is your problem—you are lacking the right information. You are fortunate that I am here because I can tell you everything you need to know to make sense of your life and why you are here."

He stood and opened the door. The light was faint now. The day was dying. He checked the hallway and then closed the door again.

"I have to go shortly, and I need to make certain no one will hear any of this. It is for your ears only."

He sat back down and leaned forward, shifting his head to the side just long enough to smother another cough with the back of his hand.

"Your father and I were hunting a vampire, a Baron, who called himself Vrolok. That was why your father spent a few weeks lecturing in Budapest the year before you went to Libya. Vrolok was hiding in Hungary. I discovered him there and brought your father in to help me. Vrolok fled, but none of us knew where.

"When he surfaced in Libya, your father followed. He tracked Vrolok to those Roman ruins. The Baron was using one of the temples as a hiding place. When your father discovered this he moved in. I wish that he had waited for me, but he didn't. Still, he did remarkably well on his own. Vrolok was cornered. It was daytime, and he was weak and tired. Your father nearly finished him, as far as I can tell. But a vampire is not easy prey. Vrolok caused the temple to collapse. It was a desperate gambit, but it paid off. It killed your father. But it also forced Vrolok into the light. He would have perished had it not been for a small boy who happened to run past."

He paused. We were thinking the same thing, my uncle and I.

"I was bitten by a dog," I said. It was barely a whisper.

My uncle shook his head and mouthed a silent "No."

"Perhaps your memory is faulty. The mind can be like that. Tell me what you remember."

I told him. There were eyes in the shadows. I moved closer and the dog crawled out and bit me. It happened so fast . . .

"And tell me," he said, "when you remember this, do you see it as a movie, or do you see it as though it is really happening to you?"

"I don't understand," I said.

"Hmmm." He paused to think. "When you look at me now, you are seeing me through your own eyes. You don't see yourself. You see me, the chair, the desk, the mirror on the door, the wall behind me. When you see the dog in your mind, when it bites you, is it like that, do you see the dog and only the dog? Or is it different? Do you see yourself, as well? As though you are watching yourself in a movie?"

That was an easy one. "I can see us both. Like a movie. We're both in the picture and I'm looking from above."

My uncle nodded. "That means it isn't a true memory. Your mind has recreated the scene and you see the recreation. If the memory were real, you would see only the dog, just as you see only me when you look across the room. Of course, it wasn't a dog, was it. It was the Baron Vrolok. He must have been close to death. Very close. But he drank your blood, and it gave him the strength to survive. To dig deep into the earth and wait for darkness."

When he finished saying this, I stared up at him. It was as if I were seeing him clearly for the first time. There was truth in his words. I could see that. And I also saw another truth. One he had implied. I had been bitten by the Baron Vrolok. I had been infected by a vampire.

And so I was a vampire, too.

Chapter 10
Strange Questions

My uncle was right. Some truths could not be ignored. Not when they rolled over you like the dinner trolley.

I was a vampire. How could I have not known? It was the only thing that made sense. I couldn't go out in the sun. I needed fresh blood every few months. My body didn't like food. It made me wonder what Nurse Ophelia had been putting into those brain cocktails. I began to doubt it was strawberry syrup.

It also made me wonder how much of this she knew. I probably should have asked my uncle about it, but another thought had come to mind—something of much greater concern. After all, this man was a vampire hunter.

"Are you here to kill me?" I asked.

He smiled. His hard features softened and he looked down at the ground for just an instant. "No," he said. "I came here for an entirely different reason. I came here to take you away from this place."

"But don't you kill vampires?"

He shook his head once, slightly, with his lips pressed together. "Not always. In some cases your father and I left vampires alive because they agreed to help us, and because we were convinced they posed no immediate threat to humanity. You must understand, Zachary, vampires aren't very different from normal people. They have choices to make, just as you will have choices to make. They can choose to be good, or to be something that is less than good. I suppose the hunger for blood makes the choice more difficult for vampires, but it remains a choice."

Well, I had no doubt in my mind what I would choose. I would be good. I certainly wasn't a threat to anybody. I didn't even believe in mousetraps. But I was thinking that maybe there was another way out of this.

"Can I be cured?" I asked.

My uncle took a deep breath and put his hands on his knees. Then he pushed himself up and got ready to leave. In a second, an umbrella was hanging over his arm and a briefcase was in his hand.

"There is no known cure for vampirism. Your struggle here is proof enough of that. But there are ways of coping, obviously. You have done a remarkable job of it here, and you ought to be congratulated. In the meantime, I have set about the business of trying to adopt you. It won't be easy. Because medical science can't make sense of your condition, it will be difficult for me to prove that I am capable of taking care of you. But we will find a way . . . assuming that is what you want. You don't have to make your mind up right away. I'll come back, and we can spend some more time talking. I have an appointment right now and I can't be late. I'm on the trail of another vampire, but I'll be back to see you tomorrow. In the meantime, don't do anything to put yourself at risk. I noticed the police outside. I'm assuming there was an accident of some kind?"

"A man crashed through the doors with a stolen motorcycle," I said. Then I told him the rest.

When I was finished, my uncle stared at me for about ten seconds without saying a word. It was as if I'd just disconnected his brain. Then he snapped out of it.

"Tell me again, what exactly did he say?"

I ran through it as best I could.

My uncle looked down at the floor. He was whispering, "Thank heavens . . . Apocalypse . . ." Then he looked up at me with the same intense expression I'd seen on his face before. As though this was the most important thing in the world.

"What exactly did he look like? Describe him to me."

I started with the old man's hair and his top hat and overcoat, and finished with his eyes, but apparently I missed a lot, because my uncle asked me a lot of questions I didn't have clear answers for. Like the shape of his nose and his cheeks and how thick his neck was.

"And his voice, was there anything unusual about it?"

I shrugged. I didn't think so.

"And they shot him twenty times?"

"More or less. It was a lot. There was blood everywhere."

"Did he mention any names?"

I shook my head.

"Well," my uncle concluded, "I think I might know who the culprit is. I'll do some digging and find out for certain. It isn't Vrolok, that's the good news. And the police are here now. I recommend never straying from where they can help you."

"He told me to stay away from the police," I said. I'd forgotten to mention this.

My uncle smiled. "I think you can ignore that part, Zachary. They're usually the good guys." Then his smile tightened and he nodded a quick goodbye. "I'll try to be back before the sunrise. If not, I'll contact you tomorrow."

"Okay," I said.

I suppose I should have stood up and shaken his hand, or said thank you, or done something like that, but I didn't. I'm not sure why. I guess I was still pretty shocked. And truthfully, I wasn't used to that kind of good news—that I might soon be living in a real home with a real uncle. It wasn't as though my life was bad—I wasn't starving in some war-torn country with flies buzzing around my eyes—but it wasn't a bowl of cherries, either. So I just said goodbye.

The moment he was gone I felt a great emptiness inside. I almost jumped up and chased him down the hall. A zillion questions popped into my head. Things I should have asked him. My mother—what was she like, and how had she died? My father and his work. And about Vrolok. Was he really looking for me? Is that why the crazy old man had shown up on a stolen motorcycle? Did he know about Vrolok, too? I felt a bit ridiculous. There was so much to find out and I hadn't really asked him anything. But at least I'd met a person who might have some answers. Maximilian. Uncle Max. I liked the sound of it. And he looked tough enough to survive an alien invasion. I liked that, too.

Chapter 11
Death and Undeath

After my uncle left, I checked the time again. It was almost eight-thirty. I was still expecting Nurse Ophelia to arrive shortly. I was anxious to talk to her about all that I had learned. And Charlie. I imagined his jaw hitting his feet when I told him I was a vampire and that I might soon be adopted by my uncle, Maximilian, the vampire hunter. I had so much restless energy in my bones I could have run to the North Pole without taking a breath.

I paced in my room until the sun went down, then I headed straight for the nurses' station. Roberta was already there with one of the security guards. She was trying to get the Chicago Man to go to bed. He was doing his usual routine, spinning and waving his arms to music only he could hear. He would often stop his dancing to clap out a rhythm and sing, but his voice was just a mumble, and the only word you could ever make out clearly was "Chicago." I guess he was born there. Unfortunately, because the women all stayed on a separate floor, he never had anyone to dance with, except the staff. Nurse Roberta clearly wasn't in the mood.

"Do you know where Nurse Ophelia is?" I asked her.

As soon as I spoke, the Chicago Man turned around and started to spin in front of me, clapping his hands and laughing. I knew just what to do. I took both his hands and we turned a few lazy circles. Then we bowed to each other. It gave Nurse Roberta a chance to slip her hand inside his elbow.

"I'm a little busy right now. Can't you tell?" she said.

After several attempts, she managed to get him pointed in the right direction, and then, with the help of the security guard, started guiding him to his room. "This way, Mr. Butterfield."

I waited for Nurse Ophelia in the reception area for about five minutes. A work crew had been in during the day to replace the shattered doors. Part of the frame had been restored, but the glass was still missing, so tarpaulin had been stretched over the opening. Two policemen were there, and I noticed extra security guards, too. A few were helping the other nurses move people out of the dining hall and into their rooms.

I waited at the nurses' station for another twenty minutes. By this time, everyone was in bed, and Nurse Ophelia still hadn't arrived. With no one around to talk to, I started to get restless.

"Why don't you go blow off some steam in the fitness room?" Nurse Roberta suggested. She was filling in forms behind the counter. "I'll tell her where you are when she arrives."

It seemed like a good idea. I was feeling very irritated. I had to tell her the news. *I was a vampire*! But she must have known. She prepared my meals. Why hadn't she told me?

I suddenly felt very frustrated. How was I going to get answers if she didn't bother coming to work? So I hurried back to my room to get my sneakers. A few minutes later I was on the treadmill, running. It was the one thing I was exceptionally good at. And it didn't matter if I felt lonely, mad or just plain bored. To get my feet moving when the sun was down always did the trick.

I spent most of my time thinking about Maximilian. I imagined telling him everything about my life here. And introducing him to Charlie. As silly as it sounds, I pictured him getting married to Nurse Ophelia so that I could live with them both after he adopted me. I even imagined us hunting other vampires, like Peter Cushing and Anthony Hopkins in the movies. And avenging my father.

Five hours passed this way. By the end, the rubber track on the treadmill was smoking. It smelled like I'd set fire to it. I hadn't really noticed because I was off in my own little world. A world that was now full of vampires.

When I thought more about it, I remembered that we vampires weren't actually living creatures. We weren't dead, but we weren't alive, either. We were *undead*. Trapped between life and death forever. It seemed like a bunch of baloney to me, but in all the stories I'd ever read and the movies I'd watched, that was the word they'd used. And the first step was dying. Once you got infected, that is. Then your human life came to an end and your life as a vampire began.

I wondered when my first death had happened. My human death. It wasn't like I'd been dropped in a pit with a rabid *Tyrannosaurus rex*. Did I die in my coma? Or just after I was bitten? You'd think a guy would remember something important like that. But then again, maybe not. Death might have been so scary, my mind wouldn't let me remember.

In the end, I couldn't figure it out, mostly because the word *undead* didn't really make any sense. I certainly felt alive. But I might have been wrong about that. I'd basically forgotten what life was like for normal people, so maybe I didn't feel alive at all, I just thought I did. Maybe what I felt was something different. It took a while to put my finger on it, but then I figured it out. What I felt was excited. And alive or undead, after eight boring years in a mental ward being spoon-fed one hairball theory after another about what was wrong with me and how to fix it, well, things were looking up.

✦ ✦ ✦ ✦

As soon as my run was over, I tried again to find Nurse Ophelia. I needed to eat. Exercise usually made my appetite go away, but only while I was moving. Now that I had stopped, it was going to come on even stronger. I was in a race with my stomach. Soon it would be freaking out. I didn't see her anywhere, but I quickly found Nurse Roberta outside one of the rooms. She'd been checking up on one of the older patients I didn't know very well.

"Is she here yet?" I asked.

"No. And she didn't call in sick, either. She's a no-show. That means they'll dock her a night's pay." Then she muttered something colourful under her breath about all the work she'd been left to finish on her own. She had a clipboard in her hand. She was checking something off.

"I haven't eaten yet," I said. "I'm starving."

Nurse Roberta's head fell back just a bit and her shoulders slumped. I could tell she felt bad even before she apologized. "I totally forgot." Then she raised the clipboard and tapped it against her forehead, as though she was reminding herself not to be so stupid. "Well, come on, then. We'd better get you something."

We got to the kitchen just in time. My eyeballs were aching and my stomach sounded like an angry bear.

"I haven't done this in a while," she said. "Do you know where everything is?"

While she got the blender ready, I fished in the fridge for what I needed.

"You can't have that," Nurse Roberta said when she saw the box full of syrup bags.

"What do you mean?" I asked. "Nurse Ophelia always puts one of these in."

Nurse Roberta looked confused. Her face wrinkled up and she pointed to the label on the box. It said "Warning: Not for Human Consumption." I'd never noticed before. I guess I hadn't looked that closely.

I took out one of the bags. It suddenly dawned on me what the red syrup was, and it sure wasn't strawberries. My hands started shaking.

Nurse Roberta took the bag from me and gently squeezed it with her fingers. "Must be some kind of gel. Looks a bit like grenadine."

I had no idea what grenadine was, but I wasn't going to correct her.

"Well, sorry," she said, "but I can't let you have that." She closed the fridge and put her hands on her hips. "We'll have to think of something else."

I looked at her very closely. I had been wrong about her. She really was very pretty. But maybe I just thought so because she was trying to be helpful. Or maybe it was because I was hungry . . .

For some reason I got thinking about what Dracula might do at a moment like this. With all his bizarre talents, he was easily the undisputed heavyweight champion of the undead world. He could climb walls, turn into a bat, or a wolf, or mist. He could make himself thin and slip through cracks. He could command rats and other night creatures to do his bidding. He could even go out in the daytime.

I figured that stuff was poppycock. I'd been infected for eight years and I couldn't even keep my room clean.

But some of his talents weren't so unrealistic. And they were certainly better suited for a time like this. Hungry. Alone with a beautiful woman. He certainly wouldn't let himself starve. So I took a page out of his book and made my move.

First, I opened my eyes so they were really wide. Then I sort of raised my hand with the fingers spread wide. "You will let me have my dinner," I said to Nurse Roberta in a slow, commanding voice.

She still had her hands on her hips. Her chin dropped just a little. Then she opened her eyes very wide and raised her hand. "No, we'll have to find you something else," she said. Her imitation was flawless.

And so I learned something very valuable about my power to charm. I guess I still needed a few centuries of practice before I could command humans to do my bidding. Dracula would have been very disappointed.

I put my hand down. I must have been blushing because the skin on my face felt really tight. "I don't think I can have anything else," I told her. "All I know is that Nurse Ophelia mixes one of those in with the rest of my medications."

Nurse Roberta shook her head gently. "Zachary, you aren't on any medications. You haven't been for months. Not since last year. Didn't you know that?"

I shook my head. Then my stomach started to kung-fu my other organs. And my throat started itching as well. Like I had ants crawling around in there.

Nurse Roberta reached out and gently took hold of my hand. "Don't do that," she said.

I'd been scratching at my neck.

"We'd better find you something else," she added.

I shook my head. "Honestly, this is what she uses. I watch her. It's the same thing every time."

"Are you sure?"

I nodded.

She looked a little cross. "You'd better be. If you drop dead on me, and it costs me my job . . ."—she spread her fingers wide and made her eyes bug out—". . . I'll kill you!" Then she cut the bag open and poured it into the blender.

I realized that it didn't look like blood. I'd seen the real stuff when the old man on the stolen motorcycle got shot. This stuff was much thicker.

"We should water that down a bit," I suggested.

A few seconds later, I was drinking. It tasted exactly the same as normal. And it was gone in a blink.

"You gonna be okay?" she asked.

I nodded and smiled. Then I blushed again. I was feeling guilty. I'd been a bit too hard on her, thinking she was cranky all the time.

We left the kitchen and I made my way back to my room. With food in my stomach, I felt a lot better. And so I enjoyed another chapter of *The Hobbit*. Enough to see Bilbo and the gang safely to the house of Elrond. Then I closed my window, lowered the blinds, drew the curtains and went to sleep.

Chapter 12
The Fallen

I woke from a deep sleep around noon. Someone was knocking at the door. The cadence was hurried, but soft. Just to be safe, when I rose out of bed I picked up the chair by my desk and held it up over my shoulder. Then I asked who was there.

"It's your uncle," said a voice. "Maximilian."

I told him he could come in. He opened the door and slipped inside. I noticed his suit was different. He didn't have his briefcase with him, but he was holding a folder in one hand. When he saw me standing in the middle of the empty room, I put the chair back down.

"Redecorating?" he asked. Then his expression changed and he started to cough, worse than before. He had to work pretty hard to clear his throat afterwards.

"Excuse me," he said, thumping his chest with a large fist. "I hope it's okay that I woke you? I was going to slip this file under the door, but I decided that it made more sense to talk face to face, in case you had any questions. I didn't want you to get too worked up, although there is reason for concern."

He tapped the folder against his palm a few times.

"I have been meeting with the hospital admin all morning in hopes of getting you moved out of here," he said, "but because of your condition and your sensitivity to sunlight, they won't give me permission. Not until I become your legal guardian, and that could take some time. I don't think it's safe for you to stay here another night, but at the moment, I don't have the authority to force anyone's hand."

As he spoke, he opened the folder and removed a photograph. It was a picture of a scruffy-looking man in an overcoat. He had a cane and a long, pink scar under his eye.

"I came across some interesting information last night," he continued, "and I wanted to share it with you." He tapped a thick finger on the photo of the scruffy man. "This is Everett Johansson, former Toronto police detective. He retired to Peterborough eight years ago."

I picked up the photograph and examined it closely.

"Ever see him before?" my uncle asked.

I shook my head.

"Your father had a term he used to describe men like this. He called them 'the Fallen,' people who have forsaken humanity and entered into the service of vampires. This man is dangerous. He has eyes all over the city. My contacts tell me that he's looking for you."

I looked at the photo more closely. "Is this why the old man on the motorcycle warned me to stay away from the police?"

"I wouldn't dismiss the idea."

Everett Johansson. The Fallen. He didn't look all that dangerous. Not compared to my uncle. But if he served a vampire, he didn't have to be dangerous himself.

"Does he work for Vrolok?" I asked.

My uncle looked at me, then down at the photograph. "I don't know," he began. "I am assuming he does. Vrolok is in Canada. And as far as I know, he's never travelled to the New World before."

"New World?"

"North America. He's never before risked crossing the Atlantic. He's found out about you from someone. And I suspect that someone is Johansson."

"How would he know I was here? I've never seen him before."

My uncle shook his head slowly. "You wouldn't have to see him. He has many people working under him, in all walks of life. Maybe a delivery person saw you. Or a security guard. Or any one of the police officers who've been here. And there is no way to know, when you see someone, if they are one of the Fallen. They look like ordinary people. They *are* ordinary people. With dangerous friends."

I thought of everyone I came into contact with each day. There weren't that many. But the night the old man crashed through the lobby, there were a lot of different people on the scene, and I was centre stage. It might easily have happened then.

"I think you should stay in your room, just to be safe." Then he smiled and fished into the inside pocket of his jacket. He pulled out a small piece of paper. It had "Maximilian" written across the middle in red letters. Across the top in black was "Iron Spike Enterprises." The *I* in "Iron" was a metal spike. He took out a pen and scribbled a number underneath his name.

"That's my cell number," he said. "Don't hesitate to call if you sense trouble. Or if you get any more strange visitors, like that old man who stole the motorcycle."

"Did you find out who he was?"

"Not yet, but I will. In the meantime, we can't afford to take any chances. Experience has taught me that we should assume the worst. That Johansson knows you're here, and that he's working for Vrolok. I'm betting that's why the old man came to warn you. We'll have to get you out of here right away."

I looked at the window. It was just after noon. I didn't want to go anywhere unless it involved a tunnel or an armoured car.

"What should I do?" I asked.

"Well, sit tight for now. The sun is up. We can't risk moving you in the daytime. I'll do some more legwork this afternoon. Find out what I can, then come back later tonight. Don't worry. We'll get you out of here."

"You can do that?"

He smiled. The muscles on either side of his jaw twitched. He looked strong enough to rip the place apart, brick by brick. "I feel sorry for anyone who'd try to stop me," he said. Then he slipped the photo of Everett Johansson back into the folder. "Pack a bag," he added. "Just essentials. Be ready at sunset. I will get here as soon as I can."

I nodded.

He placed a hand on my shoulder, smiled again, then slipped out the door. I heard him cough again in the hallway. Then his footsteps faded and I was alone.

Chapter 13
Everett Johansson

My uncle had said he'd come back at sunset. *Sunset*. What a beautiful word.

Sadly, that was about eight hours away. I wasn't sure I could go back to sleep, so I started fishing under my bed for another set of clean clothes. They were all hospital scrubs. In the end, I decided the only thing I really needed were my books. I picked up *The Hobbit* and started reading. After some riddles in the dark, my eyes started to droop, so I put the book down and fell asleep.

I woke up in a panic about a half hour before dusk. Something wasn't right. My heart was pounding, for one. And the air just felt wrong. Tense. Sort of like the feeling you get when two people start having an argument.

I sat up in bed and looked about the room. Sunlight was peeking in around my blinds so I had to squint. Everything looked normal, but on instinct, I forced myself out of bed.

Then I heard someone shouting. It was coming from the hallway. If you've ever spent time in a mental ward, you'll understand that this is about as unusual as a cow eating grass. This shouting was different, though. It was the nursing staff who were raising their voices, which was rare. I stuck my head into the hall.

Two police officers were standing in front of the reception desk. A man was with them. With the light behind him, all I could see was a silhouette. He stood behind while the nurses and the officers argued. I tried to get a better look at everyone, but sunlight was reflecting off the floor. It hit my eyes like a handful of pins, so I couldn't see anything. Fortunately, one of the police officers raised his voice.

"I know he's here and I need him up now. He's got to be moved right away. Not tomorrow, not in an hour. Now."

"It's not that simple," one of the nurses explained. "If you don't take the necessary precautions, he could die. He's allergic to practically everything. Food. The sun—"

"I don't care if he's allergic to his own skin. He needs to come with us."

Well, as you can imagine, this got my attention. Even with cottage cheese for brains, I'd still have known they were talking about me. Then the man I couldn't see very well stepped closer to the others. He was dressed in an overcoat and he had a cane in one hand. He turned around and saw me. For a split second we stared at one another. When he took two steps towards me, I noticed that he walked with a limp. And even though the sun was bright enough to melt my hair, I could see the scar under his eye. It was like a thick, pink stripe. His eyes widened for just an instant, and then they narrowed as we acknowledged one another.

It was Everett Johansson. And he had the police with him.

I slammed the door shut and backed away from it. My hands and face were hurting from the sunlight that had been bouncing off the floor and walls. Ten seconds' worth, maybe twenty, and already every inch of my exposed skin was covered in red spots.

I started looking for my uncle's business card. I couldn't remember where I'd left it. As I was rummaging through my bedsheets, I realized it wasn't going to do me any good. The only phone I could have used to call him was at the nurses' station. The house phone in my room worked only inside the building. I was done for. The police were just outside the door, and I had nowhere to hide but under my bed. I was a little too big for that.

I pushed the bed in front of the door and threw my chair on top for good measure. The door opened inward, so that would slow them down for a few seconds. But I had to find a way to hold out for at least a half hour or so. Then, once the sun was all the way down, I could run away. Or maybe I wouldn't have to. My Uncle Maximilian had said he would be here. But the bad guys weren't going to wait, and there wasn't anything between us but a few inches of wood and a single bed. So I did what a lot of people do when they get into trouble and don't have a clue what to do. I looked up.

Footsteps were right outside my door now. I heard a knock.

"Zachary, are you in there?" The voice belonged to Nurse Roberta.

"Zachary," said another voice. It sounded all crackly. "It's the police. We know you're in there. Please open up. We need to have a word with you."

The next knock was loud and hard.

"I hope you're decent," Nurse Roberta said.

I was too frightened to say anything. A few seconds later, someone tried to push the door. It opened just a crack before the bed got in the way. One of the police officers said something in a loud voice and tried to force the door while Nurse Roberta asked me to "Please open up" over and over again. A few seconds later they had pushed the bed back far enough that one of them could slide it completely out of the way. The chair toppled to the floor. Everett Johansson was the first one in.

"Where is he?" I heard him say.

But Nurse Roberta didn't know. None of them did. I was gone.

Chapter 14
Emergency Exit

Perhaps you don't believe that I really am a vampire. It is a stretch, I'll give you that. But if you do believe I am a vampire, well, you can't be a numbskull about it, either. I'm not a storybook vampire like Count Dracula. I can't do supernatural. My escape wasn't all that impressive. Check the ceiling of your school someday. Or an office. If it's like mine, it's really a false ceiling. It's made of rectangular foam tiles that sit on a plastic frame. You can poke them up with a broom. Up above, you'll find the plumbing and ducts for heating that run every which way.

That's it. That's how I got out. I just stood on my desk, pushed up the tile, slid it backwards, jumped up and grabbed one of the black pipes hanging overhead. Then I pulled myself up and slid the tile back in place underneath me. *Ta-dah!*

Are you impressed? Maybe not. But I tell you, it was awfully nerve-racking hanging there, hoping the police would leave.

Everett Johansson was furious. "Where did he go?" he asked again.

"I don't know," the nurse answered. "There's no way out of here but the window, and it's barred."

The bed was moved and moved and moved again. The mattress was lifted and the sheets pulled off. The room was only about eight feet wide and twelve feet long. It didn't take them long to search it.

"I'll check the next room," the nurse said.

"No, he's in here somewhere. There's no way he could have gotten out."

I listened while they moved the bed again.

"Wait a minute," Johansson said. "Give me that chair."

I heard the sound of people shuffling around, then the tile underneath me popped up just a hair. That got a reaction. I had to get moving. Pipes ran in every direction. So did the metal heating ducts, but they didn't look as strong. I took my best guess and slid, hand over hand, foot over foot, along the pipes in the direction of the kitchen.

"Get me a light," Johansson continued. "I can hear him. He's in the ceiling."

An instant later the tile disappeared. Johansson's head and shoulders rose through the space. He had a small flashlight in his hand.

I got lucky. There was dust everywhere, and the beam of his flashlight didn't penetrate very far into the darkness. He scanned straight ahead first, then on one side and the other. By the time he looked behind him I was even farther away.

"He's heading that way," Johansson said.

A tile to my right popped up and then disappeared. Then another one off to my left. The two police officers joined the search. The beams of their flashlights lit up the dust all around me.

"Over there," said a voice. I tried to speed up, but it wasn't easy hauling myself along. Unless I found a way to turn invisible, they were going to catch me.

I kept moving in the direction of the kitchen. I was starting to slow down because my wrists were getting tired. I was breathing heavily. All the dust made it difficult to get a full chest of air. I couldn't hang on much longer.

Then a tile popped up right in front of me. I waited for the officer underneath me to look up, but he didn't, because someone started yelling at him. It was Nurse Roberta.

"You can't do this!" she shouted. "This is a mental ward. Anything out of the ordinary throws these people for a loop. Our job is difficult enough. Tearing the ceiling apart like this is out of the question."

I could have dropped to the floor and kissed her. Instead, I slid, as quietly as I could manage, back the way I'd come.

The officer ignored her. He tossed the tile to the floor and removed another. It gave me a better view of him. He was standing on something. A chair, or a ladder, maybe. I thought he might turn his flashlight on me, but he didn't even have it out any more. I scanned the darkness above the remaining tiles. The other officers must have stopped using theirs, too. The beams were no longer shining through the dust. They were simply tearing down the ceiling one tile at a time. Soon, the whole network of ducts and plumbing would be exposed. And so would I.

The officer removed another tile, and another. As the tiles disappeared, more light danced up through the dust. I was going to be in plain view very soon.

Then I heard another voice shouting, "He's in here! He's in here!"

It was Jacob, my red-haired neighbour from across the hall. I could hear him giggling.

The officer in front of me stopped pulling out tiles. A second later, I heard the heavy sound of his feet as they hit the floor. Then he ran off in the direction of Jacob's room.

This bought me a few precious seconds. I considered what to do. The dining hall would still have a few patients lingering in it.

So would the kitchen. So would the common room. There was nowhere I could drop where I wouldn't be seen.

Another voice started shouting, too. It was Sad Stephen. He had chronic depression and came in a few times a year for shock treatment. Sounds horrible, but it might have been working, because he was laughing too, just like Jacob.

"No. I see him. He's in my room!"

I nearly started laughing myself. A few seconds later, every person on the floor who could talk was shouting.

"He's in my room!"

"No, my room!"

"He's in here!"

". . . right behind you!"

In the end, it didn't make much of a difference. Johansson told his men to go back and keep pulling out the tiles. I felt a twinge of panic until I realized that what he was doing was ridiculous. The ceiling of the first floor was huge. It was going to take them too long. They were never going to be finished by nightfall. But, of course, they didn't know my uncle was coming to save me. They must have thought they'd have all night.

I scuttled back in the direction of the kitchen. My wrists were starting to burn. I couldn't hang on much longer. A few feet away was a heating duct. The metal strips that held it in place looked flimsy, but I was out of options. I slipped my leg over it. The duct seemed to handle the weight just fine. Then I slowly shifted my whole body over until I was settled neatly on top. It made some noise, but with everybody shouting, I don't think Johansson would have heard me if I'd torn the whole thing loose.

Soon the ruckus came to an end. I guess the thrill of screaming "He's over here!" only lasts so long. Shortly afterwards, security and the nursing staff started herding people back to their rooms for lights out.

Johansson and his men continued their work. The bedrooms, the lobby, the reception area, the nurses' station, they were all being done systematically. I didn't care. Dusk was approaching, and my uncle was coming. Or so I thought.

As the police moved closer, I heard the dining room clearing below me. Soon it was quiet, and I decided to make a drop. I slid a tile all the way back and looked down. It was at least twelve feet to the ground.

What was I afraid of? I was a vampire now. Couldn't most of us fly?

I let go and hit the ground with a soft thud. No broken bones. Not even a tingle. I crept towards the kitchen. A few night staff were cleaning up after dinner, rinsing dishes and putting them through the wash. Their backs were to me. Still, I watched for a few seconds to make certain they weren't glancing around. They seemed pretty busy, so I managed to crawl over to the refrigerator without being seen. I opened the door as quietly as I could and grabbed the box of food Nurse Ophelia used to make my brain cocktails.

My uncle had said to pack the essentials. Well, this would have to do. It was time to get going.

I crept back into the dining room, grateful that the lights were off and the area was empty. But the only doors that could get me outside of the building were in the lobby. If I climbed there above the ceiling, which would have been almost impossible with the box I was carrying, I still would have had to drop down right in front of Johansson and his men, assuming they hadn't finished that section completely by now. That wasn't going to get me very far. And even though there were exits at both sides of the building, they were unlocked only if there was an emergency. I had to think of something else.

So I walked to the wall and pulled the fire alarm. Instant emergency.

As soon as it started ringing, I ducked under a table and waited.

71

Almost right away, the two kitchen staff made their way through the dining hall. Neither saw me. Then I snuck back into the kitchen, grabbed an apron from the wall, tied it around my waist and walked out myself. I thought if I looked casual enough, with all the traffic in the lobby, I'd get out one of the side doors, no problem. I just needed my luck to hold.

It didn't.

They say timing is everything. Well, I don't even wear a watch, so mine could have been better. I strode out of the dining hall expecting to merge with a crowd of people, but the lobby was nearly empty. I hadn't waited long enough for everyone to figure out what was going on and leave their rooms—assuming they could do all of this without an instruction manual or a personal attendant. To make matters worse, Everett Johansson was arguing with Nurse Roberta at the reception counter, so I practically bumped into him.

"Zachary, stop! It isn't safe!" he shouted.

I ran for the closest exit, the lobby doors right in front of me. The police were close behind.

Did I mention that I was pretty quick on my feet? Running for a few hours every night is apparently very good for this. I'd never actually been in a race before, but as it turned out, none of the officers inside had a chance. I bolted through the outside doors so fast, all they could do was shout. I looked back over my shoulder for a second, and that's when I collided with the officer waiting in the parking lot. I was so surprised, I dropped my box of food and tripped to the pavement. I'd totally forgotten there were men posted outside.

I tried to stand up, but someone had taken hold of my wrist. As I twisted away, a heavy weight pressed down on my back, flattening me against the asphalt. Someone started shouting at me, telling me not to move. At the same time, I felt another officer grab one of my legs. Then a third pinned my arm. And just like that, I was in the hands of the police.

Chapter 15
The Vampire

I wrestled with the three officers as best I could. It was hard because I was on the ground and they were all sitting on me. Then they weren't. The first officer, the one on my back—he flew off into the air like he'd been fired from a catapult. He landed on the hood of a police car. The second one—he was trying to pin my legs—he flew off an instant later. Unfortunately for him, he missed the car. I heard him grunt as he landed on the asphalt.

The last guy was kneeling on one of my arms. The look on his face was one of total astonishment. He half stood up and put his hand on his holster. Then he got hauled off the ground.

"You won't be needing that gun," a voice said.

I expected it to belong to my uncle. It didn't. It belonged to the crazy old motorcycle man. He was standing in the parking lot in his top hat and overstuffed overcoat, with the police officer in one hand and the officer's gun in the other. He was actually holding the guy a foot off the ground. The old man stared at the pistol for a second, then tossed it into the Dumpster beside us. Then he ripped a set of keys from the officer's belt. "Thanks," he said. And officer number three was airborne. "Have a nice evening," the old man added as the officer soared away.

I was so stunned I couldn't move. When he looked down at me, I thought for just a second he was going to pitch me out with the rest of them, but he didn't. He reached down and helped me to my feet. He must have been as strong as an elephant.

"So . . . didn't bother fixing the motorcycle I left for you?"

I couldn't speak.

The old man started walking over to the police car near the new lobby doors. It was a Ford Mustang. "Don't forget your box," he said over his shoulder.

I picked up the carton of food, then took a few uncertain steps towards the car. The old man was trying to unlock the door with the keys he'd stolen. None of them seemed to work.

"Oh, hang it," he said. Then he tossed the keys over his shoulder and just ripped the driver's-side door off the car. No joke. Like it was made of wet newspaper.

He was climbing into the driver's seat when I heard a man shout "Stop!" It was the first police officer. The one who had landed on the car. He was back on his feet and had his gun drawn. It was pointed right at us.

"Hands on your head. Back away from the car," he shouted.

"Hurry up, boy!" the old man snapped.

My door opened from the inside and I ducked in. The cover of the steering column had been ripped off and the old man was rubbing two wires together.

"Don't move or I'll shoot," shouted the officer.

The old man turned to me and smiled. "Time to slip it into overdrive."

I smelled a spark and the engine turned over. Then I heard several gunshots. The sound made every muscle in my body jump.

"Hang on," the old man said. He was talking through clenched teeth like he'd just been punched in the stomach. A dark stain was spreading across his chest.

Blood. The smell of it filled the car. I felt the muscles in my jaw begin to twitch and my head got all dizzy. It was exactly the same way I'd felt when I first saw him bleeding, the night he'd crashed into the lobby of the Nicholls Ward. I felt agitated, too. Almost angry. There was just a flash of it, but enough that I had a fleeting urge to rip his coat off and help myself to what he'd spilled so it wouldn't go to waste.

He threw the car into reverse and spun into the cruiser behind us. The officer with the gun was standing right beside it, so he had to jump out of the way to avoid being hit. We slammed into the car and the front end caved in over one of the tires. Without a tow truck, it wasn't going anywhere. Then the old man slipped the gearshift into forward and tore out of the parking lot.

"Buckle up," he said.

I had the box of food in my lap. I was fighting with the seat belt when I felt his hand pushing down on the top of my head. An instant later, several shots hit the back windshield and pebbles of glass flew all over the back seat.

"Are you hit?" he asked me as we raced down the street. He had to shout because there was so much wind coming in through his open door.

"No," I answered.

"Good."

I noticed he was still grinding his teeth. He looked into my box of food. "Toss me one of those, will you?"

I reached into the carton and pulled out one of the square bags. When I handed it to him, I noticed his teeth. Two of them in particular. You know the ones I mean. They were twice as long as they should have been, and pointed, like a wolf's.

"You're a vampire," I said.

"Well, give the boy a cigar. What were you expecting? A cherub?"

"What's a cherub?" I asked.

"What's a cherub? Don't young people go to Sunday school any more?"

I shrugged. I had no idea what young people did.

"Of course I'm a vampire," he continued. "Did you think you were the only one in town?"

"You mean there are more of us?"

The old vampire laughed. "More of us! Vampires are everywhere. Why, I'll bet you half the bureaucrats at City Hall . . ." He bit into the bag and took a sip. A look of total disgust came over his face and he spat everything out the open door. The wind blew half of it back inside. "What is this crap?"

I looked at the box to see if it said anything other than "Warning: Not for Human Consumption."

"Blood," I said. "At least, I think so."

"Are you nuts?" he said. Then he laughed. "What am I saying? I just helped you escape from Crackerbox Palace." He held the bag under my nose. "Does this swill smell like blood to you? If this is the real deal, I'm the Master Chief and you just got powned."

The bag looked fine to me.

"Must be from an animal," he said. "Probably a pig or a cow." He went to toss the bag out of the car, but I stopped him.

"Don't, I'll have it."

"Your funeral."

He handed the bag to me. I drank it. It wasn't as filling as one of my brain cocktails, but it tasted just as good. I waited a few seconds to see if my stomach was considering any acrobatic routines, but I didn't feel so much as a cramp.

"Don't you have any of the real stuff?" the old vampire asked me.

"What real stuff?"

He looked at me like I was too stupid to be alive. I noticed his eyes again. Watery blue. "Human blood, of course. What did you think I meant?"

I was shocked. "You drink human blood?"

"Once you start, there's only one way to stop."

"How's that?"

He spun the wheel and we skidded around a corner. "You get killed," he said.

So vampires could die. Of course they could die. Wooden stakes and holy water and all that. I stared at the old vampire for a moment, wondering how much of what I'd read in books and seen in the movies was true.

"Do you hunt people?" I asked.

He looked in the rear-view mirror. It had a bullet hole in it, so he took a quick glance over his shoulder, then he started driving with one hand.

"Not unless they really get on my nerves," he answered.

I wasn't sure if he was lying or not. But he was weaving all over the road.

"What's the matter?" I asked.

"What's the matter? I got shot three times. That's what's the matter. Here, take the wheel."

I'd never driven a car before, but I'd played my share of racing games. As it turned out, driving a car in real life and driving in a video game weren't quite the same. Especially, holding the wheel in one hand from the passenger's seat. I side-swiped a parked car and knocked over a couple of garbage cans, but I didn't get us killed. I guess that was the main thing.

Meanwhile, the vampire was frantically digging underneath his coat. I couldn't tell if he was on fire or had a bumblebee in his shirt. Then he took out a bag that looked a bit like the one I'd given him, only this one was bigger. It was rectangular and had a red cross on it. It also had a bullet hole in the side, so half of the blood was gone.

The smell of it was strong, but I didn't get as worked up this time, I guess because I'd fed already. But a part of me still wanted to grab the bag from him and drain it myself.

"Damn," he said. "This was my last one." He put his mouth over the bullet hole in the side of the bag and finished the rest. By this time we were approaching Water Street, the main road running through town. I could hear police sirens behind us.

"Are you okay?" I asked.

"I'll be fine. Vampires heal very quickly, boy, much faster than people, especially if they get fresh blood. The good stuff, not that bovine crap you were pushing earlier."

He must have been telling the truth—that vampires healed quickly—because he actually managed to keep the car straight for a whole block.

"Where are we going?"

"To the river. I know a place we can hide."

"Isn't the police station this way?" I said. This didn't seem like the best route.

The vampire didn't answer. Instead, he stepped on the gas, ran a red light, then turned onto Water Street. The tires made so much noise when he rounded the corner that I was surprised they didn't fly off the car. A few blocks up the street in the other direction was the police station. I looked out the back. There were so many flashing red and blue lights, every officer in town must have been in on the chase. As it turned out, not all of them were behind us. A group appeared very suddenly around the bend. They had a roadblock in place. Several cars were parked end to end across the street.

The vampire jumped the curb so we were cruising right on the sidewalk. We were lucky—nobody was out for a stroll, just a few ducks that had wandered up from the river. Fortunately, we missed them. Unfortunately, we hit the back of a cruiser that had moved to intercept us. The hood flew off our car and the windshield crumbled into a spiderweb of broken glass. Then the engine started making clunking noises.

"That's the problem with these damn Mustangs," the vampire said. "A couple of high-speed collisions and they just fall apart."

I was gripping the handle above the door so firmly I nearly pulled the roof down on us. I expected the car to fall to pieces, but it didn't. We kept charging forward.

"What are you doing?" I shouted.

"I have a plan," he answered.

I wondered if it involved checking him into the Nicholls Ward. I was about to tell him that my room was free, but he turned and asked me a question.

"Are you warm?"

This guy really was a loon. His door was missing. The car was like a wind tunnel. With his hair whipping around, it was a wonder he could even see the road.

"No," I said. "I'm actually pretty cool."

"Well, that's too bad. I thought if you were warm, you might like to go for a swim."

I looked out my window. Like I said before, we were driving down Water Street. It had that name for a reason. The Otonabee River was flowing beside us. It looked like a giant shadow.

He cranked the wheel over. We left the sidewalk and started spinning on a strip of grass that sat between the river and the road. We did a slow three-sixty, then went over the bank. I heard myself shouting in surprise. For a moment we were airborne. Then the back of the car slammed into the river. Water splashed everywhere. The car stopped dead and the Otonabee started pouring in through the rear window and the open door.

The vampire calmly undid his seat belt. "So, did I pass my driving test?" he asked. Then he gave me a quick wink, turned and dove into the water.

Chapter 16
Creatures of the Night

As soon as the vampire disappeared out the car door, I frantically undid my seat belt. Half a dozen police cruisers were screeching to a halt where we'd left the sidewalk and spun into the river. There was no time to lose. I started to push my door open, then I realized it would be easier to swim out the driver's side, so I jumped over the gearshift, took a deep breath and pushed off against the sinking car.

The river was freezing. If you've ever jumped into cold water, you know exactly how shocking it can be. The chill goes straight to your bones and makes it hard to move. And the water was loud. That meant it was moving fast. It took me totally by surprise. The instant I was clear of the car, the river pulled me straight under.

I hadn't been swimming since my father died. I could sort of picture how the whole thing was supposed to work, but making it happen was another matter. The water tossed me back up and I managed to sneak another breath, but a half second later I was under again. Then I banged my shins against a rock and lost all my air. I tried rolling onto my back so I could keep my face above the surface, but the current made it too difficult. My head came up, slipped under again, and I took in a mouthful of water. The next time I made it up for air, a wave splashed into my face. By this time I was coughing like a pack-a-day smoker. My arms were flailing and I kicked with both legs. I might just as well have had rocks in my pockets.

I heard a muffled voice off to my right. Someone was shouting at me. With all the noise of the river, it sounded like it was coming from twenty miles away. I took a quick look around for the vampire, but with the water in my eyes I couldn't make anything out.

"Stand up," the voice shouted. "STAND UP!"

It sounded like the vampire, but I couldn't be sure. It also sounded like good advice. I put a leg down and touched bottom. The water was about four feet deep, shallow enough to touch, but deep enough that the strong current pushing at my back made it impossible to stand in place. I got knocked off balance right away, but I just put my other leg down and so managed to keep my head above water.

Eventually I got the hang of it, bounding from leg to leg as I drifted with the current. I must have looked like those guys who landed on the moon, springing up and down like I didn't weigh a thing. The only difference, aside from the fact that I wasn't in outer space, was that I couldn't see where I was stepping. There were rocks on the bottom and so I lost my footing a few times and wound up swallowing more water. But with the current pushing me so quickly, I covered a lot of ground. Enough that I could no longer hear or see any signs of the police.

I spied the vampire off to my right. He was about a hundred feet away, moving towards the shore, which was steep and high and covered in trees. From the street, he'd be pretty much invisible. I followed as best I could. By this time, I'd swallowed half the Otonabee and could see the edge of Little Lake up ahead. In a relatively short time, we'd managed to travel back up Water Street, past the police station and most of the downtown. The vampire waved me over, and as I approached, the water got shallower and shallower, so my moon-jumping changed rather abruptly into normal walking. Or at least normal stumbling.

"We should keep moving," the vampire said. "They'll have the dogs out soon."

"Where are we going?"

He nodded over his shoulder. "I want to get to the far side of the river," he explained. "It's a bit ironic, really." And he looked at me as though he'd just told one of the funniest jokes in the history of comedy.

"I don't get it."

"Don't you read vampire books or watch the movies? We aren't supposed to be able to cross running water. It's a bunch of baloney, but in this case, it's sadly true."

I still didn't get it. And I wasn't keen on the idea of leaving our hiding spot. But another minute with this kook was going to be the death of me. I was tired. What I wanted most was to collapse into a warm bed. Even a coffin would have done.

"Well, this is no good," he said at last. "There's a place we can hide on the far side of the river, but we can't get across this way, and we're still too close to the heat." He peered over his shoulder again, as though expecting the police to appear any second. Then he looked me over and smiled. "You all right?"

I nodded, shivering. "Who *are* you?" I asked.

"I have had many names," he said, pulling his tattered overcoat up around his face so that it looked like a cape. He spoke with only his eyes and matted hair showing. "But you may call me . . . *John*."

If this was supposed to be a joke, I didn't get it.

"John Entwistle." He paused, like this was supposed to mean something to me. "You know, like the bass player from The Who."

"Who are The Who?"

"*Who are The Who?* You gotta be joking! Rock band. Late '60s early '70s."

I still didn't get it.

He started shaking his head again, then he looked up at the sky. A sliver of moon shone through the thin layer of clouds overhead. He took a deep breath and let it out slowly. "Man, time moves quickly."

I'd heard other people say that, too. I'd noticed they were never young.

"How old are you?" I asked.

"Six and a half." I thought he would say more, but he didn't. At least not right away. He kept his face to the sky. His eyes were closed. It was like he was soaking up the starlight. Then he fixed me with a steady stare. "When you're as old as I am, boy, you start counting by the century."

That took a few seconds to register. Six and a half centuries. Six hundred and fifty years old?

"You're joking." I said.

Mr. Entwistle reached into his coat and pulled out a silver flask. It had a bullet stuck to it.

"Of course I'm joking. I'm really only thirty. I've just lived hard."

At this point, I really didn't know what to believe.

He pried the bullet lose and tossed it into the river. Then he uncapped the flask and held it up. "To our escape," he said. He took a swig and offered it to me. I accepted, but as soon as I got it near my mouth, my whole system recoiled.

"What's wrong?" he asked.

"I thought it was blood!"

He shook his head. "No. There's the good stuff. And then there's the *good stuff*. I guess you're a little young for Crown Royale." He took the flask back, put down another swig, then tucked it away.

"How did you do it?" I asked.

63

"Do what?"

"Get up after being shot so many times? That first night at the hospital, they shot you about twenty times. There was blood everywhere."

"The blood wasn't mine," he said. "I'd stuffed my coat with Red Cross bags, thinking you'd be hungry."

As soon as he said this, I remembered something I'd forgotten.

"I left that box of blood in the car," I said.

"That swill. Leave it. You'll never reach your potential drinking that crap. I almost feel sorry for the fish."

I'd never had anything else. "I don't want to kill anyone," I said.

"You won't have to. There are other ways of getting blood. I'll show you. Stick with me and you'll be fine."

I looked him over. He was a disaster. Still, he wasn't freaked out like he had been the night he remodelled the Nicholls Ward. It made me wonder what had spooked him so badly.

"Why did you steal that motorcycle?" I asked.

He scratched at his stubble and thought for a second or two. "I was in a bad headspace. But that was two days ago. I'm better now, as you can see."

I could see that I needed to get in touch with my uncle, or I was probably going to end up in jail, or worse.

"Do you have a cellphone?" I asked.

He laughed. "Yeah, I left it in my Porsche. Now we should get going. The cops are after us. And someone else is after you. Another vampire. A powerful one. With some dangerous friends." He looked at me closely. I wondered if he was testing me to see how much I knew already.

"The Baron Vrolok," I said. "And the Fallen."

Mr. Entwistle raised his eyebrows and nodded slowly. "The Fallen. Interesting term. I like it. It fits. But as for Vrolok, well, we can talk about him later. For now, we need to disappear. And I know just the place." He nodded towards the heart of the city and reached out with a hand to help me up the bank. "Come along, boy. Time for your first lesson."

He raised his upper lip just enough on one side to reveal the long canine tooth underneath, then he bounded off. I did my best to follow. If this was my first lesson, at least it was about something I understood. Running.

✦ ✦ ✦ ✦

That night we were like a pair of wolves. Fast. Tireless. The hours drifted by. We dodged through backyards. Over fences and hedges. Across the rooftops of downtown apartments and single-storey row houses. Mr. Entwistle was light on his feet. Nearly invisible. And he didn't really run like other people. He bounded. He loped. Half the time I couldn't see him or hear him. I think he must have been testing me to see if I could keep up.

I couldn't.

But whenever I lost track of him for more than a few seconds, he'd appear on a rooftop overhead or leap out of the darkness so that our chase could continue. He stuck to the shadows, and I followed. Up and down fire escapes. Into trees. Along the edges of buildings and rows of parked cars. I felt alive. And, as weird as this will sound, I felt as if I was somehow part of the night. That my body was just a shadow, an extension of the darkness.

After we'd put a few miles behind us, Mr. Entwistle began to speak.

"You've lived a half life," he said. "Like a caged animal, alive but not free. But you feel differently now, don't you, boy?"

I nodded. I did feel different. Excited. Uncertain. I was being hunted by another vampire, my father's killer. And his minions. An avalanche of trouble was headed my way, but I was strangely unafraid.

It was true that I had no idea what was going to happen to me, but there are many kinds of uncertainty, and uncertainty about the future is just one of them. There is also the uncertainty of where you fit in. Where you belong. Until my escape with Mr. Entwistle, I never felt as though I really belonged anywhere. My parents were dead. I had no brothers or sisters. No home of my own. And as much as I loved Nurse Ophelia, I certainly didn't belong in a mental ward. But those days were over. At that moment, I knew my place. I knew what I was. The problems that had made my life miserable back at the ward—my reaction to the sun, my food trouble, my transfusions, my bouts of anger, the need to be alone—these things had always been shrouded in mystery, because no one could explain why I was like this, why I was so different. I'd been waiting for an answer. For a cure. Well, the waiting was over. I was a vampire. A creature of the night. Inhuman. Beyond human. Stronger. Faster. Tougher. And the certainty of this gave me a profound confidence. I was finally where I belonged. In the darkness.

"To run, to hunt with another vampire, is to realize your true self," Mr. Entwistle said. "You realize how you were meant to be." He stopped to sniff the air, then glanced at me from the corner of his eye. "But be cautious. It is at moments like these that your desire to kill will be strongest." He turned and scrambled over a tall wooden fence.

We were in the old west end, a neighbourhood of century-old homes. I can always tell when I'm running in an older neighbourhood. The houses all have wide porches, whose whole point seems to be to welcome guests to the front door. It's way different in the new areas of town, where the houses are all the same and the garages jump out at you like the cars are more important than the people. Whenever I imagined living a normal life, in a normal home, it looked a lot like the one in front of me. It was set well back from the street on a large lot with huge trees all around.

And even though it was dark and a bit rundown, it had a strangely inviting feel.

"Are you ready?"

I didn't know why Mr. Entwhistle was asking me this, but I said okay anyway.

"Well then, let's go." And he started up the lane.

Chapter 17
The Safe House

While I walked beside Mr. Entwistle, our feet scuffing on the paving stones, the world of the night opened up like the pages of a book. Something—probably a cat or a squirrel—was moving quietly through the hedge off to our right. Bats hunted overhead. I could even hear the beating of moth wings; dozens were circling under the street lamp behind us. I sniffed at the air and noticed a faint trace of wine.

"Whose house is this?" I asked.

Mr. Entwistle laughed. "Mine."

He turned towards a carport on the far side of the house. There was a Porsche underneath. A cherry-red convertible. He took out a set of keys, unlocked the door and reached inside. When he resurfaced, he was holding a cellphone to his ear.

"Just need to check my messages."

I had to smile. I guess he wasn't such a disaster after all.

He led me up onto the porch, then through the front door and into the hall. I was curious to see what he'd have stored away in a house so old, so I was surprised to discover that it was nearly empty. No shelves or carpets or pictures or lamps. Only the living room had any furniture—just two wooden chairs that sat near the fireplace. There was a small, round table between them with a half-empty glass of wine on it. An overturned bottle was lying on the floor, accounting for the smell I'd detected on the walk.

"I must have been in a hurry," Mr. Entwistle said. "Never leave a glass half full."

He walked over to the table and drained the glass. I stared at him dumbly.

"Oh, sorry," he said. "Did you want some?"

I shook my head and raised my hands so he wouldn't bring it any closer.

Mr. Entwistle sat down, then he kicked the other chair over to where I was standing. The echo was loud in the empty room.

"Most vampires can't take anything but blood," he said. "The instant you're infected, a rapid metamorphosis takes place in your body. The pathogen isn't well understood, so no one knows exactly what happens. But you know the results. Most things you can do better—run, hear, see, smell, heal. But some things you can't do at all. Eating is one of them. Cells can no longer make digestive enzymes to break food down into substrate. It takes about thirty years to reactivate those portions of your DNA that produce enzymes for metabolizing alcohol."

I didn't know what he was talking about and I didn't ask. Half his words sounded made up. He bent over and retrieved the bottle from the floor. Then he peeked down the neck to see if anything was left. Apparently there was enough. He tipped the neck over the glass and a thin red stream dribbled out. Less than a sip.

"Thirty years, so you've gotta be committed."

He offered the sip of wine to me. I took the glass and sniffed at it. The smell made me think of mouldy fruit, rotten and sour. The expression on my face made him laugh. I handed it back. There was no way I was putting that stuff in my mouth.

"Thirty years to be able to drink wine again. Thirty years . . . seems like a short time to me now. But not back then." He snorted. It might have been a laugh had there been any trace of humour on his face. "Those were the plague years. The time of the Black Death. Took my wife. My son, too. But not my daughter. She lived—for about another ten years. Soldiers killed her. Burned her as a witch. Edward's men. Edward III. Ever heard of him?"

I shook my head.

"Well, that's not terribly surprising. He wasn't very popular by the end. But things were different back then. Life had no value."

He looked at me, and his eyes were smouldering.

"The place is pretty empty, isn't it, boy?"

"Yeah," I said.

"Surprised?"

I nodded, then shrugged. "I guess."

"Well, I've learned not to get mired in the past. I don't collect things. I don't need things. I have faith, and I have a purpose, and that's what matters."

He held up the last mouthful of wine so that the crimson liquid glistened in the moonlight streaming in through the back windows.

"To finding purpose," he said.

He upended his glass while I stepped over to the chair across from him. My shoes were still a bit damp and they made squelching noises on the floor.

I sat down and felt myself drifting away. I had never concerned myself with purpose. I'd spent most of the last eight years wondering what might be wrong with me and whether anyone could make it better. I had been waiting to be fixed. And while I'd waited, my only concern had been how to spend my time so that I didn't die of boredom. I tried to explain this as best I could, and I think he understood me.

"The biggest problem was that you didn't know yourself. But you're on track now that you've discovered the truth."

He looked at his empty wineglass with a sad expression. Then he stood and walked into the kitchen. When he came back he had another bottle in his hand.

"What is *your* purpose?" I asked him.

He used his teeth to pull the cork from the wine bottle and poured himself a glass.

"I help vampires," he said.

"Only the good ones, I hope."

He laughed and raised his drink. "Not usually," he answered. "It's the bad ones that need the most help."

Mr. Entwistle sat and stared at his glass of wine. After seeing him all paranoid in the nuthouse, it was odd to see him so relaxed. Odd and reassuring. Of course, he could have used a few hours in a hair salon and about a gallon of Miracle Glow shampoo. And with his mismatched gloves and overstuffed overcoat, he still looked the part of the crazy motorcycle man. But it didn't matter now. I trusted him.

"You know that my father was a vampire hunter?" I said.

"No," he answered. "But I can see another lesson in irony tucked away there someplace. God has quite a sense of humour."

He seemed to doze off for just a second or two, then his head jerked up. "So he's gone, your father? Or retired?"

"He died."

"I'm sorry for your loss," he said. "But perhaps it will prepare you for your life as a vampire. You will outlive everyone you know. It isn't easy."

Then he stood, removed his overcoat and held it up so that the silver moonlight shone through many finger-sized openings. They were bullet holes. When he tossed the coat to the floor, I saw what he was wearing underneath. It wasn't ten layers of clothing. It was like something out of a video game.

"What's that?" I asked.

"Body armour," he said. "Platinum." He thumped his chest. "Sewn inside a double Kevlar weave. Cost me more than my car, but it's worth it. Stops most small-arms fire. A bullet still feels like a sledgehammer, but it keeps the blood where it belongs."

That explained it. I'd watched him get shot so many times that all the wine in his stomach should have been streaming out onto the floor.

"Do you have another set?" I asked.

He shook his head.

"So, what do we do now?"

Mr. Entwistle looked around. "You don't have to decide on anything at the moment. Just relax. You're in a safe house. No one knows you're here. You can rest and get used to being a vampire. It's no small thing. Then, once you're ready, you can start testing yourself. See how strong you are. How fast. What it takes to exhaust you. How well you recover. How quickly you learn. What your strengths are. And your talents."

"What do you mean by 'talents'?"

"That's a loaded question." He picked up his wineglass and spun it in his hand, then he put it under his nose and inhaled deeply. "All people have talents. Things they're naturally good at. But when it comes to vampires, that word has a special meaning. You know, most people who get infected, they don't become vampires. The body's immune system fights it off, as it would any other disease. I think that's why, in all the old stories, people had to be bitten so many times."

I remembered that from *Dracula*. It seemed to take three bites.

And you had to lose a lot of blood too, which I guess made you weaker. It made me wonder: if you were healthy, how many times could you get bitten and still stay human?

"I only got bitten once," I said.

Mr. Entwistle's eyebrows rose in surprise. Then his face relaxed. "But you were young. Maybe that had something to do with it. Vampires don't usually bite children."

I nodded.

"You are the only child vampire I've ever seen who has survived," Mr. Entwistle continued. "But that's not what I'm getting at. The whole talent thing has to do with the pathogen. From what I can tell, it's like a kind of retrovirus. Do you know what that means?"

I shook my head.

"It means it's a kind of virus that alters the DNA of the host. Sometimes the results are bizarre, the sort of stuff that fills fantasy stories. Witches. Wizards. I've met vampires that could breathe underwater, walk through fire, pass through walls, make themselves as light as air, rip steel, travel out of their bodies, change their shape, read people's thoughts. There are as many talents as there are vampires. We are unique, after all, like the rest of God's creatures."

"What's your talent?" I asked him.

"I can drink," he said, and laughed. Then he stopped abruptly and cleared his throat. "Well, that's more of a hobby than a talent, really. No, I see things. Visions. Snippets of the future, the past, the present. That's what led me to you. I had a vision of a boy. Oh, it was months ago now. A child vampire. I was amazed at first. Then saddened. He was starving and lonely. Then I had one again last month. And another. And another. Just about every night, come to think of it."

"What did you see?"

"I saw you alone most of the time. Reading. Running. Boy, for a young blood, you've got some speed."

I looked away, a bit embarrassed, but the tone of his voice drew me back.

"I saw you chased from your room by the cops. And I saw . . ." He stopped to clear his throat. "I saw what is hunting you."

Chapter 18
The Boogeyman

M r. Entwistle let out a deep breath. His head tilted sideways but he kept his eyes on me. "You mentioned a name earlier," he said.

"The Baron Vrolok."

He shook his head. "That can't be real. *Vrolok* is the Slavic word for vampire, or werewolf. Centuries ago, they were thought to be the same creature. Perhaps they are. But Vrolok is an assumed name. An alias. No one would be called 'Baron Vampire.'"

"But you've seen him?"

"Yes, if we're talking about the same vampire. Glimpses of the past, mostly. Atrocities we won't speak of. He's old, boy. And insane. They call him 'the Impaler'—for good reason. I have a book on him upstairs. Grim reading. When I saw that your paths were destined to cross, it nearly undid me. I couldn't sleep. For weeks I was haunted because I knew the danger, but I didn't know where to find you. I got frantic. Then I had another vision. You were talking to a nurse, the same one you were standing with a few nights ago. Pretty little thing."

I remembered the expression on his face when he saw Nurse Ophelia that first time—a flicker of recognition.

"Well," he continued, "once I knew you were in a medical facility, it was enough to start a search. And so it has ended." He smiled, but there was something in his eyes that made me doubt my troubles were over.

"What is going to happen to me?" I asked.

His hands moved apart just a bit. It was a kind of shrug. "Who knows?" he said.

Was he drunk already? He'd just told me he could see the future.

"I thought you said you have visions."

This made him laugh. "Yes, but I don't get to choose. I only see bits and pieces of what might happen. Possibilities. The future is never set. It moves. It changes. Most of what I see never comes to pass . . . thankfully."

He leaned forward and his head tipped up, as though what he was about to say was particularly important. "You have my protection now, which is no small thing. You'd have to dig your way to China to find another vampire as old as I am. Don't worry about the future just yet. Do what is right, for the right reasons, and the rest will take care of itself."

He got up and walked towards the stairs in the front hall.

"Time for sleep now," he announced. "I haven't done this much talking since the Nuremberg Trials."

He waved for me to follow him up the stairs, then led me to a guest room. Inside was a canopied bed. The window beside it was boarded over. A pile of magazines sat on the floor.

"You'll be safe in here," he said. Then he turned to go.

"Wait," I said.

"What is it?"

"My uncle was supposed to come and get me," I said. "That's why I ran outside when I did. I thought you were him at first."

"He'll be worried, no doubt."

I nodded. "He was coming to break me out."

Mr. Entwistle turned his head just slightly, as though he needed to look at me differently to see if this was true.

"To break you out?"

"Yes. He was worried, just like you were. He told me about Vrolok. And about Johansson."

"Who's Johansson?"

"One of the Fallen," I said. "He's with the police. I was running from him when you arrived."

"And who is your uncle?"

"Maximilian," I said. "He's a vampire hunter. Like my dad."

Mr. Entwistle looked at me with an expression of disbelief on his face. He put a hand against the wall as if to steady himself.

"Maximilian is your uncle?"

"You know him?"

"Know him? Know him! He's like the Boogeyman to us. *Maximilian.* And I practically kidnapped his nephew. Great. Just great." He pushed his hair back from his forehead and looked down at the floor. "Wait a minute," he said. "He must know you're a vampire."

"Yes. He was the one who told me."

"And he didn't kill you for it. Well, that's promising." He walked to the hall window and looked outside. "We'll need to get in touch with him. But not right now."

"Why not?"

He raised his hand and gestured towards the backyard. "The sun will be up soon. If I've learned anything in the last six hundred and fifty years, it's this: don't tempt fate. Your uncle is a vampire hunter. The most feared man in the western world. He has contacts everywhere. And he kills people like us. You'll have to forgive me for not inviting him into my house just before the sun rises."

I was surprised to hear him talk this way. And embarrassed. I'd always thought I read people very well. I trusted my uncle. Truth is, I trusted most people. But in his case, I believed he had a genuine interest in my safety. If he'd wanted me dead, I'm sure he could have managed it quite easily by now.

"Sorry," Mr. Entwistle said. "We can talk more about it tomorrow night. There will be a way to get in touch with him, but I'd rather err on the side of caution. For vampires, this is a sanctuary. No one can know about it. Especially not people like your uncle." He leaned forward and raised his eyebrows. "Or it won't be safe."

I nodded. Then we said good night.

A few minutes later I was stretched out on the guest bed. It was the first time in recent memory that I'd spent a night outside of the ward. I wasn't exactly nervous, but it did feel a bit weird. And not just because the room was different. My mind was muddled. Mr. Entwistle's comments about my uncle had made me see things differently. I guess I couldn't blame him for being worried. I hadn't really seen Maximilian from a vampire's point of view. Things were obviously more complicated than I'd thought. My life had been so simple before. And easy. But not any more.

Chapter 19
The Vampire Problem

I slept late the next day, probably because of all the running Mr. Entwistle and I had done the night before. The sun had been down for about an hour when he came to wake me. He was dressed in his body armour.

"Sleep okay?" he asked. He had his hand on the doorknob and was leaning in from the hallway.

I stretched and yawned, then clamped my eyelids down to try to wake myself up.

"I have to go out," Mr. Entwistle continued. "I'm going to try to get us some blood."

I sat up. "Good," I said. "I'm starving."

Mr. Entwistle looked at me funny. "Starving?"

"Yeah."

He stepped into the room. "You're starving?"

I nodded again.

"But you drank yesterday. I watched you."

"So did you," I said.

"Yes. But I won't need blood again for another week, at least. I'm just getting more because I've run out and some might be available, not because I need to drink it right now."

Well, this was weird.

"I usually drink twice a day," I said.

He looked at me like I had two heads. "Twice a day?" He thought for a moment. "Must be that cow swill you were drinking. Vampires don't need that much blood. Not when they get the real stuff."

"Really?"

"Haven't you seen the movie *Dracula*? He drinks a woman dry and sleeps for a hundred years."

"I thought that was just a story."

"Well, it is. Or that part of it."

"Have you ever slept for a hundred years?"

"Well, no. But . . . but you can't do that nowadays. The world changes too quickly. If I'd fallen asleep a hundred years ago, I wouldn't know what a car was. Or an electrical appliance. Or airplanes, movie theatres, radios, televisions, push-up bras, computers, telephones, Velcro. Why, I'd be useless. But that's not the point. A vampire should be able to drink and coast for a while. Twice a day!"

I guess as a vampire I didn't quite have my act together yet.

"So you're going out?" I asked. "Should I come?"

He shook his head. "No. Too dangerous. You need to relax. Think. Sleep some more. Start writing the great Canadian novel. I won't be long. An hour, tops."

"Where are you going?"

"Blood donor clinic. They're closing in another half hour, so I've got to hurry." He turned to the door, then stopped. "By the way, I've been thinking about your uncle."

"What about him?"

"I think it's time for Maximilian and me to sit down and settle our differences."

"What differences?"

He took a deep breath and let it out slowly. "There are a lot of opinions about how to solve the vampire problem."

I sat up and swung my legs out of the bed. "You mean that we exist?"

"More or less. Some people want to see us wiped from the face of the earth . . ."

"I don't think my uncle is one of them," I said.

Mr. Entwistle cleared his throat. "Maybe not. But it is how he deals with the rogues."

"The bad ones."

"Exactly."

I think I understood this. After all, weren't most vampires evil? "How else are you supposed to deal with them?" I asked.

"In a word, forgiveness. 'Am I not destroying my enemies when I make friends of them?' Abraham Lincoln."

Abraham Lincoln. I'd heard that name somewhere. "Is he that guy with the beard?"

Mr. Entwistle shook his head in disbelief. "Guy with the beard? Guy with the beard! Is that what they're teaching you kids in school these days?"

I shrugged. "I don't know. I've never been to school."

This seemed to stump him completely. He was speechless for about ten seconds.

"Never been to high school?"

I nodded.

"It's the most important time of a young man's life!"

He must have seen that this bothered me, because he flipped his hand through the air like it didn't matter at all.

"So what? I never went either. And I'm richer than Bill Gates."

"Really?"

"Well, rich in memories." He smiled again, then his face flattened out and his voice got a little more serious. "Don't worry, boy. There's a reason for everything. Why my wife and son died. And my daughter. Why we have this contagion. And if there is a reason for your being here, it might just be so that your uncle and I can find a way forward without having to declare war on each other."

I was scratching my head when he said this. I stopped and looked at him carefully. What did he mean? I was afraid to ask. In his body armour, he looked more formidable than anyone I'd ever seen. But it was more than that. He had a kind of inner strength. A confidence. My uncle had it, too. I didn't want them to be enemies. And I didn't want to be stuck in the middle. It was bad enough that Vrolok was after me.

"Where does the Baron Vrolok fit into this?" I asked.

"That conversation will have to wait." He pulled up his sleeve and checked his watch. "Yeah. I need to boogie. Clock's ticking." He stopped in the doorway. "We'll get in touch with your uncle when I get back."

"Is that a promise?" I asked.

"I make no promises. My word is my bond." He smiled a tight-lipped, goodbye kind of smile, then nodded. "And until I get back, you're grounded."

"What does *that* mean?"

"You can't leave the house. That's the way it is when you go underground. You have to stay out of sight until the coast is clear."

"For how long?"

"No idea. But the library's down the hall. That should keep you out of trouble for at least a few centuries. Hopefully, by then your troubles will be over." Then he grunted a goodbye and slipped out the door.

Chapter 20
Collision

After Mr. Entwistle left, I lay in bed for a few minutes flipping through magazines and thinking over what I should do. My brain kept taking me back to the vampire problem—about the rogues, the bad ones—as though that was somehow the secret to figuring everything out. I was going to have to ask Mr. Entwistle more about it. And about Vrolok, in particular. If that wasn't his real name, I had to find out who he was and what powers he had. Talents, Mr. Entwistle had called them. Was he a shape-shifter? Could he walk through fire or breathe under water? It made me wonder what *my* talents might be. Before long I was out of bed and pacing the room.

Walking up walls. That would be cool. Just like Spider-Man. Maybe I could build my own web-shooters, too. Of course flying would be better, but I couldn't really imagine how that would work. I mean, if you were light enough to fly, wouldn't you sort of float around all the time? Maybe there was more to it than that.

I'd never even had any flying dreams, so I wasn't exactly qualified to say. Charlie got them all the time, so if he became a vampire, maybe that would be his talent. Then he'd never have to worry about getting caught. Of course, if I could turn invisible, that would pretty much solve things, too. And getting blood wouldn't be a problem. I could just sneak into the civic hospital and drink it out of bags.

As I pictured myself gorging on a huge stash of blood, my stomach rumbled. A hollow spasm followed. It was time to feed. I stepped out into the hall to have a look around. I thought there might be a supply of blood hiding someplace. And if not, then at least I was moving. That might take my mind off my hunger.

I started my search in the kitchen, but the only thing in the fridge was wine. The cupboards were empty, too—nothing but dusty plates and a box of light bulbs. I went down into the basement. Three doors opened off a central hall. The first room had padded walls and a padded floor and ceiling. I'd seen a couple of these back at the ward, although I didn't remember the ceilings being padded. I guess when vampires got put in time-out, they were a little more jumpy than normal people. Next to the padded room was an office. The computer on the desk wouldn't have been out of place on the Starship *Enterprise*. Newspaper clippings were tacked to the wall beside it. Most of them had to do with people disappearing. The last room was full of filing cabinets. They were all locked.

I went back upstairs. There was nothing in the bedrooms but magazines and closets. Then I found the library. It stretched the whole length of the house and was lined with wall-to-wall bookshelves. Other volumes were piled in stacks on the floor. The room was practically groaning from the weight of them all. Mr. Entwistle wasn't kidding—it would have taken centuries to read them all. Most of the books were old. *Very* old. And even though I've heard a lot of people say you shouldn't judge a book by its cover, well, you sort of can with an old book, because if it was crummy someone would have thrown it out a long time ago. So you can bet I was pretty excited.

The only light in the room came from a gas fireplace that was set in the wall opposite the door. Two windows sat on either side, and through these I could see the yellow glow of a streetlight outside, and the dark silhouettes of leaves and branches. It was like they were waving to me, begging me to come outside and join them. Plunging into the darkness for a long run would have to wait. Without Mr. Entwistle, I wasn't going anywhere.

I was just deciding where to begin my search for books about vampires when something fluttered across the window. I caught a glimpse of a dark shape out of the corner of my eye. When I turned it was gone, so I moved closer, to get a broader view of the yard outside. The night air was so thick with fog you couldn't see the sky. It made the neighbouring houses look hazy and ghostly. Bats were diving under the streetlight in search of food. That must have been what caught my eye. In the shadows below, two green, glowing eyes blinked up at me. It was a raccoon. We stared at each other, then it bolted from its hiding place and disappeared. As I watched the fog roll past, the porch lights across the street faded to a soft white. The street lamp all but disappeared. So did the bats. I thought at first that they were just hard to spot in the haze, but when I listened for them, I couldn't hear anything. A chill went through me and I shuddered. A cold had settled into the room. And a quiet. I held my breath, but all I could hear was the sound of my heart and the wooden floor creaking under my feet.

I backed away from the window. I probably shouldn't have been so close to it anyway, in case someone saw me. Then I realized I was being silly. With all the fog, anyone in the yard would have needed X-ray vision to see up here. Still, I couldn't shake the feeling that something wasn't quite right. I snuck back to the window and edged one eye past the frame. Something flew past and I jumped back again. It was a large bat. The biggest I'd ever seen.

I hid behind the rocking chair so that the back of it was between me and the window. The flapping of large, leathery wings returned. This time it didn't go away. And it was much louder than it should have been. I peeked around the edge of the chair. The bat was hovering right outside the window. Wait a minute—hovering? That wasn't right. I was hardly what you'd call an expert, but I'd spent enough time running the city streets after midnight to know that bats darted. They were always on the move. You'd never see a bat soar like a hawk, that's for sure. They sort of flopped through the air, instead. They could do it pretty quickly, but you'd never call it graceful. This one just . . . *hovered*. It was unnatural. And it raised goosebumps on my arms and neck.

I stayed hidden behind the chair until I heard the sound of tires crunching on gravel. Someone was pulling into the driveway. I stiffened at the sound. Then I noticed that the flapping had stopped. A car door slammed. Then another. I didn't want to risk going to the window to see who it might be, not with that bat outside. It looked big enough to tear the beak off a bald eagle. It didn't take a genius to figure out what that meant. Not after listening to Mr. Entwistle's description of vampire talents. Some were shape-shifters. He'd said so himself, and the stories were full of things like that. It seemed crazy, but then again, three days ago I'd been nothing more than a kid with a bad sun allergy. I couldn't take anything for granted any more.

I quickly tiptoed out of the room. I reached the top of the stairs just as several sets of feet climbed onto the porch. The old planks creaked. I heard whispers. I hesitated. There was no way I was going to go down into the hall. But I had to know who it was. A sinister thought had taken form in the back of my mind. Dracula, the same vampire who could turn himself into a bat, couldn't enter a stranger's house without an invitation. That usually meant having a human servant break in first, then open a door or window. Once he'd even got a dog to break in for him, or maybe it was a wolf. I couldn't remember.

I bent down so I could see through the hallway onto the porch, but there were no windows set in the door and none beside it, either, so there was no way to see who was lurking outside. I did notice that a steel bar had been set across the back of the door, sitting in a pair of brackets. I didn't remember Mr. Entwistle barring the door when we came home. He must have set it up that way before he left.

I strained to listen, then something crashed against the door. It sounded like a wrecking ball. The whole place shook. A crack appeared in the middle of the door and bits of plaster dropped from the hall ceiling.

The people outside were smashing their way in!

I tore down the stairs just as another crash sounded from the porch. The door broke apart, but the bar remained in place. Through the opening I could see two policemen. They were holding something between them that looked like a small battering ram. Off to one side was a man in an overcoat with a thick, pink scar under his eye. Everett Johansson. Somehow, he had found me.

I ran out of the hall, through the living room and into the kitchen. I had to find a back door. It was on the far side of the stove. I could see another pair of brackets and a steel pipe lying on the counter. Since this door wasn't barred, I figured Mr. Entwistle must have left this way.

I could hear voices shouting behind me, then a loud clank, which I guessed was the steel bar on the front door falling to the floor. The men were coming inside, only seconds away.

I yanked on the handle of the back door, but it didn't open.

"Come on," I shouted. I kept pulling, then noticed it was locked. None of the rooms in the Nicholls Ward had locks, so I'd sort of forgotten about them. I twisted the deadbolt and pulled the door open. Then I grabbed the steel bar, just in case, and darted outside.

Men were entering the kitchen as I cleared the landing. In four steps I was around the side of the house. I coiled my body for a mid-stride leap, then launched myself up onto the lower branch of a tree. I used this as a springboard and cleared the neighbour's fence. I couldn't tell if anyone had seen me, but I wasn't taking any chances. I just kept running through the fog. Full blast.

I jumped another fence, and another. It made me think of men running hurdles at the Olympics, only these were six feet high. When I reached the last property on the block I ditched the pipe. It was slowing me down. Then I tore across the road and into the next yard. I wanted to stay off the streets. There was too much light. I ran through people's yards instead. Dogs barked. Lights came on. People shouted. I didn't stop, not for anything. My feet were moving so quickly that, if the earth had opened up below me, I would have run through the air. And the whole time, I had only one thing on my mind.

Vrolok had found me. My father's killer.

Wasn't that place supposed to be a safe house? And where was Mr. Entwistle?

I laboured on. All I could hear was my own frantic breathing. I thought it best to hold a straight line and put as much distance between me and the bad guys as I could manage. Soon, it was like I was running in a tunnel. My eyes took in nothing that wasn't right in front of me. So I didn't react when I heard a loud roar and a scream. It took me too long to sort out what it was. The roar turned out to be a car horn, and the scream was skidding tires. It was a police van. I'd reached the end of someone's property and had run onto the street without looking. The police must have been searching for me. They were moving quickly. And so there was little I could do. I just lifted my feet and curled up into a ball so that my legs hit the grille and my shoulder hit the windshield. And then I was airborne.

Chapter 21
Homecoming

I remember an explosion of light. Pain followed. Then a sharp snap from inside my body somewhere. And more pain. Then darkness.

When my eyes started working again I was lying on my back with my arm twisted underneath me. It was broken. My stomach was bucking. Even though it was empty, it still wanted me to throw up. The whole world was spinning around me. Even when I closed my eyes.

I managed to sit up. The pain in my broken arm made my vision go black and for a few seconds I think I was unconscious again. Then I put my one good hand against the side of my head and rocked back and forth, moaning.

I was vaguely aware of people approaching. I didn't know who. I didn't care. I just wanted them to go away. I wanted to be back at the ward. To have my dinner with Nurse Ophelia. And ping-pong fights with Charlie. And I wanted the pain to stop. What I got instead were two voices just above me.

". . . not your fault. Came out of nowhere."

". . . kid move so fast!"

". . . never seen anything . . ."

"Are you okay?"

". . . look like anything's broken?"

"Can you hear me?"

". . . neck seems fine . . ."

". . . at his arm . . ."

". . . kid from the ward . . ."

Then one of them touched me. That was a big mistake.

I'd always suspected that I was much stronger than other kids my age. This wasn't just a vampire thing, it was also because I lifted weights every night. Turned out my strength was off the charts. I didn't really understand that until I felt the policeman's hand on my shoulder. He was wearing a bulletproof vest. I think they all wear them now, which is good. It probably saved his life. I balled my fist and smashed it into his chest. I didn't even see where he landed.

Then I screamed. It wasn't a shrill scream, the kind of sound a person makes when they're afraid. It was more like something you'd expect to come from the mouth of an angry predator. I was furious. Then I was back on my feet, running. I can guess that the police tried to catch me. They never got close.

In time, maybe an hour, my rage started to subside. I slowed and listened. Cars. Distant voices. The hum of electricity. Feet shuffling on the sidewalk around the corner. Rustling leaves and creaking branches. Nothing out of the ordinary. I was alone. And I had no idea what to do. I should have asked Mr. Entwistle before he left where the blood donor clinic was. If I had, maybe I could have figured out why he hadn't come back.

I decided to keep running.

More time passed. I looked at my arm. It was black just below the elbow, and it had a crook in it. I'd been cradling it in my other hand. It didn't feel as painful now. More itchy than anything. And it throbbed as I ran.

What I needed was blood. According to Mr. Entwistle, that would speed up my healing. But I also needed a safe place to hide. So I kept running, oblivious to the houses and blocks as they passed, until I found myself in familiar territory—my old neighbourhood. I turned a corner and just like that, I was standing in front of our old house on O'Carroll Avenue.

I don't know why I chose to go there. Maybe a part of my memory decided for me. I think it must have remembered that I'd once been safe there. And loved.

I stood at the end of the front walk, uncertain. Now that I wasn't moving, I felt very exposed, so I dashed over to the neighbour's place and hid behind a tree. Then I just stared at the house, thinking. The lights inside were off, but it was late. Maybe eleven o'clock. The older couple who lived there now must have been sleeping. I crept out from behind the tree, then I noticed that the big RV that was usually parked in the driveway was gone. It probably meant that they were away. I'd just have to chance it.

I sprinted into the backyard. I hadn't seen it in eight years and it was totally unfamiliar. Everything looked smaller than it should have been. Our old apple tree was gone, and instead of the hedge there was a fence. I crept up to the back door and tried to open it. It was locked. Even with one arm broken I probably could have torn it off the hinges, but I didn't want to damage anything if I didn't have to, so I tried the basement windows. The first one was locked too, but the second one wasn't. It was one of those sliding windows. The wide and short kind. It made a hissing noise as I opened it, and it seemed so loud to me that I was afraid the whole neighbourhood might wake up.

I had to slide in feet first. There was a huge laundry sink underneath, the kind that's made of cement and looks like a big feeding trough, so I didn't have far to go. Fortunately the sink was empty. As soon as I was inside I turned around, slid the window shut and locked it behind me. Instantly, I felt safer. I could actually breathe without worrying about all the noise I was making. After a few deep breaths, my heart began to settle. As it did, the throb in my arm returned.

There was a washing machine beside me. The floor was covered in stuff, mostly boxes and clothes. The room didn't seem familiar, especially the smell. It wasn't foul, but it wasn't a clean smell, either.

I stepped out of the sink and listened. Nothing. To my left was a set of wooden stairs that led to the back hallway. It didn't look as familiar as it should have. Too small. Too worn. I climbed them slowly, cringing each time the old wood creaked. At the top of the steps was a door. I tried to push it open quietly, but it was stuck at the bottom, so when I put some weight behind it, it opened with a pop. And that's when I discovered what the strange smell was. It was a dog. A big husky. It was waiting for me in the back hall. And it didn't look happy.

Animals are a bit like people. You meet some nice ones and some that are a little prickly. This dog was a walking cactus. Its eyes didn't even get along—one was blue and the other was green. But I could see right away that all of his teeth were alike. Long and sharp and white. The way he showed them off, you could tell he was very proud of this.

He snarled, took a few quick steps and lunged at me. I was just fast enough to back up and close the basement door. My heart started pounding again.

The dog was now barking loudly and scratching at the door. With the luck I was having, the neighbours were probably going to show up any minute with torches and pitchforks. There was no way I could stick around with Barky making so much noise, so I ran down the steps and climbed into the sink again. I was aiming to crawl out, but my broken arm was still useless, and the window was too high for me to manage without something taller to stand on. The lights were still off, so I had to fumble around looking for a chair or a stool to put in the sink. In the end, I found something else, and I decided to go upstairs instead and try my luck with Barky.

I'd once read a book by Jack London, *The Call of the Wild*. Actually, my dad read it to me. And we watched the movie on TV. The story is about a dog, Buck. In one scene, he gets thrashed by a man with a stick. Apparently, that's how you establish who's boss. Well, I figured there were lots of ways of showing someone who was boss. And whoever heard of a vampire running away from a dog?

Barky was still scratching at the door when I hit the top of the stairs. He was making more noise than a police siren. I turned the door handle and pushed it open with all the strength I could muster. It wasn't easy. I was carrying an awkward load in my one good arm. But even with all my heavy breathing, and Barky's barking, I could still hear his claws scraping over the tile floor as I forced him backwards. The door opened just enough for me to lean my shoulder in. That was all the space I needed.

I leaned over and dumped my awkward load onto the floor. It was a big bag of dog food, one of those fifty-pounders that old people buy because it probably saves them ten cents. Kibble spilled everywhere. About ten years' worth. And just like that, Barky was my best friend. I didn't even need a stick.

I waited behind the door while he filled his belly. I was feeling jealous. Without a blender and a bag of blood, I wasn't going to be eating anytime soon. And that meant my arm was going to be useless for a while.

After a minute, I stuck my head out and said hello. Barky ignored me completely. He wasn't eating the kibble so much as he was vacuuming it up with his mouth. This gave me a chance to look around. And that was when they hit me. Old memories. I guess it happened because my nerves were a little more settled, but a flood of things I'd forgotten all about came back from some part of my brain I hadn't talked to in a long while.

I could hear my father's voice calling me for dinner. I remembered how he hummed or sang whenever he cooked. Just bits of songs. Never a whole one.

Other things came back. The sound of the back door slamming, all the times I'd gone crashing out into the yard. Coming in from the cold and kicking off wet winter boots. How my dad used to straighten them all the time so that they were always waiting in a row. The vent we dried our mittens on.

My stomach began to tighten.

I left Barky in the back hall stuffing his face. There was a door separating the back hall from the rest of the house, so I closed it to keep him from following me, then I made my way to the stairs. I didn't bother going into the living room or exploring the rest of the house. You would think it might have made me happy to be home after so many years, but it wasn't like that. I felt like an intruder. Or a ghost. Like my body was in the present, in the house as it was now, but my mind was stuck in the past, in my home as it used to be. It made me feel very lonely. Like my life was gone somehow.

At the ward, when I felt this way and got all quiet, it wasn't really because I didn't want to talk to anyone, it was because I only wanted to talk to my parents. My father, as I remembered him. And my mother, as I imagined her.

So I was talking to them as I climbed the stairs and turned down the hall to my old room. I opened the door and stared inside. It looked like a guest bedroom now. Right in the middle was a tall brass bed. It smelled dusty. Unused. I sat on the edge of it and looked out the window at our neighbour's house. Its two front windows loomed on either side above the door. As a kid, I thought it made the house look like a face. And there it was, staring at me again. It was the only familiar thing there.

More memories came back. I couldn't turn them off, even though I was tired and my head felt thick, like it was full of jelly. Mostly I remembered stories my father had read to me. When I couldn't sleep, I'd creep into his room across the hall. Sometimes he'd have fallen asleep watching the news, so the TV would still be on. Other times, after we'd been watching a movie, the room would still smell like buttered popcorn. I thought it was funny that he always cooked it in a pot on the stove even though we had a microwave.

I didn't sit still for very long. I was exhausted. I couldn't feed, so I decided the next best thing was to get some sleep, even though the sun wouldn't be up for a long time. I considered lying under the bed, but then I remembered my dad's closet. It was big, the kind you could walk right into. But more importantly, it had no windows, so when the sun came up it would be pitch black in there.

My dad's closet had always been off limits. One time, I snuck in just before Christmas to see if there were any presents hidden there, but I didn't find anything. Just the same, when he found out, he exploded. It was the only time I remember being afraid of him. He was furious.

Like everything else, the closet was much smaller than I remembered, but it was deep enough for me to lie down flat. There were two rows of clothes hanging inside, and everything smelled like mothballs.

I lay on my back and rested my broken arm on my stomach. The bone might already have mended, I couldn't be sure. The black coloration was gone. It was yellow now. And the odd crook in it had fixed itself somehow so it didn't have that funny bend to it.

I was feeling beat, but I wasn't really sleepy, for some reason. My body was certainly happy to be resting, but my brain was still going sixty miles an hour. I wondered what Charlie would have made of all this. And Nurse Ophelia. Chases and escapes and more chases. And vampires and giant bats. I wondered if they were all right. If they knew I was in trouble. If they were worried.

I let out a deep sigh and turned my head to the side. There wasn't much to look at, just a baseboard running along the wall, so I ran a finger over the cool wood, tracing the pattern in the grain. Then I noticed there was a seam in it that was nearly invisible. Just a thin, vertical crack so slender you'd have needed eyes like a hawk, or a vampire, to see it.

I lay there for a time, rubbing my fingers over the seam in the baseboard. It was strange that my father never wanted me to see the inside of this closet. There was no way it was just about Christmas presents. This place was off limits all year round, even in mid-July. Who does their Christmas shopping in the summer? As I was thinking this over, my finger kept rubbing the seam, until I got a sliver. I don't know if it was because I was still hungry or what, but I got angry again, so I banged my fist against the wall.

A piece of the baseboard slipped forward. I thought at first I must have broken it. Then I noticed that it had separated where the seam was. A little farther down was another. The board was obviously meant to come loose. I rolled carefully onto my side and pulled it free. In behind was an empty space. I stood and turned on the closet light so I could see better. Then I got down on my knees and reached in. The space wasn't even two feet wide, but it was deep enough to hold a box about the size of a chessboard. I pulled it out carefully and set it on the closet floor. It was covered in dust and looked to be made of tin. I blew the top layer of dust off, then pried up the top and looked inside.

Chapter 22
The Journal

Money. The tin was full of it. Some old. Some new. And it was from all over the place: England, Germany, France, Spain, Italy, Hungary, Nigeria, Libya, Turkey, even Malaysia. Sadly, none of it was Canadian. And there were passports. Four of them. All of them had my father's face, but the names were all wrong: Charles Montagne, Jean Levasseur, Frederick Steinke, Thomas Richardson. There was an empty holster, too. It had been folded and the leather had dried so that it was too stiff to be useful. I guess this didn't matter because there was no gun, but there were several boxes of bullets inside. Many of the bullets had spilled out and were rattling around with all kinds of coins and tokens. No wonder my father never wanted me to go in the closet. If I'd found this stuff as a kid it might have been a disaster, especially if the gun had been there, too. I don't remember my father ever having one, but he must have had a weapon of some kind when he went hunting for vampires.

On the bottom of the tin was a notebook. The cover was a collage of coloured squares. Some of them had neat designs that reminded me of far-off places, like India and Egypt. I recognized it right away. It was my father's journal, the one he wrote in when I was a kid. He always encouraged me to keep one too, but I never got in the habit.

I carefully removed it. The cover was soft and a bit pliable. I lifted it to my nose. It had a musty smell. I flipped it open to the first page. It was dated September 14. I started reading.

Out for Chinese with Jake. Michelle was furious when we got back. Charlie had fooled her into answering the door. By the time she realized nobody was there, he'd locked her out on the porch. We found him and Zack asleep on the sofa watching Invasion of the Body Snatchers. *If we can't get these kids to behave, we're going to run out of babysitters . . .*

I tried to remember what this was about, but I couldn't. Charlie and his father were over a lot when I was a kid. And Michelle? That must have been the babysitter's name, but my mind couldn't dig up a face to go with it. Still, it was kind of funny. Charlie was always getting into trouble as a kid. Not much had changed.

I kept reading, hoping to find something about vampire hunting. It was slow going. My father's handwriting was terrible, as though he'd done most of his writing in the back seat of a car. I had to guess at every fourth or fifth word. And my arm was still throbbing. Still itchy. I had to stop frequently so I could find a position that would make it more comfortable, or just flex my other muscles and try to drive the dull ache somewhere deep where it wouldn't distract me. So that first night I didn't get very far. Although I did discover this one gem. He'd been writing about some work he was hoping to do in Kashmir, and then his writing style became choppier.

Got an emergency call from Mutada in Damascus. N spotted outside village near Kandahar. Will fly out tonight with Max.

The next entry was a few days later.

Cornered N at dawn in a cave. Max flushed him with a gas bomb. Mutada immobilized him perfectly with a Taser. N refused amnesty. Chose to watch the sunrise. Recommended scattering ashes but Mutada took them to villagers instead. They mixed remains with cattle urine and lime dust and painted village gates. Evil to ward off evil, Mutada said.

This was about a vampire. It had to be. I put the book down and tried to picture it. Chasing a vampire from a cave. And a gas bomb. That sounded cool. So did the Taser. I'd seen them on television. They give you a whopper of a shock. I guess they worked on vampires, too.

I read some more, but the next few entries were about a lecture my father was preparing to give on European megaliths. Still, it was better than lying in the dark with nothing to think about but my troubles.

I fell asleep well before the sunrise. I next remember being in my old room. My Spider-Man poster was back on the wall. Toys littered the floor. I was looking over the edge of the top bunk at Charlie, who was just waking up below. Everything looked just as it should have. Only the smell was off. Like mothballs.

"Rise and shine, lazybones," I said.

In an instant the two of us were standing shoulder to shoulder, looking out the bedroom window, only we were in Mr. Entwistle's house, in the library. And Charlie had turned into my dad. He was wearing the suit he usually wore when he gave lectures. It was grey and had flecks of white and black in it.

"Look at all that fog," he said. He reached down and put a hand on my shoulder. "It's like a werewolf movie."

I could hear the flapping of large, leathery wings.

"We should get away from the window," I said. I knew the bat was coming. And I knew what it would turn into.

My father shook his head. "Those aren't bats. Look!"

I pressed my face closer to the glass. A wind was blowing up. It cleared the fog away. Instead of Mr. Entwistle's yard, there was an open field below us. The ground looked charred, as though all the crops had been burned. And it was stained with the blood of dying men and women. As far as the eye could see there were bodies impaled on long stakes. Some of the people were still alive, screaming and quivering. Birds pecked at their eyes and lips.

My father started to laugh. It didn't sound right at all. I turned to look at him but he was gone. In his place was a shorter man. He was thick, like a bear. He stared at me with large, deep-green eyes that were wider apart than they should have been and set above hard cheekbones. Under his pointed nose was a dark moustache. He was wearing a fur cloak, and a red shirt with big gold buttons. Over his heart was a brooch in the shape of a dragon. The dragon had a cross in its mouth. The man's hair was long and flowed from under a hat that reminded me of the spires you see in pictures of far-off churches. But what I noticed most was his mouth. His lips were thick and blood-red. And when he smiled at me he had the teeth of an animal.

I was too scared to move. He reached out and took hold of my arm. Pain ran up my elbow and into my chest. When I tried to pull away, the pain intensified. Then I snapped awake.

There was nothing around me but darkness. And the smell of mothballs. I was back in my father's closet. All I could hear was my heavy breathing. In my sleep, I'd rolled onto my injured arm and it was throbbing painfully. I sat up, grimacing, and tried to cradle it as best I could. It was as if the man's thick fingers were still digging into my skin.

I wondered who he was. And about the bodies. I'd never seen anything like that. My head shook for just a second. A quiver of revulsion. Then I stood up too quickly. My head went dizzy for a few seconds and I had to lean against the door. I needed blood, badly. But the only food in the house was doggy kibble, and I wasn't about to go three rounds with Barky just to get his leftovers. He would have chewed me into Spam.

I decided the best thing was to get moving. Put some distance between me and my nightmare. Those awful images, the bodies and the vampire, had left me feeling nauseous. My belly was empty too, and screaming for blood. Running would cure that, at least for a time. And I still had to find out what had happened to Mr. Entwistle and why Nurse Ophelia hadn't come in to work, and I needed to get in touch with my uncle. It wasn't going to happen if I stayed hidden in a closet.

I turned the light back on and started repacking my father's box. Once all the phony passports and money were in place, I hid it behind the baseboard again. I kept the journal for myself. Then I straightened things up as best I could and went downstairs. I had just decided to go out the front door and risk being seen, rather than go out the back and risk being bitten by Barky, when someone opened the front door.

Chapter 23
A New Plan

I was standing face to face with an elderly man. He was bent slightly at the waist and looked so frail that a gentle breeze might have swept him off the porch. He stared at me for a second. His glasses were so thick they were probably bulletproof. They made his eyes look humongous.

"Who are you?" he asked. "What are you doing here?"

He didn't sound angry, but he was obviously surprised. Since he didn't seem like a mean person, I decided to tell him the truth.

"I was just feeding the dog," I said.

"Oh!" The man looked surprised. Embarrassed, even. He peered back over his shoulder for an instant as though he wasn't sure if he should be there.

"Well, Bert asked me to feed Chaucer. I've been doing it for the past few nights." He cleared his throat. "Who did you say you were again?"

I raised my hands to show him the hospital duds I was wearing. "Just a guy who escaped from the nuthouse," I said.

He laughed.

"I have to be honest," I added. "That dog makes me very uncomfortable. I've fed him, and I was thinking he should be let out, but I don't want to go near him. Do you mind doing it? There's no way he dislikes you as much as he dislikes me."

The older man moved past me into the front hall. "Ah, he's not so bad. He just has to get used to you, that's all." He held out his hand. "It's Al," he said.

"Zachary," I told him. "I'm Dr. Thomson's son."

We shook hands.

"A doctor's son. That would explain the clothes," he said.

I smiled, raised my hand in a quick wave, then slipped out the door. As soon as I hit the street, I felt my lungs expand with a huge breath of relief. Then I started off again.

A plan was taking shape in my mind. I would need food soon. And a safe place from the sun. For that I needed help. I needed my uncle.

I headed to the Brookdale Plaza. It was a strip mall on the edge of my old neighbourhood. There was a bowling alley in the back where Nurse Ophelia took Charlie and me once in a while, and a handful of stores and restaurants. There was also a phone booth near the corner gas station. If I could get a number for Iron Spike Enterprises, my uncle's business, I'd be set. Maximilian would know what to do.

I searched the phone book but found nothing. Then I dialled 411 and got an automated voice. It asked me for the person I was looking for, and the address. When I said I didn't know, it kept asking me to repeat myself. Eventually I got transferred to an operator.

"Iron Spike Enterprises?" she said. Then she asked me what city. I had no idea, so we tried Peterborough, then Toronto, then Ottawa, then Kingston. We found nothing.

"I think the best thing would be to try an Internet search," she said.

I almost bit the end off the phone.

Then I thought of Charlie. He was at his cottage on Stoney Lake. He might have a computer there. I managed to find the number for his cottage in the phone book, but since I had no money, I had to call the operator again. Unfortunately I got a different person and had to go through this whole song and dance about how I was in trouble and needed to make a local person-to-person call. Charlie had once told me that his older brother Dan drank too much wine one Christmas Eve and tried to call the Pope that way. He probably had an easier time of it than I did.

Charlie picked up the phone and the operator asked him if he would accept the call. He didn't seem a bit surprised to be hearing from me.

"I'm glad it's you," he said. "You won't believe what happened. My mom called. She said the cops came to her house. They were looking for you."

"I know," I said. Then I corrected myself. "I mean, I'm not surprised. They came looking for me at the ward, too. I had to run away."

"Wow. The cops. That's sick! What did you do, switch everyone's medication?"

I didn't feel like explaining it to him right then and there. You don't feel terribly safe in a phone booth. The walls are see-through, for one thing. And I kept expecting to hear the sound of oversized bat wings.

"Can I explain later?" I said. "I just have to get out of here. I'm at the Brookdale Plaza. Is there some way you can come and get me?"

"I don't think so. I'm here by myself. Dan won't be back with his kids until tomorrow. He's off riding the roller coaster at Canada's Wonderland."

"Well, I need a place to hide," I said. "I'm in a lot of trouble. I need to get to a computer. I need to call my uncle."

"You have an uncle? Wow! Where's he been all this time? The moon?"

"That's what I thought. It's a long story. Can you come and get me? I don't feel safe here. And I'm starving."

Charlie took a moment to consider.

"Suki might have a car, but it's a bit late to wake her family up . . . Could you take a cab or something? I could pick you up at the marina."

I'd forgotten for just a moment that his cottage was on a small island.

"I don't have any money," I told him.

"It's okay. I've got some. Just get here."

Chapter 24
Charlie's Cottage

The scariest part of that night was waiting for the cab. I suppose it took only two minutes or so to arrive, but every second felt like the tense moment in a horror movie. All that was missing was the creepy music. I hid behind a Dumpster until the cab arrived. Once we got moving, I felt a lot safer, which is usually about that time in the movie when the bad guy jumps out with a chainsaw or something and hacks you to bits. Fortunately nothing happened, and the cabbie got me there in about twenty minutes.

When I climbed out of the car, Charlie was waiting on the dock. He saw me, waved and came over to pay the fare.

"How much is it?" he asked.

I don't know what the cabbie said, but Charlie pulled a wallet out of his back pocket and took out some bills. He handed them through the window to the cabbie and then pushed me roughly on the shoulder.

"Run," he shouted, stepping past me.

I didn't move right away, so he pulled me forward.

"Run!"

I don't know why it is that I don't always do what I'm told. I suppose it's because I usually want to understand what is going on before I make a decision to do anything. It seemed strange that my friend was pulling me towards the dock and screaming in my ear like that guy with the chainsaw had just appeared, but when I saw the cabbie open the door and get out, well, the look on his face told me everything I needed to know. It was pure rage. There's probably a picture of him in a dictionary somewhere under *maniac*. I can picture the words underneath it: "Don't ever, ever cheat this man of his cab fare!"

Charlie must not have had enough money.

I ran. Fortunately, Charlie was ahead of me by quite a bit and had untied the boat. It was a small tin boat with a bright orange engine that made me think of a pumpkin. He didn't bother trying to start it. He just pushed off from the dock. I had to leap.

I was excited, so I jumped too far. Fortunately, I had the presence of mind to drop my father's journal into the boat as I flew over it.

My feet hit the water on the far side, but I managed to turn and grab hold of the boat as I dropped past. An instant later, the coolness of the water seeped through my pants. I kicked my legs and tried to pull myself over the side, but Charlie didn't give me the chance. He fired up the motor, put it into gear and took off. I could hear the cabbie swearing at us from the dock, but I didn't look back for even a second. As soon as the boat started moving it was all I could do to hang on. After my adventures on the Otonabee, I was so scared of drowning that I dug my fingertips into the metal. I could feel it bending from the pressure.

Charlie didn't slow down. Even though there was water spraying everywhere and we were too far out for the cabbie to get us, or even hit us with a rock, he kept the throttle turned up to full. I'm amazed I didn't tear the boat in half. Finally I started shouting at him to slow down, and he cut the engine. He was laughing hysterically.

There must be something contagious about laughter because a second later I started up, too. We were a pair of hyenas. The whole time, I kept trying to climb into the boat, but I was laughing too hard. After a minute, Charlie reached over the side and helped me in.

A second later we were heading down the lake again. I was clutching my father's journal against my stomach, which was grumbling so angrily I'm surprised it didn't crawl out and attack me. And I was getting cold. My clothes were soaked right through. So was the journal. I'd splashed so much water into the boat that it was drenched. I hoped I hadn't wrecked it completely.

Charlie must have known I was really bummed out, because he didn't say a word to me once we were moving. He just let me shiver. All I could think about was how awful things were. My life had gone from painfully dull to totally out of control. And I felt ridiculous because it was what I'd always wanted—an adventure just like Bilbo's. Well, I imagine you've heard the saying "Be careful what you wish for." The wise guy who came up with this one must have had a brain the size of a watermelon. My own adventure had arrived like a kick in the pants. Baron Vrolok and his servants were after me. I was soaked, freezing and penniless, with no way to feed myself. I didn't even have a change of underwear. If there was an adventure survival guide out there someplace, I'd already broken every rule in it. And that wasn't all. While I was screwing up left and right, the people I needed most were disappearing, one at a time. First Nurse Ophelia. Then Mr. Entwistle. It made me really nervous because I was with Charlie now, my best friend. If things kept up the way they were going, well, we were both in for it.

The boat ride to Charlie's cottage was mercifully short. I was shivering so much I'm surprised I didn't chip a tooth. But Charlie's place was warm and cozy. I'd never been in an old-fashioned cottage before, but I'm sure if you ever have, you know exactly what it's like to walk into one for the first time. It has this wonderful smell, like old, sun-baked wood. The design was simple: just a porch, a kitchen, a living room and a master bedroom, all laid out in a row. I'm betting it was just what the survival guide would have recommended.

"I'll get you a towel and some clothes," Charlie said. He disappeared into the bedroom. While he was gone, I sat on the kitchen floor against the cupboards and tried to figure out what to tell him, but it was hard for me to concentrate. The hunger was coming on. Pinched eyes. Churning gut. Itchy throat.

I didn't notice that Charlie was back until he grabbed my wrist.

"What are you doing?" I snapped, jerking my hand away.

"Relax. You want to scratch a hole in your neck?"

I don't know about you, but whenever someone tells me to relax it always has the opposite effect.

Charlie tossed a dry shirt and pair of pants on the floor beside me. "Man, who's pulling on your tail?"

I closed my eyes and took a deep breath. I even tried counting to ten to settle myself down, but I only made it to three. Blood. I swear I could smell it right through Charlie's skin. It made my teeth grind together.

"I need to eat." I kept my eyes closed when I spoke. I was sure if I looked at him, I'd bite him.

"What do I have that you can keep down? You're allergic to everything but air."

"I need blood," I said.

There was a long pause after this. I opened my eyes just to make certain Charlie was still there.

"Blood?" he said.

I nodded. "Yes. Blood. Now. Like, *right now.*"

Charlie was sitting in a kitchen chair. He stood up so that he was looking down at me.

"Oh, blood. Right. Of course, blood. What was I thinking? Well, we just happen to have a huge barrel of it in the back. Do you want some fries with that?"

What should I have expected? But I did need to eat. I didn't want some part of my mind taking over and forcing me to do something unspeakable to my best friend, so I told him the truth.

"I'm a vampire. I got infected eight years ago. I need blood."

We stared at each other for a few seconds, then Charlie started shaking his head.

"You lucky duck," he said.

Chapter 25
Food Trouble

Charlie kept staring at me. I couldn't tell if he was stunned or jealous.

"You believe me?" I asked.

He put his hands on his hips and flashed me a grin like he heard this sort of thing every day. "What do *you* think? I told my dad I thought you were a vampire years ago."

He walked across the kitchen to where I was sitting on the floor, then he reached down and offered me his hand. He was very trusting. If he'd known how much I wanted to help myself to what was flowing through his wrist, he might have run for his boat.

I took his hand and stood up. Then I started changing out of my wet clothes and into the dry ones he'd brought.

"I can't help you with the blood," he said. He started digging through the refrigerator, then he stopped to look at me. I was hopping up and down trying to get my foot through the second pant leg. It was tough because my skin was wet and the material kept bunching up. I bumped into the counter and slipped to the floor.

"Aren't vampires supposed to be super-coordinated?" he said.

What could I say? I was having an off-day.

He turned back to the refrigerator. "What have you been living on?" he asked.

I had to answer him with my teeth clenched. I had never been this hungry. Not ever. "Animal blood of some kind. I don't really know. From a cow, maybe? I thought it was strawberry syrup."

"Would Nurse Ophelia know?"

I nodded. "But she's gone. She never came back to work."

"What do you mean, she never came back?"

"I mean she never came back. The night before I left, she didn't come in. I think something happened to her."

Charlie walked over to the telephone. "I hope not," he said. "Maybe she just got sick."

"She never has before."

"Well then, she was overdue." He picked up the phone and started dialling.

"Who are you calling?" I asked.

"You," he answered.

He waited, then started speaking.

"Hi. It's Charlie Rutherford. I'm calling for Zack Thomson or Ophelia. I was hoping someone could let me know what is happening. If someone could call me back as soon as possible, I would appreciate it. My family is very worried. Thanks." Then he left a number and hung up.

I slipped back to the floor and put both hands over my stomach. I was so hungry I nearly bit myself. I couldn't move. I couldn't lie still. It was worse than being hit by that van.

"Do you know her home number?" Charlie asked me. "Or her last name?" He must have meant Nurse Ophelia.

I shook my head and grunted a no.

"Damn . . ."

Charlie walked over to the fridge and opened the freezer. He took out something that hit the counter like a big block of ice. I heard scraping noises. When I looked up, he was jabbing something with an ice pick. Then he reached down and handed me a cold chunk of pink stuff that looked like part of someone's brain.

"What is it?" I asked.

"Frozen hamburger," he answered.

I knew better than to eat it, so I just sucked on it. It didn't do much. At least, not right away.

"So, you can drink animal blood?"

"I guess so." I waved my hand like I was hailing a taxi. "Keep 'em coming."

For about an hour or so, he fed me frozen hamburger, then frozen steak, then frozen pork chops. I didn't chew on them, I just did my best to drain every bit of moisture from each piece. It helped pass the time while my stomach went nuts.

We talked the whole time. I told him everything, starting with Mr. Entwistle's motorcycle stunt and ending with my flight from Al and Barky.

"I've got an idea," he said. He handed me another piece of frozen pork, then he slipped on his windbreaker and headed for the back door.

"What are you doing?" I asked him.

"Ordering breakfast," he said.

I waited while Charlie did something behind the cottage. He was making a lot of noise. The sound was metallic, like someone shaking cymbals. Then I heard footsteps on the roof. A few minutes later, Charlie came back.

"What was that all about?"

"Squirrel traps," he said.

I fired the last piece of frozen pork into my mouth. "You've gotta be kidding," I said.

"Hey, I'd rather rid the island of squirrels than watch the neighbours' dogs disappear one at a time. Unless you have plans to rob a blood bank?"

He had a point. "Do you think it will work?" I asked.

"What, the traps? Yeah, better than throwing rocks . . ."

"No," I said. "I mean squirrel blood. Do you think I can drink it?"

"I have no idea." He threw up his hands. "Who do I look like, Anne Rice?"

He didn't look a bit like Anne Rice, but I didn't think there was any point in saying so. Instead, I just sat on the floor and held my stomach.

"Here, try sipping this," he suggested. He handed me a glass of water.

I shook my head.

"Blood is mostly water," he said. "If you can drink cows' blood, you should be able to handle this."

That made sense. I put a few drops in my mouth and let them slide around. Then I swallowed. Nothing happened. Nothing bad, anyway, so I took a few more sips. I nodded to Charlie. I was going to be all right. At least for a while.

"So, what will you do in the morning?" he asked me. Morning was about two hours away.

"I need to get in touch with my uncle."

"I was thinking more about the sun," Charlie said. "What are you going to do when it comes up and you can't be in the light?"

"Have you got a place I could hide?" I asked. "Somewhere that's dark?"

"There's the tool shed."

"Won't anyone look in there?"

Charlie laughed. "Dan's a pencil-pusher. Do you think he knows a hammer from a hamster? He spends so much time at the office he barely has the energy to lift a mug of coffee when he comes up. I don't think he's ever been in the shed. But if I tell him there's a vampire in there, I'm sure he'll steer clear of the place."

Chapter 26
Bad Press

I suppose I should have been happy about sleeping in a shed. It was better than turning into charcoal when the sun came up. But there were two windows—one in the door and one above the workbench—and they made me very nervous, even though Charlie had taken a staple gun and nailed garbage bags over both of them.

Around noon the next day he knocked and walked in. I refused to come out of my sleeping bag until he'd closed and locked the door.

"What is it?" I asked from behind my pillow. I was using it like a shield.

Charlie didn't answer, but I heard a racket, like someone dropping a whole bag of silverware down a flight of stairs. I peeked out from behind the pillow. Charlie was holding up his traps, with a triumphant smile on his face. Each had a red squirrel inside. They were making more noise than a marching band.

"What am I supposed to do with those?" I asked.

He shrugged. "Hey, this is *your* thing. What did you expect? Was I supposed to serve them up with some spider goulash?"

He said he'd come back after sunset, and closed the door behind him. I tried going back to sleep, but the squirrels were trying to escape. I was worried the sound of their frantic scurrying would reach the far end of the lake. I considered putting them outside, but I couldn't risk it. The summer sun was strong. And now that I was awake, and there was food in the room, my stomach started barking orders.

You can guess what happened next. I don't want to go into detail, but if you've ever eaten meat, you can't hold this against me. And if you are a vegetarian, well then, I'm really, really sorry. I cried afterwards. I couldn't help myself. I'd never hurt anything before. I'd seen nature shows on TV. Survival of the fittest and the law of the jungle—these weren't new to me. I needed blood to live. And to heal. But knowing this stuff didn't help. Reaching inside a cage to kill a defenceless animal just felt wrong. I swore right then and there that I wasn't ever going to fish for my dinner in a rodent trap again. Preying on the helpless was out. There had to be a better way.

I fell asleep feeling distraught.

Charlie came back just after the sun went down. He was carrying a flashlight and a newspaper. When he opened the door, I could hear other voices coming from the cottage, but I didn't recognize them.

"Dan's back with his kids," Charlie said. "He said there were cops all over the marina. They were passing around photos."

"Of me?" I asked.

"Probably. Dan just said it was a kid. I guess it's lucky he hasn't seen you in a while or he might have told the cops you were a friend of mine."

"How did they get here so quickly?" I asked.

Charlie shrugged. "Must have been the cabbie," he said.

It made sense. If he'd called the police after we took off without paying, he might have identified me.

"Did you hear back from the ward?" I asked.

"No," he said, "but I'm going to try again. I thought I'd wait until Dan is asleep. It won't be much longer. I'll come back when the coast is clear." He passed me the newspaper and smiled.

"What's so funny?" I asked.

Charlie crouched down in front of me. I was sitting with my back against the shed wall. He reached over and opened the paper. Several pages in was a caption that read "Escaped mental patient still at large." There was a small photo of me beside it.

"Zack," he said, "you've been stuck in the nuthouse for eight years. You're out on the weekend for the first time in your life. Did you think you'd be this famous already?"

I folded the newspaper up so that the article was easier to see. Charlie handed me the flashlight.

"Try not to get too bent out of shape about it. Suki's family is here. You can meet Luna. There'll be a party somewhere we can crash. It's time for you to live a little. Have some fun. Whatta you say?"

I nodded. I sure needed something good to happen.

"I'll be back in a bit," he said. Then he slipped quietly out the door.

I turned on the flashlight and read under my sleeping bag. The article was short on detail. It explained how I had escaped from the Nicholls Ward with the help of another man who was involved in a suspected arson downtown. It referred to a second article. I made a mental note to look at that one too, then kept reading. Apparently, I was pretty much guilty of every crime but treason. I'd stolen a car, some hospital supplies, assaulted police officers, resisted arrest, destroyed private property and been an all-around bad person.

I flipped to the other article. "Fire levels Salvation Army: Arson suspect killed in blaze." There were before and after pictures of the Salvation Army. The first one showed a red-brick building with flowers blooming in beds near the door. The second one was a photo of the charred remains. Beside these was a thumbnail sketch of Mr. Entwistle. It made him look like a drugged-out hobo. Underneath was a caption that read, "Do you know this man?" along with a number for Crime Stoppers.

According to the paper, the fire had started shortly after nine o'clock, about the same time Mr. Entwistle had left the safe house. The fire had spread quickly to all four corners of the ground floor, so the Fire Department was pretty sure an accelerant was used. I figured that meant gasoline or something. The article didn't say. But it did say that a few witnesses saw Mr. Entwistle entering the building just before it caught fire and collapsed. He was one of three people crushed or burned. The other names I didn't recognize, but they were apparently Red Cross volunteers.

I read and reread the article, hoping there was something in there that would say for sure what had happened to him. I had to know if he was really dead. But there was nothing in there about finding his body. And no one had actually seen him die. At least, it didn't say so. They didn't even know his name. But there was a reference to the first article about my escape from the Nicholls Ward and his role in that, so they knew something about him.

I couldn't believe he was dead. A man who'd lived for six hundred and fifty years wasn't going to die in a fire. What was the point of having visions if you couldn't see when the building you were in was going to collapse?

I put the paper down and lay back. I didn't want to read any more. I needed to take my mind off things. I was getting sick of getting bad news everywhere I turned. Fortunately, Charlie came back less than a half hour later, so I wasn't stewing by myself for too long. Even before his hand touched the door I could smell something funny. It was either cologne or bug repellent.

"I have some good news and some bad news," Charlie said. "The good news is, I have Dan's BlackBerry. We can use it to get a number for Iron Crown Enterprises."

"Iron *Spike* Enterprises," I said.

"Whatever."

"What's the bad news?" I asked.

"We're out of squirrels," he said. "Just kidding. I got in touch with someone from the Nicholls Ward. Nurse Ophelia hasn't been to work since you left." Then he said something about the woman who'd answered the phone that I won't bother repeating. "She said if Ophelia doesn't show up today she's getting fired."

"Has she called in?" I asked. "Has anyone spoken to her or called her house?"

Charlie shrugged. "The way it sounded, no one has spoken to her."

"What about her last name? Did you find out what it is?"

Charlie shook his head. "No. That stuff is apparently confidential, and the woman wouldn't tell me. Maybe if you called she'd tell you. I don't know."

I tipped my head back against the wall. My heart must have known what my brain was thinking, because it started to pick up the tempo. "I think something's happened to her," I said.

"I hope not. I'll call again tomorrow and see what I can find out." He sat down and let out a long sigh. "Does she know you're a vampire?"

I shrugged. "I think she must."

"I wonder why she didn't tell you."

I wondered that, too. But mostly, I wondered if she was okay.

Charlie put his hand on my shoulder to push himself back up to his feet. Then he offered me his hand and pulled me up from the floor.

"Why would she go back there anyway?" he said.

"What do you mean?"

"Think about it. If she knew you were missing, she'd look for you. She wouldn't go in to work knowing that you might be in trouble. As long as you're gone, she'll be gone."

This made sense. Sort of. Nurse Ophelia wouldn't go back if I were missing. But she'd disappeared before I had, so she might not even have known I was gone. I didn't mention this to Charlie. I figured it would only make him worry more.

"My uncle can help," I said. "Mr. Entwistle said he's the most feared vampire hunter in this part of the world and that he has contacts everywhere. If anyone can find her, he can."

Charlie took out Dan's BlackBerry and started searching for my uncle's business number on the Internet. We tried all the major cities we could think of. Charlie eventually got a hit in Montreal and dialled the number. As soon as it started ringing he handed me the Black-Berry. No one answered. It made me wonder if he'd disappeared too, just like Ophelia and Mr. Entwistle. Then his voice came on and told me I could leave a message.

"It's Zachary," I said. "I'm at a friend's cottage. Please call back as soon as you can. There's been a lot of trouble, and I need your help." Then I left Charlie's number.

"Now what?" I asked.

Charlie took the BlackBerry from me and crammed it into his pocket. "Now?" he said, clapping me on the back. "Now it's time to experience the true joys of having no adults around."

Chapter 27
Meeting Luna

Charlie and I snuck down to the water and climbed into his boat. Within seconds we were speeding off to Suki's cottage. Fortunately, my hunger was gone, which was a relief to both of us, but neither of us had any idea how long that would last. Charlie had brought a couple of the squirrel traps with him. I didn't think it was necessary—I was more or less decided on the rodent issue—but nothing I said would change his mind.

Suki's place turned out to be a house-like cottage on the mainland. I didn't get a look at the inside of it because Charlie didn't think it was a good idea for me to come up to meet her family. Even though it was very unlikely that they'd been to the marina and seen the photo the police were passing around, there might have been something on the news. So while he visited Suki, I sat on the dock and swatted at mosquitoes. It made me wonder what happened if any of them got infected with my blood. Could a mosquito be a vampire? What difference would it make, since they all sucked blood anyway? And what if it delivered my blood to someone else? Could vampirism be spread through mosquitoes, like malaria? It seemed to me that it wasn't too likely, or there would have been a lot more of us around.

About ten minutes later, Charlie came back down to the dock. "We're going to an island party," he said. "Unless you want to try your luck with the cops at the marina?"

An island party sounded like a pretty dangerous idea to me. After all, if you want to avoid attracting attention, bury yourself under a tree or something. Don't go to a party. But I wasn't about to argue. I didn't have anywhere else to go. I was like a guy on a train. I could ride it to wherever it was going or I could take my chances and jump off somewhere along the way. An island party sounded pretty stupid, but it also sounded like fun, so I wasn't quite ready to jump.

Suki came down to the dock a few minutes later. She didn't really walk, she sort of bounced everywhere. Charlie introduced us.

"So you're the famous Zachary," she said.

I didn't know if this meant that she'd read about me in the paper. All I managed was a limp smile.

"Charlie's told us all about you," she continued.

Well, that was awfully nice of Charlie. I sure was hoping he hadn't mentioned the squirrels.

"It's nice to meet you," I said. And it was. She had a friendly way about her. Sometimes you can tell that about a person straight off.

I didn't notice Luna until she was practically on the dock. She crept down as Suki and I were talking. The way Charlie had talked back at the Nicholls Ward, it was as though we were destined to be the next Romeo and Juliet or something. Well, if you were picturing a romantic first meeting like the kind in the movies where two people gawk at each other because their brains are melting from too much happiness, you're way off. She looked at me and said, "Hi."

That was it. I might have been a fence post. I'm not sure what I'd been expecting myself. That she'd be so pretty my jaw would dislocate when I saw her? It didn't. She looked pretty normal. Two arms, two legs, one head. Long copper curls. Then she looked at me. Her eyes were an emerald green. They suited her.

"We've come to fix your squirrel trouble," Charlie said. He held up the two traps like they were God's answer to the rodent crisis.

Suki laughed so loudly I thought all the squirrels on the mainland might lose their hearing.

"I'm just going to leave these out back," said Charlie. "Nothing like a good bit of roast squirrel to start the day, eh, Zack?"

"You said it."

As soon as Charlie disappeared around the edge of the cottage, the rest of us fell quiet. I stood there feeling very foolish because I had no idea what to say, so I just helped Suki climb into her boat, which looked a lot like Charlie's except the motor was newer and less pumpkin-like. I offered her my hand.

"What a gentleman," she said. Then the boat lurched and she kept herself steady by grabbing my arm. She gave the muscle there a squeeze.

"Wow," she said.

I was really glad it was dark because I'm sure I lit up like a Christmas candle. Then I helped Luna in. Too bad, her balance was a little better.

Finally Charlie came back. He hopped into his boat and asked the girls where we were going.

"Elephant," said Suki. Then she and Luna sped off.

"What's Elephant?" I asked, stepping into the boat.

Charlie fired up his motor. "It's an island," he said. Then he twisted the throttle and we bounced down the lake, chasing the girls.

✦ ✦ ✦ ✦

Driving down the lake was like navigating through a dark maze. Islands and rocks and buoys were scattered around like they'd just dropped from the sky. Soon the channel opened up, however, and I could see where we were going: a small shadow of an island that looked like it was on fire.

It *was* on fire. Apparently, this was the whole point of an island party. You made a fire so big the rocks practically melted. As we got closer, I could see the boats and the silhouettes of a few people walking around. Woodsmoke hung in the air, mixing with the odours of gasoline and what I later discovered was beer. But the focus was the bonfire. People orbited around it all night, some sitting, some standing. It was strangely alluring. Curls of orange, red and yellow light, and even small flashes of green and blue leapt from the wood, popping and sparking.

Charlie had beer in his boat, which made him as popular as the ice-cream man. He was generous and fun and everyone knew him, so I was considered all right just because of that. I showed up like his sidekick, and if Batman and Robin had followed us in, I doubt anyone would have noticed. We were that cool. Honest.

Luna sat across from me. She seemed to know everyone, too. And when she laughed, I laughed with her. They were real moments. I'd never really understood that word, *real*. As in "Get real." Or "He was so real." I understood it that night. I was undead, but I was alive, too. And nervous. This was probably a good thing. It kept me from opening my mouth too often, which would have crushed all my coolness to smithereens.

"So, Charlie's one of your friends?" someone asked me.

I decided that when people spoke to me, I'd just answer honestly. "He's my *only* friend," I said.

Everyone thought this was funny.

It was much later at this point, and there were only six of us still sitting around the fire: Charlie, Suki, Luna and me, and twins whose names I've totally forgotten. All I remember was that they had a place on the same shore as Suki and Luna. And one of them had dark hair and the other had bleached his so that the tips were yellow. It was the only way I could tell them apart.

"How did you get to be so . . . ?" Suki held her breath and flexed her arms in a circus-strongman pose. She had downed a few drinks by that time and was speaking very frankly.

"I used to live in a mental ward," I said. "They have a great fitness room there."

She thought this was hilarious.

And so the party continued pretty much like that. It was almost perfect. I didn't get to talk to Luna alone, which would have been nice, but we did talk. At one point, she saw my necklace and asked me what it was.

"It's a full moon," I explained. "It belonged to my father. There's another piece, a gold crescent that fits along one side, but my mother had that part. I've never seen it."

She was sitting beside me. When she spoke she had this habit of reaching out to touch my arm, as though she needed to get my attention every time she had something to say. It made my insides tumble.

"May I?" she asked.

I didn't know what she meant until she reached around my neck. She undid the necklace clasp at the back and pulled the chain free. For just a second her face was so close I could feel her breath on my cheek. Then she sat back down and held up the necklace for a closer look. Although the moon charm was made of silver, the red and orange flames of the bonfire made it look like burning gold.

"It's beautiful," she said.

"I think so, too."

"And you never saw the other part?" she asked.

"No."

"But your mother had it."

"She died when I was two," I said.

"Oh, that's so sad," she said. But she dragged the "so" out for about five minutes, which I guess meant that it was *soooooooooooooooo oooooooooooo* sad. Then she asked me how my mother had died.

I wasn't sure what to say. Once, when I was a young kid, I'd asked my father about it, but he never really answered. He just said that sometimes people go away and you never get to see them again. It upset him so much to talk about her that I never asked again after that. I think he would have told me, eventually, if he had lived longer.

"I don't know how she died," I said.

Charlie was surprised by this. "What do you mean, you don't know?"

"I never got the chance to ask my father again before he was killed."

"Your father was killed?" The question was asked so quietly, I don't think anyone heard it but me. Luna spoke in a whisper. She cleared her throat. "Someone killed him?" She was louder the second time.

I nodded.

"Do you know who it was?"

I don't remember who asked this question. Everyone was suddenly part of the conversation. I think it must have been one of the twins.

"Yes," I answered.

"Did they ever catch him?" Suki asked.

I shook my head. "No."

"You must just want to kill him," the blond twin said.

I wasn't sure if it was a question. If it was, I didn't answer it. I didn't even want to think about Vrolok.

"If anyone killed our parents, and I got my hands on them, I don't know what I'd do," Suki said.

This started a conversation between the twins about what they would do if they caught their parents' killer. It sort of turned into a competition. They carried on for a while, until Luna interrupted.

"You don't know what you'd do," she said. I can't remember which twin she was speaking to. It might have been both of them. "Until you're really in a situation," she continued, "you just don't know."

The blond twin disagreed. "If someone killed my parents, they'd have it coming."

Both twins seemed to agree on this. But Luna wasn't finished. "Killing is killing. If it's wrong, it's wrong."

At this point Charlie stood up and heaved another log on the fire. A fountain of sparks exploded into the air. "Enough already," he said. "If you can't agree to disagree, I'm going to have to start chucking people in the lake."

And that was the end of it. For a few quiet minutes, we all just stared at the fire.

I thought about what Luna had said. That killing was wrong. I couldn't imagine arguing against it. But a part of me understood what the twins were saying, too. Vrolok *should* pay for what he'd done. Still, if I got my chance and took revenge, would it make me just as bad? I couldn't decide.

When the blond twin got up for another beer, it seemed to wake everyone up. "Anyone else want a drink?" he asked.

"No thanks," said Luna.

"Come on," said Suki. "One won't kill you."

"I don't like it."

"I don't either," I said. "It smells like water someone boiled running shoes in."

Luna smiled when I said this. I'd seen her smile before, but this one was different. I guess I'd just gotten her off the hook, so this smile was just for me.

Not everyone looks better when they smile. Everyone looks worse when they frown, but not everyone is fortunate enough to have a really good smile. Luna would have given Nurse Ophelia a run for her money. When her lips came together and turned up, her face widened just a bit and her eyes kind of squeezed shut. It was perfect. I guess I must have been staring, because I stopped paying attention to everyone else until Charlie slapped me on the shoulder.

"You get used to it," he said.

"Used to what?"

"The beer. You get used to it."

"Apparently, it takes thirty years," I told him.

He looked at me funny, then nodded over to the dark twin. "You want one?"

The dark twin shook his head without taking his eyes from the fire. He was thinking about something, you could tell.

"What kind of a nutcase kills someone, anyway?" he said to no one in particular. It seemed an odd remark from someone who had just spent the better part of a half hour defending his right to take revenge. I almost told him to go examine his reflection in the lake.

"Luna could tell you about some nutcases," said Suki. "She used to work with young offenders."

Luna had her arms folded across her knees. They made a cradle of sorts for her head. She looked ready to fall asleep. "None of them ever killed anybody," she said.

Charlie took a haul from his beer, then spoke as if he was holding in a burp. "Still, you must have met some headcases."

Luna shook her head. "Not really. But some of them were pretty rough."

"Pretty rough?" Suki said. "One of them robbed a bank with a shotgun."

"Is that true?" asked Charlie.

"Yeah."

"And your parents let you work with people like that?"

"It was a summer camp, not a mercenary camp," said Luna. "It was totally safe. And the kids were great."

"They sound great," said Charlie. The twins laughed. Charlie clapped me on the back. "Well, we've found the way to her heart, Zack. All you need is a shotgun."

I think I must have blushed when Charlie said this, like the whole point of the night was to set me up with Luna. I guess in his mind it was.

Suki tried her best to look miffed. "I think it's very brave that my sister worked with young offenders."

"It's not that big a deal," said Luna. "They aren't much different from any of us."

Charlie wasn't buying it. "Has anyone here robbed a bank lately?" he asked.

"That's not what I mean," said Luna. I could tell she was frustrated. She looked as if she were about to say more. Then she changed her mind.

"I know what you mean," I said. I hadn't spoken in a while. It seemed to surprise everyone. "I used to live in a mental ward," I added, and everyone went quiet.

The twins looked at each other and then at Charlie. They laughed. He didn't.

"I thought you were joking about that," said Suki.

I shook my head. "I was seven when my father died," I explained. "I got really sick and went into a coma. When I came out of it, I was angry all the time. And there was no one around to look after me. I guess I had nowhere else to go." I talked a bit about how nice everyone there was. Jacob and Sad Stephen. Even the Chicago Man. "They don't have easy lives either," I added when I was finished.

Luna was looking at me. She must have understood. I guess the same was probably true for the kids she worked with. Their lives weren't easy. But you can find a reason to like just about anyone. You just have to do a little digging sometimes.

"You seem pretty normal," Suki said to me.

"He's anything *but* normal," said Charlie.

Suki laughed. She had her arms around his waist. It looked very comfortable. She gave him a squeeze.

And that led to a discussion about what "normal" is, which led to families and home life and whatever. I guess that's when I learned that talking in groups is really hard because everyone has to have their turn, and so you don't always get to say what's on your mind, and you have to listen to everyone when you really only want to listen to one person. I kept asking Luna questions about her old job and the kids she worked with, and other things, but with four other people chiming in, I didn't get as much from her as I would have liked.

Then suddenly it was time for everyone to go.

Charlie and I escorted Luna and Suki home, which basically meant we followed them in the boat. Luna and I did the driving because neither of us had been drinking. I'd never driven a motorboat before, but it was a little easier than steering a Ford Mustang at eight hundred miles an hour from the wrong seat. Charlie helped me navigate so I didn't hit a rock or an island, and that was the main thing. As I got close to their dock, I didn't know what to do, so I just cut the engine and we drifted in.

"That was a lot of fun," said Suki. Her voice was so loud, I noticed, that even the bats in the air turned away from us. Luna must have been worried about waking up the rest of the lake because she put her arms around her sister, then shushed her by lifting a finger to her lips.

Suki started giggling. "Sorry," she whispered.

Charlie climbed out of the boat. I was amazed he didn't fall in. "Gonna get me some squirrel meat," he said.

"What's with the squirrels all of a sudden?" Luna asked.

"We've run out on the island," Charlie explained. "It's thrown off the whole food chain. We have to restock before the ecosystem collapses." Then he burped, waved his hand in front of his face and walked into the dark.

"He's the one who should have been in the mental ward," said Suki.

I was about to disagree. Then he came back to the dock with a trap in either hand. It would have ruined my argument. Inside one trap was a red squirrel. The other had a chipmunk in it. Each was trying frantically to find an exit. It sounded like a circus. Charlie held them up like trophies.

"You're taking our chipmunks, too?" said Suki. "You should be taking deer instead. They're all over the place this year."

"No room for deer. Just rodents. Rodents of every variety."

"Why?"

"I just bought a pet fox," said Charlie. "You don't want him to starve, do you?"

"You're joking," Suki shouted. "You wouldn't dare." She tried to grab one of the cages. When she put her hands on it, the squirrel inside nipped her fingers, so she shrieked. That's when the light came on in the cottage.

"That's our cue," said Charlie. "Time to run." He yanked the traps away and scrambled into the boat. Then he leaned out to give Suki a kiss, which ended when Luna yanked her sister away by the arm.

"On behalf of the island, I thank you," Charlie said. "In fact, the whole ecosystem thanks you. No, the whole *planet* thanks you."

The two sisters were running away. Actually, it was more like Luna was dragging her sister away by the arm.

"See you tomorrow at the Yacht Club," Suki said over her shoulder. "And bring your friend with you."

I was glad she'd added that, even though I wouldn't be able to go.

As soon as Charlie sat down, I pulled the ripcord on the motor and we puttered away.

"So, what do you think?" Charlie asked me.

I was thinking that his pet fox was hungry, but that wasn't what he was really asking me.

"They're nice," I said.

Charlie threw up his hands. "You say that about *everybody*!"

Chapter 28
A Warning from My Father

When we got back to the island, Charlie went to bed straight off. Since it was at least four or five hours before sunrise, I decided to sit down on the dock and read more of my father's journal. The pages were all crinkled now because they'd gotten soaked from my first boat ride when I'd jumped into the lake escaping from the cabbie, but at least I could still read the writing.

My father talked about some archaeological work being done in England along the Fosse Way, which sounded like an old road. I was skim-reading at this point. Then a short entry caught my attention. I was pretty sure it had to do with another vampire, because my father stopped using proper names.

I received an urgent call from Dr. Q regarding one of his patients, a recent carrier named C. He is having difficulty adjusting to the contagion. I have called Max in for support.

My brain went into computer mode when I read this. Carrier? What did that mean? A vampire? Could it have been something else? I didn't think so. I quickly skipped ahead. After an entry about a trip to the Tower of London, the story continued.

C has gone missing. We suspect he is responsible for the recent deaths of two women near Hyde Park. We have several agents posted in the neighbouring boroughs. I hope this will be adequate.

Well, any doubts I had that C was a vampire were gone. And agents? Did that mean my father had people working for him? Perhaps he and Maximilian were part of a much larger organization. I read on. There was nothing for a week, then this.

Got a call from Dr. Q near midnight. One of our agents discovered C's body near the rail yard in Egham. Most of his bones are shattered. Suicide is the likely explanation.

I felt my stomach sink when I read this. Who ever heard of a vampire committing suicide? I started to close the journal, but as the facing page turned towards me, I noticed another entry with the initial *C* at the bottom. I guess the story wasn't over.

C is recovering well. His damaged tissues have completely regenerated. (Ratio 1kg:5L is consistent with past cases.) The process was completed in less than 2 days.

Two days. Wow! Vampires really could heal quickly when they got the good stuff. A person with shattered bones would have spent months in a hospital getting better, if he lived at all.

There was more on the following page.

With the hunger issue resolved, C's rationality is returning. It confirms my deep suspicion that without adequate nutrient and guidance, few carriers adjust well to the symptoms of their infection. C has agreed to assume a role in a donor clinic. Max is skeptical, but Dr. Q has every confidence that C will not regress.

And that was it. But it was plenty.

The first thing I thought was that my father was dead-on about feeding. It *was* difficult to be rational on an empty stomach. It explained why I'd been so angry eight years ago when I came out of my coma. And why I'd bitten that nurse when I was ten. My hunger issue hadn't been resolved. But that might not have been the most important idea buried in these entries. It was clear that my father didn't see himself as just a vampire hunter. He helped them find their way. I should have guessed as much. My uncle had suggested that not all vampires were bad. I guess this meant my father helped look after the good ones. It was comforting. And a bit alarming, because it sounded as if they needed lots of help. C had more or less gone off the deep end. It made me wonder how many vampires had similar problems. I suppose I should have been grateful that I'd been living at the Nicholls Ward. When I'd needed help, Nurse Ophelia and the rest of the staff had been there. I might not have managed so well anywhere else.

I decided to flip through the journal to see if there was anything else written with capital letters instead of names. I scanned each page as quickly as I could manage, but the writing was so messy, and the pages so wrinkled, it took a long time to find anything. Then about three months later there was this short entry.

Flew in to Heathrow. One of our agents is missing. There are three other victims in the Dartmouth area, all women. Evidence suggests possible WW.

"WW." That had to be something special, or my father would have just spelled it out properly.

The next entry was short.

Met Max in Torquay. Tracks outside of Plymouth confirm our suspicions. We set bear traps and doubled the watch.

I skimmed a whole page that described a boat trip up the Dart, which I guessed was a river. Then I found this.

Success and disappointment. The bear traps have ended our hunt.

Bear traps? I tried to imagine the kind of creature you would catch with one of these.

Identity of WW impossible to determine. Dr. Q determined his psychosis is incurable. Despite availability of nutrient, killing urge cannot be suppressed. Hemlock administered. Body cremated. Ashes scattered in the Dart.

Was this about a werewolf? I flipped quickly through the pages ahead, searching for another WW, but I didn't find any more. Then I put my hand against my forehead and closed my eyes. If only my father had told me what he was doing when he was still alive. If we'd just been able to talk about it. There were so many things I might have asked him that could help me now. But I guess I was way too young back then. And I probably wouldn't have believed him. Werewolves? It was nonsense. Then I laughed. I was a vampire now. It was sort of like a doctor not believing in a dentist. Of course, I *would* have believed my father.

I reread the last few lines: *"His psychosis is incurable . . . killing urge cannot be suppressed . . . Body cremated . . ."* I was noticing a very disturbing trend in these entries. Insanity. And death.

My father had had no way of knowing what I would become. And still, he had left a warning for me that was probably more important than anything he'd said to me when he was alive. If I wasn't careful, I might turn out like these others.

I started reading again, then my stomach grumbled. I was getting hungry. After all this reading about vampires going crazy, I wasn't about to let my belly complain without doing something right away. The journal would have to wait.

The squirrel traps were still in the boat. I reached in and lifted them onto the dock. Mr. Chipmunk was eyeing me from the farthest corner of the cage. He could probably guess what was coming. So could Mr. Squirrel. I don't think any of us were happy about the arrangement, so I opened the cages and let them go. There seemed to be no point in killing two rodents when an army of them wouldn't have satisfied my appetite for very long. And I didn't want to have to cope with the guilt of killing something so small and helpless.

Still, I had to feed. I didn't want to turn into a monster. I decided it was time to follow Mr. Entwistle's advice and test myself. And I needed to stretch my legs. I was used to burning lots of fuel every night. All this sitting around was making me restless.

I zipped on a life jacket. I felt a little nervous about being on the water by myself, so I put a second one on overtop. It was snug, but if the boat decided to flip over on me, I didn't want to end up as fish food. Then I untied the boat and pushed off. When I was far enough from the shore that the sound of the motor wouldn't wake anyone up, I pulled the ripcord and took off for Luna's cottage.

As I made my way past the lights along the shore my thoughts returned to the bonfire. What I'd said and heard. I forgot about carriers and agents and werewolves and psychosis and just enjoyed replaying the evening in my head. Then I started changing a few things. Mostly, I just stole a lot of Charlie's jokes and made myself a lot funnier. And I imagined supporting Luna in her argument with the twins about revenge. I shouldn't have stayed so quiet when she was really arguing on my behalf. After all, both my parents were dead and I hadn't done a thing about it. By the time I was halfway down the lake, the whole episode was completely altered. I came out looking like a saint. And a genius. And a stand-up comedian.

Then I imagined telling Luna the truth about myself. Everything. In this version, everyone had left the island but the two of us, so no one got to interrupt. I started with my father's real profession. And my condition. Then Vrolok. I think a part of my mind was preparing me for when this conversation might happen for real. It was also preparing me for disappointment. It seemed that, even in my imagination, no matter how I sugar-coated things, she just wasn't going to be interested in a guy who got angry when there was no blood to drink and who couldn't go out in the sun. We could never be like Charlie and Suki, which was too bad. They obviously liked kissing a whole lot. But who would want to kiss a vampire? It was like I had fifteen diseases rolled into one.

I stopped the motor about fifty feet from the shore in front of Luna's cottage. The water made soft lapping noises against the hull as I drifted in. I took my life jacket off, tied up the boat and slipped quietly onto the dock. There was a gentle breeze blowing over the water. I put my nose to the air and stopped breathing to listen. It wasn't long before I heard something rustling just past the cottage. I snuck through the shadows and into the laneway. Then I discovered the source of the noise. A raccoon was nose-deep in a garbage can on the back of the porch. When it saw me approach it scampered off. There must have been no shortage of garbage cans on the lake, because this one waddled like an overstuffed house cat. It was lucky. I hadn't come all this way for blood that was made from recycled garbage. I had come because of what Suki had said about the deer.

Chapter 29
The Killing Urge

I followed the driveway from the cottage to the main road. Between domes of grey and pink granite, tall evergreens grew in clumps. Most of them were cedar, I think, and pine. Where it was rocky there were clearings, and it was in one of these that I picked up the scent of something wild. Fur, I guess. Then I saw the deer. A buck with arm-sized antlers.

I approached from downwind so it didn't hear me until I was close. It bolted just as I sprang. I was fast, but the buck was faster. He outdistanced me in a few seconds. Still, I wasn't worried. Way back before bows and arrows and farming and the wheel, our earliest ancestors practised exhaustion hunting. I'd seen it on a nature program once, and it worked like this. Your great-great-great-whatever-grandfather and his buddies followed an animal for six or eight hours until it ran out of energy. Then they stabbed it with sharp sticks. It apparently worked because running on two legs is more efficient than running on four legs, so even though the animal was faster over short distances, in a long race it eventually ran out of juice and collapsed. Exhaustion hunting. Not a lot of fun. I think it was the main reason farms were invented.

Well, I didn't have six to eight hours. And I didn't have my friends with me, or a sharp stick. What I had instead was a running speed much, much higher than any ordinary human's. I was hoping this would matter, or I was going to have to consider putting rodents back on the menu.

The buck ran deeper into the woods. I followed. I'd never run in the forest at night. I wasn't sure I could manage it. My arm was better, fortunately. I hadn't really been paying attention to it, so I guess it had sort of fixed itself. That was a bonus. But the ground wasn't even. It kept throwing off my stride. There were roots and rocks lying all over the place just waiting to trip me up. To avoid these I tried bounding from one open patch to another. It seemed to be working, until I hit a clump of moss. It swallowed my foot and I nearly pitched head over heels. There was a lesson in that. Avoid the moss. I learned to spot it quickly.

Fortunately, I could see well. And my eyes could focus in a snap. I had to trust them. Look down when I needed to, but keep mapping out the best way ahead.

Rocks and roots. I'd been jumping over them. Time to fix that. It was slowing me down. I started using them as launch pads so I could cover greater distances between strides. I took powerful steps. Long and fast and smooth. I would have made Mr. Entwistle proud. It was awesome. I was where I belonged. In the dark. In the wild. And my powers of survival were being tested.

I pushed the buck over trails that wound through the forest. It was faster than I was. Over a few hundred feet it wasn't a close race, but it couldn't keep the same pace after a few miles. Gradually it slowed down. Then it stumbled.

My body went a bit haywire. It started in my mouth. I felt a sharp pain in my upper gums. Something moved against my front teeth. The taste of blood, my blood, was in my mouth. The same thing had happened during my first disastrous meal back in Charlie's shed, so when I ran my tongue over the area, I knew exactly what I'd find—two long, sharp teeth that seconds before had been the short version you would see in a normal person's mouth. These were my canines, the vampire's teeth, the ones we use for feeding. They had descended. And with them came a feeling that I could only think of as *the killing urge*. My father had mentioned it in his entry about the werewolf. It was a lust for blood so strong that once it took hold, there was no turning back.

My eyes locked on the buck's neck. An instant later, it was dying with my fangs in its throat.

I have heard people say that the best part of the hunt is not the kill but the thrill of the chase. Well, I'd bet my last pair of running shoes that none of them ever killed anything larger than a housefly. Sure, the chase was fun, exercise and all that, good for the heart. But the meal at the end was tops. It frightened me, actually, how intense it felt to surrender to that killing urge and feed.

As the warm blood coursed down my throat, it was as if my senses were waking up. Everything was magnified. Nothing moved around me that I didn't see in the clearest detail. Bats, moths, rustling pine needles. And I heard every sound. The buck's failing heart. My own heart pounding in my chest. Heavy breathing. The drone of mosquito wings. I could pinpoint every one of them. And the smells. Evergreen boughs. Musk. Fur. Damp leaves and old needles. The soil. I could even smell the lichen and the granite rock around us.

The sense of being watched was very strong—as if all the creatures around me in the forest were aware of what I had done and were afraid.

I fed like a predator. And I had no remorse. None.

I look back at this moment with a mixture of sadness and something else. Understanding, maybe. Or acceptance. I'm a vampire. Sometimes I wish I could live on tofu and alfalfa sprouts, but I can't. And I understand that I'm not consistent. I don't always act the same way. I'm a nice guy as often as I can be. As my Uncle Maximilian said, I have a choice. And I choose to be good. Until I get hungry. Then I'm something that is less than good. Then I'm a killer.

Chapter 30
Marshmallows

Charlie came to get me just after sunset the next night. "You sleep all right?" he asked.

"Yeah." I stretched and blinked my eyes. It felt good to tense every muscle.

Charlie tossed a dark bundle into the shed. It landed on the sleeping bag I was using.

"What's this?" I asked.

"Your scrubs."

"They're soaked."

"Yeah. You can thank me later. I had to clean them in the sink. You must have run about fifty miles in those things before you got here. The smell was killing all the birds."

"What's wrong with these?" I said, pulling at the collar of my shirt.

"You wore them to the bonfire last night. You want to spend the rest of your life stinking like a chimney?"

"Do you have something else I could wear?"

Charlie shook his head. "Do you want to wear a bedsheet? My clothes would never fit you."

"Then whose clothes am I wearing?"

"Those are Dan's. I scoffed them the night you got here. He was at Canada's Wonderland, remember? Well, he's in his room right now, so there's no way I'm going to be able to borrow any more. You want me to tell him an escaped lunatic is living in our shed and needs another set of duds?"

I stood and unrolled the shirt and pants from the ward. Charlie had obviously tried to wring them out because there were crease lines all over them.

"I can't wear these!"

"You can if you *believe* you can."

The boat ride was freezing. I endured it thinking about how nice the bonfire was going to be. I was disappointed when we arrived at the girls' cottage and Charlie announced to everyone that we were going sailing instead.

"I left a window in the Yacht Club unlocked so I could sneak in," he said, climbing out onto the dock. "I'll open up the doors and we can rig up a boat."

"I don't think that's such a great idea," said Suki. "If someone saw us, we could lose our jobs."

"Well, you don't have to come," said Charlie. "I just thought it would be cool to take Zack out for a sail. He's never been."

Unless he was planning to light some part of the boat on fire, I didn't have any great interest in sailing, especially if it was going to involve wind.

"We should just go tomorrow afternoon," said Luna. She was

watching me shivering in the boat. "You look a little cold for sailing. Don't you have anything warmer to wear?"

I shook my head.

"Come on," Charlie said to me. "Live a little. What's the worst thing that can happen?"

"I can't really swim, Charlie," I said. "So the worst thing that can happen is that I drown."

"You can't swim?" said Suki.

"Not really," I said. I thought of my trip down the Otonabee River with Mr. Entwistle. "My last try didn't go very well."

"Well, we'll have to fix that."

"Can we fix it later?" I said. "Unless the water's warmer at this end of the lake."

So I got my bonfire after all. It wasn't so big that you could see it from outer space, but it did the trick. A few logs were set up as benches near the shore by the dock. They were arranged around a small circle of stones that kept the fire from crawling across to the neighbours' place. While I thawed out and dried my clothes, the others roasted marshmallows and talked sailing.

"You ought to try one," said Suki, as she plucked a toasted marshmallow from her stick.

"Oh, no thanks," I said. "I ate yesterday."

Charlie plunged his marshmallow right into the coals. As soon as it turned into a torch, he blew it out, ate the char, burned the next layer, then started chewing on the sliver of black marshmallow that was left on his stick.

"No, Zack doesn't eat sweets," he said between mouthfuls. "He likes roasted squirrel."

I could have killed him.

Suki glared at us. "What did you do with our squirrels?"

"I let them go," I said. "Honestly. You can come visit them anytime."

"They're living like rodent kings on our island paradise," Charlie added.

Suki pointed the sharp end of her stick at him. "You'd better not be lying."

Charlie grabbed the stick from her and started chasing her around the fire. I noticed he wasn't trying all that hard to catch her. Come to think of it, she wasn't trying all that hard to get away. Then the two of them disappeared around the corner of the cottage. I held my breath and listened. They didn't go very far, but they didn't come back, either.

And that left me alone with Luna.

She looked up from her seat and watched me soak up the heat from the fire.

"Why didn't you come by today?" she asked.

"By the Yacht Club?"

"Yeah."

I took a deep breath and let it go.

"Am I being too nosey?"

"No," I said. "I just . . ." *Can't tell you that I'm a vampire.*

Luna pushed another marshmallow over the remains of the last one, then hung it over the coals. "Stumped on question one. Wait till I get to the hard stuff."

"This *is* the hard stuff."

"Really?" Her eyebrows flashed up for just a second. "Well, this ought to be good. You out robbing banks or something?"

I stood and turned so that my back was to the fire. Luna was watching me. Her eyes sort of moved around my face. They were curious. And bright.

"I'm allergic to the sun," I said. "I sleep during the day."

"Really?"

"Yeah."

"You sleep all day?"

"Yeah."

"Every day?"

"Yeah."

"A creature of the night?"

"Pretty much."

She was looking at me to see if I was telling the truth. I pointed to her marshmallow. The bottom was starting to blister.

"Oh," she said. "Thanks." She turned it over and began toasting the other side. "So what do you do for school?"

"Don't go."

"Get out!"

I shook my head. "Not since Grade Two."

She pulled her marshmallow stick away from the fire, reached over and offered it to me.

"No thanks."

She waved it around a few times, like there was no way I could pass up a gooey ball of roasted sugar.

"No, really," I said, lifting my hand. "I don't want one."

She gave me a look like I was putting her on. Like living with no sun and no school was easier to believe than not wanting to eat a marshmallow.

"Suit yourself."

She tested it with her fingers, blew on it a few times, then carefully pulled it off and stuffed it in her mouth.

"So how do you get your vitamin D?" she asked. The marshmallow muffled the sound of her voice.

"Squirrels," I said.

She put her stick down and stood up so that she was right in front of me. "A wise guy, huh?"

"Not really," I said. "I haven't been to school since I was seven."

"I don't believe you," she said.

I smiled and shrugged. It was the perfect thing for her to say. It meant she thought I was normal.

While I continued to dry, she stepped over the log she'd been sitting on and walked over to the front porch. A towel was hanging over the railing. She pulled it off and slung it over her shoulder.

"I think I'm going to explode," she said. She was still holding the bag of marshmallows. She tossed them back beside the fire. "You warm enough for a swim?"

The correct answer was no. I was so cold I could have crawled right into the coals and made a nest for myself, but I didn't want to miss a chance to spend more time with her, even if it meant drowning.

"I think so," I said.

She started walking around to the back of the cottage.

"Isn't the water this way?" I pointed towards the lake.

"I'm just going to see if the others are interested."

She came back a minute later by herself. I had to put my hand over my mouth to keep my smile from showing. I was so happy I thought my lips were going to crack.

"Do I need a life jacket?" I mumbled.

"You mean you really can't swim?"

"No. I can't."

I started to walk towards the dock. Luna took hold of my elbow with both hands and steered me over to the shore.

"That part of the lake is better for drowning. This part is better for swimming."

Beside the dock was a narrow ribbon of sand that stretched along the shore. I pulled off my shirt, kicked off my shoes, rolled up my scrubs and waded into the shallow water. And what a thrill. I've never had a massage, but I imagine that swimming must come very close. I lay in the water looking up at the stars. Luna had one hand under the small of my back and the other between my shoulder blades. I just floated with the water pressing around me on all sides. Then she showed me how to keep myself from sinking. Sculling, she called it. It sounded like the kind of skill every vampire should have. And all the while we talked. She told me about her school. I talked about the ward. It took a while to convince her that I hadn't been joking earlier. I really couldn't go out in the sun and I'd never been to high school. She seemed to think I was lucky, but I thought she was the lucky one. All of her close friends were people she'd met there.

"So how do you know Charlie?" she asked me.

"My dad and his dad were old friends."

"When do you see him, if you don't go to school?"

"He visits me at night. Usually over the weekends, because it's pretty late."

"That's it?"

"Pretty much."

By this time I was lying on a flutter board. It fit under my stomach and kept me from sinking.

"Don't kick so hard," she said. She walked beside me in the shallow water. "You only move your legs so that they don't sink. It's your arms that pull you forward. Just like you're crawling."

"But my legs are so much stronger," I said.

"I think your arms will manage just fine."

I was starting to get the hang of it.

"You must spend an awful lot of time alone," she said.

I mentioned Nurse Ophelia. And Jacob and Sad Stephen, too. They checked into the Nicholls Ward a few times a year, so they counted.

"Still, that's not a lot of visitors," she said. "Not a lot of company."

"There aren't a lot of people who stay up all night."

"No. I guess not," she said. "Sounds like you need to meet a nice insomniac. Or a vampire."

I fell off the flutter board.

Luna laughed. She had a hand over her mouth, but it didn't do much to hide her smile. "I'm sorry," she said. "That was my fault."

She tossed the flutter board back on shore and went over the fundamentals of the backstroke. I liked this better. She had her hands underneath me again.

We talked about swimming, then sailing, and that led us to other stuff like hobbies and things we liked to do. The whole time she kept mentioning all the people she knew. I could hardly believe it, how she kept track of them all. It was mind-boggling. She must have known everyone in the phone book.

She brought back the flutter board and stuck it under my chest. Then she taught me how to do a frog kick. I liked it the best. Once I had that down, she took my hands and showed me how to pull myself through the water.

"This is the breast stroke," she said. "It's my favourite. Cup your hands, and sweep them around so that they make a heart, then push the water down to your feet."

I let her guide my hands for a few heart-shaped sweeps. Then she let go and I took a powerful stroke.

"I think you're a natural," she said.

I didn't think so. It seemed to me the flutter board was doing most of the work.

"Do you want to try swimming off the dock?" she asked.

I stood up and we walked out of the water together. She handed me her towel so I could pat myself dry.

"I'd rather warm up for a while," I said.

"Okay. Just hide that bag of marshmallows. They're going to be the death of me."

By this time the fire had died down a bit. It was hypnotic, the way the flames danced and changed colours. The embers, too. They shifted in the breeze from red to black to orange. I imagined cavemen must have spent a lot of time just staring at these things. It made me wonder why we didn't have a fireplace back at the ward. Infomercials about Miracle Glow had nothing on this.

"The coals are perfect," she said. She reached for the marshmallow bag, stuck her hand in and pulled one loose. "I'll just have one."

As soon as it was set on her stick, she turned it carefully over the coals.

"Do you have a girlfriend?" she asked me.

I shook my head. Males and females were separated at the ward, so I'd never had the chance to talk to any girls my age.

"Are you going to come for a sail tomorrow?"

"I'll be sleeping."

"Right." She nodded.

I noticed her first marshmallow was followed by a second.

"Well," she said, "if you find a cure by tomorrow, I'd be happy to rig us a boat and take you for a tour of the lake."

I smiled. If only . . .

On the way home, Charlie grilled me with questions.

"So . . . ?" was the first one.

"So . . . ? So what?"

"So what happened?" he asked me.

I told him about the fire and the swimming lesson and our conversation.

"That's it? You just talked?" He shook his head and looked at me like I'd just slept through my last day on earth. Then he started talking about baseball and getting to all the bases, and that I hadn't even gotten into the batter's box. I had no idea what this had to do with anything, but I wasn't really listening. I was thinking of Luna.

I'd never actually *met* a person before. A stranger. Not the way they do in movies where two people bump into each other on a bus or in a café and say things like, "Excuse me, is this seat taken?" and you just know they're going to get on famously. Meeting Luna was like that. I wondered if other kids ever felt this way, if it was normal. A week ago I'd never heard of her. Now she was stuck in my head so firmly . . .

Charlie interrupted me with a poke on the shoulder. "And no biting, either," he said. "You know what I mean?"

I hadn't been listening, which wasn't like me.

"I hear ya," I said. Then I went back to thinking about Luna.

Chapter 31
The Fate of All Vampires

Just as I had the night before, I snuck back down to the dock with my father's journal once Charlie was asleep. I was hoping I might find another entry with a little more detail about—anything, really. As long as it related to vampires. Why we have such a tough time of it. Where this whole thing came from. Why we can't be cured. Or maybe something about Vrolok and what his real name might be. I just needed more.

I skimmed a few pages, then came to a passage about Malta and Gozo. It didn't say where they were, but I could see that my father was hunting again.

Bad news confirmed by Mutada. B is now connected to three disappearances in Valletta. He appears to be spreading the contagion indiscriminately. Max and I are flying out tonight.

B must have been another vampire. One who was apparently doing a lot of biting. A few entries later, my father continued with this.

B found impaled and decapitated in Ta'Braxia cemetery.

There was more, but I stopped reading.

Impaled. The word stuck in my head like a shard of glass. *Impaled.* Like those people in my nightmare. There had been thousands of them writhing on those long stakes. Screaming. Bleeding. Dying. The memory was vivid, as though I'd really been there. And that strange man who had appeared beside me, laughing. His face was perfectly clear, too. Large green eyes. Wide face. Hard cheekbones. Dark hair and moustache. And the teeth. I wondered if he was real. Well, not real, exactly, but maybe a person I'd seen on television, or in a picture I couldn't quite place, someone ordinary that my mind had twisted a little so that he fit in with the rest of the nightmare.

A voice inside me said no. He wasn't a person I'd invented or rec-reated. And he was connected to that bloodstained field of dying bodies. The two belonged together.

Impaled.

Who ever heard of a vampire dying that way? A stake through the heart I understood. If you really wanted to go overboard you cut off the head too, and put garlic in the mouth, like Van Helsing did to Lucy in *Dracula.* But impaled? It seemed like a disgustingly cruel end, even for a rogue vampire.

I read on.

Of B's servants, we can find no trace. The lack of evidence suggests the Coven of the Dragon has been at work here.

The Coven of the Dragon? That sounded ominous. Like a secret society. I kept skimming, hoping to find more. Then my uncle's name caught my eye. And the letters *EP*, which I assumed at first were the initials of another vampire.

Max returned from Turgovishte last night in great dismay. Of the Coven of the Dragon, nothing can be confirmed. Like early stories about carriers, there is much rumour and few hard facts. In addition, our friends have concluded their research. If their findings are correct, the inevitable fate of all carriers is insanity, a condition they refer to as "Endpoint Psychosis" (EP). This confirms our worst fears—a carrier's madness cannot be prevented, only postponed.

I read it a second time, then a third. I kept reading until I'd practically memorized every word, but only two stuck out. *Endpoint Psychosis*.

I couldn't believe what I was reading. Did my father really believe that *all* vampires went crazy? Like I wasn't in *enough* trouble?

I started flipping frantically through the journal to see if he'd written any more about this. *Endpoint Psychosis.* When did it happen? Was I close? Was there any way to tell? My hands were shaking so much I had to set the journal on the dock just to keep the pages still.

I got to the end and had found nothing. I started flipping again from the back. Then again from the front. Nothing. Maybe this was how I was going to go crazy. I was going to get so worried about Endpoint Psychosis that I'd keep turning pages until my brain snapped in two.

I slammed the journal closed and slid it away from me. Then I flopped back on the dock so I was looking up at the stars. The sky was full of grey-blue clouds, but Cassiopeia was in full view, floating upside down in her orbit around Polaris, the North Star. I thought for a minute how cruel it was that she had been in my life longer than my father. It made me furious. Why hadn't he explained things properly? Why was his journal so vague? Why did he have to go off in the first place and get himself killed?

I balled my fists and tried to squeeze the frustration out of my body. My heart was pounding against my ribs like it wanted to escape, and who could blame it? If my father was right, I was going to go crazy. After spending eight years in a mental ward, I knew exactly what that meant—confusion and anger and pain. Or hopelessness and despair. I'd seen both. And because I was a vampire, it would be far worse. I would become a creature so terrible even my own father would have killed me.

I tried to slow my breathing so my body would stop shaking. It took a few minutes. Then I folded my hands under my head like a pillow and closed my eyes. The water was shifting gently underneath the dock. Normally, the subtle rising and falling would have calmed my nerves, but now it just made me nauseous.

For a time I just lay there, wrestling with my nervous stomach and listening to the sound of the bats hunting overhead. The needles of the trees made soft swishing noises that blended with the chirping of insects. My thoughts drifted and I found myself wondering about Nurse Ophelia. She'd vanished just after Mr. Entwistle crashed into my life. When all the trouble started. There was no way this was a coincidence. Her disappearance and my dilemma had to be connected. And Mr. Entwistle? He'd died by arson the day after saving me. That couldn't be another coincidence. Someone had to be responsible.

Maybe my Uncle Max would know. But he hadn't called back yet, so maybe he was gone, just like the others.

Thank God for Charlie. I wondered how much I should tell him. If I was in danger of going bonkers and biting everything in sight, I should warn him, at least. Or just go away by myself. That would keep him safe.

But I didn't want to go away. I'd spent enough of my life alone.

Mr. Entwistle had survived for over six hundred and fifty years. If that was true, then it *was* possible to stay alive and stay sane . . . if you could call him that. But Mr. Entwistle was gone, and his secrets were gone with him.

I thought back to the night of our escape, when he'd told me about his purpose: that he helped other vampires. Even the rogues. That must have been one of his secrets. And he didn't attach himself to things. And he drank. A lot.

Well, one of those things was possible for me. I could find a purpose.

I stood up and retrieved my father's journal. That would be my first purpose. I would finish reading it, all of it, not just the vampire parts, and learn all that it could teach me. Then I was going to find my uncle. That was goal number two. I had to find somewhere safe to hide, and then I could figure out how to deal with Vrolok. Find out who he was and if he had a weakness. That was goal number three. And I had to see Luna again. In fact, *that* was goal number two. My uncle and Vrolok could wait. As soon as I was done with the journal, I had to find a way to tell her the truth.

I looked up at the sky. Cassiopeia was still sparkling overhead. I felt a sudden swell of confidence, as if my Miracle Glow, fairy-tale ending was only minutes away. I smiled and started leafing through the journal to find my page.

No sooner had I started reading than a sudden coolness crept over the dock. A chill went through me, raising goosebumps on my arms. I looked out over the water. A fog was moving down the lake. It curled and tumbled like a living thing, clawing its way toward me. The wind picked up, lifting the back of my hair and causing the pages of the journal to flutter.

Something wasn't right here. I held my breath to listen, but heard nothing. The bats were all gone. The insects had stopped their chattering. The fog moved closer, swirling more violently now as it met the same breeze that stirred the pages of the journal and blew my hair down over my eyes.

The fog was moving against the wind.

I took a step backwards, and another. Then I heard it. The flapping of leathery wings.

I turned and ran. Trees and rocks passed me in a blur. So did the cottage. I followed the path straight for the shed, bounding with long, powerful strides. As I drew closer, I felt an icy cold against my skin, as if tendrils of fog were reaching out to snare me. I was panting loudly. The shed was close now. Just a few more steps. When I reached the door, I nearly tore it off the hinges. It snapped closed behind me and I fumbled with the latch. Then I held my breath and backed away. Although the window in the door was covered, in my mind's eye I could see the eerie luminescence drifting past outside, rolling, searching.

My lungs were burning so I sucked a quiet breath in through my teeth. I kept backing away until my foot hit the edge of my sleeping bag. Then I buried myself underneath and waited.

Chapter 32
Problem Child

Sometime during the early-morning hours I fell asleep. My dreams were frantic and confused. I couldn't find anyone. Everywhere there was shadow and fog and the sound of bat wings. I could feel an evil presence hunting me, but the more I ran, the closer it seemed to come.

It ended when Charlie ripped open the door of the shed the next day. I could hear his heart. It was doing a drum solo. He was so agitated, he actually pulled the latch right out of the door frame.

"We've got a problem," he said.

The sun was still up, and light was bouncing all over the place, so we had at least two problems. I buried myself under my sleeping bag and waited until he closed the door.

"Suki just called," he said. He made it sound like a bad thing. "The cops were there. They're on their way over right now. We've got to get you out of here. They could arrive any second."

I stood up and grabbed my shirt. Then I started looking for my father's journal. As soon as I'd found it, I lifted a corner of the garbage bag that Charlie had stapled over the window frame. My fingers started to burn right away, so I let it go.

"What time is it?" I asked.

"I don't know. It's evening, just after eight, maybe."

That meant the sun would be up for another half hour or so.

"What do I do?" I asked.

Charlie shrugged. "Can you wrap yourself up in that?" He flicked a finger towards my sleeping bag.

"Where am I going?"

"That's another problem."

"Can I talk to Luna?"

"And that's another problem."

"How did this happen?"

Charlie took a deep breath, then leaned back against the workbench under the window. "Their father read that article about you in the *Examiner* the other day. The one that said you're an escaped mental patient with psychotic tendencies. Who knew? Well, apparently he overheard the girls talking about you. Once he put two and two together, he detonated and called the cops. So we gotta get going. If the police catch you here, they're going to lock you away for about eight million years."

That didn't sound too appealing. But that wasn't what really bothered me.

"So Luna knows?" I asked.

"Yeah." Charlie nodded. "Sounds like she was pretty upset."

"I've got to explain."

Charlie shook his head. "No way. The girls, Suki . . . You've got to stay away."

I let out a deep breath. I felt as if my whole body was going to collapse. I looked at Charlie, and then at the floor, and then at the shelves. I don't know what I was expecting to see, like the key to my future was going to be written on a half-used can of spray paint. I was lost. The police were coming. The sun was still shining. I'd run out of hiding places. Funny thing was, I didn't care about that. I just wanted to talk to Luna. I couldn't have her believe all those things about me were true.

"Does your brother know I'm here?" I asked.

"No."

"Isn't there another place I can hide? Maybe at the other end of the island? I could sneak away as soon as the police are gone."

Charlie shook his head. "What are you going to do, make yourself invisible? Suki said they've got dogs with them. This isn't *The Hobbit*, Zack. This is for real."

"So what do we do?"

"We get in the boat and take our chances."

Charlie picked up the sleeping bag and handed it to me. I passed him my father's journal, unzipped one side of the bag and put it over my head like a giant cape. As soon as I was outside, it would be the only thing between me and the sun.

"Is that going to work?" he asked. "You aren't going to go up like a torch, are you?"

"We'll see," I said. I sounded braver than I felt.

I waited in the shed for Charlie to go down to the dock and get the boat ready. Then he whistled. That was the signal. I was supposed to take off.

I couldn't.

The light outside was just too bright. Why couldn't it have been cloudy?

Charlie whistled again.

I took a deep breath. Then another. I had to go, but my feet wouldn't move. The sun was out there. The sun was death. Painful death.

Charlie whistled a third time. I imagined him waiting in the boat. Then I imagined Luna at her cottage. If I stayed here, if I chickened out and hid in the shed, the police would find me and I'd never get the chance to set things straight.

Charlie whistled a fourth time. I pulled the sleeping bag tight around my shoulders, took a deep breath, then kicked the door open and ran outside.

Chapter 33
On the Run

I'd never been out in the full sun before. Even with the sleeping bag over my body and clothes protecting my arms and legs, I still felt like I'd just jumped into an oven. My eyes burned. My skin tingled. Everything was hot. Then I felt jabs, like pinpricks, spreading over my hands and neck. All the while, I ran as fast as I could. I kept my eyes on the ground, but even that was blinding. And so I didn't see the little boy until he was right in front of me.

He must have been one of Dan's kids. He just popped out of nowhere as I rounded the cottage on my way to the dock. I didn't hit him, or he would have landed somewhere in Saskatchewan, but I tripped and fell getting out of his way. The ground came at me quickly, so without thinking, I stuck out a hand to break my fall. The effect was dramatic. In less than two seconds, the skin turned red, blistered, then charred to black and cracked open.

I screamed.

Behind me, up in the cottage, someone started shouting. I pulled my hand back under the sleeping bag, but the damage had been done. My hand was a mess, and I'd been spotted.

A second later, Charlie was beside me. I could only see his feet. He was trying to help me up by the arm, but it was the bad one, so I just shouted, "Don't!" and ran down to the boat. I ate up the last fifty feet in about two strides. A moment later I felt the boat lurch as Charlie jumped in after me.

"What happened?"

All I could say was, "My hand." I leaned out of the boat so that the shadow of the sleeping bag was over the water. When I stuck my arm in, it made a hissing noise. It wasn't like swimming. It didn't feel like a massage. It was more like acupuncture. I got dizzy and fell back against the side of the boat.

By this time, Dan was calling for Charlie. I could tell by the sound of his voice that he was coming towards us.

Charlie didn't answer. He just gunned the motor, and we took off. I had no idea where we were going. I turned the sleeping bag into a cocoon and waited for the sun to set. I didn't say anything, I just gritted my teeth and rocked back and forth, doing my best to keep my hand from touching anything that would make the pain come back.

As soon as Charlie told me that the sun had gone down, I poked my head up from under the sleeping bag and looked around. My head was still buzzing. Or maybe it was the flies. We were in a swamp, with reeds and drowned trees in the water all around us. It was like something out of a Tarzan movie. Charlie had pulled the motor up so that the prop was sticking out behind the boat. He was using a paddle to push off the spongy bottom. The smell of rot coming up from the water was enough to singe your nose hairs.

"Where are we?" I asked.

"It's a bird sanctuary," said Charlie. "My dad calls it the Lost Channel, I guess because no one uses it any more."

"Where are the cottages?"

"You can't build in here. And you can't come in with motorboats, so we should be safe."

"Isn't this a motorboat?"

"If we get caught by the cops, that will be the least of our worries."

That made sense.

"So now what?" I asked. I had to speak through clenched teeth because my hand was still on flame-broil. "Can we go back to your place?"

Charlie shook his head. "No. The cops might still be there. We're going to feel awfully stupid if we go back and they nab us."

I was already feeling stupid, but I didn't say anything.

Charlie smiled. "I have a plan. I used to play hide-and-seek with my brothers all the time. You know the best place to hide?"

I blew on my hand. "In a cave?" I said.

"Look around, chowderhead. Do you see a cave anywhere? I mean in general."

I had no idea. Hide-and-seek wasn't too popular at the ward. Most patients couldn't remember what they were doing for more than ten seconds. And they got spooked super easy. Hide-and-seek would have looked more like hide-and-freak.

"The best place to hide from someone," Charlie explained, "is in a place they've already searched."

He paddled us out of the bird sanctuary and dropped the motor.

"So where are we going?" I asked.

"To see Suki and Luna. Where else?"

That definitely sounded better than a cave. And since the police had already searched there, it was probably safer than anywhere else. If he was concerned that the girls didn't want me around, he sure didn't show it. I was definitely more worried than he was. Of course, he wasn't an escaped mental patient with a warrant out for his arrest. But his confidence helped convince me things might turn out all right.

We drove with the lights off. It felt good to be moving, even if it brought us closer to trouble. It was a distraction from the pain in my hand.

We were lucky. The police were gone from Luna's part of the lake. We didn't see any of their boats. It was still early when we arrived at her cottage. Ten o'clock, maybe. All of the lights in the cottage were still on, so Charlie cut the engine and we drifted in to the dock.

"Are you sure this is a good idea?" I whispered.

"What have you got to lose? They already want to kill you."

Charlie stepped out of the boat and grabbed the rope to tie it up.

"What are you doing?" I asked.

"I'm going to knock at the door," he said.

I hadn't really considered what we'd do once we arrived, but I didn't think the front door was the best option.

Charlie motioned for me to get under the sleeping bag. "I'll see if Luna can come out. Just be ready. Their old man's pretty good with a shotgun. We might need to make a quick exit." I couldn't tell if he was joking.

He slipped up onto the front porch and knocked at the door. Suki answered. She took one look at him and folded her hands across her chest. I crouched under the sleeping bag in the front of the boat and watched.

"Well?" she said.

"Hey, it's me. It's Charlie. You don't have to look at me like that."

"Like what? Like you set my sister up with a crackpot?"

"He's not a crackpot. He's my best friend. And you were all wild about him until a few hours ago. You really think he's crazy? Come on!"

"He lied to us. You both did."

"That's a bunch of—"

"You *did!*"

"Zachary's got a lot of problems right now, but he's never been a liar. Never."

"Yeah, he said he lived in a mental ward. He never said he escaped! You let on like he was fine. It was in the newspaper. He attacked four police officers. Explain that one, Einstein."

I listened, but Charlie didn't say anything for a few seconds. I could hear the porch creaking under his feet as he shifted around.

"I can't explain it. But Zachary can. I know we can clear all of this up. Is Luna here?"

There was another long pause.

"Where is he?" Suki asked. "Is he here? Did you bring him here?" Her voice sounded like she was trying to yell and whisper at the same time.

"He's in the boat. He wants to talk to Luna."

"Forget it!" said Suki.

She backed up and started to close the door. Charlie stopped it with his hand.

"That's no good," he said.

Suki put her hand against his shoulder. "Not tonight, Charlie. Not tonight."

Then she closed the door.

Chapter 34
Explanations

There was nothing we could do but go back to the bird sanctuary. We waited there until just after midnight, then we headed back to the girls' place.

"Persistence is the key," said Charlie. He cut the engine and we drifted in, this time to the beach.

"I don't know about this," I said. "I have no idea what to say."

"Knowing what to say is a lot less important than making sure we go to the right window."

We snuck around the side of the house. Charlie pointed to a screened window on the second floor of the cottage. "That's the one, I think."

"You *think*? You're not sure?"

"Do I look like I designed the place? Here." He put his hand on my shoulder to get me to bend down, then he stood on my back and tapped the screen several times. Then several more. I heard a creak and a voice. It was Suki.

"Charlie!" She made his name sound like a swear word. "God, you're impossible!"

The screen slid open. I couldn't tell what Charlie was doing. It felt like Suki was trying to push him over. I heard a sound like kissing, so I started to back up. I wasn't here for this.

"Hey, hey!" he whispered.

I stopped.

"Wake your sister," he said to Suki.

"She's awake already."

"Well, come out then."

Charlie didn't wait for an answer. He just jumped down.

A half minute later Suki swung a leg out of the window and then lowered herself down so that we could catch her.

"You'd better have a good explanation for all of this," she said. She spoke to Charlie, but I think her words were really for me. She didn't look very angry, which was encouraging. Charlie grabbed her hand and pulled her towards the front of the cottage.

I stared up at the window. "Luna," I whispered. My heart was beating so hard, I think it was louder than my voice.

"I'm right here," she said quietly, circling around from the back of the cottage.

I turned. She glanced at me and glanced away. Her mouth was a flat line and her eyes were red-rimmed and watery. Neither of us spoke for a while.

"I heard you had a tough night," I said.

She nodded. "We shouldn't talk here."

We passed Charlie and Suki on the way down to the lake. I avoided looking at either of them. I thought Luna was going to sit down when we reached the end of the dock, but she turned and faced me instead.

"Is it true?" she asked. "Did you really do all of those things?"

I took a deep breath. *Here goes.*

"I ran away from the ward. I had to. I couldn't stay there another day. A friend helped me. We stole a car. Well, he stole it, and I was sort of along for the ride. I don't know how to drive."

I paused to make sure she was with me.

"They said you assaulted some police officers."

This was a tricky one, because I *had* assaulted a police officer, but not on purpose. I explained as best I could. I started with the three officers who'd pinned me in the parking lot of the Nicholls Ward. It was difficult, because I didn't want to mention any of the vampire business, so I couldn't say why I had to resist arrest. Fortunately, I had Mr. Entwistle to blame, since he'd really done all of the assaulting and I'd just watched. Then I told her about the fourth officer. The one I'd punched after he and his partner hit me with their van.

"It hurt so much," I said. "There was pain everywhere. When he touched me, I lashed out without thinking. Then I took off."

"You mean you got hit by a car and just ran away?"

"A van."

"Car, van, what's the difference?"

"I don't know," I said. "I've never been hit by a car."

That made her laugh. She was starting to come back.

"Why don't you just explain this to the police? It's not like they're going to toss you in jail."

I wasn't worried about jail. I was worried about Everett Johansson and Baron Vrolok, neither of whom I'd mentioned.

"I can't," I said.

Luna looked down at her feet, then out over the lake. The moon was bright, but hidden behind a thin layer of cloud that shone silvery-white along the horizon. We didn't speak for a moment, but we glanced nervously at each other and then out over the water. Then Luna noticed my hand.

"Oh my God! What happened?"

"I had a bit of an accident leaving Charlie's. The sun wasn't down all the way."

"The sun did that?"

"Yeah."

"You should put it in cold water."

I started to crouch down so I could dip my hand in the lake. She grabbed my other elbow with both hands.

"No. The lake water's got bacteria and stuff in it. You might get an infection. I'll get some ice water from the kitchen."

"Won't your parents hear?"

She laughed. "They might. But as far as I know, it's not illegal for me to get ice from my own freezer."

A few minutes later I was sitting on the dock with my hand in a pail of ice water. It was numb, which was an improvement. Luna sat beside me, looking at the lights of the far shore as they shimmered on the surface of the water.

"Here, let me check that," she said.

I pulled my hand out.

"It's a lot better than I thought. It looked black before. Must have been the light."

My hand was now an angry red. The blisters were gone and the cracks were all sealed over. I was healing, albeit a lot more slowly than if I'd fed. I put my hand back in the pail and looked up at the sky. With the clouds, it wasn't the best night for stargazing, but it was perfect for watching the bats hunt. I saw one do a half barrel-roll that ended with a dive and a mouthful of moth. I had to smile. It was impressive.

"What's so funny?" Luna asked.

"The bats." I followed the same one as he continued to stalk insects through the air. "They're unbelievable. That one in particular." I pointed. "He's an ace compared to the others."

Luna was looking in the same place I was, but she had no idea what I was talking about. The cloud-covered moon was like a giant night-light, but still she couldn't see them.

"I don't believe it," Luna said. I couldn't tell if she was impressed or irritated.

"How can you not believe in bats?"

She started laughing. "You obviously see much better in the dark than I do."

"Well, if you stayed up every night like me . . ."

She nodded. "I've heard that blind people hear and smell and taste better because their brains just adjust somehow. I guess it's the same kind of thing."

"Hmmm."

Her head flopped onto my shoulder.

"Did you get a bug bite?" she asked. "If you rub it, it just gets worse."

I stopped scratching my neck. I hadn't fed since I'd killed the deer. That was the night of the bonfire, almost two full days ago. I guess because I'd drunk so deeply, my hunger had stayed away for much longer than normal, but it was returning with the same impatience it always had. I took a piece of ice from the pail, wiped it across my forehead, then popped it into my mouth.

"Do you know what time it is?" she whispered.

I looked at the sky and then at the neighbours' cottage, where the twins lived.

"Almost one."

"And you know this how?"

"The kitchen clock."

Luna glanced over at the neighbouring cottage. "Zachary, they don't even have the lights on."

"I told you I see well in the dark."

"Apparently." She let out a deep sigh.

"Are you okay?" I asked.

"Yes. No. I don't know."

She stood up and offered me her hand. I took it, not because I needed to, but just so I could hold it. I'd never held a person's hand before, well, other than my father's. Then I stood so that we were facing each other. She was close enough that I could feel her breath on my neck.

"It just bothers me that you can't have a normal life," she said. She moved a bit closer.

"I'm not a normal person," I said.

"I got that much."

She was looking straight at me. I didn't know what to say.

"I have to go soon," she added. She was standing so close, I don't think even the wind could have snuck between us. I would have backed up a step, but then I would have fallen off the edge of the dock.

"You've never had a girlfriend, have you."

I shook my head. I started to say "No," but it got stuck on the way out.

I don't know how she managed it, but her hand was suddenly on my good arm. The way my legs were feeling I'm surprised it didn't knock me over. My heart started pounding so hard it was practically bruising my stomach. I felt dizzy. I could smell the blood coursing under the skin of her neck. It was right in front of me. I could hear her heart racing. She was still staring right at me. Her emerald eyes were beautiful. Soft and warm. Almost luminous. My hand rose to the side of her face and I heard her take in a quiet breath. *I could do this thing and I wouldn't have to be alone ever again.*

Luna closed her eyes and tilted her head back. I felt my teeth slide down through my gums and my mouth opened just a sliver. She was so close . . .

What was I thinking? I was a vampire. Cursed to endure a slow descent into madness. I shouldn't have been near her. I shouldn't have been near anybody.

"I can't do this," I said, pressing my lips closed.

Luna's eyes opened. I couldn't tell if she was confused or upset. She looked down, and then looked away, and then looked at me again. She started to back away, but I pulled her close and put my arms around her. I had to. I lifted my chin so that her head was cradled against my neck. Then I closed my eyes and just soaked up the feel of her. Warm skin. Soft hair. Her hands on the small of my back. It was the closest I had ever been to another person. It was wonderful.

"I wish I could explain," I said. "But I can't. I'm sorry."

I had a full minute of bliss. Of being alone with another person. It was the exact opposite of what I had experienced on the hunt. I didn't hear or see or smell anything around me. There was only Luna. Everything else had vanished.

And then the air went frigid and a deep chill ran through me. Everything suddenly felt wrong, the way it had in Mr. Entwistle's library, and the night before on the dock. There was no wind this time, not even a ripple on the water, but an icy cold made me shudder inside. I let go of Luna and sniffed at the air. I didn't smell anything unusual. I didn't hear or see anything unusual. Then I noticed the bats were all gone again, and a fog was beginning to rise from the water near the shore.

"We've got to get out of here," I said. I looked past Luna to see if I could spot anything in the shadows near the cottage.

"What is it? What's wrong?" she asked.

"I don't know. But you'd better get inside. And lock the door."

"You're making me nervous."

I pushed her gently towards the front steps. Then I heard a noise coming from behind the cottage. It was raspy. Like the sound of someone choking. Or being strangled. That was where Charlie and Suki had gone!

"Oh my God," I whispered.

A part of me that didn't think took over. I bared my fangs and bolted. I don't imagine you've ever seen a creature move so fast.

Just behind the cottage I found Charlie and Suki. They were lying on the ground. Their faces were glued together at the mouth. They were fine. Suki shrieked when she saw me.

"Get her inside," I said. "Hurry."

Charlie wasn't too happy about the interruption. "What's gotten into you?"

Then he saw my fangs.

"Get her inside and lock the door," I said. "Lock all of them."

"What is it?"

"Evil," I said. "I can feel it. It must be Vrolok. It isn't safe for you to be out here. You need to get inside."

A light came on in the cottage.

"And call the police," I added.

Suki ran for the door.

"Are you sure about the cops?" Charlie asked.

"Yes. Yes. Call them." I waved for him to go. "Just get moving."

I watched while Charlie followed Suki up the back steps. Then I thought I detected the faint beating of leathery wings. When I listened for it again, I heard another sound. This one made my teeth hurt. It was a scream, long and shrill. I followed it to the other side of the cottage.

It was Luna. She was standing on the porch facing the neighbours' place. And she was covered, head to toe, in blood.

Chapter 35
Helpless

Maybe you know this already: the human body contains about five and a half litres of blood. That might not sound like a lot, and I suppose it isn't. In a bathtub, it wouldn't look too impressive. But when it's all over the place, five and half litres of blood will blow your eyelids clean off. That much paint could cover half a football field. You can picture this, I'm sure. Half a football field painted red. Now change the image a bit. Imagine you're looking over a rocky clearing with a sandy shore on one side and a forest on the other. The bark of the pine and oak trees is covered. Blood is dripping from the leaves and needles. It's soaked into the moss and soil. It's pooling in tiny cracks in the rock. It's all over the porch steps.

And it was all over Luna.

I didn't know what to do. There was so much blood, you couldn't tell where it had come from. At least it hadn't come from Luna. She would have been empty. It must have come from somewhere else.

Luna started running down the front steps. I moved to follow, but as soon as I reached the bottom of the porch I saw the body. It had been stuffed under the stairs. Blood was everywhere. The sight of it and the smell stopped me dead. I'd never fed on human blood, but for eight years it was what my body had been craving, every day, day after day. It brought on a hunger so intense it was a kind of pain. Sharp and nasty. Maybe I'd have felt differently if I'd had a transfusion at the ward just before my escape, or if I'd just finished a brain cocktail or killed another deer, but that's not the way it was.

And so I did exactly what I shouldn't have done. I slipped under the shadow of the stairs to feed.

I recognized the body. It belonged to one of the twins. The blond. His brown eyes were glazed over in death. Blood ran in red ribbons down his neck, which I could see had been snapped and torn open. The flesh there was marked by dark bruises, and all of the vessels were exposed. The person who did this must have been a powerhouse.

I should have felt sorry for the twin, but all I could think about was the blood. How wasteful it was. And how angry it made me to see that it had been sprayed everywhere when I wanted it all for myself. So without a second thought, I drank every drop that was left in his body.

Blood for a vampire is life. Another day. Another week. Another month. Another year. You can't imagine how this felt, to drink life. I was undead, and then for a moment I was more than alive. Let's leave it at that. And that was when the police arrived.

Most vampires fear bright lights, which makes perfect sense. Nothing is more dangerous to us than the sun. So when that police boat appeared out of nowhere and turned its lights on me, I felt as if I were staring death straight in the face.

I am told that when people panic they have one of two responses: fight or flight. They either dig in like a wolverine and take on all comers, or they bolt like a gutless chicken. I discovered a third response that night, which is to stand still like a total idiot and not move a muscle.

Someone started shouting through a megaphone. He said they were the police and not to move. Well, I don't think they could have moved me with a battering ram. Other voices joined in. Some were coming from the porch behind me. Others were coming from the boat. I couldn't pay attention to what they were saying. I was too busy trying to hide my face from the light, so I remember only fragments. Things like "What's going on here?" and "Good God . . ." and "It's him" and "We're too late" and "Get them back inside."

Suddenly men were all around me with guns and lights and loud voices. Only when I felt someone grab me did I struggle. Then my whole body went stiff with pain. I found out later that they had used a Taser on me, like my father used when hunting vampires. It's a weapon that delivers a very powerful electric shock. Had I been Count Dracula or the Baron Vrolok, or even that vampire from the cereal box, I might have put up a better fight, but I had been raised on animal blood. "Bovine crap," as Mr. Entwistle would have said. Not the real stuff. It is human blood that takes a vampire to the next level. I had tasted it for the first time just moments before, and it might have done wonders for me, but I couldn't overcome so many full-grown men. Not when they had that Taser. Every time I moved, I felt the burn of electricity shoot through my body, paralyzing me with pain.

And so they chained my arms and ankles and stowed me away.

The boat ride was terrifying. There were so many lights trained on me, I don't think I could have blinked without the whole world seeing. All the time I heard two officers talking. One kept insisting that they "do it now," another that they "wait." I think they meant to kill me.

The same two officers lifted me out of the boat and onto the dock when we arrived at the marina. Each had a hold of one arm. They shocked me before we got out onto the wharf and again as soon as my feet touched the wooden planks. I was so scared, I think if they'd let go of me I might have turned into a puddle of goo and dribbled back into the water. I couldn't move. I couldn't run. There was only pain. Pain and bright lights, so I couldn't even see where they were taking me. I remember staring down at the gravel parking lot and at the feet of the police officers. It was easier than looking up at the lights. The stones made crunching noises under their shiny black shoes. And I remember when they stopped. A man was standing in front of us. He was leaning on a cane and had a long, pink scar under one eye. It was Everett Johansson.

When he saw me he grunted. There were bright headlights behind him so I couldn't see the expression on his face.

"Has he fed?" he asked.

One of the officers must have nodded, because I didn't hear them answer.

"Well, don't take any chances with him," Johansson continued. "If he moves, shock him."

Then he stepped to the side and opened the back door of a cruiser. I was pushed in, then the door was closed and locked. I was feeling very sick, as if someone had been kicking my stomach.

"What are you going to do?" I rasped. The men were still outside the car talking to Johansson, so I didn't get an answer. Then Johansson walked off towards the water and the other two climbed in the front seat of the car. I heard the engine turn over. Then we lurched forward to the sound of tires on gravel.

"Where are my friends?" I asked.

I was worried they were still back there with whoever had killed that boy. My instincts told me it was Vrolok. What chance would they have against him? A creature from a nightmare . . .

"Where are they?"

The two officers looked at each other. I got my answer when one of them reached back with the Taser. It looked like an electric shaver. Purple sparks crackled from the end of it. Pain followed, and for a few minutes I couldn't talk, so I just sat back against the seat.

As my strength returned, I tried to break my cuffs. It was no use. I was too weak. At least in the arms. But my legs were strong enough to snap the chain that bound my ankles. So I did. Then I turned sideways to try to kick the back door off its hinges, but the officer with the Taser reached back and jolted me again. He said something to me, but I couldn't make it out.

I realized a second later that he wasn't talking to me at all. He was swearing. Two bright lights were coming up behind us. They lit up the interior of the car so that everything looked white. The seat covers, the dashboard, the rear-view mirror. Everything. The officer who was driving stepped on the gas, but it didn't matter. Something slammed into the side of the car just behind the back wheel. My head nearly snapped from my neck as the back of the car skidded sideways towards the ditch. I could hear the tires screech. Then the car started to roll. I've never been on a roller coaster, but it couldn't possibly be as frightening. Or as fast. A car flips so quickly that you barely have time to panic.

In an instant, broken glass was everywhere. The top of the car smashed down against my head. My arms, which were still handcuffed behind my back, were practically wrenched from their sockets. Had I not been so strong, I think they would have ripped clean off. Fortunately we landed upright. I could feel my cheek swelling under my right eye. I think it had slammed into the door. And I must have had a cut on the top of my head, because blood was dripping down past my left ear. A loud noise was coming from the front of the car. It was the horn, which must have been broken, because it didn't stop. The driver's forehead was pressed against an airbag. I was guessing that he was unconscious. The officer beside him looked like he was out of it, too. His head kept shaking back and forth as though he was going to vomit.

Then I heard the sound of feet crunching on gravel. It stopped, and the door beside me began to groan. Metal was being bent. An instant later the door opened.

And there he was. My Uncle Max. He had come to save me.

Chapter 36
Flight

My uncle was holding a crowbar in his hand. He was dressed all in black. There was a belt around his waist with a whole slew of gadgets hanging from it. One of them was a gun. He looked like a commando. I wondered for a brief moment if my father had ever dressed that way when he was hunting vampires. It was like something out of a comic book.

He set the crowbar on the ground, then reached in to pull me out of the police car. When he leaned across my torso, for just an instant his neck was exposed. In the movies, that was where vampires did most of their biting. I'd never really thought about why, but after seeing that boy under the porch, I understood. The neck is the highway to the brain, and the brain needs blood, buckets of it. And unlike the brain, which is surrounded by a hard layer of bone, the vessels in the neck aren't protected at all. Blood there runs very close to the surface, so it's pretty much a bull's eye. When Uncle Max leaned past me, I was tempted to stretch out my teeth and chomp away. I was bleeding and bruised. My body wanted the good stuff so that it could start to heal. But I resisted. It helped to remember what he'd told me—that even vampires have a choice: to be good, or to be something that is less than good. I wanted to do what was right. I wanted to be good.

"Are you all right?" he asked me. "Is anything broken? Are you hurt?"

"I have a cut on my head," I told him.

He took me by the elbow and helped me carefully from the car. Then he inspected my scalp closely and made certain I wasn't cut anywhere else.

"We'd better get something on that. It's bleeding heavily," he said.

He took my elbow to steady me while he led me to his car.

"We'd better get those off of you first," he said. He was talking about my handcuffs. "Can you break them?"

I strained. My arms were aching, but I tested myself, just as Mr. Entwistle said I should. Still, I wasn't quite strong enough.

Maximilian reached down to his belt and removed a canister of something. I heard a hissing noise.

"Try again," he said.

I didn't have to work too hard this time. There was a loud crack and my arms jerked apart. The cuffs were still circling my wrists, but the chain between them was now broken.

"What did you do?" I asked.

"Liquid nitrogen," he replied. "When the metal's frozen, it's easier to break. Now wait here." He stepped quickly behind his trunk, opened it up, pulled out a red case and removed a wad of small, white squares. They were pieces of gauze.

"Hold these against your head," he told me. Then he motioned for me to get in the car while he walked around to the driver's side. "We've got to hurry."

And so I got in, and it was like stepping straight into a spy movie.

The car was unreal. I'd never been in an airplane cockpit before, but I'd seen them in movies, and I'll bet you this car had more dials, buttons and screens than a space shuttle. And it had two steering wheels. I knew this was a little weird. What kind of car had two steering wheels? And they weren't even wheels, really. They were like wheels with the tops cut off so that your hands fit on either side, like the controls for an arcade game, the kind you sit in.

There was no window behind me, just a solid wall of black. I wondered how he saw out the back. Then I noticed that in place of a rear-view mirror there was a small video screen. There must have been cameras in the back of the car, because you could see the road behind us. It was all tinted green.

In front of me on the dashboard was a screen covered with white lines. I figured out straight off that these were roads. A red light appeared on one of the lines. It was beeping and flashing and it moved quickly towards another light, a blue one that was sitting in the middle of the map.

"What's that?" I asked.

"That's either a police car or a car with a police radio," my uncle said. "Either way, we're getting out of here. Now buckle up."

I put the seat belt on. It was padded. Then he stepped on the gas, and the car whined like a jet engine.

"Will they catch us?" I asked.

My uncle smiled, then shook his head. "Not in this car." He coughed a few times into his sleeve, then pushed the pedal to the floor.

My head was forced back against the seat like I'd been shot from a bazooka. I'd driven a few times with Nurse Ophelia when she'd taken me out to the movies, or to bowl or whatever, but she never liked to break the speed limit. Uncle Max didn't break it either. He shattered it to bits. The road was winding, and I kept thinking we were going to fly off into the woods, but somehow he kept us from wiping out.

"Don't worry," he said. "The car has a vacuum in the bottom. The faster we go, the more firmly the car is held in place." Then he asked me how my head was.

I checked the bandages. That was when I noticed for the first time that my burnt hand was better. It must have healed when I drank the boy's blood. But my head wasn't doing quite so well. There was a long, red blotch on the bottom of the bandages. The blood had soaked right through.

"Keep it on," he told me. "It will probably heal before we get to my office, but if not, we'll stitch it up there." Then he pressed a button and a drawer opened up in front of me. He reached inside and pulled out a Kleenex. "Here," he said, "take some. Your chin is covered with blood."

I did my best to scrape it off. Once blood dries it's like paint. I'd have needed a chisel to get it all. There was blood on my shoes as well. And my scrubs. His car looked like it had just about every gadget you could think of, but I doubted a sink was one of them.

Uncle Max reached for the dash and started adjusting a dial. "I went back for you at the hospital," he said, "but I was too late. You'd already run. You can't imagine how relieved I was when I learned that Johansson didn't have you."

I told him about my trip through the ceiling, and that made him smile.

"You did well," he said. "But we were lucky, too. I thought Johansson was retired. I didn't expect him to be working so closely with the police. It must give him access to all kinds of information. We'll have to avoid the authorities for now."

"They can't all be bad," I said.

He shook his head. "No. You're right. But we don't know what Johansson might have told the others about you. And now . . ." He looked me over. "Now he's free to make up all kinds of nonsense. No, let me clear this up. I'll get you to a safe location, then I'll take care of the rest of this mess."

After I got as much of the blood off my face as I could, my uncle asked me what happened the night I escaped from the ward. I told him about Mr. Entwistle. About our escape from the police. And about his death.

"You have to find out if he's all right," I said. It seemed an absurd thing to suggest. Apparently, a whole building had fallen on him. How could he be all right? Unless his body armour was made on the planet Krypton, he'd probably been flattened.

Maximilian coughed quietly, but he kept his eyes glued to the road. "If what they printed in the paper is true, I think you should prepare yourself for the possibility that he didn't survive," he said. "Vampires are just as vulnerable to fire as normal people. And Entwistle kept some nasty company—"

My uncle stopped talking to have another coughing fit. He smothered his mouth with his sleeve, then cleared his throat. I waited for him to say more about Entwistle and what he thought might have happened, but he was apparently finished. I'd forgotten that the two of them were at odds, to say the least.

"Did you find out anything about Nurse Ophelia?" I asked.

My uncle shook his head.

I closed my eyes and let my head fall back against the seat. So Entwistle was gone. And Nurse Ophelia was still missing. She'd done more for me in the last eight years than everyone else in whole world put together. And I hadn't done a thing to help find her. Instead, I'd spent the last few nights thinking of myself and having fun. She deserved better.

"One thing at a time, Zachary," my uncle said. "One thing at a time. You can't do a lot for others when you're running for your life."

"I tried to call you," I told him. "I left a message at your office."

"And I got it. I called the number you left as soon as I could. When I didn't hear back from you right away, I started to get nervous. Your face has been all over the news."

I hadn't realized that he'd called me back. When I told him this, he looked surprised.

"It was later that night," he said. "About ten after eleven."

I wondered why Charlie and I hadn't heard the phone ring. We'd had Dan's BlackBerry with us all night. Then I remembered that when I'd left him the message, I'd given him the number for Charlie's cottage. That was the night of the island party, so neither of us would have been around at eleven. And Dan would have been asleep. He must have picked up the message the next morning, figured it was a wrong number and simply erased it.

"Don't be too hard on yourself," said Maximilian. "You're in good hands now. And I've just secured a deal that should keep us out of trouble. You're going to do just fine. I'm certain of it."

It was hard not to believe him. He looked like he was ready to storm the Batcave.

"Did you tell anyone?" he asked me. "About your condition?"

I nodded. "I told Charlie."

"Anyone else?"

"No."

"Did he believe you?"

"Yes." Then I told him about our conversation in his kitchen. And how I had stalked the deer. Finally, I told him about the body at Luna's.

"It was one of the twins," I said. "And he'd been strangled. I think it was Vrolok."

"What makes you think so?"

I told him about my encounter with the bat at Mr. Entwistle's house. And the fog. And how I'd seen them again at the cottage.

"So you've been there?" my uncle asked.

"Where?"

"Entwistle's house."

I nodded. "Yeah."

"Would you know how to find it again?"

"I think so."

My uncle seemed pleased by this. But it brought on another round of coughing. This was the worst bout yet. He actually had to slow down the car. When it was finished, he ran his tongue over his teeth. I could smell blood in his mouth. He must have been really sick.

"Is that the first time you've tasted human blood?" he asked. "Back at the cottage?"

I nodded. "Is that bad?"

He took a deep breath and checked a few of his gauges. Then he let out a big sigh.

"Yes, it is bad," he said slowly. "It is bad, and it isn't." And he explained to me how human blood made a vampire stronger, which I knew already. But he also told me that once you drank it, you craved it more and more.

"And therein lies the problem," he said. "You need it to be strong and so you will come to hunger for it. If you don't get enough, your desire might drive you to desperate lengths. You might even kill for it, if your hunger can't be controlled."

Well, I had felt the hunger, but I wouldn't kill a human being. Not ever. Or so I thought.

"I didn't kill that boy," I told him. "I found him like that. Maybe I shouldn't have fed . . . but I didn't kill him."

My uncle's head moved up and down slowly while he watched the road. "I know, Zachary," he said. "I know."

I relaxed when I heard him say this. I put my head back and watched the road.

"Do you think my friends will be all right?"

My uncle didn't have a chance to answer. A yellow light started flashing on the dashboard. He took his foot off the gas pedal and the car slowed just a little.

"What's that?" I asked.

"Someone's using a radar gun up ahead," he said. "Probably the police. I'll just have to slow down for a few minutes until we drive through their speed trap."

I checked the electronic map on the dash. Sure enough, a red light had appeared ahead of us on the grid of white lines.

The engine was quieter now that we weren't driving so quickly. I thought I heard something behind me. There was no back seat, just lots of trunk, but I was certain I'd heard a muffled voice.

"Is something wrong?" my uncle asked.

I nodded. "I thought I heard a voice behind us."

My uncle smiled, then reached up and pulled a wire from his left ear. He'd been listening to something. The earpiece was connected to the dash, and when he pulled it out, the sound of people talking came through the rear speakers.

"Is this what you heard?" he asked, turning up the volume.

I listened. "What is it?"

"A police radio. It's how I found out where you were. It and the radar detector will help us to avoid their patrol cars. I'm not taking any chances."

About a second later, we passed a police car parked along the side of the road.

"Will they come after us?" I asked.

My uncle looked over and smiled. "You don't need to worry about them."

"But you wiped that other car right off the road!"

My uncle nodded. "True. But no one saw us. So as far as anyone is concerned, we're just another car on the highway."

My uncle didn't speed up until the patrol car was miles behind us. Then he turned on an interior light and leaned closer. "Let me check that again, would you?" he said, nodding towards my head.

I lifted my hand so he could get a better look at my gash.

"It looks quite a bit better," he said. "I think the bleeding has basically stopped. You might want to get some rest now." He opened a compartment near his elbow that was hidden between our seats. Then he reached in a pulled out a small bottle. "Take one of these. It will help."

I looked at the bottle. The label said "Zaleplon," which sounded to me like a city on the planet Venus or something you would use to de-clog a drainpipe.

"They're sleeping pills," my uncle said. "If you don't feel you need one, don't take one, but I imagine that with all the excitement you've had in the last few days, it might help."

Had I known that I would die the next day, I would never have chosen to go to sleep. I would have stayed awake and asked questions about my mother and my father and what it's like to hunt vampires. And I would have asked to steer the car. I might even have suggested we stop somewhere along the highway so that I could just run for a while under the moon—run so fast that tears would spill out of my eyes. And I would have called Luna, or at least written her a note or something. But I didn't know. And so I swallowed two pills and fell asleep.

Chapter 37
Iron Spike Enterprises

I woke up feeling like a bag of cement. I was lying on a sofa. The room I was in could have fit neatly into an art or history museum. It was as big as the common room in the Nicholls Ward. Oil paintings and masks covered the walls, and busts and statues and carvings stood along the edges. There was even a suit of armour. And weapons, too. When I sat up and rubbed my eyes, I caught a glimpse of two crossed halberds. The wooden shafts were about six feet long, and the iron heads—a wicked blend of axe, hook and spear—had been polished to a deadly shine. When I looked more closely, I could see they were actually on the wall behind me, reflected in a mirror that hung on the opposite side of the room. And I guess I ought to mention that I could see my reflection, too. Because of the movies, some people think a vampire can't see himself in a mirror. It's a neat special effect, and I guess it ties in with this idea that a vampire doesn't have a soul. Well, I don't know anything about that, but I can tell you that I saw myself, and I looked like I'd been attacked by Mr. Entwistle's hairdresser. While I patted down my bed-head, I got up and looked around some more.

The room, long and rectangular, was obviously an office. Adjacent to the sofa was a desk that faced the expanse of the room. Sitting on one corner was a golden cup that must have been worth a fortune. On the wall just behind it was a large painting of a battle scene. Men in red with iron breastplates, long pikes and fin-like helmets were fighting against a bunch of men on horseback. There were muskets and cannons, and it looked like total chaos. I had seen it once before, but I couldn't remember where.

Then I spotted the windows. They sat on either side of the mirror on the wall opposite the sofa. The panels of glass were enormous, running from the floor to the ceiling. Even though no light was coming through them, I could somehow feel the sun shining from behind. I walked over to inspect them and noticed that they were covered with a thick layer of black paint. The only light in the room was coming from two candles, on either side of the couch.

I heard a knock and looked around. There was a door in the far corner of the room opposite the desk. It opened and my uncle came in. He was wearing a suit and looked the way he had when he'd first come to see me, like a man in charge of a bank.

"Just checking in," he said. "I trust you're feeling better?"

I nodded and told him I felt fine.

"Do you need anything?" he asked.

I was a bit dopey, and after getting tossed around in the back of a police car, my body wanted a little blood for repairs. "Something to drink?" I said.

"I suspected as much, but I don't have anything here at the moment. Once the sun goes down, we'll see what we can do."

I asked him where all the stuff in the room had come from.

"Oh, no one place, of course," he answered. "Some items were gifts. That bust of Napoleon, for example. And this cup." He held up the golden chalice I'd noticed earlier. "I received this just yesterday. A present to seal a new contract." Then he raised his hand to indicate the rest of his pieces. "Some I bought overseas while your father and I did our work. That painting I inherited from my parents." He nodded at the battle scene hanging above the desk, the one that was familiar to me. "It used to hang in their living room. You must have been there a few times as a young boy. And truthfully, some of this stuff your father and I took."

He looked at me and smiled. He must have seen the surprise on my face.

"Some vampires are old, Zachary. Not many, but those who survive the first few months of infection can live decades, even centuries beyond a normal human lifespan. And they collect things, as people collect things, to stay connected to the past."

I thought of Mr. Entwistle and his empty house. He was an exception, and he'd wanted me to know it. It made me wonder if a vampire's best hope of survival was to not be connected to anything at all.

Maximilian was looking at me carefully. When he knew he had my attention, he continued.

"Sometimes your father and I found ourselves in possession of old artifacts and paintings, things that once belonged to vampires. Since they technically weren't ours, we gave most of them away to universities or libraries or museums. But we also kept some for ourselves as a payment of sorts, because no one had any idea about the work we did. No organization paid us. No government. We were a secret to all but a few, and our operating costs were very high, so we took artifacts from time to time in order to sell them or keep them as a reward. I hope that doesn't sound inappropriate. I would hate for you to think of your father and me as thieves, just because we sometimes kept what belonged to those we killed." He crossed his arms and looked over the artifacts in the room as though he'd made them all himself. "Perhaps it would help if you thought of these as the spoils of conquest."

I nodded as though I'd understood every word, but between you and me, he didn't seem right in the head all of a sudden. Something about his tone had changed. It was nothing major. He just seemed a little more aggressive than normal. More excited. Like he was about to sit me down to explain his plans for world domination.

"We should have a talk," he said, and as he moved to sit behind the desk, he motioned for me to sit on the sofa. "You must have some questions. Now is the time to ask."

I sat back and thought for a moment. There were so many things I wanted to know about the secret world of vampires. Maximilian probably knew as much as anyone about Vrolok. About the Coven of the Dragon. And Endpoint Psychosis. But he wasn't just a vampire hunter, he was my uncle, and so he knew personal stuff, too. About my father and mother. I didn't know where to begin, so I decided to start at the beginning.

"How did they meet?" I asked.

"Who?"

"My mom and dad."

"They met at Trent University. Your mother studied anthropology, your father archaeology, and so as undergraduates they had a few of the same classes."

"How did she die?"

"Your father never told you?"

I shook my head.

My uncle looked down at his desk. He seemed uncertain about what to say. Then he reached to a console on his desk and flipped a switch. A light came on behind him. It was mounted on the wall, so his whole body became a shadow. One elbow was propped on his desk, and he rested his chin on his hand, between his thumb and index finger. I imagined that he must have spent long hours in this pose. I'd seen it before, back at the ward. It was a thinker's pose.

"There is someone who is better qualified to answer that question," he said, watching me. "Someone who would like to talk to you, if you're feeling up to it."

I nodded.

My uncle stood and stepped over to the wall behind his desk. He reached up and grabbed the light fixture. I noticed that his hand was shaking. When he pulled the light down, a panel in the wall opened. A secret door. He turned to face the opening.

"We are ready for you to join us now," he said.

Then the vampire from my nightmare entered the room.

Chapter 38
Betrayed

The vampire stood just inside the room. Although I had been watching him closely, I never actually saw him move. I would say that he drifted in, but it was more as if the room itself shifted. He was hidden in the corridor one moment, and standing in front of me the next. It left me feeling dizzy and confused. I imagine it's the way someone feels when they drink too much and can no longer trust their own eyes. In place of the fur cloak and gold-buttoned shirt of my dream, he was wearing a suit with long tails that reached past the backs of his knees. Underneath was a lacy shirt with a puffy collar and puffy cuffs. I would like to be able to tell you that it was a Victorian suit in the Balderdash style from 1857, but I don't know anything about that. To me it was just old. Old and purple. To one of his lapels he'd fastened the brooch, the one with the dragon holding a cross in its teeth, the one he'd worn in my dream. He saw me staring at it and a glimmer of amusement flashed in his large eyes. He stroked his thick moustache, then nodded to my uncle, who lowered his head very solemnly.

Uncle Max raised a hand and gestured towards me. "This is my nephew," he said. "Daniel Zachariah Thomson, son of the late Dr. Robert Douglas Thomson, famous archaeologist and vampire hunter, and my former partner. Zachary, this is a new business associate of mine. Former Count of Wallachia and the Grand Master of the Coven of the Dragon. His real name is Vlad. Vlad Tsepesh. You know him as the Baron Vrolok."

The vampire had been watching my uncle as he spoke. Then he turned his eyes on me. I couldn't move. It was as if Mother Nature had forgotten to equip me with any real tools for dealing with trouble. I wondered if this was a human failing. In nature programs, other animals could do all kinds of things when they were threatened. Squids squirted ink and scooted away. Chameleons changed colour. Possums played dead. Hedgehogs rolled into spiny balls. Lambs and rabbits shrieked. Skunks sprayed. Snakes bit. Dogs barked. Cats hissed. Stink bugs stank. The list was endless, really.

Well, if I could have chosen any response at that moment, standing face to face with my father's killer, I would have gone with the mountain gorilla. They go berserk and kill everything that moves. Unfortunately, that isn't what I did. I guess I was just too surprised. I'd never been betrayed before. I understood the word, but there is a huge difference between knowing a word and living it. This was terrible. I was cornered. My uncle was on one side, the Baron was on the other, and the sun was at my back. And it had all happened at a moment when I'd thought I was safe. So I was sort of frozen with disbelief. Like—how did I get here? Then I realized it didn't matter. Unless I tossed myself through the window, there wasn't going to be an easy way out.

The Baron looked me over without speaking. There was a power in his eyes that made it impossible to look away. He seemed to grow taller, more ominous. Then he spoke to my uncle, although his eyes still held me paralyzed. His voice was deep and seemed to come from inside my own head.

"My necklace, does he have it?"

"Yes," my uncle replied.

The Baron reached under his shirt and pulled out a necklace of his own. It was a golden crescent moon. Even though I had never seen it, I recognized it right away. It was the matching piece to the charm around my neck. And just like that, I knew how my mother had died. The Baron must have killed her—killed her and taken the necklace. The instant my mind zeroed in on this truth, a part of me just turned off. Sound disappeared. It was as though I was suddenly deaf. My vision started to narrow, as if I was seeing both my uncle and the Baron through a long tunnel. They were the only two things in the room. A surge of anger made my fists shake. I wanted death. To kill. In ancient times, they called this "blood lust." And that's when I ripped the halberd from the wall above the sofa and started swinging.

I would like to tell you that my first fight was a smashing success—that I was a mountain gorilla and didn't stop until everything around me was kaput, but that isn't what happened. The truth is, I was exhausted, still smarting from the car accident, and up against a true vampire, a creature who had fed for centuries on the blood of humankind and was stronger and faster than anything you've ever seen. So I didn't start a fight so much as I initiated what was to become a dreadful beating.

Vrolok became the kind of evil creature you'd expect to see in a horror film, a being unmoved by the suffering of others. He was fast. I could barely see his ghost-like movements. He took the halberd from me before I could even scrape the dust from his old purple coat. Then he tripped me to the ground, put a hand on my chest and pushed all the air from my lungs.

Through it all, my uncle watched with a face like a statue. I don't think he blinked even once. His eyes were focused on the two of us as though he needed to memorize everything that happened. But it was like he was watching us and *not* watching us, because his face just stayed blank.

When I said at the beginning of the story, way back at the Nicholls Ward, that my uncle had come to the right place, that he was nuts, well, I was right on the money. He really was crazy. He must have been. He'd just rescued me from the Taser-happy police, then looked after my injuries. Why? So I could get flattened in his office? It didn't make a bit of sense. And he didn't seem to care a pinch about what was happening. He didn't lift a finger.

The fight ended seconds later. I fastened both hands around Vrolok's wrist and tried to pry his arm away, but without any air, it was as if someone had flicked a switch and turned off the power. My strength vanished. The room started spinning and my eyes couldn't focus properly. Then I blacked out.

Chapter 39
The Coven of the Dragon

I don't know how long I lay on the floor. I drifted in and out of consciousness, and you can't really keep track of time when that happens. Some time later, my uncle came back into the room. He stood over me with his hands on his hips. I still couldn't see well. My eyes were watering and everything looked blurry.

"Get up," he said. Then he turned his back on me and walked behind his desk. There was a cigar in his hand, which he lit with something that looked like a miniature cannon. He took a big puff and turned to face the painted windows.

"Get up," he said again. "We don't have much time."

I wanted to tell him to leave me alone, but I was too tired, and when I opened my mouth to speak, the pain of moving made me gasp.

He looked down at me with the same blank expression he'd worn during my fight with the Baron. "In life, the only person you can really count on is yourself. Others will abandon you, betray you, disappoint you. You have to learn to depend on yourself. GET UP."

I couldn't believe that he was shouting at me after what had happened. It made me so furious I did stand up. Then I coiled myself for a charge. He probably had a gun handy, so I'd have to be quick.

"Don't be foolish," he said. He had a small black box in his hand. There was a switch on it. "One false move and I blow out the windows. And you know what that means."

I did. The sun would stream in and I would go up like gunpowder, so I straightened up as best I could.

"That's better," my uncle said. "Now, take a seat." He nodded towards the couch.

I shook my head. I wasn't sitting down. I wasn't going to do another thing he told me.

"Fine," he said. He took a haul on his cigar. The end of it glowed an angry orange. It lit up his face, and for just a split second he looked more like a devil than a person.

"That was incredibly foolish, what you did earlier. Reckless . . . mindless . . . stupid . . . I can't imagine what would have happened if I hadn't been here."

He paused. I knew he was giving me a chance to respond, but I had no idea where to begin. For starters, he was making it sound as if he'd saved my life, when he hadn't done a thing. And he was angry. I was the one who was half dead. What did *he* have to be so mad about? Had he forgotten that the Baron killed my mother and father? What was I supposed to do when I met him, snuggle up for a cozy hug?

"I didn't rescue you from Johansson to watch you get flattened in my office," my uncle said. "Another mistake like that, and it might be your last."

He took another puff on his cigar. The smoke brought on a series of coughs that shook his broad chest. Once he'd fought them down, he reached into the drawer of his desk and pulled something out. It took me a moment to recognize my father's journal. He stepped out from behind the desk and walked over to where I was standing.

"You left this in your friend's boat. The Baron brought it here. I flipped through it while you were sleeping. I've found some interesting passages I think you should read." He handed me the notebook.

I snatched it away and stumbled into the sofa. "You don't deserve to touch this," I said.

He blew smoke out through his nostrils. I guess he didn't care.

I stared at him. He stared back.

"Do you want me to read it for you?" he asked.

I looked down at the journal. There were yellow sticky notes marking several of the pages. I opened it to the first and glanced over the writing until I found a passage that had been underlined with a pencil. This is what my father had written.

Max is a true evolutionist . . .

And later, on the facing page, was this passage.

Because of his belief that the fittest will survive, and the confidence he has in his own abilities, he is willing to place himself in the most dangerous situations. I fear for him. At times, he shows a total disregard for his own safety. And yet, if he were not like this, we would never have achieved so many victories over those carriers who have fallen into darkness, who refuse redemption. And so, indirectly, he has saved hundreds, if not thousands of lives . . .

I shook my head. What was this supposed to tell me? Was I supposed to forgive him or something? Did he think it would explain why he had betrayed me and given me over to my father's killer?

I read the rest of the page and the one following.

"Why am I doing this?"

"Just keep reading," Maximilian said.

I found the next passage.

Max put forth the suggestion today that instead of merely monitoring those carriers to whom we have granted amnesty, we use them to hunt other carriers. I am reluctant to endorse this strategy. It seems a dangerous risk, given that we know so little about Endpoint Psychosis and what triggers its onset.

And that was it. He'd marked only those three entries. Well, perhaps my brain had been bruised, or maybe it was still disconnected from my wrestling match with the Baron, but I didn't get it. I looked up at my uncle. His eyes were dark and focused.

"Your father was a very conservative man, Zachary," he said. "Perhaps too conservative. The truth is, the best vampire hunters in the world are other vampires. You have the potential to be counted among them. But you must be able to prove that your mind is healthy. Uncorrupted by the pathogen. Another ridiculous stunt like the one you pulled earlier, and I won't be able to do a thing for you."

He went on to say other things, about Endpoint Psychosis and suicide and spreading the infection, but I wasn't really listening. I was thinking of my father. That he wouldn't have wanted me to bite Maximilian, which is what I wanted to do most at that very moment. I wanted to kill him. I'd like to think it was my hunger that made me think this way. I was a little short of juice, and after tasting human blood for the first time at Luna's cottage, my desire for more was making me furious.

When I looked up at him he must have noticed the change in my expression. That my rage was closer to the surface. Still, he didn't seem worried at all. Who would be? He had the sun as his ally. It was waiting to kill me, hidden behind a thin layer of glass.

"How much do you know about the Coven of the Dragon?" he asked me.

What did this have to do with anything?

"We don't have a lot of time," he said. "Answer me."

I shook my head. "Nothing, really."

My uncle pressed his lips together and nodded slowly. "They are an elite group of vampire hunters. They keep the pathogen from being spread recklessly by those who go insane. Baron Vrolok—Vlad—is the Grand Master of the Coven." He stared at me for a few seconds. I couldn't tell what he was thinking. That this excused the Baron for killing my mother and father and squashing me into submission?

My uncle turned and walked back behind his desk. He was practically shaking with excitement. "Your father and I tried for years to penetrate this organization. It is cloaked in secrecy. We only knew that it existed. And could move with terrible swiftness. On more than one occasion, your father and I started a hunt only to discover that the Coven had finished it for us. Always very thoroughly."

He stopped talking and opened one of the desk drawers. I expected him to remove something, but he didn't. He closed the drawer instead.

"And do you know how I made contact with them?" he asked.

He looked at me as though I was supposed to guess. Like I should have been as excited as he was. I barely had the energy to see across the room. Why should I care?

"I didn't," he said. "He came to me. Vlad came to me. He came with an offer, and I have accepted it."

He looked at me and started coughing. The coughing turned to hacking. He had a handkerchief in his pocket. He removed it and covered his mouth. When he pulled it away, I could see the crimson stain of his blood on the cloth. For just an instant, he looked like a wraith. Shrivelled and decayed. Then he straightened up and thumped his chest with the side of his fist. It helped him clear his throat.

"You're dying," I told him.

He nodded. "Yes. Yes, I am. But I'm taking steps to ensure that my work will continue."

Steps? What did that mean? I took my best guess.

"You want to become a vampire!" I said. "You want to enter the Coven of the Dragon. You want to work for *him*!"

Chapter 40
Abandoned

My uncle shook his head. He was still fighting with the disease in his chest. For all his strength, I could see it would soon get the better of him.

"I will not be working *for* Vrolok, but *with* him. Together, we will be unstoppable. Perhaps you have heard this maxim: *The enemy of my enemy is my friend.* Well, the Baron and I have many of the same enemies. Those, as your father says, who refuse redemption."

My hands were shaking. I almost dropped my father's journal. "But he's the worst—"

"No," my uncle interrupted. "No, he isn't. In time, you'll see how depraved the worst ones get. You don't—"

"But he killed my father. And my mother. Your sister. Your very own sister!"

"Well, he shouldn't have," Maximilian snapped. "Your headstrong father should have done a better job of protecting her. He failed, and we both paid for it. And taking off to Libya without me—it was foolish. Even so, he almost pulled it off. If you hadn't come along, Vrolok would have died."

"That's not my fault," I said, although I realized it probably was.

"Not your fault?" my uncle said. He snorted. Then he took another puff from his cigar. It seemed to calm him down a little. "No. Maybe not. But it *is* what happened. Vrolok survived. And yes, he did kill your father. And he killed my sister. But he was different then. Now he is back with the Coven. They would not accept him as a member if he wasn't mentally sound."

I started shaking my head, but my uncle ignored me and kept talking.

"Nothing can bring your parents back, Zachary. I know this must be hard for you to understand. But my work must go on. Since your father's death, I have been searching in vain for a competent ally. As the Grand Master of the Coven, Vrolok has a network of informants greater than most governments'. The Coven's eyes are everywhere. Places your father and I couldn't possibly have gained a foothold. Iran, China, Russia . . ."

He pulled out his chair and sat down. His eyes never left mine, even when he puffed his cigar.

"You asked me back at the Nicholls Ward how I had found you. It was an accident. I was searching for a different vampire. Even now, Vrolok's informants are gathering information to aid my search. This one has proven to be extremely elusive."

"Is it Mr. Entwistle?" I asked.

My uncle shook his head. "No. Entwistle is out of the picture now."

I took a step forward. It wasn't an aggressive move—I was still wobbly—but Maximilian raised the detonator to remind me who was in charge. Still, I had to do something. The expression on my uncle's face, it had changed slightly. Or maybe it was the tone of his voice. There was guilt in it. I could just tell.

"You killed him?" I said.

He paused, then nodded. "It wasn't intentional. I was trying to shut down an operation that provides blood to a number of dangerous vampires. Ones who have reached a point of mental decay that makes them unmanageable. Entwistle was trying to protect them. He has several houses in the city where he offers them refuge. You stayed in one yourself." He paused to take a deep breath. "He wasn't the intended target. He was just unfortunate. When he showed up, there was nothing I could do. The die was cast."

I watched my uncle's face as he spoke. He wasn't lying. Mr. Entwistle was really dead. All the hope just drained out of me.

"I don't understand why you would kill someone like him and help someone like the Baron. He's evil. Can't you feel it?"

My uncle butted the stub of his cigar in an ashtray. Then he folded his arms across his chest.

"You are wrong about the Baron. He's not as he once was. Despite his past crimes—and I know they are many—he is willing to redeem himself. To help control the spread of this pathogen. It is important work. More important than the life of any one man. Or any one vampire. You or your father, John Entwistle or anyone."

"So you don't care that he killed my parents? My father . . ." I was clutching his journal so hard that my fingers began to press through the cover. I wanted to add that Vrolok had killed me too, that he had ruined my life, but I couldn't speak.

"I am not going to be consumed by thoughts of revenge, if that's what you mean. I have to weigh the lives of your parents against the lives of those I will save by killing other vampires. As a member of the Coven, I will be in a position to do immeasurable good. As will you. I've told the Baron about you. We both think you have extraordinary potential. Few vampires live past the first year of infection. Did you know that? The fact that you have survived for eight years on your own is incredible. But it is not enough. You won't be accepted in the Coven unless you can prove that you can control yourself. And work with the Baron. And that means you must forgive him for what he's done."

My uncle stood up. Then he pulled down the light behind his desk to activate the secret door in the wall.

"Where are you going?" I asked.

"It's daytime, Zachary. You can feel that, can't you?"

I nodded. The sun was strong behind the blackened windows.

"This is the best time to hunt vampires. I am after one in particular. One that got away from your father many years ago. With the help of the Coven, that hunt will end today."

"And what is going to happen to me?"

"That is the Baron's concern now," my uncle said. "You may be my nephew, but that is less important than the fact that you're a vampire. As Grand Master of the Coven, it is the Baron who will decide your fate."

"What does that mean?"

"The pathogen you carry causes insanity in most people who get infected. Given your recent behaviour, your mental state is being called into question. So the Baron is going to test you. I suggest you prepare yourself. He will be here shortly."

He must have seen the look on my face when he said this, because he didn't head for the secret door. Instead, he walked over to where I was standing and put his hands on my shoulders.

"If I didn't have the utmost confidence in you, Zachary, I would never allow this." His grip was firm. He looked straight into my eyes. Then he nodded and walked to the doorway.

Just before exiting he turned back to me and made a fist. I could see the muscles in his arm ball tightly inside his sleeve. "You are your father's son, Zachary. And we will be great hunters together, you and I. Keep your head and you'll do just fine."

He looked me over once, then left. I heard the panel close behind him. And that was it.

I couldn't believe this was happening. I stumbled to the couch and eased myself onto the cushions.

I had been so hopeful after my uncle's first visit. A normal life seemed to be just around the corner. And now this. I put my head into my hands and felt my whole body shake. I couldn't make sense of anything. What was my uncle thinking? Was he bewitched? Charmed? If Dracula could make you do things you weren't supposed to do, why not the Baron? He was evil. How could Maximilian not see?

Endpoint Psychosis. The Baron was there. I wasn't. And still, my uncle trusted him to pass judgment on me.

Maybe that had nothing to do with it. Maximilian was dying. He was looking for a way out. And Vrolok was offering him just that. And more. Entry into an organization that would put him at the top of the food chain. A perfect place for an evolutionist, a man who believed in survival of the fittest.

I looked at the windows. The sun was still up. It would be for another hour. I couldn't leave. I couldn't stay. The parts of my body that weren't in pain were numb. I wanted desperately to talk to someone. To have Charlie cheer me up with a wisecrack, or to feel Luna's hand on my arm. I would have settled for a familiar face from the Nicholls Ward, even the Chicago Man, but I was totally alone.

It wasn't until that moment that I really understood what it meant to be an orphan. To know that there was no one alive in the world who had the power to save me. My father wasn't going to kick in the door. Mr. Entwistle was finished. My friends had no idea where I was. My uncle was right. There was only me. And I was a mess.

I had to get out somehow. Find a place to hide. I couldn't let Vrolok find me like this. I put my hand on the arm of the sofa and pushed myself up as quickly as I could. Too quickly. I got dizzy. My vision started to go spotty and I tripped over the carpet. And so I was kneeling on the floor when the Baron came back into the room.

Chapter 41
Reunion

Vrolok moved into the office dragging two long black bags, one in either hand. Unlike my uncle, who made me think of a stone statue when he walked, solid and purposeful, Vrolok seemed to shift from one place to another without moving, as though the room just bent and allowed him to be wherever he wished. It was soundless, and the sight of it was nauseating.

I turned my attention to the bags he was carrying. They looked like the kind of thing the police would put a dead body in. I could tell by the way they were moving that people were struggling inside. The Baron pushed each to the floor and I heard two muffled cries. The people inside, their mouths must have been gagged. I recognized that sound right away. I'd heard it before. During the drive with my uncle, noises just like that had come from inside his trunk. He'd covered it up with a bunch of hooey about the police radio, and I'd fallen for it. But it wasn't the police radio I'd heard. It was these two.

The Baron looked down and saw me on my knees. "Ah, a true penitent."

The words stabbed inside my mind. His voice seemed to come from everywhere at once so that you couldn't really tell where he was.

"Such faith is a rare thing in this age of skeptics. In a vampire, rarer still. Do they not call us soulless creatures?"

I had no idea what he was talking about. Then I realized that he thought I was praying. I probably should have been.

"You do well to concern yourself with such things," he said. "You will be meeting your God soon. I hope you will send Him my regards."

The Baron started moving towards me. I tried to stand up, but my head was reeling and I fell over sideways.

"It is just as well, my son," he said. "God cannot help you here."

He reached down, grabbed the front of my shirt and hauled me off the floor. With his other hand he snatched my necklace, then he tore it over my head and let me drop.

"This was a gift to my wife . . ."

He paused and stared at the window. It was exactly where the sun would have been. His expression was vacant.

My wife . . . The words echoed in my head almost too quietly to notice.

He saw me on the floor and seemed to remember where he was. When he spoke, the necklace dangled from his fist.

"Your father killed her. Then he stole this necklace and gave part of it to your mother. He had no right!" When he looked at me his eyes were black. His lips moved a little, revealing the long incisors underneath. I couldn't tell if he was smiling or snarling.

"I understand you have been talking to your uncle. A most useful man . . ." The Baron bent so that he was crouched down beside me. "But perhaps a little too trusting?" He reached out and brushed the side of my cheek. The touch of his skin made my insides squirm.

"You must forgive him for his weakness. Few men cope well with death. Only those of unwavering faith. Or those who have suffered much. He is neither. He seeks immortality. I have offered him this, in exchange for you."

He picked me up and set me on my feet. When he let go, I fell to my knees again.

"For what has happened, blame no one but yourself," he continued. "The day your father died, I should have perished. Burned to ashes. But fate brought you to me, and with your blood I endured. What an irony! To become that which your father once hunted. And to fall into the power of a vampire he himself would have destroyed had you not interfered. God is quite a trickster, is He not?"

He turned his back to me and drifted away. As soon as his eyes were off me, it was like I could suddenly breathe again. But the feeling of relief didn't last long. When he turned and fixed me with a dark stare, I froze again.

"Fate has bound us together, my son. I am your doom."

He then bent and picked up one of his hostages. With his other hand he ripped open the black bag so that I could see the person inside. It was Charlie! He was bound and gagged, and his eyes were wide with terror. I could see two small, red dots on his throat, as though he'd been bitten, and his skin was horribly pale. Vrolok pushed him to his knees, then grabbed the second bag and tore it open. It was Luna. She didn't look frightened. She was past that. She was in shock. Her clothes were still covered in blood. I could see the same red holes in the side of her neck. She glanced around the room with a face as white as chalk. I couldn't tell if she had any idea what was happening.

The Baron pushed Luna to her knees so that she was shoulder to shoulder with Charlie. "To see old friends, is it not wonderful?"

I raised myself to one knee. I could almost stand up. Almost.

He shook his head, as though I'd disappointed him somehow.

"You know the fate of most vampires. I see that. But no one recognizes madness in themselves. That is for others to discern. And so we have brought your friends along to test you."

He sucked a breath in past his teeth. The sound of it made my stomach tighten. He watched me with his bulging eyes and I felt them burning into my head.

"You were careless, you see." He scratched a finger under Charlie's chin. "You told this one you were infected." Then he glided past Luna and grabbed a handful of her hair. "And this one saw enough to divine the truth herself. Tragic, but fate isn't always kind . . ."

He raised one hand towards me. His fingers were long and gnarled with age, but I had felt them pressing down on my chest. They were strong. His eyes widened for just a second, and again I couldn't breathe.

"It isn't safe for humans to know this about us, and so I am giving you a choice. Consider carefully." He flicked a finger towards Charlie and Luna. "There were two halberds on the wall earlier. It was most kind of you to bring them to my attention. I had them fashioned into blunt stakes. There are three of you here. Two will be impaled for my amusement. It is for you to decide who will receive this honour."

The Baron stared at me while I crouched on the floor. I didn't whimper, but I couldn't stop tears from rolling down my cheeks. I pushed myself to my feet. I wasn't going to face him on my knees.

"Good," he whispered. "Good."

He waited while I got my balance. The whole time I kept wondering if this was really happening, if I really had to choose. My uncle's words kept coming back to me—that this was a test. It was about my mental state. What was I supposed to do? Argue? Fight? I looked at the Baron to see if there was something in his face that might give me a clue. It was a big mistake. His eyes dug into my brain. What he saw there made him smile, and that's when I realized that my uncle had been duped. My sanity was just fine. I didn't need a test to tell me that.

Neither did the Baron. This was about revenge. It was about cruelty. It was about evil and torture and death. And unfinished business.

The Baron nodded. "Quite right," he said. "Now make your choice. Who lives? And who dies?"

Chapter 42
The Test

I couldn't speak. My lips moved, but no sound came out. The Baron must have seen. Or maybe he just knew what I was thinking. He answered my silent question.

"Why? You ask why? Is the answer not obvious? Your father robbed me of a treasure beyond price. His debt has passed to you. You are here to suffer. And you will. But perhaps not in vain. You could save yourself . . ."

I shook my head. I didn't want his voice in there, telling me lies. He wasn't going to spare anyone.

"Of course I will," he said. "I am not without honour. And I believe God speaks to all of us in His own way. There were two halberds. Was that not a sign? Two long, wooden shafts for two blunt stakes for two slow deaths. It can mean nothing else."

I looked at Charlie, then at Luna. I wanted them to understand how sick I felt.

"You can let them go," I said. "They haven't done anything."

The Baron shook his head. "No," he whispered. "They haven't. But you have. You revealed yourself too carelessly." He looked at Luna and Charlie with contempt. "You must learn to see people for what they are. Food. A resource to be exploited. A source of amusement, perhaps. But never more than this. A hard lesson to learn, but a vital one, if you wish to join me and become a member of my Coven."

I saw his fingers twitch slightly when he said this, as if he was getting ready to slash something.

"Your father believed a vampire could be tamed. 'Redeemed,' he called it. A life spent pilfering donated blood. He was a fool. What kind of vampire sucks blood from a bag? We are predators. And a predator makes no apologies. You don't expect a wolf to repent for killing a *deer*, do you?"

The Baron stared at me. I couldn't look away. It would have been a denial of the truth. I had killed a deer in the forest, chased it down and fed. I had been a predator. And I hadn't felt the slightest bit sorry for what I'd done.

The Baron looked amused. He began to circle me. He drifted past one shoulder, then the other. "We are more alike than you realize. The spirit of the hunter is in us both. It stirs in your heart. I see it. Embrace your true nature, and together, we can transform you into something divine. Something eternal. All it will take is a little sacrifice, and a few more nights like the last one, when you found that gift I left for you."

I had no idea what he was talking about. Then I remembered the boy, the blond twin, whose body I had found at Luna's cottage. Was that what he meant? I saw him nod. He was right behind me, speaking straight into my mind.

"It was good, wasn't it? That first taste of human blood. Why deny it? It is ambrosia to our kind. And it is the only thing that can sustain you now." The smile on his face slipped away. The look that replaced it was one of exaggerated pity. "You are weak. That is why you suffer. And yet, only through suffering does one become strong. Don't you wish to be strong?"

The Baron stood in front of me and put his hands on his hips. His head tilted up as he spoke.

"I can make you so much more than you are. But you have to give up your past, starting now. So make your choice. Who dies? Tell me now, or I will have you all impaled."

I nodded, as though I finally understood what he was getting at, but I was careful to look down at the floor so he couldn't see into my eyes. I couldn't risk that he would sense what I was thinking. That there was a way out of this. I needed the Baron to get angry. So I did my best to irritate him. I made like the Chicago Man and started muttering incoherently. The only thing I left out was the tune.

"What was that?" the Baron said.

I mumbled again, making sure my mouth was moving but my head was down so he couldn't lip-read or look into my eyes and see that I was speaking gibberish on purpose.

"At me, pup," he hissed. *"Look at me!"*

He stepped forward, grabbed me by the throat and hauled me off my feet so that they were dangling above the floor. It hurt and I couldn't breathe, but it was working. I was so close. All he had to do was toss me against a wall, any wall. Then I could throw something at the windows. A statue. A candlestick. Anything. The sunlight would stream in and kill us both.

Instead, the Baron stared straight into my eyes. He glanced at the painted windows and smiled. Then he turned me around so that my back was against his chest. He wrapped the other arm around me so I couldn't move.

"Clever boy," he whispered. "Our weakness is known to you. And my strength, you sense that too, do you not? Indomitable. Eternal.

You desire this, too. You cannot hide it. You fear your end. But to hunt through the ages, your mind cannot be mired here. You must let go of all this." He waved a hand at my friends. "You cannot be connected to anyone but me. Only I will endure."

The Baron still had his hand around my throat. He let go so that his arms were around my chest in a bear hug.

"Because you are a vampire, because you are immortal, you think that time is not your enemy, but it is," he said. "Time is a thief. It will take everything from you. All of your friends, the ones you love, they will die centuries before you. All that you value will be stripped away. Music will change. Your language will change. Your country will change. Your religion. Everything will change but you. Cling to the past and it will drive you insane. I am doing you a favour. I am teaching you how to give up that which you care most about. You will thank me for it in time. When you are more evolved in your thinking. More detached and independent."

He held me up so that I was suspended at arm's length above the floor, then he set me down. By the time I had my balance, he was standing behind Luna and Charlie.

"You will choose," he hissed. *"Now."*

I was out of time. We were done for.

Then I heard a knock. Four quick raps. The secret panel opened and Maximilian stumbled in. I recognized him only by his suit. There was a black bag over his head and his arms were tied behind his back. He struggled to keep his feet, then tripped and fell against his desk.

The Baron dropped me. I heard another familiar sound—heels clicking on a hard floor. And that was when Nurse Ophelia walked in.

She wasn't dressed like a nurse when she came to save me. She was wearing a dress. An old dress. And nothing I'd ever laid eyes on was as beautiful as she was that day. Nothing. Not in any painting. Not in any movie. Not anywhere.

The Baron looked absolutely shocked.

"Ophelia . . . How is this possible?"

Ophelia looked at him and smiled. It was a smile unlike any I'd seen on her face. I can't imagine what she was feeling. Regret, maybe? Sadness? Disappointment? I don't know. But an instant later it was gone and her face hardened. When she spoke next, her voice was like granite.

"I have come to offer *you* a choice, *husband.*"

Chapter 43
Choices

Ophelia and Vrolok stood face to face for a few seconds. Neither moved. Then the Baron drifted past me, but Ophelia raised her hand and he stopped.

I started backing away as quietly as I could. Luna was curled up on her side. I think she was shaking, but I couldn't really tell. I didn't want to take my eyes off the Baron in case he noticed I was sneaking off. Charlie was still on his knees, doing his best impression of a mouse in a reptile zoo. When I put my finger to my lips in the universal "Be quiet" sign, he shook his head. I didn't know if he meant "No, I won't make a sound" or "No, please don't come anywhere near me if that freak behind you is going to turn around and notice I'm still here!"

Then, while we both watched, stupefied, Ophelia reached down, grabbed my uncle by the shoulder and hauled him from the floor so that he was half sitting, half leaning against the side of his desk. She pulled off his hood. Blood was dripping from a welt on his forehead, but he ignored it. His eyes were alert and focused. I could tell he was thinking. Calculating.

"I am giving you a choice," she said. "Give up the boy and his friends and we will leave quietly and disappear. Then you and this worm can go back to doing whatever it is you do."

The Baron had his back to me, so I wouldn't have been able to see his face even if I'd wanted to. The tone of his voice was one of total disbelief.

"Ophelia . . . how?"

"How? How am I still alive? It's simple, really. I never died. Dr. Thomson didn't kill me. He let me go."

As soon as Nurse Ophelia spoke, I asked myself the obvious question. Why would my father have wanted to kill her? It made no sense. And then it did. Ophelia was a vampire, just like me! She always worked the night shift at the Nicholls Ward. She could see in the dark as well as I could, and she knew what to put in my brain cocktails. She could toss a boy into a trash bin. It made me wonder if she was the vampire Maximilian had referred to, the elusive one he believed had escaped my father.

"Dr. Thomson gave me a choice," Ophelia continued. "To hide and never again take a human life, or to be destroyed. I chose to hide. And I sealed my contract with a gift, as is the custom. I gave him *my* necklace. And after you killed him, I chose to look after his son, who is the most decent boy on the face of this earth, and if you don't agree to let him go, you're going to die in this room."

"So that is my choice?" the Baron said. "To let this boy go, or be killed by my *wife*?"

He sounded amused by the whole thing. But just like that, he changed, and his voice was so angry I'm surprised the light fixtures didn't shatter.

"You Judas! You had me believe you were dead!"

I was shocked that Nurse Ophelia could stay so calm in the face of his rage. His voice was an explosion. It made me wish I was on the other side of the planet. But when he spoke again, he sounded hoarse. Deflated.

"How I have suffered. You cannot imagine."

"I don't have to imagine," she said. "But I made a promise—to disappear and have nothing to do with you. And I have kept that promise."

"And what of your promises to me?"

"We both made promises," she said. "To love each other forever. To give up the old ways. And to be decent. But you broke your promises. You became what you are. What you were. You gave up your goodness, and so you gave away the only part of you that was worth loving."

"Oh, spare me the melodrama," he snapped. "We are vampires. You know what this means. To live—to be truly alive—we must hunt and we must kill."

"And since when did that include terrorizing children?"

The question hung in the air, unanswered, for a long time.

"So you would choose this boy over me?" the Baron asked.

Nurse Ophelia looked at him squarely, then her eyes slipped past him to where I was waiting. Her head shook slowly and she smiled such a perfect smile I could have cried.

"Vlad, you demented sadist, I would choose a sewer rat over you."

I cringed when I heard Ophelia speak. Then I felt Vrolok's hate and anger swell. I was overcome by the feeling that the most terrible things I could imagine were about to happen. The presence of evil that had nearly undone me at Stoney Lake filled the room until it was practically bursting.

Vrolok rose. He made no effort to disguise the malice in him. Instead, he unleashed it. It was foul. You could hardly breathe the air.

"There is a third option," he said. "I could rip this boy's throat out and feed his friends to the crows." Then he turned around to grab me.

Well, the look of surprise on his face when he saw me is difficult to describe. He'd forgotten about me, and I'd been busy. For a moment he was too confused to act. He had expected to find me curled up at his feet, exhausted and humbled, but I wasn't there. I was right in his face, chest to chest, eye to eye, tooth to tooth, and I was so angry, so ready to go berserk, that I'd have made the most insane mountain gorilla proud. My body was healed and I was strong again. Supernatural. And I can tell you, if the Baron had been given a choice right then and there to face me or dive into a pool of hungry sharks, he would have been wise to go find a bathing suit.

So while he stared at me in amazement, I wound up and threw a punch that nearly broke the sound barrier. And when it hit him in the jaw, he flew clear across the room.

Chapter 44
My Second Death

You have to be wondering how I managed this. Perhaps you've figured it out already.

While the Baron and Ophelia were having their argument, I was trying to convince Charlie and Luna to crawl out the door with me. But Charlie wouldn't move. He just shook his head like I was asking him to jump off a cliff. And I couldn't get Luna to even acknowledge that I was there.

"Come on," I whispered, "hurry!" But I might as well have been speaking Swahili. She didn't respond at all, even when I untied the ropes around her wrists and shook her gently by the shoulders. When I shook her again, she just squirmed back against the wall. So I had to come up with another plan.

This whole time, I was still listening to the conversation between the Baron and Ophelia. I didn't think he was going to let us go. And

I knew Ophelia wasn't going to leave us there. They couldn't both have their way, so things were going to get messy.

Well, there was no way I was going to let Ophelia face the Baron alone. He wasn't like that boy she'd tossed into the trash—a drunken teenager armed with nothing but a foul mouth. He was a killer. And my uncle—underneath that suit he was a piece of iron. If he got his hands free, he could certainly tip the balance. And so I did the unthinkable.

I bit Charlie and I drank until he died.

I hope you can forgive me for this. He was my best friend, and I loved him. I didn't mean to do it. I just needed enough blood to fix myself. I thought that if I took just a little, Charlie would be fine. After all, it was supposed to take more than one bite to turn someone into a vampire. But that's not what happened. I started drinking and I couldn't stop myself. The killing urge took over. And it felt so intoxicating that I didn't give my friend a second thought, not until he started having a heart attack. Then I looked into his face. I wish I hadn't. It was the most tragic thing I'd ever seen. His fear and confusion. It gave way to a terrible pain. He looked as though someone was pulling his insides out. His back arched. When he settled back to the floor, he was gone.

This should have crushed me. My best friend. And it was all my fault. But all I felt was rage. And power. I had tasted human blood only once before, and that was a very small dose—the body at Luna's cottage had been nearly empty. This rush was on a different scale. I gorged until my body swelled. Charlie's blood went to work right away. My exhaustion and soreness vanished. Dark bruises faded yellow and then disappeared entirely, as though someone had taken a cloth and just wiped them away. In seconds, I was filled with an energy that you have never possessed and never will. And so when the Baron turned around I was supercharged. He looked at me with total disbelief in his eyes, and then he was airborne.

This started an avalanche of events that fell so quickly, one after the other, you would have needed a vampire's eyes to sort it all out. The Baron hit the wall behind the desk and fell to the floor. An instant later he was on his feet, moving like a blur. He had a stake in his hand, the remnants of one of the halberds. The head had been removed from the shaft, so it looked more like a blunt spear now. Fortunately, another blur got in his way. It was Ophelia. She met his charge like a rock. The shaft of wood flew to pieces. Ophelia stumbled. The Baron tried to move past, but she grabbed one of his legs. I guess she knew more than one way to stop a man in his tracks.

The Baron raised his hand to strike her, but he didn't. "Insufferable woman!" he snapped.

I picked up a small statue to use like a club, but I didn't get to do anything with it, at least not right away, because the Baron's charge had stalled. Then I noticed that my uncle had somehow freed himself. His hands were loose and he was opening one of the drawers in his desk. I whipped the statue at him, but he ducked out of the way and it exploded against the wall behind him. He rolled to his feet. The little black box, the detonator, was in his hand. I met his eyes from across the room. He nodded, smiled, then flicked his head towards the door. *"Get out,"* he seemed to be saying. Then he threw the switch.

Pain. It started with the blast. A shock wave followed that knocked me to the ground. It made my ears bleed. Then glass showered everywhere, tearing through the skin of my hands and face. But none of this compared with the sun.

The windows were facing west. As the light of the setting sun streamed into the room, I caught a brief flash of my uncle as he tipped the light on the wall, the one that activated the secret panel. Then he disappeared.

I started to burn.

Someone took hold of my arm. It was Ophelia. She was running for the door. We were almost free when I jerked to a halt just inside the threshold. The Baron had crossed the room and taken hold of my other arm. He was screaming too, or maybe he was laughing, I couldn't tell, but I'd never heard anything that sounded so insane, so malicious. Not during eight long years in a mental ward.

And so a tug-of-war began. I was the rope, with Ophelia on one side and the monster on the other. It was excruciating. But Ophelia and I were close to the doorway and the dark hall behind. The Baron was standing directly in the sun. He wasn't going to last as long as we were.

I felt his fingers dig into my arm. All the while, he screamed his insane scream. Then he let go, and for just an instant, I thought Ophelia and I were going to make it to safety.

It shames me to be saying this, but in my panic, I had forgotten about Luna. The Baron hadn't. He must have realized he was close to death. His body was a torch. He needed blood, and she was the only source in the room, so he made straight for her.

Luna was still lying on the floor beside Charlie's body. I could see that she was bleeding heavily from the explosion of glass. I felt Ophelia pull me towards the door. She had hold of my wrist and was trying to get me into the hall and out of the sun. I twisted my hand away, then used her momentum to push her out through the door. She turned around as she fell. Surprise was all over her face. For a second our eyes met. She must have realized right then that I wasn't coming with her, because she reached out for me and called my name, and there was great pain in her voice.

I slammed the door shut and tipped a large statue in front of it so that she couldn't get back in. My skin started cracking. It was black. Charlie's blood was keeping me alive, but I didn't have long. I grabbed a picture from the wall and held it over me like a shield, then I crouched and ran for Luna.

She was kicking her way across the floor like a crab, trying to escape the Baron, who was crawling towards her. His clothes were on fire. The sun was setting, and so the last rays of the day streamed in. They had burned through the muscles of his legs, neither of which was working. I could see some of his bones as he dragged himself farther away from me.

Luna reached the wall and couldn't go back any farther. Her emerald green eyes were wide. Her shock was gone. She knew exactly what was about to happen. She was kicking at the Baron. His moustache and hair were gone and the skin on his face was burned black so that his head looked like a charred skull. He pushed her feet out of the way, put his hands around her shoulders and pulled her neck towards his mouth. Then he stopped.

He stopped with my hands around his throat.

After feeding on Charlie's blood, catching a half-baked corpse with fried legs wasn't all that difficult. I hauled him off the ground as if he were made of straw. He scratched at my face, but his strength was gone. Mine wasn't. Not quite. I held him at arm's length and looked him straight in the eyes. I can't tell you what I saw there. Insanity, perhaps? Pain? Or fear? There was so little left of him that was recognizable, there was no way to know.

The only thing that wasn't charred was the necklace he was wearing. I'd never seen the two pieces attached as they were now. The golden crescent fit perfectly along the edge of the full silver moon. Both reflected the fading orange light of the sun. It had nearly set, and the same rays that were stretching out to warm the bottoms of the clouds were streaming into the room, killing me.

There was little left to the Baron now. He weighed less than a child. Still, there was something in him, an awareness, a soul. I can't say. But he was still alive, or still undead. I thought of what my father would have done. And I thought about what Mr. Entwistle had told me in the safe house when we'd discussed the vampire problem. I looked out the window, then spun and threw him as far from me as I could.

I picked Luna up in my arms. I needed to take her somewhere she could get help. The pain nearly finished me. I stepped towards the secret passage, hoping it might take us somewhere safe, but I didn't have the strength. My legs buckled. I fell and dropped her to the floor. We landed in the shadow of the desk. She moaned softly and her eyes fluttered open. I would like to tell you that she recognized me, that there was understanding in her expression, but that's not what I saw. She was scared stiff. And who wouldn't have been? I must have looked like something straight out of a zombie movie.

I wished at that moment that there were some way to go back in time. I would have returned to the bonfire and started all over again. I felt cheated. Like this could have been a different story if I'd just done a few things differently. It seemed a terrible injustice—that I'd spent all those years alone in a mental ward only to die so soon after tasting real life for the first time. But life is like that sometimes. The things you want most are impossible and there's nothing you can do about it.

Life is also about choices. That's what my father believed. He chose to offer vampires a shot at redemption. He respected their right to decide for themselves whether they could give up the hunt. Nurse Ophelia had made her choices. To leave the Baron. To look after me when my father died. The Baron had made choices, too. Cruel ones. And Maximilian—he had chosen survival.

Me? I had one last choice to make. As my uncle had said: to be good, or to be something that was less than good. You see, all I could smell was blood. Old blood on Luna's clothes from the twin's body, and the fresh stuff that had leaked from the cuts on her neck and face. I was almost finished, and the hunger in me was more intense than the fire in my muscles and bones. All I had to do was pull her in and drink. She was weak, barely conscious. She wouldn't have been able to stop me. But she was alive. And she looked as though she was going to make it. Maybe. Once I'd started feeding, it would have been impossible for me to stop. And I would have needed all of her blood. It would have killed her, just like Charlie. So that isn't what I chose. I chose to be good. I chose to die.

I reached up. I was still holding the necklace. There wasn't much flesh left on my fingers and I nearly dropped it. I wanted her to take it. If anyone should have it, I thought, it should be someone who believed in giving people second chances, people like the young offenders she worked with. My father would have liked that. He believed in second chances, too. And I wanted her to know she'd be okay. That I wasn't going to hurt her.

I think she must have understood, because her expression changed. She took the chain that was hanging from my hand and held it up so that the moon charm caught the fading sunlight, just as it had caught the light of the bonfire that first night on Stoney Lake. The night I discovered real joy. She must have remembered too, because she smiled. It was the tired smile of a friend in pain. But it was still perfect, and it made everything all right.

And that was the last thing I saw before I died.

Epilogue
Life After Death

I have heard people say that religion was invented because people are afraid of death. They can't face the idea of not existing. They need to know that there is something after. Something more.

There is.

Many people have described it. Hearts stop beating and death occurs. Some people remember leaving their bodies. Most remember a tunnel of light. Then the heart starts up again and they come back. And they are never the same.

What I remember most about the tunnel of light is that I was not alone. I became a part of something much greater than myself. And I felt that it was good.

But you know that my second death wasn't my last. I'm not a ghost writer. I left the tunnel of light, or I passed through it, and I woke up in a warm bed. My chest was rising and falling in a comfortable rhythm. I could hear the familiar hum of electric lights. My eyes were slow to focus, but I saw beside me the faces of those I knew and loved.

Charlie. Then Ophelia.

"Hello," said Ophelia. There were tears in her eyes.

"Am I in Heaven?" I asked.

"Close," said Charlie. "You're in Peterborough."

"Charlie . . . you're alive . . ."

"Not quite," he said. He was sitting in a chair next to me. I felt the mattress shift when he lifted his feet and rested them on the end of the bed. "I'm undead. You bit me. Remember?"

Parts of that last day came back to me.

"But I killed you. I watched you die. It was awful."

"You're telling me. Painful, too. But I guess that's how it works."

He looked at Ophelia. She nodded.

"No one becomes a vampire from a mere bite," she said. "Even the old stories are consistent in this. The human immune system is too adept at fighting off the disease. Unless you drink a vampire's blood directly, you have to be bitten many times and lose a lot of blood before your system is overwhelmed. In Charlie's case, he was bitten twice. Once by Vlad, and then by you. But you drank too deeply and it was fatal, leaving the pathogen free to take hold and transform him. I suspect when Vlad bit you, it was much the same. Infection followed by extreme blood loss. Then death. Then life."

"I don't understand," I said.

Ophelia smiled. "You will, in time."

I remembered what my uncle had told me—that if you didn't understand something you needed more information, or you had to think about it a bit longer. I think I needed both.

"Why didn't the sun get you?" I asked.

"Who, me?" said Charlie.

"Yes," I said. "It was still up when I bit you."

He shrugged. "I guess it takes a while for your body to change. The sun was long gone by the time I woke up." Charlie had always been a late riser.

"Luna?" I asked.

Ophelia looked at Charlie. A sheepish expression came over his face.

"I woke up hungry—I mean, *really* hungry," he said. "So, she's one of us now."

One of us. I smiled. That meant she wasn't dead. I might see her again.

My lips cracked. I tried to moisten them with my tongue but it was too dry. My head fell to the side. I could see a red tube running into my arm. There was one in the other arm as well. Blood seeped into my charred body. But I needed more. Much more.

I looked at Ophelia. "Why didn't you tell me?"

She smiled, then reached out and put the back of her hand against my cheek. "Oh, Zachary, if only you knew what happens to most of us. There are no good endings. I hoped that you could be cured. I wanted to save you from what is coming."

I knew what she was referring to. Endpoint Psychosis. The descent into madness. It would happen to me. To all of us. Just as it had happened to the Baron.

"Where is he?" I said.

"Who?"

"The Baron. Did he make it?" I wanted to explain everything, but the right words were still scrambled in my mind. "I tried to save him."

"What do you mean?"

"I threw him through the secret door into the dark."

I felt the mattress shift as Charlie lifted his feet off and set them back on the floor. "Why?" he asked.

I didn't know what to say. I suppose I could have offered many reasons.

Maybe because my father believed in redemption. And Mr. Entwistle, too. Forgiveness, he'd told me. That was how you dealt with rogues. If there was even a small chance that they were somewhere watching over me, how could I disappoint them? I couldn't kill the Baron without offering him the choice my father would have. Or maybe it was because I'd spent my undead life in a mental ward. The Baron was mad. You don't judge people like that. You help them. But at the time, there was really only one reason.

"I don't want to hurt anyone," I said. "Never again."

I looked at Charlie. The memory of his death was clearer now. I had killed him. And the pain and confusion on his face was something I didn't ever want to see again.

I think they understood me. Ophelia reached up and put the back of her hand against my forehead as though checking my temperature.

"There was no trace of the Baron when I returned," she said.

I wondered what this meant. Perhaps the Coven of the Dragon took care of their own. Maybe Maximilian had come back for him. Or perhaps he had servants, like the vampires in the movies. The Fallen. Men like Everett Johansson who were ready to die in his service.

"Did I make a mistake?" I asked.

Ophelia checked the tubes running into my arm. "Time will tell, Zachary," she said, stroking my forehead again. "But for now, you need to rest."

That sounded like perfect advice. But it wasn't going to happen just yet. Someone was coming into the room. My vision was still too blurry to see all the way to the door. All I could make out was a tall, dark blob. As he approached, I could see he was walking with a limp. Then his face came into focus. What stood out most was the thick, pink scar under his right eye.

I struggled to rise, but Ophelia put a hand on my chest. "Relax . . ." she whispered. "It's okay."

"What is *he* doing here?"

Johansson barked a laugh but didn't say anything. He just hobbled over behind Ophelia and looked down at me.

"You don't need to worry about Everett," Ophelia said. "He and I have been working together for many years."

I couldn't believe it.

"How's our patient?" he asked. His voice sounded like sandpaper. "Blood supply okay?"

"We should be all right," Ophelia answered.

Johansson grunted, nodded once to me, then hobbled towards the door.

"My uncle said Johansson was one of the Fallen," I told her. "That he served vampires."

Ophelia smiled. "He does. He works for me."

This took a moment to register.

"But they kept shocking me," I said. I thought of the Taser the police had used the night they captured me on Stoney Lake.

"You must forgive the police for their excesses," Ophelia said. "After seeing you feed on that boy's corpse, can you blame them? It is not an easy thing, controlling a crazed vampire." She pressed her lips together in an arrangement that might have been a smile had it not been so full of regret. "I just wish you hadn't run away from him. I sent him to the ward to get you."

"Where were you?"

"Avoiding your uncle. He was getting dangerously close to me. And I didn't want to lead him to you. Not until I knew his intentions. I was also trying to get in touch with my husband. Not an easy thing, given that he and Maximilian started working together shortly after you ran off. In the end, I decided to risk a confrontation. I guess I arrived just in time. I should have come to the ward myself, but I didn't want to put you in danger. And it didn't occur to me that you would run from the police. As a rule of thumb, they're the good guys." She stood and smoothed out the front of her uniform. "But we're all here now. For better or worse."

She then excused herself and crossed the room.

"I need to have another word with Everett," she said at the door. "I'll be back in a minute."

I thought about what Maximilian had told me about Johansson. I'd assumed he served Vrolok, but he'd really been working with Ophelia the whole time. So my uncle had basically turned my life upside down to save me from a woman who was practically my mother. I was beginning to understand the whole *irony* thing.

I turned back to Charlie. He was a vampire now, a carrier, like me.

"Have you told your parents?" I asked.

He shook his head. "Nope. Not looking forward to that conversation." Then his face brightened up a little. "But on the plus side, at least it will explain why I lost my job." He laughed. Then he sighed and looked around the room. "What am I supposed to tell them? They can barely deal with me as it is."

I had no idea what to say to this. My instinct was that he should just tell them the truth. That it wouldn't stay hidden for long. But offering advice was beyond me at the moment, and I had other things on my mind.

"Tell me what happened," I said.

"When?"

"After I died. How did I get here?"

"Luna. She dragged you under the desk. I found you two after the sun went down."

"So she was still alive?"

"Barely. She was bleeding to death. There was only one way to save her. I had to kill her. So I drank. Man, the hunger . . ." He shook his head.

I understood.

"Then Ophelia showed up and took care of things."

"But I died," I said.

"Yes, you did."

"So how am I here?"

Charlie stood and leaned on the metal rail that ran along the side of the bed. "You were pretty crispy on the outside, but on the inside, you were still medium rare. Ophelia brought you here and gave you a blood bath. It seemed to do the trick. You started to heal right away. You still look like you've been sleeping in a sauna, but it shouldn't take too much longer to get you back to normal."

"How long have I been here?"

"Two days. Not even. A day and two nights."

"I don't understand how it's possible," I said.

"How is any of this possible? I can see in the dark now. And run all night. I'm faster than a rabbit. And that's just the tip of the iceberg."

"I know all about the iceberg."

"Oh, right."

"What happened to my uncle?" I asked. "What happened to Maximilian?"

"He's still a loose end waiting to be tied up."

"A loose end . . . ?"

"I wouldn't worry too much about it. Ophelia and Johansson are quite a team. And I'm a sailing instructor, remember? Tying knots in loose ends is supposed to be my specialty."

I didn't think tying up Maximilian was going to be that easy for anyone.

"Charlie," I said.

"Yeah?"

"You're a good friend."

"So are you."

"I mean it."

"So do I."

I tried to sit up in the bed so I could look at him more closely. I wanted to see if he had changed, but that was going to have to wait. It was all I could do to keep my eyes open.

"Oh," he said. "I almost forgot." He dug into his pocket and took something out. It was my necklace. He put it in my hand.

"Where's the rest of it?" I asked. The part that had belonged to my mother, the golden crescent, was no longer attached to my full moon.

"Where do you think, you goofball? Luna has it."

My heart went into overdrive when he said that.

"I'd like to see her."

"And she wants to see you, too," he said. "I'm sure Ophelia can arrange something." Then he looked me over. "On second thought," he added, "I'd recommend waiting a few days. Love may be blind . . ."—he shook his head—"but it's not *that* blind!"

Acknowledgments

Thank you to Janet Shorten for her early edits; Mark Swailes; Kathie Stevenson; my brothers, Charlie and Jake; my father, Robert Douglas; my wife, Joanna Richardson; and especially my mother, Julia Bell, for many invaluable contributions. Thanks also to Sharon McKay and her husband, David, for their interest and support; Catherine Marjoribanks for a fantastic copy edit; and to Lynne Missen, Patricia Ocampo, and HarperCollins Canada Ltd. for this wonderful opportunity.

end of
days

CHAPTER 1

BEING A TEEN VAMPIRE

I'm told vampires are popular in books these days. I'm not surprised. The perks of infection are pretty sick. Awesome physical power. Highly tuned senses. The ability to recover from almost any injury. Good dental hygiene. A simple diet. And that immortality thing—very impressive on a résumé.

My name is Daniel Zachariah Thomson and I'm living the dream. I have been for over nine years. Having said that—the first eight of them weren't what you might imagine. I was orphaned, living in a mental ward, and sick all the time from medications that would never cure me. Then I found out what I was, met a girl, fell in love, and died.

For a while afterward, I'd say life was almost perfect. Then I discovered that every silver lining has a cloud. Does this sound like a complaint? I guess it does. But being a vampire isn't a free ticket to Boardwalk. Those perks I mentioned earlier come with a heavy price tag. If you don't believe me, just think of all the wonderful things you did growing up. How many of them were outside on a beautiful day? For a vampire, the UV index never drops below *deep-fry,* and they don't make sunscreen for that, so once you get infected—no more warm, tingly skin on the beach, no more ocean sunsets, no more afternoon road hockey games, and no more sneaking into your mother's room to look at her Victoria's Secret catalogs. Actually, I guess you could still do that, but it would have to be at night. Still, you get the point. Life without the sunshine is tough. Just look what it did to Gollum.

And the sun is just the tip of the iceberg. I'm sure you've seen the movies. There are lots of ways for us to die, and some are pretty nasty. Forget about holy water and silver bullets. Water of the regular kind scares me, and bullets don't need to be silver, they just need to be airborne.

Then there's the angry mob. Scores of people armed with sticks and pitchforks and torches. They got the Werewolf. And Frankenstein's monster. And the Phantom of the Opera. They almost got Homer Simpson, too. For a vampire, fear of discovery, fear of the mob, is constant. It's why we work so hard to stay hidden. Vampire hunters are another reason. And they aren't all as cute as Buffy. In fact, most of them aren't human. They're vampires, which means most of us are killed by our own kind. Does this seem wrong? It certainly does to me. But if I understand it correctly, it's a matter of necessity.

Imagine a berserk gorilla. Now take off some of the hair and give it rabies. That's the future of every vampire in a nutshell. My father called it Endpoint Psychosis. The stuff of horror movies. No one really understands it. Some vampires get it right away, and others put it off for centuries. But eventually the stress of change, of hunger, of fear, and the loss of light and normal relationships—it unhinges us. Death is never far behind. A small number choose suicide, but as I said before, most are murdered by other vampires. Older ones who've lived for centuries and want our existence to remain a secret. They can be ruthlessly efficient at removing those who might give them away—or who might spread the infection carelessly. To top it off, they really have it in for child vampires: at least, they did before The End of Days. I guess the theory was, a young vampire was pretty much guaranteed to do something stupid and give himself away. And young vampires had a history of spreading the infection too quickly. Given that I turned my friend Charlie last year, and he did the same to a girl named Luna on the same night—well, it would have been hard to argue our case.

Everyone imagines being a vampire would be cooler than joining the Justice League, and it is. You're practically a superhero. But you have to be able to cope with what you lose. It's a kind of culture shock. You need lots of support from family and friends. Sadly, when Charlie turned, he didn't have that. At the time, his father lived in Halifax and his mother was in rehab, his friends were still in school, and his girlfriend, Suki, lived with Luna in New Jersey. Without me, he would have been a hermit. He got angry often and it made him careless about keeping his condition a secret. I had hoped he would keep it together for a few more centuries, or at least until someone invented the jet pack, but at the rate he was going, a ride on the crazy train was just around the corner. Of course, you could argue he was a crackpot even before he turned, but guys can be loo-loo in a lot of different ways. He was giving up fun-loving-reckless for angry-young-man, and it had me worried. If he didn't get himself under control, someone was going to notice and take the *un* out of his undead. What he really needed was a *Chicken Soup for the Vampire Soul*. Something to calm him down and help him come to terms with what he'd given up. The sunshine. Safety. Sports. And school.

I know what you're thinking. *He had to give up school? What a heartbreaker! What could be worse, winning the lottery maybe?* Well, he didn't exactly love the place, it's true. But he was popular there. He was a great athlete, so he got to be in the spotlight often. He'd given that up for the shadows. And so Charlie Rutherford, Detention King of Adam Scott Collegiate, now talked about school as if it were the Land of Chocolate. If that's not a sign a guy's gone mental, what is?

I wasn't sure what to do to help him. Fortunately, I still had Ophelia in my corner. She was a vampire, too, and for nine years after my father died, she was the closest thing I had to a family. The night this story started, she was leaving to meet someone. I didn't ask whom. With Ophelia, if she wanted you to know, she told you up front.

Before she headed out the door, she reached up, pinched my cheek, and smiled. "You can't fix his problems overnight. Just try to help him reconnect with people. Take his mind off of things. But don't put yourselves at risk. If you sense he's getting a bit hot under the collar, get him home. I'll be out for a while, but I need to talk to you both before sunrise. It's very important."

I understood, so after I said good-bye, I wandered down to Charlie's room in the basement so we could work out a plan. Right after that, things started to go haywire, although as I look back, our problems really began long before that—with two murders in Toronto. Like a pair of dominoes, they set off a sequence of events that led to Peterborough and pretty much flattened everything in sight. But we didn't know that was coming so, for us, the End of Days started with a rave.

CHAPTER 2

PARTY CRASHER

Charlie was on his cell when I knocked on the door and stepped into our room. He'd been living with Ophelia and me for a few weeks now, ever since his mother checked into the clinic. She'd been fighting with the bottle and losing. After drinking herself into the drunk tank for the upteenth time, Children's Aid had given her two choices—quit the drink or lose custody of your son. She made the right decision and entered a rehab program. While she was away, Charlie was rooming with me.

"Sounds great," he said into his phone. He looked at me and quickly pointed to his bed. A black T-shirt was lying there, so I tossed it over. He slipped it over his head, then said, "Yeah . . . See you later," and hung up.

"What's going on?" I asked.

He turned and started sifting through his clothes. Like mine, they were in mixed piles all over the floor. I caught the smell of leather and looked up as he slipped his coat over his shoulders.

"There's a rave on River Road out past Trent," he said. "You feel like taking in some local wildlife?"

"You wouldn't rather go later? *A Fistful of Dollars* is starting in a few minutes." It was a Clint Eastwood duster. One of Charlie's favorites.

"Those old spaghetti westerns are on all the time. You'll like this better. You can work on your dance moves."

I'd never been out dancing before. My best move would have

been to find the closest chair. "I don't know how to dance, Charlie. You know that."

"Then it's a perfect night to learn." He smiled and headed for the stairs. "And you're going to love the scenery."

"Um . . . okay."

"You don't sound too keen."

I guess I didn't. I was worried that if he lost his temper, he'd have a fairly large audience. And I wasn't exactly thrilled at the prospect of dancing for the first time with a bunch of people watching. But this was what he needed—to get out and mingle.

"Come on, chowderhead. Fortune favors the bold. Get your boogie shoes on. This will be fun."

Well, it would be for him, and that was the main thing. I followed him upstairs and through the kitchen.

"Where's Ophelia?"

"She's gone to meet someone."

"Who?"

I shrugged. "She didn't say."

He didn't look surprised to hear it. Ophelia was a private person, and I wasn't one to pry.

We slipped out the front door and took off down Hunter Street. It was where we were living now—one of Peterborough's old west-end neighborhoods with huge trees and houses that were each different from the next. Some big. Some small. Some palatial. Some set back so far from the sidewalk it was a workout just getting to the door. Our place was a modest brick bungalow, the house on the block you were least likely to notice. Not too large or too tiny. Nothing fancy, but not uncommonly plain, either—or its plainness would have made it stand out. Around here, it was all about blending in.

"How far is it?" I asked.

Charlie set out at an easy jog. I let him set the pace so he'd be comfortable. "Close," he answered. He was right. Sort of. Maybe you know this, maybe you don't. Vampires are a lot stronger than normal people. We see better, hear better, move faster, heal faster.

We do everything better except suntan. So the two of us were across town and past Trent University faster than a Greyhound bus. About four miles. For us, it was barely a warm-up.

The rave wasn't quite what I expected. Speakers, lights, artificial smoke, the air so thick with body spray it was a wonder anyone could move. But people did. Perhaps a hundred. Maybe more. They jumped and danced and collided to music that thumped right through my chest. So much energy was in the place, even my hair was tingling.

I wasn't used to crowds, so I stood off to the side and watched for a few minutes while Charlie disappeared into the writhing mass of dancers. He was smooth. No herky-jerky. Like a normal person caught with a slow-motion camera, only he was moving at regular speed. Other people around me noticed, too, those on the periphery who were resting, or refueling, or looking for friends. A girl a few feet away was staring so intently I wondered if she'd forgotten how to blink. This happened often. It was the same way with Ophelia. When we went out shopping at night, even the blind gawked.

In little time, Charlie was surrounded by a group of people, mostly girls that I guessed were either friends or hopefuls. He looked at me and waved me over. I shook my head. I wasn't ready to brave the dance floor. Not yet, even though it didn't seem all that difficult. By the looks of things, the music and the crowd sort of pushed you around. Still, if there was a way to look ridiculous, I was sure I'd find it.

I pressed the charm of my necklace between a finger and thumb. It was a full moon fashioned of silver, etched and polished to a perfect shine. My father gave it to me when I was seven. I could still picture him bending down to fasten it around my neck. He pressed it against my chest, messed my hair, and stood. Then he left. And died. It was the day I became an orphan. And a vampire. Aside from a few old photographs, the necklace was the only thing of his I still had. There was another piece to it, a golden crescent that fit along one side, but that part was with Luna.

I thought of her and felt a smile creep up my cheek. Pretty soon my whole face was involved. I'd say I thought of her often, but it was more like I thought of her constantly and just got interrupted by other things. I wondered what she was doing, and if she was thinking of me. I pictured the two of us dancing. Would she have liked it here? I wasn't sure. Like me, she was comfortable when other people took the spotlight. It was even more true now that she was a vampire. Sadly, she was in New Jersey. A million miles away.

My smile faded. Then someone touched my arm, a tall woman with dark hair and black lipstick. She was carrying a tray of drinks. Her eyes wandered over me, then she offered me one. I raised my hand and shook my head. My drinking habits stayed at home. She wasn't gone a second when a strange feeling came over me. An absurd amount of body heat was being generated in the room, but for all that, I felt a chill. I was being watched.

I quickly located Charlie and his friends. They were in a tight circle, each taking turns dancing through the center. The guy in the middle, who might have been a lineman from Charlie's old football team, was doing something that I could only describe as the Cyborg Chicken. I scanned the rest of the floor. A guy with blue hair was jumping up and down like a spawning salmon. In another corner, a group of girls were dancing so close together it was a wonder their jewelry wasn't tangled. Farther on were a bunch of guys, some with spiked hair, others with shaved heads, who were all jumping up and slamming into one another. It was all alien to me. But certainly no cause for concern.

Then my eyes drifted upward. I thought I saw something in the lights. It was hard to tell. Even if you're from the planet Krypton, your eyes aren't much good with strobes flashing in them. But my instincts told me I was getting warm, so I made my way onto the dance floor to get a better look. I was staring up at the ceiling, not watching where I was going, when I bumped into a girl. Her red hair was cut like a lampshade and she was wearing high-heeled boots that went right up past her knees. Before I could reach out, her drink spilled. I started to apologize.

"That's fine," she said. She moved closer so we were almost touching. "Don't worry about it."

I offered to get her another drink, but she smiled and shook her head. She seemed cool with things. Her boyfriend wasn't. I hadn't noticed him at first. He stepped toward me with a scowl on his face. His hair was gelled down the center like a giant fan and he was wearing a Ramones T-shirt. The people around us backed away just enough that I could tell there was going to be trouble. Then Charlie slid in beside me. His eyes had the same look I imagine Roman gladiators wore when they went into the Colosseum. A kind of focused intensity that was a three parts anger and one part crazy.

"Back off, Romeo," he said. His teeth were starting to drop.

I felt the bottom fall out of my stomach. This was the last thing we needed. A free-for-all that would make the *National Enquirer. Teen Vampire Starts Riot at Small-Town Rave.*

"It's fine, Charlie," I shouted in his ear. "It was my mistake."

I think we could have made it out cleanly at that point if the girl I'd bumped into hadn't been staring at Charlie with a look of dazed euphoria. Whatever cologne he was wearing, it was working overtime. Charlie smiled at her. She smiled back. Then her boyfriend stepped closer so the two of them were chest to chest. *Here we go,* I thought. Charlie's eyes were like two black disks. I hadn't seen anything like it since Shark Week on the Discovery Channel.

Then something bizarre happened. A shadow fell to the floor on the far side of the hall. It happened quickly. With the lights doing a kooky flash dance above, I wasn't sure if I'd actually seen anything, but then the people on that side of the floor began to part. They were staring at a man who was moving toward us. With the light behind him, all I could see was a tall silhouette, but it was enough. His movements were fluid. Effortless. Perfectly balanced. Driven by tremendous strength. There was none of the stiffness you see with normal people. It was another vampire. He'd obviously spotted us. If he was one of those elders who didn't like kids, we were going to go straight from rave to grave.

I wasn't about to take any chances. "Charlie, we've gotta go." I grabbed the sleeve of his jacket and started pulling him to the door.

"That's right, pretty boy, take a walk," the guy with the fan-shaped hair said.

I'd hoped Charlie would just fall in step, but I should have known better. He resisted. Fortunately, I was a lot stronger and jerked his shoulder back. He shot me an angry look, but when he noticed I was staring past the guy with the fan-shaped hair, he turned and saw what I did. Right in front of him, the girl with the red lampshade hair was smiling and waving. Her boyfriend was smirking. Then the tall vampire, little more than a shadow, shouldered past a guy just behind them, spinning him like a turnstile.

Charlie looked back at me, panic all over his face. "Zack, that's a vampire."

"I know!"

We raced for the door.

"How did he know we were here?"

I had no idea. But it didn't matter. We'd been spotted. So we ran.

CHAPTER 3

RUNNING SCARED

We were just outside when I heard a sound like a flag rippling loudly in the wind. I looked up to see a second shadow drop from the far corner of the building, about a hundred feet away. He was wearing something that might have been a cape, or a loose cowl. It snapped in the night air as he fell.

"There's two of them," I said.

Charlie put it into high gear and I followed. Neither of us spoke. We were both terrified. Our lives were at stake, no pun intended. Our fear was so strong I could smell the sharp tang of it in the warm night air.

To avoid being seen, we didn't follow the road, but stuck to the banks of the river. When we reached the Riverview Park and Zoo, we stopped.

"Are they following us?" Charlie whispered. "Do you hear anything?" He pushed so little air past his lips that it made less noise than a pair of moth wings, but to my ears, it was crystal clear.

I tested the air. Smelled sweat. Charlie's cologne. Zoo animals and rotting straw. Our strained nerves. The wind in the trees was loud. So was the babble of the river. I heard nothing else and didn't expect to. Vampires are predators. Fast, silent, and lethal. We wouldn't hear them until it was too late. Not if they were elders. Over time, the pathogen responsible for making us vampires changed us in ways that stretched the imagination. Talents, they were called, but they were more like the special powers you'd expect to read about in comic books and fantasy novels. Turning into mist. Blending into shadows. Reading people's thoughts. Shape-shifting. Even flying.

I scanned the treetops overhead, then started running again. In minutes we were downtown. We headed for the rooftops. Up and down, block to block. Trees, fire escapes, phone poles, and fences, we scampered over all of them, sticking to the shadows, jumping store to store, row to row, house to house. We were two foxes who knew the hounds were right behind.

We never made it home. About a block from our house, I stopped. Charlie was looking over his shoulder and nearly plowed into me. I tested the air with my nose.

"What is it?" he whispered.

I could smell blood. Normally, it has a distinctive odor—much like everything does. But because it's our only food, we'd never confuse it with anything else. It always set off a chain reaction, in me at least, that usually started in my mouth and spread like a jolt of electricity to every muscle in my body. But I wasn't reacting this way because the odor was a bit off. My mind took a few moments to sort out the reason why.

Charlie poked me in the shoulder. "Wake up, Sleepy Dwarf. Why have we stopped?"

"Can't you smell that?"

He tested the air. Then his eyes widened.

"I think it's from a vampire," I said.

"Yeah." He nodded. "Smells wrong."

The wind changed and the odor grew even stronger. I raced to the tallest house nearby, scampered up the wall, pulled myself up onto the roof, then perched on the chimney. Our place was just down the street. Ophelia's car wasn't there. Did that mean she hadn't returned? I was hoping so, because the odor of blood was coming from our driveway. A telltale crimson smear covered the asphalt.

I heard Charlie below me. He was climbing up the side of the house. I waved him off, then dropped as quickly as I could to the ground. Once I was hidden in the shadow of a tree, I pulled out my cell phone and called Ophelia. Her number was at the top of my call list, right under Charlie's. I hit send and waited. The ring sounded louder than a church bell. I figured every vampire from here to the moon could hear it.

"Can't you set the volume lower?" Charlie asked.

I shook my head. Then Ophelia's voice mail came on. "Call me immediately," I whispered. I nearly snapped the phone in half folding it up.

"Let's get home," Charlie said. He started off toward the house.

I grabbed his arm and pulled him the other way. "We can't," I said. "That's where the blood is coming from. I think they might have arrived ahead of us."

"What? Those vampires? How would they know to come here?"

I had no idea.

"Perfect. I knew this night was too good to be true. We were finally having a bit of fun." Charlie was starting to raise his voice. I waved for him to be quiet. The wind picked up and the smell of vampire blood intensified. "You don't think it might be . . . ?"

He didn't finish, but I knew where he was going. That the blood might be Ophelia's.

"I don't think so," I said. "Her car's not back. And I don't think she was planning to come home this early."

"Let's hope that's not wishful thinking." He stared up the block, then checked over each shoulder. What now?"

I had no idea, but standing still wasn't an option. I turned toward my old neighborhood, where I'd once lived with my father.

"Wait . . . not that way." Charlie pulled me around so we were backtracking downtown. "If we want to hide, the best place is somewhere they've already looked."

Did he mean back at the rave? We'd done this sort of thing once before, last year on Stony Lake when the police were looking for us. We went to a cottage they'd already searched. It seemed a good idea. I fell in step beside Charlie and we headed back to the rave, back to the rooftops.

"It's him, isn't it?" he said.

Him . . . He could only mean one person. Vlad Tsepesh—the Impaler. His real name was Wladislaus Dragwlya, but to the modern world he was Dracula. Not a creature of fantasy but a scourge. When I'd first heard of him, he'd used an assumed name, the Baron Vrolok. My uncle Maximilian told me about him. That he'd killed my parents and infected me. Later, Vrolok tried to kill Charlie and me. And Luna. But, thanks to Ophelia, we'd survived. So had he, but only because I didn't have the heart to kill him. Now he was missing, or his body was. It meant he might still be out there. Although he'd almost burnt up in the sun, nearly dead for a vampire isn't really dead at all. Unless the head is cut off, or the body is incinerated, all it takes to bring us back is a bit of time and blood. Lots of it.

"We should never have stayed in Peterborough," Charlie whispered.

It was hard to disagree at the moment.

We ran over the downtown and sprinted along the river until we reached a picnic area between one of the city's hydro stations and a row of houses. Then the smell of vampire blood returned, stronger here than at the house. I slowed, then stopped. Charlie pulled up beside me. The way his nose flared, I could tell he'd noticed, too. His teeth were down and his pupils were two black disks again. Wide. Alert. Nervous. I felt the same.

I scanned the shore and the grass around the trees. A few picnic tables sat near a trash can. Drops of vampire blood ran past them in a straight line toward the river.

"Over here." Charlie pointed to a large bootprint in the grass a few steps away. "Do you think it's from one of those vampires at the rave?"

I had no idea.

"Look, it leads straight into the water."

In the mud on the lip of the bank was another print. I set my foot in it, then backed up and looked for another. Whoever it was, he'd lost a lot of blood here. Then jumped into the river. It made no sense. Blood doesn't clot underwater.

"What can do this to a vampire?" Charlie asked.

I shrugged. "A stronger vampire maybe."

He kneeled down and smeared his fingertips with blood, then raised it to his nose. He was about to stick it in his mouth when I grabbed his arm.

"Oh, right," he said.

I let go of his arm. He wiped his fingers on his pant leg and stood. A vampire's blood could be fatal to another vampire. I wasn't exactly sure why.

"He was motoring." Charlie stared at the bootprint in the grass. The other print, the one in the mud by the water, was at least twenty feet away. "You think he was being followed?"

My eyes swept over the grass. "I don't see any other footprints, do you?"

Charlie went back to the bank where the ground was softer and shook his head. Then he kicked off his shoes and waded out to his knees. A few seconds later, he pointed to the ground at the lip of the river. I saw a hollow depression. A few inches of water had washed inside, obscuring the bottom. We found several more. They were deep, as if someone had pressed a large tin can into the muck.

"What makes that kind of mark?" he asked.

I couldn't say. I stared at the round hole and tried to imagine what might have done it. It looked almost like a bear print, but was wider at the front, with no toe markings, though the river might have washed them away.

Charlie slapped my shoulder gently with the back of his hand. "Don't go catatonic on me now."

I wasn't planning to. But I often got quiet when I was thinking and sometimes forgot to answer people when they spoke to me. I'd picked up this bad habit from living in the Nicholls Ward. Half the people there couldn't carry on a conversation. They just muttered all the time or repeated themselves or completely ignored me. Since it didn't really make a difference what I said to them, I got used to keeping my mouth shut and thinking about things in my head. The busier my mind got, the less likely I was to say anything out loud.

Charlie gently punched my shoulder. "Say something, turkey meat. Your tongue's frozen."

"Sorry. I'm just trying to figure this out."

I tested the air. I could smell the damp grass, car exhaust, rotting sticks and leaves along the bank, my deodorant, vampire blood . . .

"What is it?"

"Wine," I said. "And a sweaty, leathery kind of dog smell."

We stood for a few moments, not speaking.

"You want to get your feet wet?"

I shook my head. I didn't like the water.

Charlie looked farther up the shore. "Should we keep checking along the bank? Whoever jumped in had to come out somewhere."

"If he came out at all. You really want to find him?"

Charlie shook his head. "Not really. But if he's injured, this might be the best chance we have. He's weak. If he feeds and regenerates, we're going to be in trouble."

I had a feeling we were already in trouble. I turned back to the street.

Charlie stayed for a few moments to tie up his shoes. Then he just stared out over the river. In his first life, he'd been a water baby. Swimming. Canoeing. Windsurfing. He used to be a sailing instructor. Before that, he raced Lasers, single-sailed boats you could skipper by yourself. It was all part of a life that belonged in the sunshine. It was gone and never coming back. I didn't know what to say to him. These were all things he'd lost because I'd infected him, and there was no easy way to set it right.

I heard him take a deep breath, then he turned so we were standing shoulder to shoulder. "Any more clues, Sherlock?"

Before I could answer, a howl ripped through the air. Another answered. Wolves. They were close, only a few blocks away.

"That's weird," he said.

And unsettling.

"Let's go." He started forward.

I didn't move.

"What is it?"

Did he really have to ask?

"We have an advantage, Zack. He's hurt."

"That only makes him more dangerous," I said.

"Or more likely to kill someone."

Charlie had a point. An injured vampire needed human blood to regenerate. If his hunger was strong enough, it might push him over the edge.

"Who else is going to do anything?" he added. "What if he's gone crazy?"

That clinched it. "You're right. We'd better check things out."

Charlie laughed.

"What is it?"

"You sound like you're auditioning for the part of Superman in the school play."

"Very funny."

Another eruption of howling. It sounded as if the entire cast of *White Fang* were having a feeding frenzy just up the street.

"Well, now is our chance, Clark. Up, up and away."

Charlie brushed past me, then raced off into the dark along the river. The howling continued.

CHAPTER 4

SURPRISE ATTACK

The Riverview Park and Zoo was less than a quarter mile down Water Street. And yes, they had wolves. Two of them. Whenever Charlie and I came by on a late-night run, they were always up, padding their cells, restless to join us on the hunt. They would have been disappointed. We never killed anything larger than mosquitoes. But tonight was different. We were hunting an injured vampire.

I took off. I'd been infected much longer than Charlie. Even though we'd been drinking human blood for about the same length of time, my transmission had a few extra gears. I wanted to arrive first, just in case there really was trouble. By the time he caught up, I was standing outside the wolf pen. It was empty. The chain links of the outer fence and the taller, inner fence had been ripped apart. The smell of vampire blood was in the air. I ran my fingers over the torn metal. I couldn't make sense of this. If a vampire was injured, why would it mess with two wolves?

"Why would someone do this?"

Charlie shrugged. "Like I'm supposed to know?" He nodded toward a hole in the ground. "One of the posts is missing."

We heard another howl. And a squeal.

"That way," Charlie said, nodding past the animal cages to a play area full of monkey bars and swing sets. He bolted. I got swept up in his turbulence. We passed a goat and donkey pen—they were bleating as if the world were going to end. Then we entered the kids' park. Every animal in the zoo was awake by this time. It sounded like the inside of Noah's ark. Then I saw the two wolves. They were dead. Both had deep rows of gashes along their flanks, as if they'd been run over several times by a lawn mower. I scanned the ground looking for footprints, then sniffed at the air to try to find any trace of where the vampire had gone. With so much blood everywhere, I couldn't tell what was what. My senses were on overload.

"He's definitely gone bonkers?" Charlie said. He had to raise his voice over the sound of the buffaloes, which were sounding off like a pair of foghorns.

I surveyed the mess and nodded. Most vampires hid their tracks. This one was advertising, a sure sign of Endpoint Psychosis. Whoever it was, Vlad or someone else, we had to catch him quickly or he might easily start the kind of pandemic you only saw in bad Hollywood horror films.

Charlie slapped my arm gently with the back of his hand, then flicked his fingers toward the edge of the park. "The prints lead that way."

The children's area was a sandlot. I could see a pair of boot markings—the same from the riverbank—leading past a tube slide to a set of steps that ran down the hill. The river was that way. As we were following the tracks, I heard the sound of sirens approaching.

"Hurry," Charlie said.

I took off at warp speed, following the blood trail to the bottom of the stairs. Then I slowed. I'm not sure why. Was it fear? Or perhaps a deeper instinct. Trouble was waiting ahead. The hairs on my arms were standing up, and the eerie chill I'd felt at the rave returned—as if I was being watched. Charlie was right on my heels. As I slowed, so did he. We crept along the path, then I felt his hand on my back. I flattened out on the ground so I was hidden in the long grass. Ahead, by the riverbank, we could see the silhouette of a man.

"Who is it?" Charlie whispered. "Can you see?"

I couldn't. He was about a hundred meters away, and the light of the moon was behind him, so his face was just a shadow. His hair was long. A mix of black and white and gray. He was wearing what might have been a cape, or maybe a long overcoat. As we watched, the man dropped to a crouch and looked back in our direction. By his movements, I could tell it was a vampire.

"It doesn't look like Vlad," Charlie said.

He was right. Vlad was short and thick with a neck like an ox. This man was taller. Leaner. This should have brought me some relief, but it didn't. Maybe because the vampire had the missing fence post—the one from the wolf pen—and was holding it like a baseball bat. He began to circle, his eyes scanning the grass where we were hiding. The trees to our right were suddenly looking like a much safer place to hide.

"I think he can see us," Charlie said. "What do we do?"

I didn't know. But if we didn't make up our minds soon, we were going to run out of choices. The vampire would decide for us. His eyes were still searching the shadows. Then he started toward us, first at a jog, then a sprint. I felt my stomach twist. Suddenly a shadow shot out of the darkness. It froze the air in my chest. I'd never seen anything move so quickly. I took it from Charlie's reaction, he hadn't either. He jumped as if I'd jammed a pin in his ribs. I wasn't even certain how the thing was running, on two legs or four. There wasn't time to tell. Whatever it was, it collided with the approaching vampire about a stone's throw in front of us. The two shapes rolled over the top of one another in a blur. A lethal dance started that was so quick, even my vampire eyes had difficulty following it.

"What is *that* thing?" Charlie asked, his eyes open wider than his mouth.

I couldn't decide what it was. It might have been another vampire, but it seemed too large, and the shape was wrong. Had I been able to see it more clearly, I might have been able to make up my mind, but it was moving too quickly. The vampire with the post was swinging for the fences as if this were game seven of the World Series. They were two overlapping ghosts. Snarling shapes that were impossible to separate.

I started creeping back to the stairs. Charlie was right behind me. We were way out of our league here. It was time to run. Then the fight ended. I don't even know how. I glanced up the hill toward the zoo and missed the grand finale. There was a splash in the river. When I looked back, the vampire was gone. The larger creature from the shadows craned his neck and let out a roar that would have scared the ears off a Kodiak bear.

"I think that's our cue," Charlie whispered.

As soon as he spoke, the thing turned and saw us.

Charlie froze. I didn't. I was the Night Runner. My feet were already moving. I grabbed an armful of his coat and hauled him back toward the steps. If we didn't slip it into overdrive, we were going to be next on the menu. We bolted up the steps. Ahead, at the zoo, the red and blue lights of police cars were reflecting off the leaves of the trees and sumac along the hill.

Charlie slowed when he saw them. "Are you sure you want to go that way?"

I wasn't sure about anything, but it seemed the safest place to go, and I said so.

"I don't think I'd feel safe in a bank vault right now," Charlie said.

The sound of soft footfalls behind us was all the motivation we needed. So we fled up the stairs in the direction of the police.

CHAPTER 5

INSPECTOR JOHANSSON

When Charlie and I topped the steps and entered the zoo play area, we nearly collided with a young officer who was standing near the mouth of the slide. He was stocky, with hair that would have looked perfect on a mannequin. When he saw us, he raised one hand in a "Halt" gesture. The other was pressing the buttons on a radio pinned to his shoulder. I felt Charlie tense up beside me.

"We should hustle," he whispered. "That thing is coming."

I quickly glanced around. Five other cruisers were in the lot, plus two more on the road, and three near the fountain. A group of officers were inspecting the wolf pen. Others were sealing off areas with plastic yellow tape. One was snapping pictures. At least a dozen officers had to be within earshot. And gunshot. Even Godzilla would have thought twice about making trouble up here.

"What are you two doing?" the officer asked.

Charlie looked at me. I looked at him. We both looked at the officer. There was no good answer for this. Fortunately, the conversation got cut short by a voice that crackled like a dry flame.

"I'll take it from here," a man said.

A dark shape hobbled out from behind a car that was more rust than paint. It was Everett Johansson. He was a police inspector and a good friend of Ophelia's—part of a network of supporters who helped supply us with blood so we didn't have to wander the streets at night looking for people to bite. He moved awkwardly, leaning hard on his cane. The injury was old, from when he'd worked as a homicide detective in Toronto. A bullet through the knee had helped him decide to get out before the locals learned to shoot a little higher.

"You sure?" the young officer asked him. "I was going to wait and turn them over to Baddon."

Inspector Johansson grunted. It might have been a yes, or it might have been a swear word. Then he started hacking. He had a smoker's cough from years of wine-tipped cigars. "Baddon's busy," he said. "I'll handle these two critters."

"They're all yours." The officer glanced at us once before walking away. I couldn't tell from his expression whether he felt relief or disappointment. It might have been heartburn.

I waited until he was out of earshot before speaking. "Thanks. I wasn't sure how I was going to explain this."

Inspector Johansson grunted again. He did most of his talking this way. Then he turned back to his car, one of those ancient muscle machines people bought before anyone knew what global warming was. For just a second, the streetlamp overhead lit up the bright pink scar under his eye. It made him look tough. I'd once mistaken him for a bad guy. He certainly looked the part. He cleared his throat, then pulled a cigar from a carton inside his coat pocket and lit up.

"What were you two doing here?" he said with the cigar pinched between his teeth. Without waiting for an answer, he opened the back door of his car and told us to get in. I slid through the door and across the seat. The inspector waited for Charlie to climb in, then closed the door and grunted his way into the front. Once settled, he rolled down his window and blew a plume of smoke from the side of his mouth. When he turned the key, I winced. The engine burped, hiccuped, detonated, then a cloud of black soot flew out the tailpipe. As soon as the car recovered, he slid it in gear and stepped on the gas. My whole body shook as if I were sitting on a paint mixer. It was easily 6.2 on the Richter scale.

"So?" Johansson said. We pulled out of the lot and turned onto Water Street.

"We were following a vampire," I said.

"Vampire?" The inspector pulled the cigar from his mouth and cleared his throat. "Are you crazy?"

After living eight years in a mental ward, I was pretty sure the answer was no.

"Do you know who it was?"

"I don't think it matters now," Charlie said.

A deep grunt followed. "Why not?"

"Because something showed up and carved him into fish food."

The inspector's eyes flashed up to the rearview mirror. He glanced at Charlie, then at me. He looked exhausted. His eyes were two slits. "*Something* showed up. *Something?* What do you mean *something?*"

"I didn't get a good look at it," I answered. "It was moving too fast. But we did see some weird footprints."

His eyelids rose to half-mast when he heard this. "Where?"

"The picnic tables by the hydro station," Charlie answered.

The inspector's hand disappeared into his overcoat and came up with a cell phone. He started dialing. When someone picked up at the other end, he said, "Yeah, it's me."

It was difficult to listen in. The car sounded like two chain saws trying to cut each other in half.

"Have you got them?" said a voice.

I looked at Charlie.

"Ophelia?" he whispered.

I nodded. It was her. It meant she was safe. She said something, but I missed it, then Inspector Johansson answered by saying he was bringing us home.

"That's a mistake," Charlie said.

The inspector hung up, then dropped the phone onto the seat beside him. "What was that?"

"That's a mistake," Charlie repeated.

"The vampires were there," I added.

"What vampires?"

"Two of them followed us from the rave. That's why we didn't go home. There's vampire blood all over the driveway."

"Great," grumbled the inspector. He hit the brakes and our heads jolted forward. He picked up the phone and made another call. No one picked up. "Well, that's not good," he muttered.

"What is it?" Charlie asked.

"Ophelia's place was under surveillance. An old friend of mine from Toronto. He's not answering." The inspector tried his car radio, but didn't have any luck with that, either. "Dammit!"

"What's going on?" Charlie asked.

"And where's Ophelia?"

Inspector Johansson ignored us. He just stared at the radio. "Let's hope he's at the hospital with his son," he muttered. I had no idea whom he was talking about. Then he turned so he could see us better. "What happened tonight?"

We did our best to explain. His eyes bounced from me to Charlie as we took turns running through the night's events.

"What do you think it was at the zoo?" the inspector asked me. "What killed those wolves? Was it the vampire? Or was it this *something* you were talking about?"

I shrugged. "I don't know."

"You said there were two vampires at the rave. What happened to the other one?"

I looked at Charlie. He shrugged, then glanced at the inspector. "You didn't answer my question."

Inspector Johansson responded by hammering on the gas pedal. The engine grumbled and we lurched forward. "What question?"

"What's going on?"

His eyes rose the rearview mirror. "The Underground is collapsing. No—let me rephrase that. It's going to hell in a handbasket."

"What does that mean?" I asked.

"The Underground has been compromised. We're under attack."

"*Underground?*" said Charlie. "You hanging out with mole men or something? What are you talking about?"

We drove in silence for a few blocks. The inspector was looking at his phone. He seemed to be debating another call. He put it down and sped up instead, then glanced back over the seat.

"Don't pretend you've never heard of the Underground."

"Who's pretending?"

The inspector grunted his surprise. "You've heard of it. You just never put the right name to it maybe."

"Then what is it?" Charlie asked.

"All the people who help look after vampires."

"Aren't they called the Fallen?"

Inspector Johansson started coughing. He hurried an answer in between a few loud fits. "That was a word Zack's father used, but it only applied to the bad ones. We're the good guys."

"You're part of it then?" Charlie asked.

"The Underground? Yeah. A small part."

"How big is it?"

The inspector put his lips together and frowned. "Global. But I only know what I need to know. A handful of names. Some are police. Some are vampires. Some are normal people. It's supposed to be a secret, but someone must have let the cat out of the bag. Our supply systems are falling apart. Blood has been tampered with. Poisoned. Other shipments have been stolen. A vampire in Havelock disappeared yesterday. Another in Lakefield last week. Bridgenorth before that. Just vanished. And they were good ones, like you two slack-jawed nincompoops."

He took his cigar out of his mouth. His hands were shaking—only a slight tremor, but I noticed. The window was still rolled down. He blew another lungful of smoke outside.

"Is that why the vampires showed up at the rave? Are they behind it?" Charlie asked.

"Who knows?" Inspector Johansson said. "Maybe they were trying to warn you."

I hadn't considered that. I looked at Charlie. Judging by the look of surprise on his face, he hadn't either.

The inspector stopped the car a block from our house. Then his phone rang. "Go," he said.

It was Ophelia again. She sounded alarmed. "Where are you?"

"I'm a block from the house with Tweedledumb and Tweedle-dumber. Looks like a hot spot. I think it's been compromised. Any other suggestions about where to take them?"

"Is Burnham safe?"

"I don't know if anywhere is safe, but it's probably the best option." He mashed his cigar into the tray under the radio.

"I need you to drop them off, then swing by right away," Ophelia continued.

"Where are you?"

"London Street."

"What's up?"

I held my breath and waited. Charlie was listening, too. For a few seconds, all I could hear was the sound of the car idling and the inspector, who was grinding his teeth and feeling about his coat pocket for another cigar.

"You need to come quickly," Ophelia said. "There's been another murder."

CHAPTER 6

THE SAFE HOUSE

The inspector looked at his cell for a few seconds as if it were guilty of a heinous crime, then he disconnected it and tossed it on the seat beside him. A string of swear words erupted from his mouth. He pulled the last cigar from the box in his coat pocket and started chewing on the end of it. He didn't light up, he just rolled it from one side of his mouth to the other, then chucked the empty carton to the floor.

"Who just got killed?" Charlie asked.

The inspector shook his head. "I'll find out later. Once I've dropped you two off." He slipped the car into gear and headed back toward the downtown. We crossed the Hunter Street bridge, drove past a baseball diamond, then pulled onto a quiet side street.

"That's it." He nodded out the window toward a tiny brick bungalow that looked just big enough for a family of ants.

"We're staying *here*?" Charlie asked.

"Unless you had other plans . . ."

We didn't, so we followed Inspector Johansson around to the back door. He reached into his coat and pulled out a key ring that would have given Governor Schwarzenegger a workout. "Give me a second."

There were four dead bolts to unlock. As soon as he opened the door, I saw why. The place was like an antiques shop. It was packed floor to ceiling with swords, helmets, armor, busts, carvings, statues, old candlesticks, furniture, and carpets. Everything looked as if it had been stolen from a museum. Or a medieval castle.

"Where did you get all this?" I asked, bumping into a coffee table that might have belonged to Moses at one time.

"It's Ophelia's," the inspector said over his shoulder. He was punching numbers into an electronic box near the door. It must have been a home security system.

"Did you know about this?" Charlie asked me.

I shook my head. Ophelia wasn't into clutter. Our house had no knickknacks or collectibles. Not unless you counted books and music and the odd painting. This clearly wasn't a place she expected to be living in anytime soon. The sheer volume of stuff would have driven her into an insane cleaning frenzy—one that wouldn't have ended until nothing was left in the rooms but air and dried paint. But Luna would have loved it. And my father. He used to obsess over anything old. Or well made. Things that were lasting.

I don't know how long I stood there. Eventually, I felt the tip of Johansson's cane tap gently against the bottom of my arm.

"Come on," he said. "Ophelia's waiting for me."

I nodded, then followed him through the hall to the far end of the house. Just past the kitchen, a door led down to the basement. The inspector opened it for us, flicked on the lights, then nodded for us to go ahead.

If the first floor of the safe house was an antiques store, the basement was a Future Shop. Everything was state-of-the-art. High-def TV. Surround-sound stereo. A computer that looked as if it belonged on a spaceship. A weird sofa that had a thin, contoured back. A bed folded up against the wall. A funky reading chair with a spiral metal base that I was sure I'd seen in an episode of *Star Trek*. Several glass and wire bookcases with small lights built in. The only things that didn't look as if they were made in the year 3000 were the books. There were even game consoles. Charlie saw them and his eyes lit up.

"Now this is more like it," he said. "I could survive a zombie apocalypse down here."

"No windows," I whispered. Another plus.

"You aren't the first vampires we've had to hide." The inspector handed me a remote control. "Try not to break anything." He grunted and turned to go.

"Wait," I said.

He turned back. He was leaning hard on his cane.

"When will I see Ophelia?" I asked.

The inspector scratched at the stubble on his chin, then positioned his cigar at the side of his mouth. "We'll be back before dawn."

"She mentioned she wanted to talk to Charlie and me about something. Do you know what it was?"

"Yeah." He nodded. "A few things. The Coven was one of them."

The Coven . . . He meant the Coven of the Dragon, a team of powerful elders who were like the secret police of the vampire world. An invisible network of executioners. They were the most dangerous organization on the face of the earth, at least for Charlie and me, because they were the ones who were most likely to come after us. I didn't know much about them, only that their seat of power was overseas in Europe somewhere. Vlad had been their Grand Master. With him gone, I didn't know who was in charge.

"We weren't sure if the Coven were behind these disappearances," the inspector continued, "but I had my doubts, even before you saw that thing at the zoo."

"Why?" Charlie asked.

The inspector took out his cigar. "The Coven always impale their enemies. They cut off the head, stuff the mouth with garlic, cut out the heart, burn it, and put the corpse on display as a deterrent to others. The vampires who have died lately, they just disappear. Nothing is left but a stain on the sidewalk. And they were all stable. Discreet. That's not the way the Coven operate. They only go after the crazies. Or the ones who don't stay incognito. You were an exception. Vendetta. And an age thing. The Coven don't permit child vampires. But you knew that already." He grunted, then spoke with the cigar pinched at the side of his mouth. "And the Coven are in disarray right now. Infighting. Vlad is still missing. Even if he comes back, and let's pray he doesn't, he'll have a hell of a lot of reorganizing to do."

"What do you mean *reorganizing*?" I asked.

"Vlad's underlings are all fighting to see who gets to be the top dog. Vlad would have a lot to do to bring them back under control. Ophelia and I thought their lack of leadership would keep you out of trouble for a while."

Obviously not.

"So what happens now?" Charlie asked. He made his way over to the game console under the television.

"You two stay out of sight," the inspector said. "There's a phone by the bed, but I don't want you calling out. And don't answer it unless it's me. When I call, I'll let it ring twice, then I'll hang up and call again. Two rings, pause, pick up on the next one."

"Don't we have caller ID?" I asked.

"Yes, you do. But someone else might be using my phone. You never know. . . . Two rings. Pause. Then pick up the next call. Got it?"

"Yeah. I got it."

He grunted, then looked us over again. His head tilted forward a bit. I'd seen his expression on a lot of adult faces. *Be careful,* he was saying. Well, how much trouble could we get into in a one-room basement? I nodded back and he turned to go. Then he remembered something.

"One more thing. The alarm. It'll be on upstairs. If you try to leave the house, it will go off. So stay put. Is there anything else you'll need?"

"Yeah," said Charlie. "Could you send for some backup? Someone to watch the place from outside—raise the alarm if trouble arrives. We aren't going to see anything from down here. And once the sun comes up, we're toast if someone breaks in."

The inspector grunted a negative. "We're out of backup. Every cop

I know in the Underground is dead or missing. And I can't get anyone else involved on short notice. I have to keep you guys off the radar."

He walked over to me and reached into his coat. From the holster around his shoulder he took out his gun, a semiautomatic. He handed it to me. "The clip is full. The safety's on. You ever fire one of these things?"

I took the gun and shook my head. I'd never even held one before. Then a jolt of pain ran down my arm. It took root in my chest. My heart began to burn. I pinched my eyes shut, and when I opened them, everything was an agonizing haze. All I could see were spots. It was a few seconds before I could speak.

"Take it back," I whispered.

"I'll take it," said Charlie.

The inspector glanced down at the gun and removed it from my hand. Instantly, the pain began to ebb. Nerves stopped burning. My blurry eyes cleared.

I watched him reholster it. He was watching me intently. "You okay?"

I didn't know how to answer that, so I didn't. After a few seconds, he grunted a good-bye and started hobbling to the stairs.

"Two rings, pause, pick up," he reminded me.

I nodded and he closed the basement door. Then his footsteps clumped across the floor above. The back door opened and closed. The house shuddered. Dead bolts followed. A minute later, I heard his car roar. I could picture every animal in the neighborhood running for cover.

"What was that all about?" Charlie said.

"What?"

"With the gun. Your face . . ."

I rubbed my arm. It was still pins and needles. "It didn't feel right."

"You should have given it to me!"

I had no answer for this. I trusted my instincts. Something about that gun was just wrong.

"You want to play some?" Charlie turned the game console on. Then he started opening drawers in the TV cabinet, no doubt looking for games.

I wandered over to the desk. It was covered with open books. Loose-leaf pages were scattered everywhere. "There's a note here." A yellow sticky was pressed to the bottom of the computer keyboard: *Knowledge is your best defense.* The writing was tight and neat. I recognized it as Ophelia's right away.

"What does it say?" Charlie didn't look up from the drawer he was sorting through. "Man, all these games are old. We've finished them already."

I read him the message. "It's Ophelia's writing," I added.

"How long ago did she write it?"

"Beats me." He walked over and I handed it to him. He glanced at it, then down at the desk, and froze. I followed his gaze to the open book. There, staring at us from the page, was Vlad Dracula.

CHAPTER 7

PROPHECIES

Charlie and I stared at a picture of the vampire who had almost killed us.

"A little light reading, I guess," Charlie said. "Man, that dude is scary-looking." He closed the book.

Underneath was another note. The handwriting was larger than Ophelia's. Messier. More frantic.

THE END OF DAYS IS COMING.

Charlie picked up the note, read it over again, then handed it to me. "What kind of gobbledygook is this? The *End of Days*—isn't that an Arnold Schwarzenegger movie?"

It was. Not his best work. I started leafing through the other open books. One showed a page full of ideograms.

"Is that Chinese?" Charlie asked.

I shrugged. It might have been Martian. I couldn't read it, but Ophelia obviously could. Notes were in the margins. The writing was hers. I looked at the shelves. There were hundreds of other books. And more open on the desk, *Geschichte der Moldau und Walachei* The book beside it had a passage underlined: *i nu este revelat omul nelegiuirii* . . .

It meant nothing to me. I started looking at the others. I needed to know what the note meant. What the End of Days referred to.

"Oh, no, you don't," Charlie said.

"What?"

"Zack, it would take you ten years to read through this stuff."

I sighed. "Then I guess I'd better get started."

I didn't have much luck at first. Of all the volumes on the desk, only one was in English—the phone book.

After a couple of minutes, Charlie started walking back to the television. "I need to get doing something or I'm going to start gnawing on the furniture."

I gathered up Ophelia's notes. "Just wait a second. Give me a hand. I have a feeling . . . There's got to be something here." Charlie turned back and I handed him half of the pages.

"What am I doing, exactly?"

"Just look for something useful," I said.

"Like what? A recycling bin?"

I started flipping through the sheets. Charlie held his first one up. The page was covered in curvy letters that wound all over one another.

"What is this? Snake?"

"I don't know. Persian maybe."

Charlie gave me a look. "Zack, I'd have an easier time translating a Klingon war manual. Let's do some gaming."

"No. Wait wait wait." The words came out like machine-gun bullets. "I've found something."

Charlie reached over and pulled the top page down. The words on it were in English. Typed. A letter. It started in midsentence. I set it flat on the desk so we could both read it.

> ". . . bears a shocking similarity to 2 Thessalonians, chapter 2, verse 3, "for that day will not come until the rebellion occurs and the man of lawlessness is revealed.""

The man of lawlessness . . . Who could that be?

Charlie nudged me. I read on silently.

The verse goes on to say that this man, presumably the Antichrist, is doomed to destruction, which is missing from Baoh's prophecy. The chapter continues by suggesting that the Antichrist will claim to be God, which Vlad has never done.

I hit the name Vlad and stopped again. So did Charlie. He looked at me. "Does this make sense to you?"

Not yet, so I kept going.

Regarding the other symbols, I have taken great care to translate them. I see definite parallels with the Revelation of Saint John the Divine, but there is no doubt in my mind that the prophecies of Baoh do not concern the Great Beast, the Antichrist, or the End of Days.

"Who is Baoh?" Charlie asked.

I shook my head. I'd never heard of him. But he sounded like a kind of prophet. Maybe he was a friend of Ophelia's.

Charlie pointed to the text at the end of the last sentence. "There's 'the End of Days' again."

I nodded and kept reading.

... but there is no doubt in my mind that the prophecies of Baoh do not concern the Great Beast, the Antichrist, or the End of Days. Not as it pertains to the human world and the Second Coming of the Messiah. Rather, I think these prophecies concern the fate of carriers, and more specifically, your ward.

Carriers. That was the word my father used for "vampires." Carriers of the pathogen. Those who were infected. My eyes gobbled up the rest of the text.

I have included my translations below. They are in no way complete. Even with the help of modern recording devices, we have been unable to decipher most of what Baoh said. I will forward more should we manage to transcribe them.

"The great hunter shall be sacrificed and make his son an orphan. The sun shall be given the power to scorch him with fire."

"The orphaned son who is and was and is to come shall not be hurt by the second death, though the sun will beat upon him."

"The Lamb will be their shepherd [indecipherable muttering follows] . . . a scourge. He will lead them to springs of living water . . . to destruction. Behold, he is coming soon."

And that was it. Charlie finished. We looked at each other.

"Are there other pages?" he said.

I started looking.

"We need to find more." He searched around the desk. On the floor.

I rifled through the stack one more time to be sure I hadn't missed anything. I came up empty. Charlie didn't. He found another from the mess I'd handed him. He waved the page like a winning scratch ticket.

"It must come right after." He spread it on the desk.

All of our far eastern agents are aware of Baoh's disappearance. Given his power and resources, it is unlikely we will find him. Rather, he will emerge at a time of his own choosing, though the Coven may possess the power to drive him out of hiding and compel his service. Whether they can do this without Vlad is doubtful. His whereabouts remain a mystery. No sign of him has been seen by any of our agents, in any corner of the world. If he has risen from his most recent death, he has chosen not to reveal himself.

The future of the Underground is uncertain. This would seem a prudent time to seek out those carriers with the power of prophecy and those who travel the Spirit Planes.

Be careful. You are now the rock upon which our future rests.

May God's blessings be upon you.

The name at the bottom was handwritten and difficult to read.

"What does it say?" Charlie asked. "Who's it from?"

I lifted the paper. Turned it sideways. Squinted. "I think it says Mutada."

"Mutada? Isn't that from *The Lion King*?"

"No, that's Mustafa. This is one of my father's friends. They hunted vampires together in Afghanistan. My father mentioned it in his journal."

"And this Mutada guy knows Ophelia?"

"It looks that way. We need to find the first page." I flipped through the rest of my pile. "I can't find it."

"Maybe she has it with her. Or it's in one of these books."

There was no way to know without a lengthy search.

Charlie was still staring at the pages. He spread them out so they were side by side. "I can't believe this stuff. This is about you, isn't it? You're the orphaned son. The Lamb. Ophelia's ward."

"Do I look like a lamb to you?"

"No. More like a reject from *Planet of the Apes*."

"Thanks."

"Don't mention it. I wonder who this Baoh character is?" he asked.

I did, too. He was obviously important.

Charlie elbowed me gently on the front of my shoulder. "You're off in la-la land again."

"Sorry. I was just wondering who he could be."

He picked up the note we'd found under the book on Dracula.

THE END OF DAYS IS COMING.

"That's the end of the world, isn't it?"

I wasn't sure. "We need to find Ophelia to see what all this means."

He nodded, then walked over to the phone. "Johansson said they'd be here soon. Why don't you call her?"

The inspector didn't want us calling. Not with the landline. But he didn't say anything about my cell. I picked it up and hit redial. Her voice mail came on straight off.

"It's me again. Please call me right away." I followed this with a text message, just for good measure.

"No luck?" Charlie asked.

"She must be talking to someone. I'm sure she'll call right back."

Charlie plopped down on the sofa and put his feet up. "We should phone the girls."

The girls. He meant Luna and her older sister, Suki. She and Charlie had fallen in love last July. If Stony Lake had been blessed with a tabloid, the two of them would have made the weekly cover. But she wasn't doing well, and it was largely my fault.

The past summer had ended in a night that belonged in a hack-and-slash horror movie. One of Charlie's close friends was brutally murdered. Shortly after that, I went berserk and got arrested. Suki had a front-row seat for most of it. Then, when it seemed things couldn't possibly get any worse, Charlie and Luna were abducted by my uncle Maximilian and handed over to Vlad, who wanted to impale them. Ophelia saved the day. I turned Charlie, and he turned Luna. But Suki was still human. And she was a mess.

I'd spoken to Luna about Suki many times since, and I know Charlie sent her lots of e-mails and called as often as he could afford to. But she just wasn't the same after *that night*. She felt like an outsider. With her living so far away, in Newark, New Jersey, there wasn't a lot we could do. I felt awful about it because I'd gone to

Charlie for help. If I'd done the right thing and stayed away from him and his friends, everyone would still be nicely tanned and living on easy street. Instead, I'd turned his world upside down. Suki's, too. There was no quick fix for this.

"You want to send her a text?" I said.

Charlie shook his head. "I could . . . I'd rather hear her voice. I haven't talked to her in a few days." He took my cell and started scrolling for the number.

It looked as if he was about to say something, but then the other phone rang—the landline that Johansson had told us not to use. We waited. Counted two rings. The pause was supposed to come next. It didn't. The phone just rang and rang and rang. Then it stopped. I waited to see if it would fire up again. It didn't. I snatched it out of the cradle.

"What does it say?" Charlie asked.

"One missed call."

"Can't you see who it was? There's a call display."

"All it says is *unavailable*."

"Who would call us?"

It obviously wasn't Johansson. Someone else from the Underground maybe. I set the phone back in the cradle. Then a loud boom shook the house.

Charlie and I stared at each other. "That came from upstairs," he said.

A second later the front door crashed in. Several people entered. Their footfalls were loud, as if they were wearing Frankenstein boots. An alarm started ringing. That had to be the home security system. They didn't have the password. Not good. Voices started shouting.

"What do we do?" I whispered.

"Look for something we can use."

We both glanced around the room. Charlie grabbed a table lamp. He unplugged it and wrapped the cord around the neck. Then he swung it, testing its weight. Ophelia's note sprang to mind.

Knowledge is your best defense. What did that mean? Was I supposed to hurl books?

The alarm stopped. More people came inside. It sounded like an open house. "Should we go upstairs?" I asked.

Charlie was still thinking. Listening. All I could hear was muffled chatter. And my heart. It was winning the Kentucky Derby. Several sets of footsteps walked across the floor above. They stopped at the door by the top of the stairs. It opened with a creak and the lights flicked on. First one police officer, then another started down the stairwell. Both were wearing bulletproof vests. And both had their guns drawn. The first officer saw me and aimed at my face. Another took aim at Charlie.

"Put that down," he said.

Neither of us moved.

The first kept his gun trained on me. The second stepped down into the room, then spoke into a radio attached to his vest near the shoulder.

"They're in the basement. We're going to need a few more bodies down here."

"Are you Daniel Thomson?" the first one asked me.

I nodded. Daniel was my first name. Only people who didn't know me used it.

"Get down on your knees and put your hands behind your head." The officer's voice was louder this time. He pointed to Charlie. "And you, drop the lamp and do the same. On the ground, hands behind your head."

"We haven't done anything wrong," I said.

"That's for the courts to decide," the policeman replied. "Now do as you're told. Down on your knees. Hands behind your head. You're under arrest for the murder of Everett Johansson."

CHAPTER 8

ARRESTED DEVELOPMENT

I'm sure you've seen this in the movies or on police shows. The bad guys or, in this case, our two innocent heroes get down on their knees, put their hands behind their heads, then get cuffed and hauled away to be interrogated. Things didn't quite follow the script. They never did with Charlie.

He set the lamp down and got on his knees. So did I. A second later, I felt the cold steel of handcuffs circle each wrist. Two other officers were coming down the stairs so that four were now surrounding us. I heard a loud ziplike sound and watched while Charlie's hands were cuffed behind his back.

"We didn't kill Johansson," he said. The end of his tongue was rubbing underneath his upper gums. I'm guessing his teeth were dropping. By the look on his face, he was trying to stay calm. I couldn't actually tell if he was nervous or scared. Then I realized he was angry.

"Deep breaths," I whispered. I made certain I was quiet enough that only he could hear me. "You have to fight it."

He kept his mouth closed. His jaw muscles were tense. His pupils were widening. He was snorting like a bull just before it charges the matador. The officers were watching him. I had to draw their attention.

"Where are we going?" I asked loudly.

No one answered. One of the officers took my elbow instead and lifted me to my feet. They did the same to Charlie. I thought he was going to freak, but he didn't. Then we got escorted up the stairs. One officer was in front of me and another was behind. Charlie was ahead, sandwiched between the two other officers. When he topped the last step, he dropped his chin and whispered so quietly I almost missed it.

"Let's ditch these turkeys. Right now. Come on. Follow my lead."

I heard a snap. It was the sound of Charlie breaking the chain of his handcuffs. He grabbed the officer in front of him, spun, and tossed him back so that he hit the officer behind, who hit the officer in front of me. Charlie was so fast, none of them had time to react. I did. I dropped a step and braced myself so I wouldn't lose my balance when they slammed into me. It was a mistake. I absorbed their momentum, and so the officer behind me wasn't affected by the avalanche. He had time to draw his gun. I caught a glimpse of Charlie's coat. Then the back door was ripped off its hinges. The pistol went off an instant later, right beside my ear. I had no doubt the officer missed Charlie by a mile, but the shock wave from the exploding bullet hit my eardrum like a wrecking ball. Sound disappeared. All I could hear was a shrill ringing. My head began to throb. The officer fired twice more. It made me so dizzy I fell into him. He must have thought I was trying to knock him over—to escape. He started yelling at me. I could see his lips move, but I couldn't tell what he was saying. Then electricity jolted through me. I was paralyzed. I tumbled down the stairs. Aftershocks followed. And more pain. I felt another powerful jolt. And another. Someone was hitting me with a Taser, or a stun gun. I couldn't breathe. I couldn't move. Then my head said, *Enough is enough,* and it turned out the lights.

My ears were still ringing when I came to. I was sitting in a chair, my arms behind my back. A table was in front of me. I tried to stand, but I'd been chained in place. I looked over my shoulder. The wall behind me was a mirror. I turned and gazed at my reflection. A young kid with a stunned expression stared back. His face was bruised. His lip was split. His eyes were bloodshot and tired. I took a deep breath, locked it in my chest, tensed my muscles, and tried to break loose. Iron bit into my wrists. Three or four sets of manacles had to be in place. I held my breath and tried again, but nothing happened. I tested the air with my nose. Smelled coffee and gunpowder. The room was small, off-white, square, with plaster walls, cheap ceiling tiles, and a cement floor.

My ears were still ringing from the officer's gun. It was all I could hear until footfalls approached from the hall. The door opened and a man wearing street clothes and tiny, round-rimmed glasses walked in. He was squat, maybe a foot shorter than me, totally bald, with tree trunks for legs and skin that was well tanned. He might have been a professional wrestler at one time. For just an instant, I was reminded of the Nicholls Ward. I wondered if I'd ever seen him there, then I realized it was his scent. Something on his clothes, like antiseptic or some kind of cleanser, made him smell as if he'd just stepped out of a hospital waiting room. He had a folder in one hand. In the other was a Tim Hortons mug. He raised his index finger, which was easily worth two of mine, pushed the frames of his glasses farther up his nose, and took a cautious sip of coffee. Then he set his drink on the table, pulled out the chair, sat down opposite to me, spread the folder open, looked at it, took a deep breath, and waited. After a cold minute, he looked up at me.

"You're Daniel Zachariah Thomson?"

I nodded. "I go by Zack."

"I've been told that. I'm Detective Baddon."

Baddon. I'd heard that name at the zoo. But I'd never seen this man and didn't know anything about him. He laced his fingers together and set them on the table. A wicked scar was on one of his wrists. I took a closer look at his face. He had to be in his forties. Tired, but alert. His eyes drifted up to the ceiling, then back to me.

"You know you were fingerprinted when you came in?"

I didn't know, but I said nothing. He took off his glasses and rubbed his temples, then slipped the glasses carefully back on. I noticed his eyes were watering. I couldn't tell if he was upset, furious, or just plain exhausted. "You're being charged with murder?"

I nodded. And swallowed.

"The top of Johansson's car was torn off. Like paper. Only a vampire is that strong, Zachary."

Vampire! I heard that word and my heart started to throw two-punch combinations against my rib cage. He knew what I was! I could feel his eyes probing. They were intense and focused. Searching for clues. My mouth was open. It had dried up like the Sahara. I had to clear my throat before I could speak.

"I didn't do it."

He didn't look convinced. "This is a complicated situation, Zachary. You're going to have to give me a little more than that." He flipped through the folder, then rubbed his hand over his head. "Why should I believe you?"

Why would he think I was guilty? Moisture started beading on my forehead. Isn't that just like the body? It takes all the water from your mouth and sends it to your sweat glands.

"Inspector Johansson is a friend."

I paused. He waited. His fingers were tapping on the plastic top of his coffee cup.

"That's it?" He leaned forward on the table again. "You've been accused of murder. You're not going to get a scolding and a slap on the wrist for this. . . . You have to give me more than that."

What else could I say? That the inspector was my supplier? Would that make sense?

"He dropped Charlie and me off at the house, then left. He was fine the last time I saw him. Well, tired. But he's always tired. He was going to look for . . ." I stopped to think. He'd gone to look for Ophelia. I wasn't sure if I should mention her name.

"For whom?" I waited just long enough that he answered for me. "For Ophelia?"

"Yeah."

He nodded and stared. His eyes ran over my face. He wanted to know if I was lying. Or if I knew something else. I looked down at the table and the file spread across its surface. A picture of me was paper-clipped to one side. I tried to see what was written there, but the words were upside down in messy writing. Not the best for a speed read.

"Why would your fingerprints be on his gun?" he asked.

My hand and arm twitched when he said this, as though they remembered the terrible discomfort I'd felt when I'd held the inspector's pistol.

"Did someone shoot him?" I asked.

Detective Baddon shifted in his chair. I'm amazed it didn't collapse from the weight of him.

"No. He fired several shots before the gun was taken from him. Everett said you were the fastest vampire he'd ever seen. Who else but you could have moved so quickly? My bet is, you snatched it away from him, which is why your prints are on the gun. Unless you have another explanation."

I did. But after living under Ophelia's watchful eye, I'd learned the value of keeping my mouth shut. Only a select few were supposed to know about us. I doubted Detective Baddon was one of them. Not if he threw the word *vampire* around. We weren't ever supposed to refer to ourselves that way. Ophelia and the inspector insisted upon that. Part of our secret. I wasn't going to tell him anything.

He waited for me to answer the question. When I didn't, he asked, "What were you doing at the zoo?"

We stared at one another. I wasn't sure if I should trust him. If I told him the truth, he might just use it to fabricate a story that would make me look guilty.

He looked down at the file, then up at me. "It says here you tried to run from the house. Is that true?"

There didn't seem to be any harm in denying this, but I was worried that if I started talking, I might not stop and would say something I wasn't supposed to.

"And your friend. He assaulted several officers and ran. Why would he do that?"

I'm guessing it was because he didn't want to wind up chained to a chair at the police station. I should have followed Charlie's lead. But the mention of his name got me thinking about what he would do in this situation.

"I want to make a phone call," I said.

The detective shook his head. "I can't do that. And you know why?"

I didn't know why, so he explained.

"You aren't a typical prisoner, Zachary. I'm not taking any chances with you. We're going to be moving you to a special detainment center until we get to the bottom of this. Given your special condition, you've been labeled a terrorist—a threat to national security. You won't be afforded the same rights as other prisoners."

A threat to national security. That was nonsense. Chained to this chair, I was about as dangerous as a wet paper towel.

He sat back and looked at me. "Everett trusted you. He was a good friend of mine, and now he's in pieces. I want to know why. I want to know why your fingerprints were on the gun. I want to know why you were at the zoo, and I want to know why Charlie ran. You answer some questions and I'll think about letting you make a phone call. In the meantime, you're going to stay chained up behind bars." He stood up, closed the folder, tucked it under one arm, then picked up his coffee and walked to the door. "I understand as a child vampire, you're an endangered species. Don't make things difficult for us, Zachary, or I'll do the worst thing imaginable. I'll let you go. Given what I know of the Coven, you won't survive a week."

He turned and left me alone in the room. I looked around. My instincts were telling me to pay attention, that I'd missed something on my way down to rock bottom. But my processor had more to consider than it could handle. Inspector Johansson was dead. For some reason, this hadn't really registered, maybe because I didn't see him die, or because I wasn't the one responsible, and so I'd been thinking of the whole thing as one big mistake. But now I was stuck here. And he was really gone. Poor Ophelia! She'd be sick with grief.

And worry. I had to get in touch with her somehow. I pulled the chains so they were tight between my wrists and tested them again. And again. The cuffs bit through my skin. I didn't care. I had to do something. But it was no use. Without a hacksaw or a magic wand, I wasn't going anywhere.

About ten minutes later two officers walked in. They were dressed up like grunts from a video game. Body armor, helmets with face shields. One was armed with a long stick—like a light saber. A Taser. The second one had a shotgun out. He did the click-click routine to get my attention. It worked. Then came the superzap. All I could think was *Not again*. Pain burned through every nerve. The room spun. I gasped and pitched forward. My head hit the table. It made a dull thud. Then my eyes closed and I went under.

CHAPTER 9

THE DREAM ROAD

The room was too bright. I turned away from the light and fell on the floor. It was either daytime or I'd been relocated to a tanning salon. I squinted and looked around. I was in a jail cell. Light spilled through a window set high in a concrete wall. A rough cut of cardboard had been crammed through the bars, but it stopped the light much like a screen stops air. Another wall behind me was made of cinder blocks. I sat up, still squinting. The light was unbearable. It made the skin on my face and neck itch. I could barely see, not that there was much in the way of scenery. A sink. A toilet. A narrow metal bench set into the wall. I had been lying on it until a second ago, before I rolled off onto the floor. I reached up to rub my eyes, but my hands were still chained together, manacled to my waist. My ankles, too. With three sets of chains. I guess Detective Baddon was being true to his word. He wasn't taking any chances.

The itch of my skin became a burn. I rolled underneath the bench set in the wall and pressed my back against the cold concrete. It was the only shaded place in the room. As soon as I was out of the light, the stinging began to subside and I was able to look around more comfortably. Outside my cell, at the near end of the hallway, was a desk. An ordinary-looking police officer was sitting there. His dark skin was wrinkled around his eyes, and his tight, curly black hair was receding up his forehead. He was flipping through pages on a clipboard.

I glanced at the window. It could have been noon or anytime

after. I wasn't going to last a day in this place. Then the light faded. I guessed a thick cloud was moving in front of the sun. It gave my eyes a much needed break. I tried to remember what I knew about jail from movies and TV. Then I stood up and walked over to the door of the cell and cleared my throat. I had to take advantage while the sun was hiding.

"I'd like to make a phone call."

The officer ignored me, so I said it again. And again.

Then he put down his clipboard and pen and stood from his desk to face me. His name tag said OFFICER M. LUMSDEN. "No can do."

"But I haven't called anybody, yet."

He grabbed another chart from his desk and examined it. Then he looked at me as though he'd just exposed a plot to overthrow the government. "Says here it's not permitted. I can't help you."

"Why not?"

He thumbed through his papers and shook his head. "Baddon doesn't want you calling out, plain and simple." He turned around and tossed his clipboard down on his desk. It sat near an exit. Like my cell, it had a door of metal bars closing it off from a short stretch of hallway behind. That meant to escape, I'd have to get through at least two sets of bars: the ones of my cell, and the one for the whole jail.

"It's one phone call. My family needs to know where I am."

Officer Lumsden picked up the clipboard again, then stopped and read for a few seconds. Whatever was written there made him scowl. "Says here you murdered Everett Johansson. Now why, if you killed a good friend of mine, would I reward you by breaking the rules?"

"You aren't breaking any rules. I get legal counsel. I get to talk to a lawyer. I get a phone call."

The officer snorted, then turned back to his desk. "You watch too much television. You got the right to sit on your butt and chill. Says here you're a terrorist. A threat to national security. That means no guests, no phone calls, no legal counsel, no chocolate pudding, no bedtime stories, and no favors."

"I didn't do it."

"Right. Like I'm going to take your word over Detective Baddon, who feeds my cat when I'm out of town. Whose son used to play minor hockey with my son. Who's an honest cop. Like Johansson was—before you killed him." Lumsden scowled at me. "You don't have a lot of friends in this place. Don't be bothering me again."

I wanted to tell him that the inspector was a friend of mine, too, but I sensed I would have had an easier time convincing him I was the king of Spain. "Can I have some water?"

I didn't get an answer. It didn't matter. What use was a glass of water? I'd be better off asking for some sunscreen. I went back to the metal bed and lay down on the cold floor underneath. With the manacles around my ankles and no pillow, it was about as comfortable as a bed of sharp stones.

Time passed. I drifted off. I dreamt I was back at our house running on the treadmill. My trial was on television. First I was accused of vandalizing the zoo. Then I was accused of killing Everett Johansson. I was also charged with breaking into his house and wrecking one of his lamps. As if that really mattered. The prosecuting lawyer was Clint Eastwood. He was wearing his cowboy outfit and riding on a mule. Every now and then he'd pull out his gun and shoot someone's hat off, and the jury would shout things like "What a classic!" and "Go ahead. Make my day." My lawyer was a Ken doll. The judge was charging him with contempt of court because he wasn't wearing any pants. Don't ask me what it all meant. I only mention it because one second I was sitting alone on my couch watching the fiasco unfold, and the next minute Ophelia was sitting beside me.

"Interesting program." She was dressed in her old nurse's uniform.

"They're about to announce the verdict." I turned back to the television. My stomach was trying to tear itself loose. I knew I was going to get put away for life if they found me guilty.

Ophelia stood up and turned the TV off. "Asleep or awake, television is generally a waste of time."

I sensed I wasn't dreaming anymore. I wasn't exactly awake, but dreams have a certain quality, and so does real life. I would have put this somewhere in the middle. Then the scenery changed. The walls of the room faded to black and the comfortable bedroom around me transformed itself to the outdoor play area of the zoo.

"What just happened?" I asked.

"I just turned off the television," Ophelia said. "And you changed the scenery."

I looked around. The two dead wolves were lying on the ground, their blood oozing into the sand. I could hear a rusty set of swings creaking in the wind.

"We're examining the crime scene." Ophelia kneeled on the ground and began inspecting the bootprints that led to the water where Charlie and I had seen the fight.

"That's not what I mean. I know where this is. But it's not right." I waved at the play structures and the teeter-totters.

"We are walking the Dream Road together."

"What's that?"

Ophelia smoothed out the folds of her skirt, then looked at me flatly, as though we were talking about the weather. "The Dream Road is one of our best-kept secrets."

That didn't tell me much. She kept everything a secret. My curiosity must have been obvious because she followed this with an unusual amount of detail.

"When you dream, your mind enters a different state of consciousness. One that allows me to enter your thoughts and direct them somewhat. It's my talent."

So that was it. Charlie and I had never been able to figure out what she could do. Vampire talents were a real fascination for us. Charlie thought Ophelia had the power to charm people, like vampires in the storybooks. They could often get people to do things with the force of their minds. Everyone did backflips whenever

Ophelia gave the order. We figured there had to be more to it than just good looks and a strong will.

"Why haven't you ever visited me before?"

She smiled. "I used to do it all the time when you were young. It kept you from having nightmares when you first moved to the Nicholls Ward. But as you got older, there wasn't the same need. And it does involve a slight invasion of privacy, which became harder to justify. I only like to do it if it's necessary. And it doesn't always work."

"So you can visit people in their dreams? Anyone?"

She shook her head. "Not anyone, only vampires. Visiting normal people is forbidden. This is not something they can know about. But I can visit those whose minds I know well enough to navigate. It is a tricky business, getting in. And getting out. It's easy to become trapped."

I didn't get it, but I nodded anyway.

"Are you okay?" she asked.

"For now. But Detective Baddon says I'm going to stay in jail until I cooperate."

"*What?*" she shouted. It was so loud I was sure it shook the nearby trees.

"I said—"

"I know what you said. Are you telling me you're *in jail*?"

"Yeah."

"You're supposed to be in one of my safe houses! In East City!"

"I was, but I got arrested."

"For what?"

"For murdering Inspector Johansson."

I watched her face shift from surprise to shock. She looked at me carefully. My expression must have convinced her that I was perfectly serious, because her eyes drifted down and lost their focus. This happened when her thoughts turned inward. Charlie said it was exactly what happened to me. A second later, she reached up with one hand and started rubbing at her temples. I called this her headache pose. A short breath escaped her lips. I could hear two quiet words. "Oh, no." She didn't speak for another half minute. Then she came out of it and started asking questions.

"Are you sure he's dead?"

I wasn't, and I said so.

"When did it happen?"

"Last night. Right after he left Charlie and me."

"Why do they think it was you?"

"His car was torn apart. And my fingerprints were on the gun."

"How is that possible?"

I explained how he'd offered it to me because no one was available to watch over the house, and that touching it had caused me pain, so I'd handed it back.

Ophelia started chewing on the inside of her lip. "You are starting to develop a kind of instinct that Vlad had about things. Objects and their feel."

"Is it my talent?" I asked, surprised. I thought you had to be alive a lot longer for this kind of thing to happen.

"Not exactly."

I tried to keep my disappointment from showing, but Ophelia didn't miss much.

"It's something I don't really understand, Zachary. I get bad feelings about things, too. Nothing that approaches pain, but I've learned the hard way that these feelings shouldn't be ignored." She glanced around the children's playground, then down toward the river. "I need to know what happened here. Can you show me?"

"How?"

"Just think about what happened."

That was easy enough. I started with the rave. Being seen by the first vampire. And the second one that dropped from the roof. Running away. Arriving home and finding blood in the driveway, then again at the river. The torn wolf pen. Following the vampire's trail to the water. As I remembered things, the dreamscape around us changed. Everything I thought took on shape and color. It was like being in a movie, only it was my life happening around the two of us, unfolding just as it had. The creature emerging from the woods to attack the vampire. When she saw it, Ophelia was so startled she took a step back.

"What do you think it is?" I asked.

She shook her head and started chewing her lip again. "It might be a vampire. The pathogen does strange things in some people. But it's possible he's a lycanthrope of some kind. A shape changer. That is our best hope."

"A lycanthrope. You mean a werewolf?"

"Yes."

"I thought werewolves turned into wolves."

"I think, like vampires, the range of possibilities is broad. Your father once hunted a werewolf, did you know that?"

I did. My father had written about it in his journal. I wished I still had it, but it had disappeared from my uncle's office, along with Vlad's corpse. According to my father's narrative, he and my uncle Maximilian had used bear traps to catch it. In the end, because it wouldn't stop killing, they had to poison it with hemlock.

"Did you tell Detective Baddon about this?"

"It didn't come up."

"Well... He'll find out soon enough." She raised a hand and started rubbing at her temples again, then stopped to stare at me. "Where is Charlie?"

"I don't know. He ran when we were arrested."

"You don't know?"

"He ran off."

"Oh, no," she whispered. Her hand rose to her forehead. "That means he's alone. With that thing out there."

I'm ashamed to admit this, but I'd been so concerned about myself—that I was under arrest and in jail—I hadn't considered that Charlie might be in more trouble than me. "Can't you find him on the Dream Road?"

Ophelia's eyebrows rose just a fraction of an inch and she stared off into space. "It's possible, if he's sleeping. But I don't know him well enough to find him or get inside his mind. You'll have to do that."

"How?"

"I'll show you." She tipped her head down the street. "This way. We should hurry."

We started walking back in the direction of Trent University. "Where are we going?"

"To a window. Do you see it?"

A small patch of landscape was shifting in the air. It looked like shimmering water. That had to be it.

"When you visit someone on the Dream Road, you must leave a window behind, an exit, so that you can leave."

"That's a window."

She nodded, then stopped in front of it. The shimmering patch was about the size of her hand.

"So how do we fit through it?"

Ophelia smiled. She reached in with a finger, then pulled her hand down to the ground. It left a seam in the air, like a rip in the fabric of space-time. Stephen Hawking would have jumped out of his chair if he'd seen this. She stepped through as if she were walking behind a curtain.

"Quickly, Zachary, before it closes."

I followed. A film like a soap bubble passed over me. I reached up to touch my face, but it wasn't wet. A soft, warm glow was around me.

"I've been here before." My voice echoed through the light. I was walking, but nothing was under my feet but a hazy white glow. No walls were around me. Nothing above. Just the same pale glimmer. It was coming from a long way away, in every direction. I tested the air with my nose, but smelled nothing. It was like having a cold.

"Yes, you have been here," said Ophelia. "But not since you were a child. This is the Nexus of the Dream Road."

She was beside me. Shining, as I was. My skin and clothes were luminescent. We were two glow-in-the-dark ghosts.

"What is it?"

"The Dream Road? It's a series of conduits. Like highways that connect the minds of all sentient beings. The Nexus is where they all come together."

"I don't get it."

She smiled. "You don't have to. Just like the waking world, you are part of it, whether you understand it or not."

"This is some talent."

She laughed. Then she answered the question I was getting ready to ask. "You will discover your true talent in time, Zachary. Be patient. You're still young. It might be years before it is fully manifest."

Years? I didn't think I was going to last the week.

"So how do we do this?" I asked.

She looked away and closed her eyes. "Listen."

I strained to hear. My heart was beating. My lungs slowly expanded. Air rushed in through my mouth and nose, then rushed out again. Eventually I heard them. They were faint at first. Voices. Thousands of them. Their words were overlapping and impossible to separate. "Who is it?"

I heard Ophelia sigh quietly. Even with my eyes closed, when she spoke, I could tell she was smiling. "These are the Dream Roads, Zachary. Everyone who sleeps and dreams has a voice here."

"Are they all vampires?"

She shook her head.

"Is Luna's in here?"

"Stay focused, Zachary. Charlie is the one in trouble right now. Keep your mind on him."

I wasn't going to start a debate. Instead, I listened to the voices. Together, they sounded like hundreds of radio stations playing all at the same time. Everything overlapped. "How do you separate them?"

"You don't have to. We simply need to find one voice. Charlie's. Then you can follow it to his dream and speak with him."

"How?"

"Think of him, and listen."

"That's all?"

"I'll handle the rest."

I closed my eyes again and imagined Charlie as if he were standing in front of me. A bit shorter. Dark hair. Serious, but silly. Eyes intense. Smiling. I pictured the two of us at Stony Lake, bombing around in his tin boat. Nothing happened.

"I'm not having any luck," I said.

"Perhaps he's not asleep. Give it one more try."

I pictured the two of us with the girls, Suki and Luna, sitting around a campfire at their old cottage.

I heard a voice. It was faint. My mind zeroed in on it and I started floating away, don't ask me how. Ophelia was speaking behind me. She told me to wait, but I didn't. I felt a strong pull and let it carry me away. Ophelia's voice faded, and the one I was following got louder, clearer, more defined. And more feminine. The white light began to change and I passed through the soap bubble again. Everything was blurry, but I could see colors now. Like a scene through a film of water.

Window . . .

The word jumped quietly into my head. I almost missed it. Then I heard someone else.

"I didn't know there was a test today!"

Panic. I could sense it. I was in a classroom, right in the middle of a row of desks. A teacher was telling people to sit down. He had a suit vest on, and bifocals. A patch of hair was missing right on the dome of his head.

"Young man," he said to me. "Would you please show some consideration for your classmates and take your seat so that we can start the test."

I'd never been in a high school before. It seemed tense. No wonder Charlie had skipped so often. I glanced in the direction the teacher was nodding. An empty seat was waiting beside me. Beyond that, a wall covered in inspirational posters was taking shape. I remembered I had to leave a window, so I stuck my hand in the colors and shapes as they solidified. It felt as if I were touching the soap bubble again. It left a clear, shimmering patch in the wall. My exit.

"Please hurry. We need to get started," the teacher said.

I angled myself sideways to slip into the chair beside me, then realized I was being ridiculous. I wasn't here to take a test. I tried to imagine what Charlie would do. Believe it or not, it helped immensely. I looked the man square in the eyes and told him I'd take the zero. He made a face. I turned and walked to the other side of the class. Luna was sitting there. I was supposed to be in Charlie's dream, but my mind obviously had other plans.

Luna had a pile of books open in front of her on the desk and was frantically turning pages. "I didn't even know I was in this course." She was talking to a girl beside her with a blond ponytail and braces.

I closed Luna's books.

"What are you doing?" Then she looked up. "Oh, Zack. Thank God. Do you know what this test is on?"

I started to laugh.

"Young man," the teacher said again. "What exactly are you doing here?"

I had no idea what to say to this, but it was just a dream, so it didn't really matter. "I need to borrow this woman. She has information that is critical to national security."

Luna had gone back to flipping through pages. I turned back to her. "It's the summertime, you know? You aren't supposed to be here."

The pages began to turn more slowly.

"And you're a vampire now. You don't go to school anymore."

That hit a button. She looked at me. Her emerald green eyes were clearer than I remembered. This time last year, they'd floored me. She tucked one of her copper curls behind her ear. She looked stunning. I smiled. She smiled. We were smiling together. It was wonderful.

"How did you find me here?"

I waved a hand at the door. "Let's get out of here and I'll explain." Then I took one last look around. The faces were pure stress. It was exactly the way Charlie described it. "Man, why do people do this to their kids? It feels just like jail."

CHAPTER 10

CATCHING UP

I did my best to describe the Dream Road to Luna.

"I don't believe it," she said afterward. "This is incredible."

I didn't really believe it, either. But there we were. She reached up and cupped my face in her hands. I closed my eyes and pressed her fingers closer. I would have been happy to just stand like this for weeks. Then she changed the dreamscape. We were suddenly back at her old cottage. Her parents had sold it after *that night*. But it was exactly the way I remembered it, the last time we were all together. A porch swing was creaking behind us. Luna took a seat, then pulled me down beside her. She started playing with the charm on her necklace. The golden crescent. It fit alongside the silver moon I wore around my neck. The two pieces made one necklace, her slender, golden chain lacing through my thicker links of silver. I'd only seen them together once, the day Vlad had tried to kill us. They were old heirlooms and had once belonged to Ophelia. She'd gifted them to my parents. When they died, the two pieces passed to Luna and me.

"You seem anxious," she said.

I didn't know where to begin. "I was supposed to be looking for Charlie." I gazed out over the waters of Stony Lake. Near the dock, the image was clear. But farther from the shore, the dreamscape got blurry. Formless.

"Is he okay?" she asked.

I didn't know.

She squeezed my hand. I watched her do it, but the sensation wasn't quite right. Then I remembered we were in a dream.

"It can't be that bad," she said.

Our eyes met. My expression must have set her straight because she glanced away, nervously, then tried to force a smile. She knew Charlie had been struggling. We spoke about once a week, and it came up often. We used to text each other constantly, but her parents found out and took her phone away.

"He's missing," I said. This required a bit of an explanation. I should probably have started at the beginning and just told the whole story, but conversations don't really go that way. They sort of jump all over. We hit all the major topics. The rave. The zoo. The battle by the river between the vampire and the other creature. My arrest and interrogation. The Underground. Inspector Johansson's death. Even the letter Charlie and I had found with the prophecies. It took all day, and as I said before, the conversation bounced around like a rubber ball. She held my hand the whole time. She only had to ask me if I was serious about a hundred times. In the end, she was visibly shaken. She looked over the water, stood, then sat, then stood again.

"I guess this means I won't be able to come and visit. I was hoping my parents would let me go in a few weeks."

When she saw the look on my face, she reached down and touched my cheek again. "I'm sorry. I know we talked about it all year. Maybe you could come here?"

I wasn't going anywhere.

"Is there some way for me to get in touch with you? Get you a lawyer?"

I didn't think the regular rules were going to apply for me.

"This is a disaster." She sat down again. "Suki is already a mess. If she finds out Charlie's missing . . ."

"He wanted to call her," I said. "Maybe he managed it while we've been sleeping."

She nodded. "She wants to come up, too. I think . . . I think she wants to be turned. She's asked me to do it. I wanted to talk to Ophelia first. But I got the impression if I didn't get on it soon, Charlie would just go ahead and take care of it himself."

This was crazy. "Her timing could be a little better." I was going to mention that young vampires were an endangered species, but Luna knew this already. "What do your parents think?"

Luna shook her head. "They're helpless. Nothing is good right now. Suki has terrible nightmares. That's when she can sleep at all. Mom and Dad had to pull her from school this year, so she hardly spends any time around her old friends. She doesn't talk to most of them anymore. She says they don't understand her. And she's right. They don't. She sees a psychiatrist, but it doesn't make much of a difference."

"Does she think becoming a vampire is going to help?"

Luna looked at me. Her eyes were watering. "Could it possibly make things worse? Most days, I'm the only one she talks to. And she's madly in love with Charlie—from the minute she saw him. I'm not lying. He walked into the sailing club, and that was it. You know the goofy grin he has? He made some wisecrack and it was game over."

I'd heard this before. Charlie's version was much the same, only I seemed to recall his mentioning dimples and a pair of bronzed legs. I kept this to myself.

"So she knows you're a vampire?" I asked.

"Yeah. I know I was supposed to keep it a secret. But—I couldn't hide it from her. It just felt wrong." Luna pulled her foot up on the swing and rested her chin on her knee.

"Do your parents know, too?"

She took a long time to answer. "Not really. My dad knows what's wrong. And he knows he can't fix it. He tried a full blood transfusion, but it didn't do a thing. I guess the infection gets right into the cells."

I nodded. "Ophelia tried that with me. I used to have to get them every few months. God, I don't miss that."

"No. It was terrible. And he was crushed. He was so hopeful it would make all of this go away. But there's no cure, is there?"

I shook my head. "If there was, would you want to take it?"

She took a deep breath. Her answer took a while. "I'm not sure."

"But your father would want you to?"

"Definitely. My mother, too."

"What about Suki?"

Luna's head tipped to one side. "No. She'd rather be like me. Like Charlie. We talk about it. Joke about it. She stays up like I do so we can spend time together. Then she crashes and sleeps twenty hours in a row. It's driving my parents crazy. They fight all the time now. My dad . . . I imagine it must upset him a lot, having two daughters with problems he can't solve. He spends his entire day helping other people and he can't even help his own family."

I fell back into the swing and let my head slip down against the backrest. My stomach was a bed of thorns. It honestly felt as if I'd swallowed a cactus. I'm sure it was guilt. The mess Luna was describing came right back to me, and my decision to involve Charlie with my problems. If I'd stayed away, he'd be at Stony Lake right now, teaching sailing to kids with Suki and Luna. Instead of having to sell their cottage, Dr. and Mrs. Abbott would be up there, too, a picture-perfect American family.

"Is it serious?" I asked.

Luna took a deep breath. She put her fingers in her hair and combed it away from her eyes. Right away, it fell back. "I hope not."

"I hope not, too." I pushed my feet down against the porch to get the swing moving. I was hoping it might help unknot my stomach. It didn't work. I started feeling seasick.

"Are you all right?"

I didn't know what to say. With all the trouble I'd caused everyone else, it didn't seem right to say that I felt terrible inside, that I was feeling sorry for myself. Everyone else deserved sympathy, not me.

"I'll be fine," I said, "just as soon as I get out of jail."

Luna started to laugh. Our conversation had been so serious, I was a bit surprised to hear it.

"Of all the boys to fall for, I had to choose a vampire who ends up in jail. Boy, do I know how to pick 'em, or what?"

CHAPTER 11

VISITATIONS

Time is deceptive. Chain a guy to a chair in the police station and five minutes feels like five hours. But put the same guy on a porch swing with the girl of his dreams, and five hours passes in a heartbeat. Before I knew what was happening or why, Luna started to disappear. I remembered what Ophelia had said about getting stuck. I panicked.

"Quickly! Take us back to school."

Luna's eyes were starting to close. She was like a ghost now, slowly fading. I shook her shoulder gently. "Look at me," I shouted. "Take me back to your classroom."

Her eyes fluttered open. I could see the swing right through her body. "Your test," I said. "You still need to take your test."

That hit a note. The cottage and lake faded. Luna and I were sitting on a desk. She was reclined and falling asleep.

"Young man," said a voice. "Just what do you think you're doing?"

I felt something poke my shoulder. I turned. The teacher with the vest and thinning hair was jabbing me with a ruler.

"You make a mockery of the education system." He poked me again.

"Ah, sorry, but you managed that on your own." I reached past him to the window—the small shimmering patch I had left in the wall. The rest of the room was blurring. I pulled the window open as Ophelia had done in my dream, and I slipped through just as the teacher jabbed me one last time in the shoulder.

I woke up. Officer Lumsden was prodding me through the bars of my cell with a baton of some kind.

"Oh. I thought you were dead." He said it as if he was disappointed to learn otherwise. "On your feet."

I asked him why I had to get up, but he didn't answer. My wrists and ankles were still chained to my waist. My hands had fallen asleep and were starting to hurt. After moving unfettered through my dream, and Luna's, it was frustrating to be inhibited in this way and was a reminder of how much trouble I was in. I rose awkwardly and looked around. My fingers went all pins and needles. I clenched my teeth and waited for the feeling to pass.

A young boy about my age, maybe a little younger, was being admitted. I don't know why I had to be awake for this—maybe they didn't want me snoozing. I felt that I was on display. I probably was. The boy looked as if he was ready to have a nervous breakdown. I wondered what he'd done to get himself in trouble. I listened carefully to what the men were saying. All I caught above the rattle of my chains was that he'd stolen his neighbor's Porsche. Then Officer Lumsden signed him in, and an older guard with a mustache led him down the hall. His eyes were so wide and frightened, you'd think he was being marched to the electric chair. He slowed a bit as he walked past and looked in at me. The moment we made eye contact, the guard prodded him gently with a short baton.

"Hey! You keep your eyes to yourself, understand?"

I'm not sure which of us the guard was talking to.

The boy was taken to the farthest cell in the row. The officer waved him in, then locked the door.

"That kid down there is dangerous," he said in a quiet voice. "A cop killer. He's going away for life. You're lucky. You could have killed someone tonight. Then you'd be in the same boat."

I heard the boy swallow. He glanced my way again.

"Don't even look at him," the officer hissed. "Understand?" The kid nodded. Then the guard walked back with his baton out. It clacked against each bar in the row of cells. When he reached Officer Lumsden, he stopped.

"What is it with these rich kids?"

"Boredom," said Officer Lumsden. Then the phone rang. He picked it up and pressed a button next to the display. "Lumsden here." After a few seconds, he said, "Okay . . . sure thing." After hanging up, he looked straight at his colleague and made a face as if he'd just been canned. "You won't believe it, but that kid has a visitor already."

"Are you surprised?" the older officer asked. "The way parents bubble-wrap their kids these days. Mommy and daddy to the rescue. It makes me sick. Like they don't want him to be accountable. They probably have a high-priced Toronto lawyer who makes my salary in a day. So he gets off with nothing." The guard followed this up with a thorough description of where, exactly, he wanted to place his foot.

"So the kid's spoiled. He's still a saint compared to this other one." Officer Lumsden nodded in my direction.

"Yeah, keeps things in perspective, doesn't it?" The older guard scowled, stroked his mustache, then buzzed himself out. As he turned, I noticed he had a gun holstered to his waist. Officer Lumsden didn't have one. I wondered why.

Officer Lumsden went back to his seat and picked up his clipboard. A minute or so later his phone rang and he pressed a button. I heard footfalls coming from around the corner. The older officer reappeared with the kid's visitor a step behind. I rose and stood at the bars of my cell to get a closer look. Something about the smell wasn't right.

The two stopped at the set of bars closing off the jail from the rest of the police station. Officer Lumsden buzzed them through and I got a good look at the visitor. He was tall, even without the top hat, and was tottering on his feet as if the ground were heaving beneath him. He looked half-alive. His face was covered in short stubble, and his long hair, a mix of black and white and gray, was tangled as if a bomb had just detonated in his face. He was wearing a long, filthy overcoat. Worst of all was the reek of sweat and booze that preceded him into the hall. The older officer with the mustache started frisking him and had to turn his head away to breathe. The visitor seemed indifferent. He glanced around the jail. His eyes were pale blue, as if someone had bleached out most of the color.

I knew who he was.

I met John Entwistle last year when he stole a police cycle and crashed through the front doors of the Nicholls Ward. Then he helped me escape in a Ford Mustang—also stolen from the cops. This set off a series of unfortunate events that led to *that night*. He claimed to be the oldest vampire in the Western World—over six and a half centuries. It was hard to believe. He didn't look a day over two hundred. But he was supposed to be dead, firebombed by my uncle Maximilian. I realized when I saw him that he must have been the vampire from the river, the one Charlie and I had seen with the fence post.

He was plastered. He swayed on his feet as if he might collapse under the weight of his stovepipe hat. I felt as if I were looking at a ghost. I kept expecting him to acknowledge me in some way, to say something to dispel my shock, but he didn't.

"You here to see the Mowry boy?" Officer Lumsden asked.

"Yeah, I need to find a good car thief. I need a lift to Argentina. I hear they don't extradite." The old vampire gazed to the far end of the hall where the young boy was being held. "Yeah, that's him."

Officer Lumsden wrote something on his clipboard. Then he handed it to Mr. Entwistle, who put his signature on it. His hand was unsteady.

"You a relation?" Officer Lumsden asked.

"No. I'm his mentor."

Officer Lumsden shook his head back and forth. The old vampire started forward. "Wait," the officer told him. He reached out and stopped Mr. Entwistle with one hand. The other hand snatched a paper bag from the inside pocket of Mr. Entwistle's coat. "How did you get through with this?" Lumsden removed a bottle of whiskey from the bag and whistled in surprise. Then he opened a drawer of his desk and put the bottle inside.

"Do you have a coat check?" Mr. Entwistle swayed forward. The two men collided.

Officer Lumsden pulled his head back from the horrible smell that erupted from Mr. Entwistle's mouth and snapped, "Watch it."

Then he stood aside to make room for his colleague, the man with the mustache, who was to accompany the old vampire down the hall. I was still standing against the door to my cell.

The older officer had his baton out again and tapped it against the cell bars. He nodded for me to move away. "Back up."

Mr. Entwistle starting backing up.

"Not you."

The old vampire stopped. He was only a few feet away, but he pretended not to see me. Either that or he was seeing double and didn't know which version to look at. He took an unsteady step, then he fell down right outside my cell. His face crashed awkwardly into the bars. Something slid across the floor and hit the toe of my shoe. He was hacking too loudly for anyone else to notice. Without looking down, I stepped on it to keep it out of sight. It was thin. A coin maybe. Then he stood up. He was still swaying, but his eyes were clear and bright.

"I saw you trip me," he shouted to the guard behind him. "That's police brutality."

The older man just rolled his eyes. "Move along."

But Mr. Entwistle didn't budge. He squinted, then pointed at me. "I know you. You're the guy who murdered Everett Johansson."

"That's enough," said the escort. "Keep moving."

I looked over at Officer Lumsden to see what he was making of all this. He put his coffee down and grabbed the telephone on his desk. At the other end of the hall, the young boy was on his feet. Recognition was in his eyes. And fear. I would have bet my last night of freedom that he'd seen Mr. Entwistle before.

The old vampire started hacking as if he were going to drop dead. I wondered how he could be that drunk. Booze, I guess. He cleared his throat and wiped his mouth with the back of a glove. It was filthy. He would have been better off using the bottom of his boot. Then he glanced at me and winked.

"And you broke into that house and didn't even steal anything. All those priceless antiques. I don't care if he was a friend of yours, you could have made a fortune. Kids these days . . . Useless . . . You're worse than that Porsche-stealing vagrant down the hall." Mr. Entwistle's voice rose as he spoke.

I glanced quickly at the kid, who blanched and looked away.

"Don't worry, neighbor," the old vampire shouted, pointing a finger. "I'll get to you in a minute."

The escort swung his baton forward. It extended like a telescope into something the length of his arm. "Back upstairs," he said to Mr. Entwistle. "You're not visiting anyone tonight."

Officer Lumsden stepped away from his desk. Meanwhile, Mr. Entwistle looked back at me and shook his head as if he were totally disgusted.

"I hope they throw the book at you, boy." Then he turned to the two guards. "As a thief and a murderer, that kid is a total failure. I tell you, when they stopped strapping kids in school, this country went straight down the tubes."

He gave me one last look, then stumbled past both officers to the barred gate. He stood there, waiting for them to buzz it open, then bent over and started gagging as if he were going to throw up. Officer Lumsden glanced over at me, then pressed a buzzer to open the door. Mr. Entwistle gripped it by the bars and started pulling it toward him. A second later, he stumbled backward and fell to the ground. It ripped the bars of the gate right out of the wall.

"Oops." He stared at the ruined mess of twisted metal in his hands. "Made in China—I'd bet my hat."

Officer Lumsden put his hands over his head. Parts of the ceiling and wall pulled away. It filled the hall with dust and bits of concrete. The escort recovered sooner. He swung with his baton. Before it made contact, Mr. Entwistle dropped the gate, spun, and grabbed his arm. Then he tossed the man up against the wall. The old vampire kept a hand on his chest and forced out all of his air. The officer started to wheeze, then passed out. Mr. Entwistle eased him down. Then he kicked the ruined bars against the wall, walked over to the desk, opened the top drawer, and smiled.

"Almost forgot my booze." He took out his whiskey. "Hard to stay drunk without it."

Officer Lumsden reached under the desk. I heard a click. When he looked up, the surprise on his face was comical. Mr. Entwistle was holding a gun. He must have taken it from the other officer. How he did it without my seeing, I have no idea.

"Not a good idea—bringing guns down into a jail." The old vampire was suddenly sober. "All kinds of vermin down here. You never know what might happen."

Officer Lumsden put his hands up slowly. "Now don't do anything foolish."

"A bit late for that, wouldn't you say?" Mr. Entwistle waved the gun at me. "Well, what are you waiting for?"

I lifted my foot. Underneath was a key. I bent down and picked it up, then undid the cell door and waddled into the hall.

CHAPTER 12

ESCAPE

M r. Entwistle reached into his coat and pulled out another set of keys. When Officer Lumsden saw them, I thought he was going to fall over. While he gawked in despair, Mr. Entwistle undid all three of my manacles. Then he stepped aside so I could make my exit, but not before turning down the hall to address the kid in the far cell.

"You should be ashamed of yourself, Shawn, taking advantage of an elderly man."

The boy, Shawn, stood and grabbed the bars of his cell. He looked as if he was about to have a meltdown. "But you told me I could take it," he shouted. "You told me . . ."

Mr. Entwistle paused. "Did I . . . ? He scratched the side of his head with the gun barrel. "You know, I think you're right. I did tell you it was all right to take it. That must explain why I gave you the keys. Sorry, neighbor. I take back what I said—and all that stuff about your parents, too. I guess I'll have to drop the charges." Then he turned to Officer Lumsden. "Don't even think about calling up or setting off an alarm." He waved the gun for emphasis.

"Pull an alarm. Are you out of your mind?" Officer Lumsden said. "You're on closed-circuit TV. There's cameras all over the place down here. Everybody in the station can see you. They'll bust down here in about two seconds." He still had his hands up. He pointed one at the ceiling where two cameras were glued to both of us.

"Sneaky. I usually charge an arm and a leg to make a television appearance." Mr. Entwistle raised his hat to the cameras, then turned to me. "Do I need to say it?"

"Say what?"

"Run!"

I bolted past the broken gate and down the hall. What else could I do? My life had become too absurd to make any rational decisions. We rounded the corner. About a dozen officers were waiting at the bottom of the stairs. They were moving forward cautiously, guns out, all decked out in gas masks and bulletproof vests. The first two were carrying big see-through shields. A can of tear gas came bouncing down the hall. I started coughing. An officer started shouting from behind the shield men. He was holding a megaphone.

"Drop the gun. Down on your knees. Hands behind your heads. This will be your only warning."

Mr. Entwistle came to a stop right beside me. I couldn't see much else. I was hacking and my eyes were useless. Billows of yellow gas filled the air. The wall of police officers ahead of us became one big smear. I got down on my knees and put my hands on my head. I was getting good at this. In an instant officers were in front of me with shotguns. They were looking for Mr. Entwistle. He'd disappeared.

Several more cans of tear gas bounced down the hall and the two officers beside me started coughing. Their masks were gone. One got upended. The other turned and shot a cloud of bullets into the wall behind me. Another officer stepped forward, then flew into the air as if he'd stepped into the basket of an air balloon. I could barely see. The other officers were shouting at one another: "Where did he go?" and "What the . . . ?" and finally "Who's throwing that tear gas?"

Another can and another and another were suddenly bouncing along the cement floor. Half a dozen of them were pouring thick yellow vapor into the air. A gas mask landed near my feet. I put it on, then had to duck as a body went flying past me. Then someone grabbed hold of my collar and tossed me through the air. I flew over the other officers, the ones who were crouched at the far end of the hall. My appearance was so sudden, several had to duck to get out of my way. One shot at me with a pistol, and a bullet grazed my shoulder. Then I hit a door and took it right off the hinges.

I got up running. Somehow my gas mask was off. I'm guessing my unexpected trip through the door had ripped it loose. More shots echoed behind me. As I approached a set of stairs, a second bullet nicked my thigh. I stumbled. I might have tumbled down the steps, but Mr. Entwistle took hold of me again and I shot forward toward another set of doors. I was about to stumble through them, but they exploded into pieces just in the nick of time. Mr. Entwistle had darted past at the last second and taken them off the hinges. He was now in front of me, dressed like a one-man assault team, body armor and all. In the haze, with a gas mask on, he looked like one of them.

"The hall turns left," he said.

I slowed to take the corner.

"Oh, no, you don't." Mr. Entwistle grabbed me by the arm and pushed me forward. "The hall goes left, we go straight."

We did. Right into the wall. I turned and took most of the impact on my shoulder. A sharp jolt shot down my arm and I fell to my knees. Then Mr. Entwistle started a Bruce Lee routine that would have seen him nominated into the martial arts hall of fame. He hit the wall furiously with his fists. Cracks appeared in the mortar, then he rammed several cinder blocks out of place. In an instant, he'd made a hole. He widened it with his foot until it was big enough to duck through, then he grabbed me by the back of my shirt and pulled me along behind.

I found myself in an underground parking lot. Police cars were everywhere: SUVs, vans, cars, and paddy wagons.

"Are you all right?" he asked.

I had landed face-first on the pavement. Pain shot down my arm, and the bullet wounds in my leg and shoulder burned. I groaned.

"Is that *aaahhhh* as in *good,* or *aaahhhhh* as in *bad*?"

"Bad," I muttered.

He reached down to help me to my feet. "Well then, boy," he

whispered in my ear, "let me make it up to you. Pick any car in the lot, any car, and it's yours."

I took a quick look around. I remembered our last ride together. It had ended with the car falling apart and the two of us spiraling into the Otonabee River.

"You leaning towards another Ford Mustang?" he asked.

I shook my head.

He snorted. "Been there, done that, eh? Well, I can respect a man who learns from his mistakes. I try to do likewise. The Ford does have muscle, but perhaps we need something with a little more heft. Just give it a minute, I'm sure the car you want will leap out at you any second now."

No sooner had he spoken than I heard a rumble like an earthquake. The garage doors in front of us burst inward. Something enormous punched through and bounced over the front end of a cruiser. It looked like a cross between a monster truck and an armored personnel carrier, the kind you see troops driving in missions overseas—angled plates of thick metal. Dust, cement, glass, and steel went flying everywhere. The car was coming straight for us. I fell to the pavement. Right beside me was a Humvee. I tried to roll underneath it, but the only person I know who can move fast after he's been shot twice is Will Smith. Then the armored car skidded to a halt in front of Mr. Entwistle.

He tucked the gun behind his back. "You coming?"

I didn't answer. My mouth was hanging open. He helped me to my feet. "This is yours?"

"Yup." His eyebrows rose and he smiled. "A testament to my near infinite capacity to err and learn. Quite something, isn't it?"

"I'll say."

He looked at me and laughed. "Well, just wait till you see my chauffeur."

CHAPTER 13

MR. ENTWISTLE

The old vampire reached down and took hold of my pants at the waist. Then he tossed me on top of the car. An instant later, he landed beside me. A round hatch was between us. He twisted a handle and pulled it open, then lowered me inside. The air smelled like motor oil and steel. I looked around. There, in the driver's seat, grinning ear to ear, was Charlie.

"Man, you look awful," he said. "Don't tell me you tried the prison food?"

I felt awful. Before I could say so, Mr. Entwistle dropped down between us.

"How did I do?" Charlie asked him.

"Ten out of ten, boy. You're a natural disaster." Then Mr. Entwistle turned and helped me over to a row of seats along the inside wall. "See. Told ya you'd be impressed."

I was incredulous. Charlie was the last person I expected. I didn't know he could drive.

"Here. Sit down." Mr. Entwistle eased me onto one of the molded side benches, careful to avoid the blood stains on my shoulder and thigh where the two bullets had grazed me.

"They're just nicks," I told him.

"The bleeding hasn't stopped on this one." He was looking at my leg. "I'd better take care of it." Then he turned to Charlie. "Get us out of here."

Charlie sat down. There was no windshield, just two viewers, each

like the butt end of a pair of binoculars. Charlie pressed his eyes up
against one, then reached down and took hold of two handles that
stuck up from the floor, one on either side of his chair. "It's just like
Cyber Sled," he said, laughing. That was a video game with two joy-
sticks, one for each tread of your tank. The engine revved. It sounded
like a hungry crocodile. Then it started pinging. I wondered if it was
about to explode.

"What's that noise?" I asked.

"Bullets. They're shooting at us." Mr. Entwistle must have seen
the concern on my face. "Don't worry, boy, the only thing that can
penetrate this armor is parked in my underground garage."

Was he kidding? Before I could ask, Charlie pulled one lever and
pushed the other. The car spun. The sudden movement pressed me
hard against my seat. Then we lurched forward with a deafening
rumble. Mr. Entwistle swayed on his feet, then turned and started
nosing through a red case that was stuck to the wall. He pulled out
a bandage, wrapped it carefully around my thigh, and cinched it
tight. As I was figuring out how to quietly scream, he pulled a harness down around my shoulders, the kind stock car drivers wore on
TV. I felt like a space marine. I looked at him. He smiled and winked.

"I thought you were dead!" I told him.

"I thought so, too. But it turns out, I was only at the Olde Stone
Brewing Company. Best beer in town. You can't imagine my disappointment when I learned it wasn't heaven." He walked to the front,
waved Charlie out of the seat, pulled a harness over his shoulders,
then took over the controls.

"Didn't my uncle blow you up?" I asked.

"He tried. But why bother having visions if you can't see when
the building you're in is going to explode?"

Visions. Mr. Entwistle sometimes saw glimpses of the future.
And the past, too, if my memory was correct. It was his talent. I'm
not sure how it worked exactly. He glanced back at me and smiled
again. "You've been drinking the good stuff, I see."

The good stuff. With Mr. Entwistle that could have meant one of two things, human blood or Crown Royal. My guess was, he meant blood. When he met me in the mental ward last year, I'd never fed as a true vampire. Ophelia kept me alive feeding me hemoglobin from farm stock. Mostly cows. But the human stuff takes us to the next level. The longer we drink it, the tougher we get.

My friend walked back and strapped himself into a seat across from me.

"How did he find you?" I asked.

"I went back to the rave," Charlie said. "I didn't know where else to go. I was hoping my friends would still be there so I could find a place to crash. Figure out what to do. But Entwistle was there waiting."

"How did he know to go there?"

"Best way to find someone," Mr. Entwistle said, "go to a place they've already been. We are creatures of habit."

I looked at Charlie and he shrugged. I guess his theories about hiding needed some work.

"I still don't get it," I said to Mr. Entwistle. "How did you know to go there?"

The old vampire glanced back over his shoulder. "To the rave? I was there earlier, following another vampire. You can imagine my surprise when you two young bloods ran out of the place."

"He was the one outside," Charlie added. "The one who dropped from the roof."

"Then who was the other vampire?" I asked.

Mr. Entwistle pressed his eyes to the viewer in front of him. "The one inside. He was a Coven agent."

I looked at Charlie and swallowed. His pupils were expanding to a more frantic size. "They sent him to kill us," he said. "When we took off, he went straight to your house to wait. Entwistle got there before us, and the two of them started fighting."

"Is that why there was so much blood?" I asked.

The old vampire, grunted. "Not exactly. I was hoping to talk some sense into him. I guess I was bleeding a little. Then Mr. Hyde showed up and tore him to pieces. I've never seen anything like it."

"Who's Mr. Hyde?" I asked.

"That thing from the zoo," Charlie answered.

"What was it? It moved so fast, we could hardly see it."

Mr. Entwistle answered. "Mr. Hyde? I'm not sure, but I have my suspicions."

"Is it a vampire?"

"I doubt it."

"How do you know his name?"

"I don't, but we need to call him something. Thank God he hates the water. I damn near bled to death getting away. Even after a few pints of the good stuff and a day of sleep, I'm still not quite myself."

Well, Mr. Entwistle looked exactly the same as he had last year. A little messier perhaps. But not a day older.

"Where have you been all this time?" I asked. "I don't understand."

"Vampires my age are hard to kill, boy. Fire and sunlight might be the only sure ways. When that bomb of your uncle's went off, it buried me in rubble. I dug in deep. It insulated me from the worst of the heat. But I had to wait a few weeks to surface. My body was a mess. Burnt. Broken. It took weeks to heal. . . . The trouble was over by then, so I went home."

"Where's that?" Charlie asked.

"Merry old England. I needed information. But as soon as things started to fall apart here, I came back. That's John Entwistle in a nutshell—the best foul-weather friend you're likely to find."

"Why didn't you tell me?" I said.

"What? That I was alive. I'm telling you now. You're doing fine, aren't ya?"

The correct answer was no. I'd been gassed, shot twice, thrown through two sets of doors, and run full bore into a cement wall. My eyes stung from the tear gas, and the rumbling of the armored car had my body shaking like a pebble in a tin can. Everything but my eyebrows was sore. Still, I didn't want to complain. He'd just broken me out of jail.

"Do you have any blood?" I asked.

"No," Mr. Entwistle said. "I used the last of my stash after getting trashed by the fleabag in Round-Two-at-the-Zoo. I lost the first round near your house on Hunter. So my store is all tapped out. Except what's flowing in my veins, but that would probably kill you."

"Why? I've never understood that."

"I don't know exactly. I imagine it's because the pathogen behaves differently in different people. It changes us. And some changes just aren't compatible."

It made sense. Kind of. He eased up on one lever. I felt myself shift sideways as the car turned a corner.

"What was with the wolves?" Charlie asked.

"Reinforcements," Mr. Entwistle said. "I needed the help. But that creature is something else. Stronger than anything I've ever seen, and I've been to Venice Beach." He glanced back at me. "You sure you're all right? You look a little woozy."

He was starting to slide out of focus, but I didn't say anything. I had too many questions. "How did you know I was in jail?"

"I have a few contacts in the department. And I monitor the police radios."

"What was going on with that boy they brought in?" I asked.

Mr. Entwistle sighed. "Poor Shawn. I told him he could borrow my car, then called the cops and reported it stolen. Not very neighborly of me. But they wouldn't let you have any visitors. Some new terrorist legislation. So I needed to get someone else inside so I could visit them and scope things out."

That didn't seem fair to Shawn, and I said so.

"Oh, it won't do any permanent harm," Mr. Entwistle said. "I'll have the charges dropped, but it probably won't be necessary. The cops will put two and two together. They're not stupid. But don't lose any sleep over this. We've got bigger problems."

"Where are we going?" Charlie asked.

"Little Lake."

That seemed like an odd destination. There was nothing there but water. "Why?" I asked.

"This is an aquatic car. They won't be able to follow us."

"Are you joking?"

"You'll know when I'm joking. It will be funny. Didn't you notice the tires on this thing?"

I had. They looked big enough for a tractor. "Where did you get it?"

"The shell is military, special order. The tires are designed for a bulldozer. The electronics I did myself. The engine, too. One of the perks of being around since the preindustrial era. I've been able to follow the evolution of the engine from the steamship to the nuclear sub. Same for computers. It's what you have to do. Keep up with the times. An old dog who can't learn new tricks gets mired in the past. Then you get buried with it."

It was an odd message to hear from a guy who looked as if he'd walked straight off the set of *Oliver Twist*—with a detour through a mudslide. But I had no doubt it was true. If you were stuck in the past, and the past disappeared, where did it leave you? Floundering in an unknown world. That wasn't Mr. Entwistle. I'd once been in his house. For every old book on his shelf, he had a dozen magazines scattered on the floor. Computers, cars, science, business. Like Ophelia, he was interested in everything. It must have been how they stayed connected to the present.

The car lurched left, then right. We hit something hard and it tossed me back against the wall. Fortunately, a padded headrest was mounted right where it was needed.

"What was that?" I asked.

"Roadblock."

"Are we through?"

"Easily."

The car dropped and I heard a splash. The rumble of the wheels stopped. So did the jostling. We were bobbing, instead. "We're on the water now," Mr. Entwistle told me.

. . . on the water now. That sounded as comforting as "we're going back to jail." It wasn't that I hated the water. I just really, really, really didn't like it. Really. I unbuckled myself and walked to the front for a better view. When I pressed my eyes over the lenses, everything looked green. I could see the far shoreline, but that was it.

"Is there a way to see out the back, or to the side?" I wanted to know what kind of mess we'd left behind, and what the near bank looked like, the one that was closest to the police station.

"There are small windows on each side. You can take the helm in a second and I'll check things out." He started unfastening the harness that held him in place.

I put my eyes back to the lenses, then I started to get dizzy. The bleeding in my shoulder and thigh had stopped, but I was still sore. I was going to need blood. And a week of sleep. Charlie took hold of my arm. I hadn't even noticed him get up and step over.

"You look like you're about to pass out." He stared at me for a few seconds, then helped me into my seat.

The car was moving ahead by itself. Behind us, Mr. Entwistle removed something from his coat—the bottle of whiskey he'd brought into the police station.

"Saints preserve us!" he said, raising it to his lips. When he was finished, he walked over to the side of the cockpit and lifted a thin screen. It covered an elliptical porthole set above the bench. "Dammit," he snapped. He walked to the other side, uncovered the window opposite, continued to curse, then did the same at the back.

"What is it?" I put my hands on my knees and tried to push myself to my feet, but I wasn't feeling steady, so I stayed, unbelted, in the seat.

"The shore to either side is being monitored. Cruisers are everywhere. I'd hope to float down the river and exit farther along, where they couldn't be waiting for us, but there's a boat on the water. They can follow our every move. How could they have managed that so quickly?"

"It's the summer," Charlie said. "They always have a boat out this time of year. And usually a few Jet Skis."

"We can't outrun them in this. It's designed for power. Not speed." Mr. Entwistle took another sip of whiskey. "That Ford Mustang is looking pretty good right now."

"We wouldn't have made it out of the garage," I said. "And that roadblock would have stopped us cold."

"Quite right."

"Should we abandon ship?" Charlie asked.

Mr. Entwistle looked horrified. "There are twenty-four hundred horses under this hood. I'm not abandoning this treasure. That's blasphemy."

I stood up and looked through the window that faced the downtown. Under the streetlights a row of police cars were lined up bumper to bumper, their red and blue lights flashing across the neighboring buildings. We were crawling past.

Charlie edged in beside me to take a look. "We don't have a chance. We'd be better off getting out to swim. You can paddle a canoe faster than this thing."

"Yeah, but a canoe doesn't cost you all your Microsoft stock. Do you know how many beer bottles I'm going to have to collect before I can make another one of these?"

"So what do we do?" I asked. "Didn't you plan for this? I thought you could see the future."

Mr. Entwistle took off his hat and held it over his heart. "Of course I had a plan. My plan was to sink. I never thought these tires would keep us afloat."

"Sink?"

"Yeah. I figured we sink and swim out the top." He looked at the hatch, above. "It's why I brought the air tanks." He pointed toward the first-aid kit. I could see several small canisters strapped to the wall beside it. "The top is the only way out. You may be right. It might be time to get wet. We can leave the controls in place. That will keep the tires moving. We've got to take our chances in the water."

I was about as comfortable in the water as I was in the sun. "I can't swim."

"I know," he said. "I watched you nearly drown the last time we were in the river, remember?"

I did. It was part of our escape from the Nicholls Ward last year. It had nearly been the death of me.

"Don't worry," he said. "You can just walk on the bottom."

"Really?"

"Well, there's no harm in trying. . . . Here." He handed me his whiskey bottle. Then he started fiddling with the dash.

The engine's rumble turned into a quiet purr. Then something bumped into us. I heard a muffled sound, like someone shouting through a loudspeaker.

"Turn off your engine and come out slowly with your hands up. I repeat . . ."

"Just ignore them," Mr. Entwistle said.

"What can they do?" I asked.

He pursed his lips and thought. Then he reached out, yanked the bottle from my hand, took a deep haul, then wiped his sleeve across his mouth. "They don't have to do anything. We've got nowhere to go and no way to get there. We're going to run out of gas shortly. This thing drinks more than I do."

"Brilliant," I said. "So we're floundering in this sea cow waiting to get shot."

"Sea cow! Sea cow?" Mr. Entwistle threw up his hands. "Show some respect. This thing can bounce a plutonium-tipped warhead. We can't get shot in here."

"But we can't stay, either."

"Good point." He walked over to the hatch and undid it, then pushed it open. I moved closer and peered up through the open hole. There was nothing to see but stars and clouds. Then the beam of a searchlight bounced off the far side. Enough light leaked in that I had to squint.

"I don't suppose there's any point in waiting." He sounded painfully glum. "I don't normally get attached to things." He looked around the cockpit. "Well, I guess I owe them."

"Owe who?" Charlie asked.

"The Peterborough police. I trashed a police cycle last year, and that Ford Mustang, and a few more in that roadblock. And you demoed at least three cars tonight in that underground garage, Charlie." Mr. Entwistle took a pull from his bottle. "I guess this makes us even." Then he grunted in disgust. "I really wanted to take this thing to the Warsaw Fair."

It seemed an odd time to get nostalgic. The police were still shouting instructions through a loudspeaker and I could feel the front of their boat bumping into the car. Mr. Entwistle reached up to the roof. I was hoping he'd pull out the controls for a laser cannon, or a giant slingshot, but instead he pulled down a short ladder that was hinged near the opening. It swung into place with a click. He gave it a shake to test it, then grabbed the waist of my pants with one hand and cupped the other one around his mouth.

"Here's your man!" he shouted to the police. An instant later, he raised me off the ground and flung me up through the hatch.

CHAPTER 14

WEED WORLD

I landed on top of the car in the blinding glare of a searchlight. Even with my hands shielding my eyes, and my head turned away, I couldn't make out anything but some blurry silhouettes—maybe four, on the deck of the boat. I could hear another vessel speeding over from the docks behind us. And I could hear Mr. Entwistle laughing in the cockpit of the car.

"Don't move. Keep your hands where we can see them," someone shouted.

I don't think they could have moved me with a keg of dynamite. I was petrified. I didn't want to get shot, and I didn't want to slip into the water, so I just stood there, not moving, and waited for further instructions. They never arrived. Instead, I heard a gunshot. It came from inside the car. Mr. Entwistle was firing the pistol he'd taken from the police officer in the jail.

The searchlight went out.

A pause followed that was just long enough for me to realize I was a dead man, then the police returned fire. I suppose I should have ducked behind the open hatch cover. It was bulletproof. But I couldn't do anything but flail my arms, largely because Mr. Entwistle had climbed the ladder and was pulling my feet out from underneath me. My head shot backward and I crashed into the lake. I started to flail in the water and managed to get my fingers into the deep treads of the back tire. They were still slowly moving and pulled me to the surface. I then pushed myself to the back in a space under the bumper. The police boat was on the other side of the car, so I had a few seconds to decide whether I wanted to stay with Mr. Entwistle or take my chances with the legal system. Then a blue flame arced out from the car. It was Mr. Entwistle's whiskey bottle. He'd set fire to it and sent it somersaulting through the air. One gunshot later it exploded, showering the top of the police boat with burning alcohol.

In that instant, Charlie leapt from the car with Mr. Entwistle right behind him. The old vampire was fast, but not fast enough. A barrage of bullets caught him in the back. His dive became a tragic belly flop. I reached out and pulled him over. He was sputtering and coughing. I felt the tire shift slightly as the front of the car dipped down. Someone had stepped on the top.

"They're coming," I said. "Are you all right?"

He nodded, thumping the chest of his body armour. "I'm fine." Then he patted the top of his head. "But I'll be better when I find my lucky hat." It must have come off in the water.

Charlie swam over beside us. He looked as if he was having the time of his life. "What now?"

"Duck." Mr. Entwistle put a hand on top of my head and pushed me under. I had just enough time for a quick breath, then I dropped as the smaller, faster boat sped past. The prop cut through the water with an angry whine. When it faded, we surfaced. I had one hand on his coat and another on the tire spinning slowly beside me. I didn't want to drown.

Mr. Entwistle had his top hat in one hand. He slapped it on his head so he could tread water with me hanging from his other side.

"Did you guys grab an oxygen tank?" he asked.

I looked at Charlie. He looked at me.

The old vampire sighed, then muttered something about youth being wasted on the young. He reached into his coat and pulled out one of the small canisters. "We'll have to share. Here's the plan . . ."

* * *

I don't know how much time you've spent walking on the bottom of a lake. My understanding is that our primordial ancestors just loved this kind of thing. Needless to say, after half a billion years of evolution, I was totally out of my element. My feet hit the muck at the bottom and I thought I was in Weed World. It was as if I were on a different planet. It wasn't just the density of the atmosphere, or the weird plants and soft earth, but that sound travels well underwater, and with the police buzzing overhead, I half expected a horde of giant hornet-men to descend and carry me off.

I started walking right away, although walking isn't the best description. You had to really push and lunge. It was tricky at first, because of the weeds. They made it tough to see and pulled at my body like strands of a giant, green spiderweb. The props of the police boats were loud, but as we walked farther through Weed World, the sound faded, and my fear of hornet-men disappeared. The frantic activity above us was all centered around the car, which they started to tow away. I could imagine the headlines in tomorrow's paper: *Drunk Mercenary Frees Terrorist from City Jail.*

We went single file. Charlie was first. He more or less swam, pushing off the bottom at irregular intervals. Mr. Entwistle went in the middle and helped us pass the tank back and forth. With his long hair flowing out in all directions and his overcoat, he looked like a dangerous hybrid of lion and manta ray.

Slowly, the water got deeper, and cooler. The plant life disappeared. I guess the sunlight couldn't get down this far. The lake bottom was silt so my feet raised little puffs of dirt with every step. To anyone watching, it would have looked as if I'd gone from the surface of a strange planet filled with exotic vegetation to a desolate moon with little gravity. The only hitch was that the temperature dropped quickly. The two bullet wounds in my leg and shoulder started to ache, and the pressure from the water grew so strong that it started to feel as if I had a nail sticking in both ears. Then Mr. Entwistle pinched his nose and puffed up his cheeks. He motioned for me to do the same. My ears popped and the discomfort went away.

We didn't make it all the way across before the oxygen tank ran out, but it didn't matter. The water got shallow enough for us to walk awkwardly with our heads clear. We had to tip them back so only our faces rose above the surface. Anything else and we would have been spotted. We were nearing the far bank, a good quarter mile from the opposite shore where the cluster of cruisers were still lined bumper to bumper.

"If we go farther upriver, we'll be able to make a clean exit," Mr. Entwistle said.

I knew the area well. It was just down the hill from a kids' park with play structures and a soccer field. I did a lot of running there, and on the bike path next to the water. As we got closer to shore, we heard the barking of dogs. A crew of police officers was patrolling the bank. Mr. Entwistle waved for us to stay low.

"Keep your heads down. We'll wait for them to pass, then we run. Don't hesitate and don't look back. Can you handle that?"

Charlie nodded. I wasn't sure. I was hurt, and the water at the bottom of the lake had been frigid. My joints felt brittle. I was sure if I tried to move quickly, they'd shatter. Normally cold doesn't bother vampires. With enough human blood in the tank, I could wander into a snowstorm with my clothes stuffed full of ice and I wouldn't have come home with so much as a goose bump. But I'd lost a lot of blood from my gunshot wounds, and the cold stiffness in my bones was a sign that I was getting weak.

We waited for the police to pass, then Mr. Entwistle pointed up the bank in the direction of the park. "This way. Let's get going."

I climbed awkwardly out of the water, my knees full of cement.

"Hurry," he whispered. Then he started off at a jog. In a few seconds, he was sprinting up the hill.

Charlie kept up, but I couldn't. Normally I could have outrun him dragging Moby-Dick and half the cast of *The Lord of the Rings* behind me, but now I was spent. My wet shoes squished like sponges as I struggled up the hill, the cadence of my footfalls much slower than it should have been. My body was shivering. I couldn't force it

into overdrive. To top it off, my shoulder was bleeding again. The
water had washed the scab free and so my shirt was covered with a
deep red patch.

I wasn't at the top of the hill before I heard barking behind me.
The police officers were a long way off. I doubt they'd seen us. But
I'm guessing their dogs could hear my shoes and ragged breathing,
because a few seconds later, as I crested the rise, I heard more barking. The dogs were off their leads and on the chase.

I could see Charlie ahead. A vanishing shadow. Mr. Entwistle had
disappeared. I started across the field, then looked back over my
shoulder. Two German shepherds were racing toward me. In no time,
the first was nipping at my heels. Then I felt its teeth sink into my
ankle. I pitched forward and hit the ground hard. It snarled and went
for my throat. I got my hands up, then heard it squeal. Mr. Entwistle
was back. He'd hauled it off the ground by a tuft of fur above its neck.
Before I could blink the dog was hanging from the stump of a tree
branch, the broken shard of wood resting cleanly under its collar.
While it whimpered and thrashed, he turned to square off against
dog number two. Both had their fangs out. I was thinking four out of
five dentists would have been impressed. Then Mr. Entwistle spread
his fingers like claws, hunched down, bared his teeth, and let out a
hiss that made my hair stand up. They say police dogs are among the
smartest of their species. Dog number two was no idiot. It fled.

Mr. Entwistle turned back to help me up. "Sorry, I had no idea
you were so tired. Heavens, boy, you look like a bleached bone.
And you're freezing."

I could barely hear him over my breathing. No matter how
quickly I kept refilling my lungs, I couldn't seem to get enough air.

"Can you keep going?"

My hands were on my knees. I looked up and nodded.

"Good. Because this place is going to be crawling with cops in a
few seconds."

Right on cue, the whir of sirens and the telltale red and blue
flashes of their lights bounced up Parkhill Road beside us.

"Quickly, into the trees," he said.

He ran, half dragging, half carrying me through the kids' park and into a cluster of pines at the edge of the field. Charlie was waiting. His eyes were wide with excitement. We scrambled over a fence and started running through backyards. Our pace was slow, but it was all I could manage. At high speeds, a backyard could be an obstacle course. At the pace I was going, I wouldn't have outrun a fish, but at least I didn't stumble into a pool or impale myself on anyone's patio furniture. Soon my body started to warm, at least enough that my teeth stopped chattering.

We fled past a golf course to an area of town I didn't know well, dodging police cars and barking dogs all the way. Then Mr. Entwistle stopped in front of a split-level house near a strip mall. We slipped into the backyard and he jumped up into a tree. I scrambled up after, with help, then followed his gaze to the property behind. The two-story house was dark and empty. I listened, trying to make my breath soundless so that I could pick up anything unusual. After a few seconds, I tapped him gently on the shoulder, then silently mouthed, *Why are we waiting?*

He didn't answer. Instead he hopped down and made for the back entrance. He opened the outer screen door, then tested the knob on the storm door behind. It was locked.

"You don't have a key?" I whispered.

"It's not my house."

Wonderful. So I was about to add breaking and entering to my list of offenses.

"Whose house is it?" Charlie asked.

"It belongs to another vampire."

"Someone you know?"

"Not exactly, but rumor has it she's one of the good guys, even though she doesn't get out much."

Mr. Entwistle motioned for Charlie to bend down so he could step up on his back and reach the nearest window.

"No," I said. "There's no point. They'll all be locked." I didn't even bother keeping my voice down.

Mr. Entwistle looked at me. His forehead was creased with furrows.

"Our best bet's the doorbell." I pressed it. One ding-dong later, I heard the familiar click-clack of hard-soled shoes on the floor.

There was a short pause. The door had no windows, so I leaned in and waved at the small peephole. I heard a dead bolt slide in its casing, then a chain rattled, the door swung inward, and there stood Ophelia smiling like a sun.

CHAPTER 15

BY ANY OTHER NAME

Ophelia stared at me for a few seconds. My clothes were blood-stained, my hands chalk-white. Her smile evaporated. "Good Lord," she gasped. "What happened here?"

Before I could answer, Charlie stepped onto the stoop behind me. Ophelia saw him. Concern mixed with relief.

"Charlie? Thank heavens!"

I would have said something, but I was too busy staring at the revolver in her hand. It was like the kind you see in old gangster movies.

"Forgive me." She set it on a small table that was just inside the door. "I wasn't expecting company. I've been terribly worried about you two."

She hadn't noticed Mr. Entwistle. His back was against the brick wall beside the door.

"What happened?" she asked again. "Are you okay?"

I said I was fine, even though I wasn't. She moved aside so I could slip past. Charlie followed. Then Mr. Entwistle stepped out from his hiding place. Ophelia paused for just an instant, then tried to slam the door shut. Mr. Entwistle stopped it with his hand and forced it open, pushing her backward. She reached for the gun on the table, but he was faster.

"Excuse me," he said, "but I've been shot enough tonight."

I waited for Ophelia to say something, but she didn't. Instead, she stood there stunned while he examined the weapon. He opened the chamber, looked down the barrel, flicked it shut, then raised the hammer and gave the wheel a spin. "You've looked after this well." He switched his grip so that he was holding it by the barrel. Ophelia reached out and grabbed the handle. Her hand was a bit unsteady. He didn't let go until she met his gaze. Neither spoke.

Something odd was happening. Was this just the way it was when two vampires met for the first time—awkward, tense, uncomfortable? Then I remembered that the two had seen each other before. Just briefly the night Mr. Entwistle had crashed through the doors of the Nicholls Ward on that stolen police cycle. The police had been there, so he didn't stick around long, just enough to tell her to get me out of there. I don't know how much he knew about her, or she of him, but something wasn't right. I could feel it. I'd never seen her scared before. Not like this. When she pulled the gun away, her hand was still shaking, the barrel quivering slightly. She kept it pointed in his general direction, as if she wasn't sure if she should start shooting or not. I tried to see him as she would. Hair matted. Whiskers. Oversize boots and fingerless gloves. Weathered face. Intense eyes. Like a refugee from the Apocalypse. He took off his top hat and tucked it inside his coat. I wondered if he wanted her to see the armor he was wearing underneath. If this was a poker game, he was laying his cards down on the table, one at a time.

"How did I fail to notice?" he said. "But it makes perfect sense that it would be you."

Again she said nothing, but I thought something must have passed between them, because he nodded and a deep hum buzzed in his throat.

"The only relevant question is, what will you do now?" he asked.

Ophelia's hand was still shaking, and when she spoke it was with a quaver in her voice. "I appreciate that you've brought them back."

I couldn't remember ever seeing her this way before. Afraid. Uncertain. In the past, even when she was undecided about something and needed more time to think, there was a kind of certainty in her doubt, a confidence that she could work through the problem. Now she just seemed lost.

"It wasn't my intention to disturb you," he said. "I was told you were at your apartment on Clonsilla."

Ophelia stiffened. Her voice went cold. "How did you know about that?"

He reached into his coat and removed his flattened top hat. It looked like a black Frisbee. He started spinning it in his hands. "I've been very busy. Little happens in this city now that I don't find out about." He snapped his wrist and the top of his hat popped out. "I wouldn't impose on your hospitality, but I don't want to leave without some assurance that you can look after these boys."

"We've always managed."

"Things have changed. And they will only get worse. You know this."

Ophelia looked at the floor, then at me, then at Charlie.

Mr. Entwistle went on, "The Underground has been compromised. It's unstable. You can't depend on it. It's happening across the globe. The Coven has fractured. It is warring with itself. But they haven't lost interest in any of you. They sent an assassin to kill these two. If I hadn't shown up, they'd both be dead. And there is a creature out there killing vampires. It is intelligent and determined."

He stepped forward. Normally when he moved, it made me think of a wolf. He sort of loped. But now he was standing at his full height. I was surprised how tall he was, and how intimidating. Had I not known him better, I would have thought he was the King of Mean. Ophelia was holding a gun in her hand, but I sensed, as she must have, that the weapon was irrelevant.

"I am the oldest vampire in the West," he said. "Veteran of the Balkan Crusades, the Wars of the Roses, of World War II, and everything in between. I have never met anyone, man or beast, who was my equal in a fight. Not your husband. Not Maximilian. Not anyone—until now. This thing, the one I call Mr. Hyde, is positively lethal."

Ophelia glanced at me quickly. She must have understood that

Mr. Entwistle was the vampire from my dream. The one who had fought—and lost. The corners of his mouth turned up just slightly. It was almost a smile. Then his face flattened out and he spoke with unusual seriousness.

"I understand that you don't want me here. But how, in my absence, will you protect them?"

Ophelia's eyes were busy—alert. Her voice was quiet, but there was anger in it. "You are *reckless*. If you care about Zachary at all, about us, you'll turn around, walk out the door, and leave us alone."

Mr. Entwistle took a step forward so that the hall light was directly above him. It cast his face in shadow. His eyes looked like two empty holes. "I *have* left you alone. And since my little adventure last year with your ward, I have been traveling on my own, seeking answers to important questions. You know who the boy is. Now is not the time to isolate yourselves. Everything I have read and heard and felt and seen is consistent in this one regard—we are balanced on the head of a nail. One false move and we're finished. Now that Vlad is gone, a long-predicted war has arrived. The End of Days. And the boy has a part to play. We cannot lose him now. You know the price for all of us if that happens."

I was starting to feel like an extra in my own life story. Nothing Mr. Entwistle said was making sense to me. I looked at Charlie. He seemed as nervous and unsure as I did. As if the floor were falling out from under us.

"You have more problems than you can contend with. The Coven won't be in shambles forever. Once a new order is established, they'll come in force. For all of you. Not one assassin. An army. They don't approve of child vampires, or those who shelter them. And you've a more immediate problem—Mr. Hyde. Who else can help you? I'm your last best hope."

"No." Ophelia's voice had a tremor. "I'll take them away. We'll hide."

Mr. Entwistle's head tipped sideways just a hair. Pity was in his expression. "You can run, that's true. But where? And for how long?

Sooner or later they'll find you. Then they'll kill him, and his friends. Unless Hyde devours them first. He exists only to kill our kind. We have to make a stand. As time goes on, the situation here will only get worse."

Get worse? Unless we moved up north where there were twenty-four hours of daylight at a stretch, I couldn't imagine how things could get worse.

Ophelia was still holding the gun. She looked as if she might set it down, but she didn't. "You are asking me to trust you, and I don't. You might have changed your name and your clothes, but you are who you have always been." More certainty was in her manner as she spoke, but she was still a long way from the indomitable person who showed up to save my friends and me from Vlad.

Mr. Entwistle pressed his lips together and turned them up in a smile that had no humor or mirth. It expressed loss and disappointment. "Trust is irrelevant, Ilona. You can't protect him. There is only me."

Ilona. I'd never heard the name. But Ophelia's expression changed when she heard it. Her fear remained, and there was sadness, too. And what else? She was so practiced at hiding everything, I couldn't tell.

"Like you, I have reinvented myself. I am John Entwistle now. And I walk in the light. Well—in a manner of speaking."

Ophelia looked at me. Her expression softened. I smiled. Then she looked back at Mr. Entwistle. Her face could be an iron mask when she wanted, but not tonight. She was still shaken.

"I am not a trusting person. This is not a habit I plan to change. If you are being honest, time will bear you out. But until I am certain, I will not have you here."

Mr. Entwistle placed his top hat on his head. "I suggest you tell the boys everything. Now is not a time for secrets. Or for us to be isolated. Alone, the Beast will destroy us, one after the other." He nodded in farewell, then turned and walked out the door. I heard his footsteps on the back step, then the soft grass. A moment later he had vanished.

I glanced at Ophelia. Much of their conversation had been over my head, but it didn't change the fact that I owed him my thanks. If not for him, I'd still be stuck behind bars with the charming Officer Lumsden for company. This felt wrong. He shouldn't have left. My instincts told me he was right, and that we needed to stick together.

Ophelia must have sensed what I was thinking. "Let him go, Zachary."

"Why can't he stay here?"

"Give it a night. We can discuss matters. The situation is more complicated than you know."

Only because you never tell me anything, I thought to myself. I should have screamed it in her ear. But I couldn't. I was a bit old for tantrums. "I think you're wrong about him."

She let go of my arm. "He isn't who you think he is."

"What does that mean?"

She wiped her eyes again, then took a deep breath. "It is a common thing for a vampire to change his name."

"Is that why he called you Ilona?"

She looked at Charlie, then at me. "It was a name I used once, a long time ago, but it was never really mine."

I thought she might say more, but she didn't.

"Why don't you trust him?"

She looked at me, then at the floor, then pinched her forehead between her fingers and thumb and began massaging her temples. "Things are worse than you can imagine."

Since I could imagine the sun exploding and destroying all life on earth, this was saying quite a bit. "Then shouldn't we accept Mr. Entwistle's help?"

"Well, that's the rub, isn't it? Mr. Entwistle isn't really Mr. Entwistle."

"What does that mean?"

She fixed me with a sad stare. "When I knew him, his name was John Tiptoft. He had many titles. Earl of Worcester, Treasurer of the Exchequer, Deputy of Ireland, Constable of England."

A constable. Wasn't that like a police officer? It didn't sound so bad. None of it did. Ophelia must have sensed my doubt because she finished with a whopper.

"As a constable, he was essentially an executioner. The people hated him for his cruelty. They called him the Butcher of England."

CHAPTER 16
REVELATIONS

I knew Ophelia as well I knew anyone. She was a serious person. She laughed often, but rarely made jokes herself. She didn't kid people. What she said you could write in stone. She'd just told me that Mr. Entwistle was the Butcher of England. Mr. Entwistle, who preached forgiveness. Who believed even the worst vampires should be nurtured back from madness. Who had just saved me from the police and a murder charge.

I looked at Charlie. He was as shocked as I was. "What did you call him?" he asked.

"John Tiptoft. But that is not his name. Not the first. Who he was in the beginning only he can say. But he was John Tiptoft, the executioner for the House of York, when I learned of him. He was ruthless, Charlie. Ruthless."

I wondered how all of this was possible. I thought she might explain, but her eyes were staring at the back door, unfocused. She suddenly looked like a stranger to me. I realized I knew almost nothing about her. Where she came from. Her family. Even her real name. It wasn't Ilona. Did that mean it wasn't Ophelia, either? She might have been born centuries ago. From an age vanished in time.

She looked at me and smiled. There was warmth in it. And love. *No,* my mind told me, *this is no stranger.* People can have secrets, but they can't hide who they really are. This was the person I trusted more than anyone else in the world. Her name was Ophelia and she was the only reason I was still alive.

"I had hoped to talk to you earlier about things," she said. "It was why I asked you to come back with Charlie. I didn't expect things to get so out of control, so quickly. And I didn't expect to see John."

"I think you're wrong about him," I said. "I think we can trust him."

"He was a monster, Zachary."

"Wasn't Vlad?"

"At times. But he was never as bad as history would have you believe." She let out a tired breath. "He was a product of his time."

I wasn't sure what that meant. "Are you going to tell me what's going on?"

She laughed. "I'd tell you if I knew." She looked at me, then at Charlie, who I'm sure was feeling as confused as I was.

"There are clean clothes upstairs. And a laundry hamper. Why don't you two get cleaned up. I'll wait down here."

It didn't take long for Charlie and me to get our bearings. With Ophelia around, everything was always well ordered—fresh towels in the closet, beds turned down, clothes laid out, as if she'd been expecting us.

"This place is like a hotel," Charlie said when he saw new jeans and a T-shirt folded at the foot of his bed. "You don't suppose there's room service?"

I didn't think we should push our luck. I called dibs on the shower and left him in his room. He was making a call when I closed the door—probably to Suki. If I was lucky, I would have time to call Luna after I talked to Ophelia. So after the shortest, most painful shower in the history of personal hygiene, I hobbled down the stairs to the living room, where she was standing near the front window, her eyes far away. Light from a streetlamp filtered in through a thin white curtain, filling the room with a soft glow. I walked over so we were standing side by side, her head near my shoulder. It almost always surprised me how much smaller she was when we stood this close. In my mind, she filled the room.

"Thanks for the new clothes," I said.

She took hold of my arm with both hands and rested her head on my shoulder. "I hope you weren't attached to the old ones. I don't think they can be salvaged."

I didn't care and said so. "I'm sorry about Inspector Johansson. I know he was a good friend."

She didn't answer. She just wiped at her cheek with one hand. I hadn't noticed, but she'd been crying. I'd never seen her do this. Not in nine years.

"Is Charlie coming down?" she asked.

"No. I think he wants to talk to Suki. Things aren't too good for her right now."

A quiet *hmmm* escaped her lips—as if she understood. "That will change. She needs more time."

Or to become one of us, I thought. I knew that was how Charlie felt. I didn't want to mention it, knowing Ophelia would disapprove. At least until we were clear of trouble. If we were ever clear of trouble.

"I don't feel right about Mr. Entwistle," I said.

"I'm sorry. I don't think I ever forgave him for taking you away."

"From the Nicholls Ward?"

"Yes. Putting all that fear into your head so that you ran off. You can't imagine how scared I was. I searched for days. In the end, I was so desperate, I turned to Vlad for help, and so I found you entirely by accident. All this time, in the back of my head, I'd blamed him for all that worry. If he hadn't shown up . . ."

I never knew this. Of course, we never talked about it. We'd both assumed Mr. Entwistle was dead, so there seemed to be no point in blaming him for anything. "I think his intentions were good," I said. "I think they are now."

"I can't risk it, Zachary. I can't. . . . I'm sorry. There is an evil in some men, and no matter how hard they try to bury it, to cover it with new clothes and good manners, it stays." She looked me straight in the eye. "And I ought to know."

I couldn't argue with that. She'd once been married to a man who'd impaled people by the thousands. I never understood how she could have loved him, but I wasn't going to ask now. I was hardly an expert when it came to relationships. I'd fallen for Luna so fast, I'm still not sure what really happened.

"The sun is going to be up soon." She raised her head from my shoulder and walked over to a sofa that was sitting adjacent to a gas fireplace. We sat. "I need you to understand the trouble we're in."

"With this thing—Mr. Hyde."

"That is part of it." She drifted away again, chewing the inside of her cheek. Her eyes were deep and unfocused.

"Would you rather wait?"

She shook her head. "I just don't know where to start."

I was going to recommend the beginning, but I held my tongue.

"When Vlad disappeared last summer," she began, "it sent shock waves around the world. Before him there was nothing. No order. No law. No safety. Not for our kind. You can't imagine how terrible it was. . . . But he changed all that. The Coven of the Dragon changed it. And now that he is gone, all the jackals he chased into the shadows are free to run amok, and his generals—the elder vampires—are fighting amongst themselves."

"What does this have to do with us?"

She took a deep breath. "Everything."

That didn't tell me much. I waited. She sat thinking. I knew our time was short. The sun would be up in less than half an hour. "Have you learned anything about that creature?" I asked.

"Not enough. I wondered at first if he was an agent of the Coven, but I think not. I have spoken with other vampires who agree. They are all scared. Or they were."

I didn't know Ophelia was in touch with other vampires. "Can't we team up with them? Get more help?"

"No."

"Why not?"

"Because he's killed them all."

She looked at me with a flat expression on her face. But underneath, I could see she was trying hard to keep herself level. I remembered what Inspector Johansson had said, that other vampires had disappeared—good ones. No wonder she was so rattled. It was all the more reason to get help from Mr. Entwistle.

"Do you think we can beat it?"

Ophelia reached down and straightened the folds of her dress. "I don't know if it matters."

That made no sense to me, and I said so.

"Have you read The Book of Revelation?"

"From the Bible?"

"Yes."

I shook my head.

"It predicts that two Beasts will emerge, who, along with Satan, form an unholy trinity that will try to usurp control of the earth from God, His son, and the Holy Ghost. The Bible predicts that good will triumph in the end. That God will reestablish Himself as the absolute holy sovereign. Many vampires believe a similar cycle will occur in our world, but the ending isn't so certain. Order will fall into chaos and a new order will emerge. This creature you call Mr. Hyde is a being likened to the Beast of the Apocalypse, and so whether we beat it or not, many have taken it as a sign that the destruction of the old order is upon us."

"Do you believe it?"

She looked at me, thinking, then gazed out the window. "It is hard not to believe it because it is happening. When Vlad was nearly destroyed last year, and disappeared, it was the first sign that the old order was failing. Now, his Coven is infighting and impotent, and the Underground is falling apart as a result. The appearance of Mr. Hyde is a sign to many that the destruction of the vampire world as we know it is at hand. Already, he is international news in the vampire world."

"Is this what Mr. Entwistle meant when he said a war has arrived? The End of Days?"

Ophelia nodded. "Vlad held the Coven together with an iron fist. Now that he is gone, the others are fighting for control. Most of this is happening overseas, so we've managed to stay clear of it. But the Coven has an interest in you. John is right. They will come for us."

"Because I'm a child vampire."

"Partly. But there's more to it than that. It has to do with your fathers."

She paused, so I could digest the word *fathers*. I knew what she meant. Every vampire has two kinds of parents. The normal human variety—and the vampire that turns them.

"You are Vlad's progeny," Ophelia continued. "And so they will fear you, because in time, you will come to have his power. But the Coven also feared your true father. And they fear you, because of him."

When she spoke about my true father, her voice changed. It always did when she talked about him—Dr. Robert Douglas Thomson, archaeologist and vampire hunter. I once thought that she must have loved him, but I wasn't so certain now. It might simply have been that she felt sorry for me. For my loss.

I felt her eyes on me again. Did she want to know if I believed her? Well, of course I did. Ophelia never lied. Never. So I believed her even when she didn't make any sense.

"I don't understand. Why would anyone fear my father? Or me?" This might seem like a stupid question considering my father's secret profession. But he never killed vampires, no matter how far gone, without giving them a chance to prove that they could be good—that they could live with the infection and not harm others. It made no sense that they would be afraid of him. He wasn't a threat unless they chose to do wrong. And I was seven when he died. Who would fear a boy that young? Only army ants and babysitters.

Ophelia managed a brief smile. It flickered across her face, then disappeared as she looked away. "The answer lies in an ancient prophecy. It concerns a messiah. A vampire who will overthrow the old order, emerge from the ashes of chaos, and re-create a new world. A better world."

Was this about the letter that Charlie and I had read the night of our arrest? About the Lamb? "What does this have to do with me?"

Ophelia sighed. "According to most versions, the future messiah of the vampire world is an orphan, the son of a great hunter. And this orphan would die and come back. Does any of this sound familiar?"

I caught myself swallowing hard. It was familiar. It fit neatly with what I'd read in that letter Charlie and I had found—about the sun scorching me with fire. And a second death that wouldn't harm me. That had happened last year. Death and rebirth.

I told Ophelia about reading the letter. "Do you believe what it said?"

"I'm not a prophet, Zachary. But there is something compelling in all of this. And I'm not the only one who thinks so. Vlad felt it, too. It was why he wanted you all to himself." Her eyes got their far-off look again.

My mind drifted back to *that night*. Vlad had wanted to kill my friends. To sever all of my personal connections so that the only future I had as a vampire was with him. And he'd wanted me to suffer, thinking it would make me stronger.

Ophelia stood up and stretched. She lifted the thin, white curtain hanging in front of the bay window and peeked outside at the sky, then across the street. "So you see why we're in trouble? It isn't just the Beast. It's the prophecy. All of the elders know about it. And so every power-hungry vampire who wants control will regard you as a threat because you are the orphaned son of a great vampire hunter. And you have died twice. Even if you weren't a child vampire, they would hunt you down. It is the only way they can ensure that you don't rise up against them, as the prophecy predicts."

I was stunned. I'd always known there were reasons for secrecy, but in the back of my mind, it was a temporary thing, based on my age. How much longer could I be considered a child, especially if I demonstrated I was stable and wouldn't attract attention or spread the virus carelessly? But if I was some kind of messiah—how could I outgrow that? I couldn't. I'd be stuck with it forever, even if it wasn't true, and it didn't seem to me that it was possible. I couldn't even keep my socks sorted.

"That makes no sense."

"That you're a messiah." Ophelia laughed quietly. "Chosen to establish and rule the new order." She reached down and took my hand, then helped me off the sofa. "Stranger things have happened. But if the End of Days for our kind is here, someone will emerge as the leader of a new Coven, because such an organization is necessary. And given what I know of our kind, I would much rather see you in charge than anyone else." She looked at me and smiled, then reached up and pinched my cheek. "But maybe that's just my prejudice." She glanced back at the window.

I could feel dawn approaching. It filled me with a mild unease.

"I think we should talk more about this later," she said.

I wasn't quite ready to end the conversation. I felt exhausted, but I knew I wouldn't sleep well until my questions were answered. "What are we going to do about Mr. Entwistle?"

"I wouldn't worry about him for today. I'm sure he can look after himself."

"But are we going to let him stay with us?"

"I don't want to have to decide anything just yet. I need to think about this a bit longer. He might be right. We might need him." She looked up at me. "I don't trust him, Zachary."

"Because of who he was?"

She nodded. "If you could have seen it—the things he did as John Tiptoft."

Well, I didn't know anything about that. I didn't want to. I liked him as John Entwistle. So did Charlie. And I think my father would have liked him. Luna, too. I'd never seen a hint of malice in him.

"I can't afford to take any chances, Zachary." Ophelia was watching me closely.

"So what are we going to do?"

She smiled, and shrugged. I couldn't remember her ever doing that. She always had a plan. And a backup plan. And a backup to the backup plan. Order. Routine. Structure. Careful planning. I fully expected that if an asteroid hit the earth and civilization ended, she'd have a spaceship handy and our destination mapped out on sticky notes.

"We'll talk some more later. Does that sound all right?"

I nodded and headed for the stairs. If I hurried, there might be enough time to call Luna. It had been a heavy night. I wanted to hear her voice. I was certain that would lift my spirits.

"Do you need anything else?" she asked.

Just a few minutes on the phone, I thought. And some blood would have been nice, but if she'd had any, she would have offered it by now. "No, but thanks."

"Sleep well. And try not to worry too much."

I said I wouldn't, which I hoped was true, then went upstairs to check on Charlie.

When I found him, he was lying sideways across his bed with his head hanging upside down over the edge of the mattress, his cell phone pressed to his ear.

"It's Zack. Just a second," he said to the person on the other end. Then he pulled the bottom of the phone away from his mouth. "What's up?"

"The Beast of the Apocalypse is on the loose and every power-mad vampire in the world wants to kill me."

"So nothing's changed?"

"I guess not. Is that Suki?"

"Yup."

"Is she doing all right?"

"Well, she's talking to me, isn't she?"

"Is Luna handy?"

Charlie repeated the question to Suki, then waited. A few seconds later he shook his head. "She went to bed. But apparently, she expects to see you in her dreams."

"Lucky me." Then I backed out the door and pulled it closed behind me.

CHAPTER 17

THE PROPHET

Growing up as an orphaned vampire in a mental institution, I missed out on a lot of things. Suntanning. Family picnics. Hand-me-down clothes. Popsicles. The list would fill an encyclopedia. Well, one of the things I'd missed out on was the thrill of nightmares.

As a little kid I got them all the time—lost dreams, being-chased dreams, scary-monster dreams, not-having-my-costume-ready-for Halloween dreams, Santa-missing-my-house dreams. But in the Nicholls Ward—nothing. Not a single nightmare. I understood now that this was Ophelia's doing. She walked the Dream Road to keep me safe, even while I slept.

So I was caught off guard when I found myself back at Iron Spike Enterprises, the office of my uncle Maximilian, having a nightmare. This was where my friends and I had been tormented by Vlad. Now, I was alone with the paintings and the statues and the antiques, the desk and the couch and the shattered windows. Everything was just as we'd left it.

I began to search for my father's missing journal, but I could feel that something was wrong. A restless presence, cold and evil, was approaching. I realized Vlad's remains should have been here. The sun had reduced his body to a roasted skeleton. I had to find it. I renewed my search, but the office kept changing. Every time I checked some area and looked up, everything else would have moved, so it was impossible to know where I'd actually looked. A sense of dread hung over me as I scrambled around. He was in this mess some-where, and I knew that the longer I took, the more likely it was that someone would bring him back—just as I had been brought back. Then he would find me and I'd have to relive the horror of *that night* all over again.

I started walking down a corridor—the secret passage my uncle had used to escape. Then I remembered—this was where I'd thrown Vlad's body. I sensed his evil here. It was approaching from behind. There was a door ahead. A way out. I started to run, but my legs were leaden, the injured one almost useless. It was bleeding and sore. The harder I tried to move, the slower I got. Vlad was getting closer. Right behind me. I wasn't going to make it.

"It's okay."

I stopped and took a deep breath. It was Ophelia.

"Thank God," I said. I ran my fingers through my hair and leaned against the wall. When I looked up, we were back at the Nicholls Ward. I had my scrubs on. I could tell by the sky outside that it was time to get ready for bed.

Ophelia had a look of relief on her face. There might have been some pity, too. "Are you all right?"

I sighed. "I am now." I started walking toward my room. Ophelia wasn't following me. "What is it?"

Her eyebrows rose and she tipped her head forward. "Zachary, you don't live here anymore."

That was true. I don't know what I was thinking. We lived together on Hunter Street now. No sooner did I imagine the inside of our house than we were standing together in the living room. "Are *you* all right?" I asked.

Ophelia nodded. "Yes. I'm fine. But I need to take you to see someone."

"Like a doctor?"

She shook her head. "No. Nothing like that."

I had hoped that if I was going to be traveling the Dream Road, I'd get to visit Luna again, but Ophelia obviously had other plans.

She asked me to close my eyes, then took hold of my hand. A warmth passed over my face. A glow.

"Can I open them now?"

"Not yet," she said, but I'd opened them anyway. I had been expecting her to say yes, so my eyelids slipped up just a crack. I didn't see much. Just soft, pale light. It was everywhere. We were back in the Nexus. I heard the voices again. A symphony of overlapping dream songs. I pinched my eyes shut.

"Now," said Ophelia.

When I opened them a second time, I was inside a dark building. I could hear birds singing outside, and the hum of insects. A huge set of double doors was open in front of me. A field stretched out to the edge of a forest, which receded down a mountain slope. The wind danced through the tall blades of grass and ruffled the pine trees. The sun was shining, but I wasn't afraid. Wildflowers were in bloom. I looked up at the decorated arches overhead. I'd seen a place like this before—in pictures.

"Are we in China?"

"No, this is Tibet, 'The Roof of the World.'"

I stepped onto the threshold so I could walk outside. Then I felt Ophelia's hand on my arm, stopping me.

"This way."

I turned and nearly tripped over a small gong sitting on the floor. Beside it was an open fireplace set deep in the floor.

"To him who overcomes, I will give the right to sit with me," said a voice.

I didn't know anyone else was in the room. My whole body jerked in surprise. I followed Ophelia's gaze to the far side of the temple. Although my eyes were usually good in the dark, I had trouble penetrating the shadows. Smoke was in the air, too, rising from two incense burners set on the floor. A pipe like a water pitcher with a huge stem was sitting between them. Only when the neck of it rose into the air did I see the man who had spoken. He was old and dressed in a robe that might have been orange at one time, but now seemed to reflect the shadows that surrounded him. He sat cross-legged on a matt. Smoke drifted in two slow ribbons from each of his wide nostrils, and more curled around his head, which was bald. His eyebrows were impossibly long and seemed to float in the air like insect wings. Stranger still were his eyes. They were missing. Skin grew over his empty orbits.

"For the Lamb will be their shepherd," he said. "And he will lead them to springs of living water." His voice was faint, but oddly musical. It was followed by a quiet sound. Almost a purr. It took me a moment to realize he was laughing. "I am Baoh, the Prophet. And you are welcome here."

Baoh—that was the name Charlie and I had seen in the letter we'd found at the safe house.

Ophelia bowed her head. "This is Zachary. Son of the late Robert Douglas Thomson, the great vampire hunter."

"You place us all in great peril, woman of the desert."

He raised a hand and waved for Ophelia to go. She was still holding my arm. She clung to it a moment longer, just so I would look at her. When I did, she nodded once, then walked toward the door.

"The first woe is past; two other woes are yet to come," the man said in a loud voice. His head was cocked to the side as though trying to get a better view of Ophelia as she disappeared across the field.

I wondered how he could see with no eyes. A few awkward seconds passed.

"Is she gone?" he whispered.

I was so surprised by his question and the change in his voice that I didn't answer. He didn't seem to notice. Instead, he rose to his feet slowly, as if his joints were stiff, and waved a hand in front of his face to clear away the smoke.

"You want a drink, gringo?"

I shrugged. "Um . . . okay." I glanced back at the temple doors. They were closed. When I turned back, the man was gone. I had a flash of panic. I didn't want to be stuck here alone. A second later he appeared at my side. The top of his head barely reached my shoulder. He had two gold goblets, one in either hand. He passed one to me. It had a red liquid inside. It might have been blood, but I couldn't tell. I sniffed at it, but my nose didn't seem to be working. He tapped the edge of his drink against mine, then raised it up.

"To eternal life. And miniskirts." He drained it in one go, then his head shook. "Whoa. That hits the spot."

I took a reluctant sip. It tasted sweet, and salty, and warm. Like blood mixed with something better than blood. I drank. A pleasant euphoria filled my limbs.

"Not, bad, eh?" Baoh said, placing his hand on the small of my back. He waved his other hand about the room as though the place was a colossal disappointment to him. "I don't know why she insists on these stuffy meeting places." He shook his head. "Poor Ophelia. Sooooo sad. Sooooo serious." He moved me gently to a door at the back. "But Baoh's a media man, eh. Give the people what they want! Doom and gloom. A little hope. Something from Revelation, maybe. And a way forward." Then he clapped me on the shoulder. His other hand reached into the folds of his robe and came out with a pair of sunglasses, which he slipped over his skin-covered orbits. "I gave up my eyes for true sight." His voice was suddenly melancholy. "And now look at me."

The door opened. Noise exploded inward. Cars. Horns. Loud music. Neon light. Wind and exhaust. Grease from a thousand deep fryers. Steam from a thousand soup kitchens. I found myself standing on top of a huge apartment building. Behind was a penthouse suite that looked to be made mainly of glass. Not a typical dwelling for a vampire.

"Ahhh, this is more like it!" Baoh shouted.

"Where are we?"

He laughed and spread his hands. His clothes had changed. He was now wearing a loose silk shirt and bell-bottom trousers. It did a perfect job of showing off his skinny legs and potbelly. "The center of the universe. Tokyo!"

"How did you do it?"

He laughed. "This is nothing. You should see me with a Ouija board."

He turned and reached for a tray. A waitress in high heels was holding it beside him. I wondered if she'd just appeared out of thin air. She had mascara plastered over her large almond eyes and was wearing less clothing than your average hamster. He reached up to a decanter, then filled two thimble-size glasses and handed one of them to me. "Drink up. You're with one of the old boys now."

My eyes were still on the waitress.

"Bah, don't mind her. She's not really here." He waved a hand and she walked away. "Come on inside." He downed his drink.

I was still looking at the clear liquid he'd handed me.

"He who hesitates is lost," he said. Then he took the drink from me, knocked it back, and tossed the empty vessel over his shoulder. I didn't hear it land. "One should never overdo opium on the first night. It can stop your heart faster than a long, tall woman in a black dress."

Opium? Was that what had made the blood taste so good? I wasn't sure if I should ask, so I kept quiet and followed him across the terrace, through a set of glass doors, and into an apartment that looked more expensive than the Vatican. At least a dozen women were inside.

"Out. Out. Out. Out. Out," he shouted. Once the room was clear, he put his hand beside his mouth and whispered, "Don't you dare tell them how old I am. It's hard enough getting a date when you have no eyeballs." He picked up a remote for the TV, which was about ten feet across and mounted on the wall.

"So, you want to talk to old Baoh, eh? Well, young man, there is a price. There is always a price."

I had no money. No valuables. This was going to be a short meeting.

"There are many ways of paying." He faced me so we were standing toe-to-toe. "I am of the ancient world—an age long past. But some things endure through time, and human nature is one of them. Pride. Courage. The need to prove oneself. Fear of failure. There are countless examples. Truths that don't change. You understand?"

I nodded.

"Cowardice, greed, selfishness. These also endure." His voice grew angry. Then he calmed. "So what kind of man are you becoming?"

I didn't have an answer for this.

"In my time, all men were tested by adversity. Pain, loss, struggle. There is less of this now. Life is too easy. But there is one arena in which a man's true nature could always be discerned, in this or any age. It is the crucible of war, of combat. You cannot know a man until you see him in battle. The truth of this endures also. And so you must be tested." He leaned forward. His voice grated against my ears. "Fail me, young blood, and you're doomed."

CHAPTER 18

THE PROPHECIES EXPLAINED

Baoh's back was to the television. The remote was still in his hand. Without turning, he reached over his shoulder and clicked it on. Then he nudged me to the side so we could stand shoulder to shoulder.

"You're a Microsoft man. I can tell." He handed me a Nintendo controller. "I prefer the Wii myself." When I accepted it, he bowed. "We shall see what kind of man you are becoming. The ancient sport of boxing. Or close enough. I much prefer this version. Less painful. But still a valid test. One you'll need to pass, if you intend to survive the End of Days."

I stared at the screen. This wasn't at all what I expected. I wondered if this was how Alice felt when she fell down the rabbit hole into Wonderland.

He turned to face the television as the game loaded. Then we chose our avatars, the little figures that would represent us in the fight. Instead of the usual dozens to choose from, there were only two—a blind monk with oversize eyebrows in an orange robe and a jogger in scrubs with a widow's peak. It seemed fitting.

As soon as the bell sounded, I stepped forward and threw a jab. I followed up with a right cross and left hook. He ducked and countered. I put up my guard, then dropped a good one on his nose.

"That was pure luck," he shouted.

I did it again.

"Take advantage of a blind man, will you? Shame! Shame!"

The third time I moved in, he pounded me back with a flurry of his own. "See? Hah. Thought you could get the better of old Baoh!"

His flurries continued. "I got you figured out, young blood. You're finished now."

He floored me. This happened again. And again. I struggled to my feet. Or, my avatar did. His eyes were crossed and he wobbled on rubbery legs.

"You're just being stubborn now," he said.

The fight ended a few minutes later with his icon, the monk, unconscious on the mat.

Baoh whacked his controller against his palm. "This thing's not working right. Must be a loose wire." He tossed it with disgust onto the sofa, then walked behind a counter and started pouring himself a cocktail. "You're not too shabby. Ophelia would be proud of you. Focused. Difficult to frustrate. Slow to anger. Little vanity. A good balance of aggression and self-preservation. Patience. Confidence. Little fear, just enough to keep you on your toes. You lack a recognizable game plan, but otherwise, she has done well."

It sounded like a compliment, so I said thanks.

"Courteous, too," he added, holding his drink up to the light. He lowered it under his nose. It wasn't quite right, so he continued to fiddle with the ingredients. "Combat, still the best test of a man. Even in a video game. Who you are—it comes through in all that you do, no?" He fixed me with his eyeless stare. "So . . . here is the real test! What did you learn about me?"

His question caught me completely off guard. I took a deep breath. What had I learned? That he could have used a bit of time in the Nicholls Ward. "You don't take yourself as seriously as I expected you to."

He nodded as if this was true.

"You've adapted to the times. You aren't stuck in the past."

"Keep going," he said.

"There's little bitterness in you." I glanced around the room. "You enjoy your life—being a vampire, having fun. You've surrounded yourself with things that are beautiful." Once I got going, I was on a roll. "You're good-humored. Observant. You see remarkably well for a man with no eyes. And you could have beaten me, but you didn't."

"And what does that tell you?"

"That you're willing to suffer a loss to learn something."

"Not bad. You missed a few things. My incomparable charm, for example. And superior intelligence. But I forgive you." He raised his glass as if he was saluting me, then took a cautious sip to test it. The face he made told me he approved. "So what did Ophelia want? Not just for us to meet, I think, eh? She had something specific in mind."

"I don't know. She's great at keeping secrets."

Baoh took a seat on the sofa. "Baaahhh," he scoffed. "All women are that way. Knowledge is power. Men have to learn it. Women know by instinct." I heard him crunch on an ice cube. "So what do you have to ask? Everyone has questions these days. Where do I invest my money? How do I lose weight without exercising or changing my diet? What's the best way to make my ex-lover jealous? You need help with your résumé?"

I shook my head. And thought. The first question that popped into my mind was *How did you get to be such a weirdo?* But it didn't seem appropriate. "Do you know anything about this Beast? The one that's going around killing off vampires?"

"What?" He spat out his ice and started hacking. It took him a moment to recover. "No one told me about this!" He looked over his shoulder as if the door to the living room were about to explode off the hinges. "I hope he isn't following you."

"No. He isn't." I had to pause to think. "You mean you don't know anything about this?"

"When you get to be my age, no one tells you anything. They just assume you know it all. Does this Beast have a name?"

"We call him Mr. Hyde."

"Does he have seven heads and ten horns?"

I shook my head.

"Well, that's a relief. Seven heads and ten horns would be bad. Where is all this happening?"

"In Peterborough."

"That is also a relief." Baoh wiped his shirt clean where he'd spilled his drink. "But not to you, I suppose. You live in Peterborough?"

"Yes."

"Is that the place with that big tower that spins?"

He must have meant the CN Tower. "No, that's in Toronto."

"Right, right." He took another drink, then pointed a thumb over his shoulder. "Want a rematch?"

I started shaking my head. "I thought you were a prophet. That you could give me some advice."

"I am! But what were you expecting? Prophecy is not an exact science. If it were, I'd have bought Microsoft stock back in the eighties. And I can't prophesy on the Dream Road."

"Oh."

"So you don't have any questions?"

I had tons, once I'd thought about it. "I need to know how to beat this thing. And how to deal with the Coven."

"Yikes. I'll need something stronger for that." He rose and went back to the bar. "Now where did I leave my opium pipe?"

"It's back in the temple."

His face sank. He started digging through a liquor cabinet.

"I read some of your prophecies. Some of them I didn't understand."

Baoh was pouring himself another drink. "I don't understand them, either." He waved his hand in a circular motion as if trying to remember something. "And those prophecies weren't really mine." He tested his concoction and made a face, then added more alcohol from the bottle he was holding. "No. They've been around for centuries. I just tweaked them a little bit. Creative license, eh. Not a bad job. Baoh aims to please."

I couldn't believe what I was hearing. Was this guy some kind of sideshow phony?

"Baaahhh. Don't get so upset. Prophecies are like that. Difficult to read. Over time, they change, or perhaps we change and see the signs differently. The originals bore no fruit, either. They were human prophecies for a human world. Or so we first thought, centuries ago. A noble hunter would die and leave his sons orphaned. It is over six hundred years old. Very close to the ones you read the other night." He reached into his shirt pocket and unfolded a piece of paper. Then he set it on the coffee table so we could both see it. It was the letter from Mutada.

"Where did you get that?"

"From your memory," he said. "This is a shared dream, after all.

"This is a mistake," he said, pointing to the page.

> The Lamb will be their shepherd [indecipherable muttering follows] . . . a scourge. He will lead them to springs of living water . . . to destruction. Behold, he is coming soon.

"Indecipherable muttering? You've got to be joking! I was as clear as the tax man." He waved a hand over the passage. "Amateurs!"

> The Lamb will be a shepherd or a scourge. He will lead them to springs of living water, or to destruction. Behold, he is coming soon.

He pointed to it, then took another sip. "There, that's better. And much improved over the original version. It was in Latin, you know, although I'm told there's a Han version that's older. No one can find it. Probably destroyed in the Cultural Revolution. But if you're a fan of irony, you'll like this little twist. In the fifteenth century, the prophets all lined up behind Vlad Dracula. Can you believe it? Your creator, no less.

"Vlad's father was a great falconer, a nobleman. One of the founders of the Order of the Defeated Dragon. And a mighty cavalryman. Dracul—the Dragon—he was called. He was assassinated, and so the great hunter died. He left many sons, the Sons of the Dragon, behind him as orphans. Vlad was a hostage of the Turks at the time. When he emerged from his prison, great things were expected. . . . Great things . . ." Baoh sipped his drink and shook his head. "But Vlad led the Western crusade against the Turks straight into the toilet." He paused and mumbled quietly to himself for a few seconds, lost in thought. "After his death, his head was taken by the Turks to Constantinople. Istanbul. My guess is, it must have been the head of a changeling. In any case, when he came back as a vampire and formed his Coven, he lost his interest in human history. It was too fleeting, too temporary for his liking. He became an alchemist, and the scourge of the vampire world. I'll bet my best tea set he's killed more of us than the Roman Catholic Church. He says it's to keep the spread of the disease under control, but I wonder . . ."

"Is he alive?" I asked.

Baoh shook his head. "Vlad? No—he sleeps, and it is always best to let a sleeping Dragon lie, eh? I hope no one wakes him, but I suspect the Baron Vrolock, Dracula, will rise again before the End of Days is concluded. But this is not the trouble you speak of, no? You mentioned a vampire hunter. A creature—Mr. Hyde. Do you think he is the Beast of the Apocalypse? The Beast that none can war against?"

"You mean he can't be beaten?"

"Yes."

"I hope not. But Mr. Entwistle couldn't beat him, and he claims to be the greatest fighter alive in the world."

"Who is Mr. Entwistle?"

"A vampire. John Entwistle."

"What? The bass player from the Who? He's come back as a vampire? Wow, that's cool! I always liked the Who. I'm a bit of a pinball wizard myself, you know."

I shook my head. This dream was getting a bit nutty, even for me. "Not the musician. A different John Entwistle. Ophelia says he was once John Tiptoft."

Baoh's eyebrows shot skyward. He swallowed an ice cube whole. I actually watched it go down his throat. "Are you certain? What does he look like?"

I did my best to describe Mr. Entwistle's appearance. His weathered features, scruffiness, and long, salt-and-pepper hair.

"You sure that isn't the Undertaker?" Baoh topped up his drink and sat back down on the couch. "Well, that explains it." He leaned forward and rested his elbows on his knees. "Ophelia insisted that we meet now—on very short notice. She is trying to hide her feelings, but not much gets past old Baoh. She is terrified. I haven't seen her that scared since your father died." He looked at me when he said this. With his sunglasses on, you could easily forget he was blind.

"I think she's worried about the Coven," I said. "And about Hyde. I don't think Mr. Entwistle is the problem."

Baoh swirled his drink delicately in his hand. The room was so quiet I could hear the sound of ice clinking against the edges of the glass. "I wouldn't assume that. No one knows who he really is. His past is cloaked in darkness. It was decades after his turning when he emerged as John Tiptoft, the Earl of Worcester. How many men he has been since that time, and how many men he was before, only he can say, but he has been a mercenary in his day, and an executioner, a warlord, a murderer. The worst kind of vampire—ruthless and cruel. Death walks at his right shoulder. She would be wise to keep her distance from him."

I felt the blood drain from my face. Without Mr. Entwistle, we didn't have a chance. "He couldn't be as bad as Vlad."

Baoh's lips turned down as if he was puzzling it over. "As a man, a prince, Vlad killed with purpose. With great enthusiasm, to be sure, but always for a reason. He was not as crazy as history books would have you believe. As a vampire, he kills with equal enthusiasm, or he did, but again, for a reason. To stop the spread of the disease. To silence those people who found out about us. Tiptoft was a different kind of monster. He killed for fun. For sport. To satisfy some sadistic craving." Baoh sat back and pursed his lips. "In the end, which is worse?"

I was speechless. Mr. Entwistle only spoke to me about forgiveness and truth and doing what was right. This had to be a mistake.

I felt Baoh's hand on my shoulder. His sunglasses were off. I stared at his eyeless eyes. "He is ancient, Zachary. And there is only one reason God permits us old-timers to live so long. It is because the sins of our first lives are so heinous, it takes us centuries to atone, to redeem ourselves. If John Entwistle is John Tiptoft, is he atoning for his past sins?"

I nodded.

"Then he might be a changed man. Never underestimate the transformative power of pain and loss and time, of love and forgiveness and faith. People can change. Why, look at old Baoh. Two centuries ago I weighed five hundred pounds." He paused and settled into the sofa cushions. "Hard to believe, eh? I look pretty snazzy for a man of twelve hundred, wouldn't you say?"

I would say, and I did. He seemed pleased.

"Now, whether you can trust this John Entwistle or not, Baoh can't say. But I would advise you to be careful. You have a role to play in the future of our kind. It is your decency that makes you suitable. Be righteous, and if you survive, you will have earned it, and if you die, you will move into the next world with a clean soul."

"Is that what it says in the prophecies?"

"Baaahhh, who knows? They only make sense when they've already come true. That's the trouble with them. But this isn't a helpful answer, eh? Let me say that the prophecies you read are as accurate as I can make them. I check often for signs and portents. I meditate. I listen to the inner voice that speaks to me, and sometimes through me. It might be God. Might be the devil. Might be a restless spirit, good or bad. I might have a split personality. Baoh doesn't have all the answers. But I can tell you this: for decades those vampires with the power of true sight have witnessed the coming of the messiah. No two seers agree on all the details. No two visions are perfectly identical. But the essence remains the same. The greatest vampire hunter the world has ever seen will die, or has died—perhaps by his own hand. His son will be orphaned and will become a blood drinker. There is some disagreement about which comes first. What we all agree upon is that the future of our kind rests with him, with this orphan—the hunter's son. And he will be a saint, or a scourge. He will elevate our kind to new heights, or lead us to destruction. A time of change is upon us. Apocalypse. An end and a beginning. Perhaps only for vampires. Perhaps for the whole of the world. God only knows, and He is usually very quiet about His plans."

God only knows . . . I looked at the floor, thinking. My head was full of questions. "Am I that messiah?"

"That is for God to know."

"So what do I do? Who can I trust? This thing, this Beast, it seems unstoppable. And the Coven wants me dead. And my friends. They've already sent one vampire. Mr. Entwistle thinks they'll send an army of them once they stop fighting one another."

Baoh put his sunglasses back on, took a sip of his drink, and chomped down on another piece of ice. "A smart warrior fights his battles one at a time. Focus on the most immediate threat."

"That's Mr. Hyde."

He sat back and thought. "Any creature that bleeds can die. You must only hope that he is not one of us—a vampire. Only against a lycanthrope will you have a chance."

I wanted to ask what he meant by this, but I was starting to fade, literally. My body was almost see-through. I looked at my hand and saw a blurry image of the carpet coming through from underneath.

"What is happening?" I asked, but I already knew the answer. The same thing had happened to Luna when I went to visit her.

"You are waking up, Daniel Zachariah Thomson. But have no fear. All will be well, if you walk the righteous path, and do not do to others that which is harmful to yourself."

CHAPTER 19

AN UNEXPECTED GUEST

I awoke a few hours before the sunset, which was unusual. I was strangely alert. My heart was beating hard. I heard footsteps in the hall. Hackles started to rise on my neck. The footsteps stopped outside my door. A series of gentle knocks followed.

"Who is it?" I asked.

"It's me, boy. You up?" It was Mr. Entwistle.

"I'm awake, yeah."

The door opened slowly. Sunlight from the hall window filtered through the dusty air. It was faint, but strong enough that I had to squint.

"I was having trouble sleeping," he said, and stepped into the room. "I thought we should talk."

I was more than a bit surprised. He was supposed to be long gone. And it was daytime. The sunlight was still strong and there wasn't a mark on him. "How did you get in here?"

"Here? Oh, simple. I never really left. I've been sleeping here all day."

"I watched you go."

"Yeah. I did. I had to see a friend. But then I came right back and cut the glass out of a basement window. I couldn't risk staying away for long. Not with a creature as dangerous as Hyde running around. I had to stay close."

He started pacing back and forth in front of the window. It was shuttered with thick wooden slats. A blind and set of curtains kept out almost every photon.

"So you stayed?"

"Yeah. I figured if Ilona found out, I'd ask forgiveness. It's easier than getting permission."

Funny, that was Charlie's philosophy. It had helped him set the school record for after-class detentions. When I thought about it, the two vampires had a lot in common.

"Why do you call her that? Ilona."

He cleared his throat, but his feet kept moving. "Ilona is her name. Or it was, centuries ago. Why? What does she call herself now?"

"Ophelia."

"Ophelia." He paused for a moment, his lips pressed together, but his eyes stayed busy. "'To the celestial and my soul's idol, the most beautified Ophelia . . . Doubt thou the stars are fire; Doubt that the sun doth move, Doubt truth to be a liar, But never doubt I love.'"

He sat down on the edge of the bed, then stood up right away and started pacing back and forth in front of the painted window again. He did this for about half a minute. He was mumbling to himself.

"What is it?" I asked.

"I've been thinking. A lot. And I . . . Well . . . About your future and what's happening and what Ophelia said, and I think she's right."

I wasn't certain what he was referring to. What was she right about? It was hard to concentrate. His behavior was distracting—his voice, his restlessness, and the rapid movement of his eyes from the floor to me, to the window, to the door. He couldn't stay focused on anything for long. It reminded me of the first time I'd seen him, when he crashed a motorcycle through the lobby of the Nicholls Ward.

"You seem agitated."

"Yeah. Happens when I get visions. Can't sleep. And I could use a bolt or two. Haven't had a drink since our Little Lake adventure." He tapped his chest. "I usually have a bottle handy, but I sacrificed my last one during our getaway."

"Maybe Ophelia has something you can take."

He shook his head and waved a hand in front of his face. "No. No, I'm not into medication. My mind needs to be alert. That stuff turns you into a zombie."

He looked to be halfway there. If he hadn't been moving so quickly, I might have mistaken him for one.

"Has Ophelia spoken to you yet?" he asked.

I wondered if that was the real reason he was so restless, because he was worried I knew about him and about his past—that he'd once been a murderer and an executioner. "Yes. I have spoken with her, and I . . ." I didn't know how to explain about Baoh. It was just a dream, but it was more than a dream. I needed a second or two to think about what to say, but I didn't get time. He kept on talking.

"I have much to atone for. I've been many people in the past. Most of them bad. There are things I hope history will forget. Things you wouldn't understand. I was raised in a different age." His voice began to waver. He stopped long enough to look at me. His pale blue eyes were watering. "I have done terrible things. Unforgivable things." He looked away again. His fingers strayed to his forehead. "And no matter how often I change my name or redirect the course of my life, I can't escape them. . . . It is my cross to bear." He waved his hand and muttered something to himself. "But that is as it should be. And it's neither here nor there. What I came to tell you was this—I have tried to make up for it. To live my life, my recent life, in a way that is fair and good. That would be pleasing to a higher power . . ." His forehead wrinkled up and he lost his train of thought.

"I had a vision yesterday. I think it was meant to show me the way forward. I have been thinking about it . . ." He looked over at me again, then down at the floor. The pacing continued. "I think this Hyde creature is my penance. A thing I have to face, alone, to atone for what I've done. I don't think I'll survive. I don't think I'm meant to. But I have to face him anyway." He looked over to make sure I was following him. Or that I believed him. I kept nodding. "I have to, because no one else can. After that, there is only darkness.

But it doesn't matter. Do you know what matters?" His eyes found me again, then bounced away. I got the sense he'd forgotten the answer to his own question. But he kept talking anyway. "There are men out there who will judge us and kill us. And vampires like Vlad, who will do the same. I believe in balance. Yin and yang. You understand what I mean?"

I wasn't sure, but I said I did anyway.

"Well, there needs to be balance in the vampire world. A balance of perspectives. I don't judge people anymore. I used to. When men called me the Butcher of England. The Butcher . . . But I'm not like that now."

He sat down again. "What I'm trying to say is this. There has to be someone out there who doesn't judge. Who will try, no matter what, to be good to everyone, whether they're good or whether they're bad." He waved his hand in the air as if he'd just said something ridiculous. "Well, we're all good and bad. Everyone. You, me, Ophelia, Charlie. You know that." He stood up. "But sometimes the evil is more obvious. The good is buried. But it's always in there. Deep down. And you can find it—raise it up. Even in your enemies. You believe that, don't you?"

I did and I said so.

"Good." He looked at me and stopped again, but only for a second. "Good. You have to. You have to believe. Believe in goodness. And forgiveness. You have to. Because when I'm gone, there has to be someone left who will keep the balance. Who will see the good in all things. In all people. I think that someone is you." His eyes flashed over to me, then shot around the room. "No. I don't *think* it's you. I *know* it's you. It has to be you."

He stopped pacing and turned to the door. More footsteps echoed in the hall—light and quick. He sat down on the edge of the bed and whispered, "Listen carefully." Panic was in his eyes. "You're going to come to a crossroads. To a decision. I've seen it."

He was interrupted by a knock at the door. "Zachary, are you all right?" It was Ophelia.

"I'm fine."

Mr. Entwistle kept whispering. He waved a hand as he spoke. "Forget about her. Well, no, don't forget about her. She needs you. You have to stick together. Charlie, too. But just listen. The Apocalypse is upon us. For our kind, at least. And the one who leads us through the End of Days, who emerges in the aftermath to establish a new order, will be a saint or a demon."

A saint or demon? That sounded close to "a shepherd or a scourge." Was he was talking about the prophecies? He must have seen the surprise on my face.

"You know this already?" he said quickly.

I nodded.

"Good." I could feel his relief. It settled him down, but only for a second. "Like I said, you're going to come to a crossroads. To a decision. Do your best to be a saint. It's what the world needs. Lord knows, there are enough demons out there . . ."

As he was reaching for the knob, the door opened. Ophelia was standing in the hall, an alarmed expression on her face. "What are you doing here? The sun is still up."

If Mr. Entwistle noticed her fear, he gave no sign. He fished into one of the pockets of his overcoat. "Just bringing him this." It was a bag of blood. I was surprised all his pacing hadn't popped it open. "I got worried that if Hyde came and he was still injured, you wouldn't be able to escape." He fished in his other pocket. "I brought one for Charlie, too. And for you."

"Where did you get these?" Ophelia asked.

"From a friend. It's clean, if that's your concern. Harvested straight from the source. They haven't passed through the Underground, so there's no way for them to be tainted."

Ophelia took the bags from him and backed away toward the bed. He stepped into the doorway and turned to face me one last time. We made eye contact. He nodded. I nodded back. Then he closed the door and walked away.

I listened to his footsteps as they faded down the hall. He was talking to himself quietly. "'Yea, though I walk through the valley of the shadow of death, I will fear no evil: for thou art with me . . .'"

. . . thou art with me. The words felt like a quiet rebuke. This wasn't right. I opened the door. "Wait," I shouted.

He stopped. An uncovered window sat at the top of the stairs. The light was too bright so I had to step behind the doorframe. I don't know how he managed to stand there so calmly. Then I realized he wasn't calm. He was the opposite.

"Don't leave. Just wait downstairs. In the basement maybe."

I was worried Ophelia would object, but she didn't. I closed the door and listened. His footfalls descended two flights of steps. Ophelia moved toward me. I held up a hand to stop her. I wanted to listen—to see if he kept pacing. He did.

"Are you sure you're all right?" she asked.

"Yeah, I'm fine."

"How did he get here?"

I wasn't sure exactly what to say, so I said nothing.

"He seemed manic," she said.

"Yeah, he did. He was like that last year, too. When he crashed that stolen motorcycle through the lobby."

She looked at the door, then at the window. I'm not sure what she saw there, but she was thinking. "It could be a seasonal affective disorder."

I'd heard of this. Sad Stephen, one of the patients I used to know at the Nicholls Ward, had the same thing.

"Could you give him something?" I asked. "I think he just needs some sleep. He was worried."

"About what?"

"He says he has to face Hyde. Alone. He saw it in a vision last night. But he can't see anything after that. It's all dark. I think it means Hyde's going to kill him."

Ophelia looked at the door. Her expression changed. Worry became alarm. "Oh . . . Oh, no."

I didn't understand this. She'd booted him out last night and might have done so again just now, in broad daylight. "I thought you didn't trust him."

She sat down on the bed. She stared at the bag of blood in her hand. Her eyes were unfocused. "I don't know what to think." She looked at me. "What did Baoh say?"

"He said I need to be righteous."

"And about John?"

I looked down at the floor. His footsteps drifted up from the basement. From two floors up, they sounded no louder than the soft patter of a cat, but he was probably carving holes in the carpet. "He said that people can change."

"But can we trust him?"

"He didn't know. But he said I should not do to others that which is harmful to myself."

Her eyes returned to the window. For a time she just sat and stared, then she looked down at the bags of blood Mr. Entwistle had given her. "And what does your heart tell you?"

"I trust him. I think he's honest."

"A person can be totally honest and still not be trustworthy."

I didn't know what she was getting at. My expression must have told her as much.

"What if a person has poor judgment? For a person to be worthy of trust means you can count on them, not just to be truthful, but to be prudent as well."

I hadn't considered that. I sat down beside her. "Do you trust his judgment?" she asked.

"No. But that's why you're here."

Ophelia laughed. She didn't do this often. Not these days. The pleasant sound made it impossible not to smile.

"He told me you were right," I said. "That I had to stick with you. I guess he wants to protect us. He's going after Hyde alone."

"What else did he say?"

"He told me about the prophecies. He thinks I'm the messiah, too. That I need to see the good in people."

Ophelia squeezed my arm, then stood up. "Perhaps his judgment isn't so bad after all." She started moving for the door. "I'll see what I can do for him."

"Thanks." I eyed the bag he'd delivered. My gums started to tingle. It meant my teeth were going to drop.

"Ophelia."

She turned.

"I think we should stay together—all of us. I think he wants to be on his own to distance us from trouble, but it won't do us any good if he dies alone. I think this trouble will find us. That Hyde won't stop until we're all dead. And the Coven. We'll need his help for that, too."

She took a deep breath. "John's behavior is reckless, Zachary. He's a magnet for attention. That makes him dangerous to us, whether he means to be or not. We need to keep a low profile for the time being."

"Would you want me to be by myself with that thing running around out there?"

She shook her head. "No . . . but that isn't the situation." She looked at the clock beside my bed. A few hours of sunshine remained in the day. "I think you should get some more rest." She backed into the hall. "Take care." Then she closed the door behind her and went downstairs to look after Mr. Entwistle.

CHAPTER 20

A TRIP TO THE HOSPITAL

If you're a vampire, when blood enters your body, every system goes wonky. Energy courses through your limbs. Sometimes the rush is so intense you think your brain might catch fire. But when you're injured, it's a different game. The pain of your injuries gets concentrated into a few seconds of intense agony. After the burn comes the itch. I guzzled the blood Mr. Entwistle had given me, closed my eyes, and tensed every muscle. Ripped tissue mended. I hissed. Pain racked my body. Then the itch came. I started scratching at the bullet wounds on my thigh and shoulder as if I needed to take the skin off. When this faded, my mind went to heaven. I sat and enjoyed the pleasant aftershocks. When they were gone, I closed my eyes. I started thinking of Luna—how nice it would be if we could visit on the Dream Road every day. I carried this thought into a sleep that took me a few hours past sundown.

I woke up with Mr. Entwistle standing over me. His eyes were still restless, and his appearance was so haggard, if you'd told me he'd been hit by a train, then dragged along the tracks for a few hundred miles, I would have believed you.

"Did you get any sleep?" I asked.

"No, but I'll be fine."

"Are you leaving?"

He nodded. "I'm going to see if I can find the Fleabag."

I didn't think it was a good idea for him to go after Mr. Hyde alone, and I said so.

He looked at me for a few seconds, his teeth clenched, the muscles at the sides of his jaw twitching. "I understand your concern, but there are greater things at stake than the life of John Entwistle."

"Where's Ophelia?" I was hoping she could talk him out of going after Hyde alone.

He handed me a note. "This was downstairs on the dining room table."

The writing was Ophelia's.

> *Zachary,*
> *Detective Baddon has asked for some assistance regarding*
> *the investigation of Everett's death. I thought it might help*
> *to clear your name. I see no sign of Mr. Entwistle. Should*
> *he return, please exercise caution. Don't leave the house.*
> *There is exercise equipment in the basement and a*
> *collection of books and movies. My recommendation is*
> *rest. I should be back from the police station in a few hours.*
> *O*

"It says here you left," I said.

"Yes, I did. I had to see someone about a lead. Before I go after Hyde, I thought it would be a good idea to put you in touch with someone who might be able to help out in my absence. Come on. We're going to the hospital."

"I'm not supposed to leave."

I held up the note with one hand like a raffle ticket. I hadn't meant for him to read it, but I guess the way I was holding it suggested otherwise, because he snatched it from my fingers and glanced it over.

"'Exercise caution,' huh? That's great advice. So . . . you coming?"

"But it says—"

"Look, boy, the toughest vampire on planet Earth is leaving. Are you safer with me or here by yourself?"

He had a point.

"There's the spirit of the law, and the letter of the law. Always go with the spirit, Zack, the spirit. Always. Ophelia wants you to be safe. You're safer at the hospital. Plain and simple." He clapped me on the shoulder and headed down the stairs. "We're going to be tight for time," he added over his shoulder, "so hurry. I'll be in the garage."

"What about Charlie?"

"He's waiting for us downstairs."

I should have known. If trouble was brewing, he'd already have his nose in it.

I was dressed and downstairs in a flash. The place was dark and empty. I made my way to the garage. I walked in and found Mr. Entwistle and Charlie digging through a toolbox. The old vampire pulled out a small tommy bar and handed it to my friend, who stuffed it into a backpack. Before he closed it, I spied the head of a hatchet and a coil of white rope that was woven with red. It made me think of a candy cane.

"What's that smell?"

"Lighter fluid," Charlie said.

"So where exactly are we going?"

Mr. Entwistle shouldered the pack. "Civic Hospital."

He stepped past me, then quietly opened the back door of the garage. Fresh air wafted in and the smell of dusty motor oil mixed with a blast of cedar. I closed my eyes. Even without looking, I knew that it was going to be a perfect night for running. The air had the right weight. Fresh and clear. Mr. Entwistle peeked outside, scanned the neighbors' yards, then nodded for us to go ahead.

"After you," said Charlie.

A second later the door was closed and we were approaching the sound barrier. I was much faster this time. Instead of struggling after, I let Charlie set the pace and tried not to run him over. We made good time and didn't let up until we were in the parking lot of the new Civic Hospital.

"Hold up." Mr. Entwistle took off the backpack. "I need to ditch this." He stowed it in the shadows against the wall, then smiled at me. "You looked better tonight. That blood did you wonders."

"I'd say so. And thanks."

"Don't mention it. But you might want to consider getting some body armor." He slapped the plate over his chest.

"How much would it cost me?"

He took off his top hat and mulled it over. "More than you're likely to make selling your life story, that's for sure. Now come on, I've got a lot to do tonight."

"How are we getting in?" Charlie asked.

"I'm using the front door. Did you have another strategy in mind?"

Charlie shrugged and we entered the lobby. A hand-wash station was set up just inside the door. It must have looked ridiculous to the people in the waiting room when Mr. Entwistle cleaned his hands. He would have needed to swim in a vat of sanitizer to get all the germs off. He looked like a dried-up mud puddle. When he was finished, a nurse at the reception desk asked us if we needed help.

"I just got a call to pick up my son," Mr. Entwistle said. "He's in detox again. Can you believe it?"

The woman took one look at him. He could have been the poster boy for a life gone wrong. "Down the hall and to the left," she said.

"Thanks."

Mr. Entwistle headed for the elevators.

"We aren't really going to detox, are we?"

"Now would a guy like me need directions to detox? No, we're going to radiology. Fourth floor. Actually, you're going. I'm meeting another contact to see what I can learn about where Hyde holes up. He has to have a den or lair somewhere." Mr. Entwistle pressed the button that would bring us an elevator, then handed me a slip of paper. It had a number scribbled in blue ink: 412.

"So we're staying here by ourselves?"

"Not counting a few hundred patients and hospital staff, Charlie, and Agent X, yes, you're all alone."

"Who's Agent X?" I asked.

"The man in room 412."

"But what about the spirit of the law—and being safer with you?"

"Didn't you spend eight years in a hospital ward? What could possibly happen here?" The elevator doors opened. He put his hand inside to keep them from closing. "Just make certain when you boys leave, that you take the stairs. Got it?"

I couldn't imagine why this was important, but I wasn't about to argue with a man who could see the future. "Got it."

He pressed the button for the fourth floor, then stepped back as the doors closed. The elevator started to rattle its way up.

"Man, that guy's a piece of work. Can you believe it, *my son's in detox again*?"

I nodded. Mr. Entwistle was a disaster. But he was also our best hope for staying alive. I wished he weren't leaving.

"Do you think he really was a butcher—like Ophelia says?"

I looked at Charlie. He knew my answer was yes. I didn't have to speak.

"Well, I'd hate to be in your shoes when we get home."

I imagined Ophelia coming back from the police station and finding the house empty. I should have left a note. "She's going to kill me, isn't she?"

"You have to die somehow."

I could have called her on my cell, but I couldn't stand the thought of hearing the disappointment in her voice. Or worse, that she might be scared. Or angry.

The elevator stopped on the fourth floor. It opened, and I followed the signs to room 412. The door was closed.

Charlie peeked in through the window. "Looks empty."

The lights were off.

I reached past him and knocked on the door. There was no answer. I hadn't been told what to expect, so I opened the door quietly. "Hello," I whispered. The room was dark except for a small red light that came from a machine of some kind. It was set beside an empty bed. I could tell by the wrinkled sheets that someone had recently been sleeping there. I listened. A tap was running in the bathroom. I could smell the chlorine in the water, clean sheets, men's aftershave, and disinfectant. I quietly entered and knocked on the bathroom door.

I heard a click and a whoosh, followed by a surprised "Ow!" I looked over at Charlie. His hand was on his neck. He looked at me, then his eyes rolled up and he collapsed into a heap on the floor.

I heard a swish of fabric at my back. Then the light flicked on and I turned my head. A man in a white hospital robe was standing behind me. He was holding a semiautomatic pistol in one hand. He took his other hand off the light switch, used it to steady the gun, then cocked the hammer and backed away, all in one fluid motion. He was just far enough from me that I couldn't lunge and disarm him quickly. He knew exactly what he was doing.

I was shocked. I'd been betrayed once before, and the feeling wasn't pleasant. My stomach felt as if it were falling out. The same question that had popped into my head the last time made a sudden reappearance: *How did I get here?*

"Hello, Zachary. I've been expecting you."

The man looked different than I remembered. Skin hung more loosely over his large muscles now, and his head was completely bald. But his eyes were just as intense as ever.

"Hello," I replied. The word barely made it out.

Then my uncle Maximilian, the vampire hunter, stared down the barrel of his gun, stiffened slightly, and pulled the trigger.

CHAPTER 21

AGENT X

In the movies, when a hero gets shot, he usually has time for some last words. The villains, if they don't drop dead like a stone, usually stay alive long enough to look dazed and confused—as if they're stunned that good could ever triumph over evil, as if it never happened in Hollywood before that one, shocking moment. I think I went out like a villain—stunned. I wasn't instantly dead! What a surprise! I reached up to my neck expecting to find a gushing wound. I didn't. Wonder of wonders! Something about the size of a cigarette butt was sticking out of my throat. What could this be? I pulled it out. A sting followed. Then I dropped, no wiser than before. Dazed and confused.

My uncle caught me. Pain was radiating up and down my neck. It turned from a burn into a warm rush. This passed after a few seconds and a feeling of pleasant euphoria took over. Lightness filled my limbs. I'd felt something like this before. A runner's high, it was called. When you run long enough, your body starts to produce natural painkillers. They act a bit like morphine. But I would've had to run to Pluto to feel this good.

"Forgive me," he said. "But all hell's broken loose. Good people are dying out there. I can't take any chances right now."

Forgive him? For what? This was heaven. My body was turning into air. The only thing that stayed heavy was my head, which was starting to feel like a medicine ball. If I didn't lie down, it was going to roll right off my neck.

"Just ride it out."

I managed to whisper the word "What?"

"Nothing fancy. Mostly sodium thiopental and a mild opiate."

I smiled. Why hadn't I tried this before?

Maximilian led me to a chair, then sat me down. I melted into it.

"Are you okay? Can you hear me?"

I could hear him, which I assumed was good, so I kept smiling. Questions formed. "Are you going to kill us?" The words came out in slow motion.

He shook his head. He was starting to look fuzzy around the edges. "Of course not. Charlie's going to have a little sleep, and we're going to talk."

"Thaaaat's goooood."

He sat on the edge of his bed and slipped something under his pillow. Then he started talking about Vlad, and how dangerous he was, and that he wasn't supposed to hurt anyone *that night*. I had trouble listening. I was staring at my hand. It looked interesting. So did my other hand. I waved them in front of my face. They were like two blobs of ice cream with peach-colored birthday candles sticking out the top. A birthday ice-cream cone . . . Why hadn't anyone thought of this?

My uncle gently brushed my hands away. Then he rolled up my sleeve and drew out a syringe. "Can you hear me?"

I had forgotten how to speak, so I just hummed—like R2-D2.

"The Coven doesn't want people to know about vampires. Only the Underground is exempt, and they are selected with great care. When Charlie and Luna found out about you, the only thing Vlad was willing to do was absorb them as agents, or make them vampires. I would never have guessed he was planning an execution."

"Two executions." My voice was coming back, at half normal speed. I held up two fingers in case he didn't understand me, but it might have been four.

"I'm going to set things right." He snorted. "Ironic. In the end, you all wound up vampires anyway. And Vlad is finished."

I shook my head.

"What do you mean?"

"His body went missing," I said slowly. "It disappeared." I spread my hands for emphasis. It felt as if I were rising out of my chair, so I flapped my hands slowly a few more times to see if I could really fly, but the weight of my head made it impossible. It tipped forward. My uncle seemed to take up my entire view. "You look terrible."

He cleared his throat. It sounded like rocks breaking. "It's the cancer treatment. If the chemotherapy doesn't kill me, the radiation will."

"I hope not."

For a long time he looked at me without speaking. I tried to stare back and nod so that he'd know I was being honest, but it was hard to focus on anything because my eyes wouldn't open all the way. The room seemed to be shifting, as if I were seeing it through a hazy waterfall. It made him sound far away.

"Are there any rumors of him? Of Vlad? From Ophelia or Entwistle?"

I shook my head. "Nothing."

"Do you know why the Coven wants you and Charlie dead?"

I tried to focus. It seemed this was important. Why did they want us dead? There could be only one reason. "They just don't know us very well. We're actually really nice guys."

"What can you tell me about this creature—this vampire hunter?"

He must have meant Hyde. "Ophelia and the others are hoping he's a werewolf. I don't know why. We call him Mr. Hyde, although he doesn't hide. He attacks people with these huge claws."

"Why does she hope he's a werewolf?"

I hummed for a while—until he repeated the question. "I don't know. No one tells me anything."

My uncle rose from his seat on the bed and started lacing up a pair of heavy black boots. When he took off his gown, I could see scars on his torso. He had lost a bit of weight, but he still looked like a powerhouse. He slipped on a shirt.

"What is Entwistle planning to do?" he asked.

"He wants to face Hyde on his own. He told me I needed to survive."

"You will. That's a promise. Why does he have to face Hyde alone? He didn't mention it to me."

"He saw it in a vision. He's going to die."

My uncle stopped. Whatever he'd put under his pillow he removed and tucked into the back of his jeans. "He told you this!"

I nodded.

"Did he say when? Or where?"

I tried to remember if he had. Nothing was coming back to me, so I shrugged.

"What did Ophelia say about this?"

"She doesn't trust him because he's a murderer."

"Who's a murderer?"

"Mr. Entwistle. But his real name is John something or other. Or it was. He was the Barber of England."

"The Barber of England?"

That didn't sound right. "No. The Butcher of England."

My uncle was putting on a windbreaker. His moving blur became a stationary blur. "John Entwistle is really John Tiptoft? The executioner for the House of York?"

"Yes. Well, not anymore."

"Who told you this?"

"Ophelia did. And Baoh."

My uncle moved closer. His face took up the whole screen. The words seemed to echo in my head.

"You met Baoh? The prophet? *Unbelievable!* So he does exist!"

"We played Nintendo. I beat him, but only because he let me win." It was funny—our little men pulverizing one another.

"What did he tell you?"

I wondered what my uncle was talking about.

"Baoh. What did he tell you?"

He told me lots of stuff, but one thing stood out. "To be righteous."

"That's it?"

I sat up. My uncle's tone was serious. "The End of Days is here. I have to die with a clean soul."

My uncle reached down to a black bag that was on the floor. "You're not dying on my watch." He took out something in a thin leather case. "I'm leaving this with you. Be extremely careful. It's lethal."

"What is it?"

"It's a knife. The blade has been treated with dioxin. It's sixty thousand times more potent than cyanide, so leave it in the sheath until you need it."

I looked at the knife. The blade was buried inside a narrow leather sleeve, but it must have been about the same length as my hand. My hand . . . It really did look like an ice cream cone, especially when I made a fist. Then I lifted my other hand and the two started waving to each other.

My uncle dug back into his black bag. This time he pulled out something that looked like a space gun I'd once seen on Teletoon. "This is going to cause some swelling." He put the gun against the back of my shoulder blade and pulled the trigger.

I felt a jab of pain. Right away the area under the skin started to bulge. It felt like a pimple.

"Don't pick at it."

"What's that for?"

"It's a microtransponder, so I can find you if I need to." He took out a small case and removed a syringe. He screwed a needle into the end and stuck it in a small bottle. After drawing some fluid into the syringe, he told me to roll up my sleeve.

"Is that poison?"

He shook his head. "No."

He helped me roll up my sleeve, then injected my arm with something.

"You're going to sleep for a while, but you'll be safe here. The door's locked. Mr. Entwistle will be back before the sun comes up.

I'd stay, but this Hyde creature appears to be nocturnal. I have to see if I can find it before Entwistle gets himself killed."

Was he crazy? My head slumped forward. It was too heavy to lift again. My eyes were starting to close. I fought against it. There were things I had to know. "How can you kill this thing?"

He grabbed my arm and pulled me out of the chair, then slipped his shoulder under me and tipped me onto the bed. "Poisons work best. Cyanide, arsenic, or dioxin. I've used *Conium maculatum* effectively in the past, but your father preferred venom from *Hydrophis belcheri*."

Hydrophis belcheri? What was that? It sounded like a burping water dragon. "Do you have any?"

"Only what I've given you. The dioxin. It's the Cadillac of poisons." He was moving toward the door.

The Cadillac of poisons? What I needed was the bulletproof, floating Cadillac of poisons with huge tires and twenty-four hundred horses under the hood. Then I could drive back to Weed World. Hyde would never find me there. I laughed. Why hadn't I thought of that before? I was full of good ideas tonight.

My uncle was leaving. I needed to ask something else. "Where have you been all this time?" I hadn't seen him in a year. He was sliding in and out of focus.

"Hunting a werewolf."

"Was it Hyde?"

"No."

Now he was a complete blur. "Did you catch it?"

He said something, but I couldn't make it out. I wanted to ask him to repeat his answer, but my tongue got all tied up and my eyes just wouldn't open. I heard the door. Then it closed and I fell asleep.

— CHAPTER 22

ABOVE THE TILES

I awoke feeling like death. My tongue was sandpaper and my head was a swollen wound. I couldn't move. I wondered for a minute if this was what a hangover was like. Charlie had once described one to me, but they couldn't have been this bad or no one on earth would have risked taking a drink. The thought of moving made my stomach tremble and my brain scream. I didn't want to move a muscle, but the clock on the wall said 4 a.m. I'd been asleep for several hours. If I fell asleep again and didn't wake up in time, I'd wind up on fire.

I sat up. This required I wait a few minutes while my head adjusted to its new elevation. *Why are you doing this to us?* it asked. It repeated the question when I stood. Then I noticed the knife on the bedside table. A parting gift from my uncle. I would say this for him, he was a hard guy to figure out. I picked it up and examined the handle. It was molded and had a compass built into the knob on the end. I wasn't wearing a belt, so I stuck the sheath in my back pocket and pulled my shirt over the top to keep it out of sight.

Charlie was asleep on the floor beside me, a towel balled up under his head like a pillow. I gently touched his shoulder.

"Ohhhh," he groaned. "Go away."

"Charlie, wake up," I whispered. "We have to get going. The sun will be up soon."

That got his attention. His eyebrows rose on his forehead as if he were trying to force his eyelids open. "What happened?"

I wasn't sure what to tell him. I suppose the truth would have worked, but Charlie hated Maximilian, and his feelings were well-founded. "You were shot with a tranquilizer."

I heard footsteps outside. Then the window in the door darkened. I ducked around the curtain—the one that you see in most hospital rooms that hangs around the bed to create the illusion of privacy.

"Charlie, someone's in the hall. We need to hide." He seemed not to hear me.

"Whose idea was this anyway?" he asked. "Can't you give me five more minutes? I feel like I just stepped off the Time Warp at Canada's Wonderland."

I heard the rattle of the door handle. It was locked, but someone clearly wanted in. We were in no condition for a confrontation. I looked for a hiding place. There was none. At least, none in the room. But the false ceiling had tiles hanging on a plastic frame so that ductwork and plumbing could easily be accessed. They had the same kind back in the ward. I'd once used it to hide. No reason it wouldn't work again.

"Keep it down," I whispered. I quietly hauled him up to his feet. Then I stepped up on the bed, onto the machine beside it, and slipped a ceiling tile out of place. Overhead were the heating vents, wiring, and plumbing for the hospital. I grabbed a pipe and pulled myself up, then hooked my legs over so I was hanging upside down like a three-toed sloth.

Charlie stepped up onto the bed, then took my hand so I could pull him out of sight. As soon as he had a hold on the plumbing beside me, I slid the tile back. My coordination was a bit off, so I didn't get it set right. It left a slender crack open.

An instant later, I heard a key twist in the door lock. A man whispered, "Thank you," and walked in. The privacy curtain slid back and he stepped into view. He was short, bald, with legs that belonged on a rhinoceros. Detective Baddon. His head was angled to the side as though expecting to find someone in the bed. When he saw no one there, he sighed, disappointed. He moved closer, checked around the bed and table, then noticed a depression in the center of the mattress. A footprint. He gazed up at the ceiling, drew a gun from a holster strapped around his shoulder, then turned and reached for a chair.

Well, I wasn't sticking around for a shoot-out. My best projectile was a spitball. I slipped the tile down.

"We've got to move," I whispered to Charlie. Using my hands, I pulled myself away. I tried to be quiet, but I think the detective must have heard us because he was looking in our direction when his head popped up above the tile. He'd used his gun to lift the near end up out of the frame. It was pitch-black. I was hoping it was too dark for him to see. We didn't stick around to find out. I kept moving until I heard the tile drop. The faint light coming in from the room below disappeared. I stopped and listened.

"Did he see us?" I asked.

Charlie was staring back through the darkness. "Well, he didn't shoot, that's the main thing!"

We were above the hallway. I could hear Detective Baddon's footsteps as he exited the room. Another set, moving faster, swishing on the floor like slippers, was coming toward him.

"Oh, hi there," said a female voice. She sounded friendly, but surprised. "Sleepwalking again?"

I heard a gentle laugh. "No," said Detective Baddon. "I was hoping to talk to a patient, but he appears to have checked out."

"Did you want me to look into it for you?" I assumed the woman was a nurse.

"No. He's definitely gone. I'm just going to check in on my son. Who's on call tonight?"

"Dr. Bell. Do you want me to send for him?"

"If you don't mind. I was hoping for some news, but I don't have much time tonight. I'm not staying long."

"Oh, of course. I read the news about the police station. I hope no one was hurt."

"Not seriously."

"Have you found the boy?"

"Not yet, but we're hopeful." The tone of the detective's voice changed. I couldn't see him, but it sounded as though he was looking up. I had a flash of panic, as if he knew we were here. Sweat started to break out on my hands and forehead.

"I'll be down the hall," he added. "I'd appreciate an update as soon as possible."

"I'll pull his charts," the nurse said. "Someone will be in to see you right away."

He said thank you, then the two headed off in opposite directions.

My mind was racing. The detective had been looking for Maximilian. Why? It must have had something to do with Hyde.

"What do we do now?" Charlie asked.

The dawn was nearing. It was time to get going. "We should split," I whispered.

Charlie nodded, but he didn't move. "What's he doing here?"

I didn't know. But there was one way to find out—follow the footsteps as they faded down the hall. Common sense suggested we should leave. Ophelia would definitely want us to play the safe card and get home. But Charlie wanted to stay. What to do? Follow the Detention King of Adam Scott Collegiate, whose decisions had, arguably, driven his mother into rehab, or go with the most responsible person I'd ever met, whose levelheaded decision making had kept me safe for almost ten years?

Naturally, I went with Charlie.

CHAPTER 23

SICKBED

Something about hanging upside down must have been benefi-cial because my grogginess vanished once I got moving. My head started to clear and my strength returned. I followed Charlie, hand over hand, down the hall in pursuit of the detective's heavy footfalls. We were quiet. The only real danger seemed to be the dust. I was worried one of us might sneeze and give ourselves away. But I'd never read about a vampire being thwarted by unclean plumb-ing, so we slothed onward.

The detective quietly entered one of the rooms farther down the hall. We had to take a detour around a heating duct, which took an extra minute. By the time we were overhead, he'd settled himself into a chair beside the room's only bed. I eased a tile up just a fin-ger's breadth and listened. A boy was asleep in the bed beside him. He might have been six or seven. Judging by his features, he must have taken after his mother—slight, with fair hair and skin. Tubes ran into his arm and nose. The detective was sifting through a stack of what looked to be magazines. Only when he took one out of the middle did I see they were children's books. I recognized the picture on the front. It was *Where the Wild Things Are,* by Maurice Sendak—one of my all-time favorite stories as a little kid.

Detective Baddon pushed his glasses up on his nose, turned on the bedside light, angled it away from his son's face, and started to read out loud. I thought it was odd he would do this with his son sleeping. He was just turning a page when a knock came at the door. The detective stood. A man entered. He was wearing a collared, short-sleeve T-shirt and a pair of slacks that were pulled up too high. He looked to be a bit older, in his sixties maybe. He was flipping through pages on a clipboard. I guessed this was the boy's doctor. After a few seconds, he peered over his glasses. "You get any sleep this week?"

"Not much. Things are a bit crazy at the moment. Any news?"

"Yes. Good news." The doctor stared at the pages a moment longer. "The cancer's gone."

The detective looked down at his son. He removed his glasses and rubbed his eyes. "I don't get it. I thought we were starting a more aggressive treatment tomorrow. You said his chances were low. That the cancer was spreading."

"I can't explain it, Adam. The cancer is in total remission. His blood sample came back from the lab clean. The tissue biopsies came back this afternoon. Also clean. His white blood cell count is off the charts. Given the medications he was taking, it should be low, almost nonexistent. Not high. I've never seen anything like it. No one around here has."

Detective Baddon rubbed a hand over his scalp. I noticed the scar on his wrist again. A nasty swath of pink skin, as if he'd been burned or cut open. He looked exhausted. His eyes were red-rimmed and bloodshot, with deep ditches underneath. He slipped the arms of his glasses back over his ears, then stared at his son. When he started to speak, his voice broke. It took him a few moments to pull himself together.

"Is he ever going to wake up?" he asked.

The doctor didn't answer right away. He looked at the charts in his clipboard one last time, then slipped them into a tray at the base of the boy's bed.

"Usually I tell people in situations like this that you can't tell. All you can do is wait. But your son's a fighter, Adam. He's not a big kid, but . . ." The doctor shook his head. "Most people would have died from a head injury like that. The MRI came back and it looks like we were off with our first assessment, because his brain tissue is in better shape than we thought. His heartbeat is more regular. His breathing's stronger. It's all good news, Adam. The only problem is his red blood cell count. We can't keep it elevated. I've sent samples to a few specialists in Toronto. We should hear back soon."

"Do you need me to leave you with some more?"

"Give it a few days. We'll see what happens to his hematocrit levels. If he needs more blood, I'll let you know."

If he needs more blood? I looked at Charlie. He looked at me. Was he thinking what I was thinking? I examined the boy more carefully. He was emaciated, his features well-defined for a child so young—just as mine were when I was that age. Was he was one of us? A vampire? His blood was our first clue. He'd obviously had cancer, then it had gone away. Could he be carrying the pathogen? That would get rid of his cancer. It would also heal a damaged brain, which wasn't always possible for a normal person.

"You need to get some rest," the doctor said. "When did you eat last?"

The detective looked as if he was about to respond, but was interrupted by the old theme song from *Hockey Night in Canada*. He frowned and reached to his belt, then unclipped a cell phone and read the display.

"I have to take this. Who's in tomorrow?"

"Dr. Spink."

The detective nodded, then pulled the cell phone away from his ear to hear the last thing the doctor said.

"You should take a day off, Adam. You look like the walking dead."

The doctor turned and left the room. Detective Baddon waited until the door was closed before he answered the phone.

"Baddon here. What's up, Matt?" There was a pause. "Good." He tipped his wrist to check his watch. "Can you give me half an hour? . . . Perfect." He snapped the phone closed and clipped it back to his belt. A lock of his son's hair had fallen over his eyes. The detective brushed it away with a thick finger, then bent and kissed the boy's forehead. A few seconds later, the book was in his hand and he was reading again.

I started backing away. This was a private moment between a man and his son. It didn't feel right to hang around. The sun would soon be up. Charlie took one last look, then followed. I turned my head to see the best route out, then reached over to a neighboring pipe. It must have been all the dust in the air because I didn't see the jagged end of the bracket holding the pipe in place until I scraped my wrist against it, cutting my skin. It caught me by surprise. I pressed my teeth together to smother a snarl. I didn't want to give myself away. Because I was hanging upside down, I couldn't use my other hand to cover the gash, so I pressed it against my mouth instead in hopes that it would quickly clot. It was little more than a scratch. The taste of my blood got me thinking about the detective's son. If he was one of us, the scent of his blood would give him away. I could probably have picked it up from his arm, where the needle was inserted under his skin. But there wasn't enough time to wait for Detective Baddon to leave.

"Why are you waiting?" Charlie asked.

"I cut myself."

"Yeah, I can smell it."

I gave the cut a few seconds to start drying, then I began crawling, hand over hand back to my uncle's room. Once there, I exited the ceiling the same way I came in, by stepping off the machine and onto the bed. Through the window, I could see the dark night sky growing lighter at the horizon. Sunrise was about a half hour away.

"What do you make of that?" Charlie asked, dropping quietly beside me.

"What? The boy?"

"No—the plastic flowers by his bed. Of course the boy, you dough head!"

"I think he must be one of us."

Charlie crept to the door. "Exactly what I was thinking." He glanced up and down the hallway, then nodded. "The coast is clear. Let's go."

We slipped out without a sound and headed for the elevators.

"What was he doing in the room?" Charlie asked.

"What?"

"That bald dude. How did he know to look for us there?"

He hadn't been looking for us, he'd been looking for my uncle. "He must have been looking for Agent X."

Charlie hit the button for the elevator. "Well, this was a wasted trip."

A bell dinged and the door in front of us slid open. Charlie stepped in and I followed. He hit *L* for "lobby."

"What is it?" Charlie said. "You look like you lost your brain."

My brain was actually right where it belonged. It just wasn't working particularly well. I couldn't decide if I should tell Charlie that Agent X was really my uncle. And I was worried about Mr. Entwistle. Why wasn't he here? At the same time, a vague uneasiness had settled over me, as if I'd forgotten something important. Did it have to do with my uncle? Our conversation was difficult to recall. Like remembering an old dream. I reached back to scratch behind my shoulder. It was sore for some reason. Itchy. The skin raised like a blister. The doors closed, and the floor indicator started dropping from 4 to 3. Had I missed something?

"Speak up," said Charlie. "You're worse than a rock sometimes."

"Sorry, I'm just thinking."

"Well, I know that, Brainiac. When are you not thinking?"

Never was the correct answer, but I didn't get a chance to say so, because the top of the elevator exploded. The overhead lights burst and an alarm started to ring. The wall behind Charlie folded inward, knocking him against the door. The elevator jerked to an instant stop, buckling me at the knees. Then Mr. Entwistle's words came back. "Just make certain when you boys leave, that you take the stairs. Got it?" Not the best thing to forget, apparently, because the elevator was flying apart. A corner of the roof above me disintegrated, creating a hole that brought the elevator shaft into view. Hairy fingers, half again as long as mine, reached down through the opening and tore it wider. Through the smoke and spark of burning wires I glimpsed an enormous, man-shaped shadow. It snarled, then dropped down beside me.

THE BEAST THAT NONE CAN WAR AGAINST

From a distance, you might have mistaken him for the world's largest vampire. His shape was human. And he was clothed. Tattered leather jacket. Harley-Davidson belt buckle. Jeans that were way too short, like Hulk pants. But the odor was wrong. Even with the elevator wires sparking, and the stink of burning plastic everywhere, I could tell he wasn't one of us. He smelled musty— like an animal. And he was huge. Seven feet at least, and so wide at the shoulders he filled the elevator. Something about his shape was off. His arms were heavily muscled, but just a bit too long. His fingers, too. The nails of each were black and tapered to a sharp point. So were his toenails, which clacked on the elevator tiles when he landed. The floor lurched and my knees gave way. It gave me a good view of his feet. His arches were all stretched up so that he seemed to be perched on the balls of his feet, his ankle a foot above the floor. It made me think of the paw of a dog, or a wolf.

He bent down and glared at me with his large, yellow eyes. They were set wide apart on his face, and the irises were covered with flecks of red, like tiny drops of blood. The rest of his face was only vaguely human. The skin, where it wasn't covered in hair, looked as if it had been pulled back, so his nose was broad and flat against his skull. His nostrils flared with each breath. His forehead sloped backward, as did his ears, which were long and pointed. The top of his head was covered with coarse, black hair. It ran down each jaw, and even down his neck, but the whiskers didn't stretch across his chin, so they looked more like long sideburns. His thin lips pulled back and a low rumble leaked from his mouth. I could see a row of teeth not unlike my own. Incisors, long and pointed. They would have been right at home in a dinosaur exhibit. It made the hair on the back of my neck stand up. Then he growled. The sound was like electricity. It rippled through the bones of my chest. I glanced at Charlie. He'd been knocked flat and was crouched behind Hyde's feet. He looked as if he'd been hit by lightning.

I had one chance—the knife my uncle had given me. It was still in the back pocket of my jeans. I reached for it, but before I could get it free, Hyde snapped out his hand and took hold of me around the throat. He was so fast, I'm not even sure I saw it. It was more like my mind took its best guess from the blur of movement and then, afterward, tried to patch together what had happened. I felt myself rise, then the air flew from my chest as he pushed me up against the elevator wall. Charlie got to his feet. I have to give him credit. He wasn't looking for the exit. He balled a fist and swung. Like his dancing, it was smooth. But Hyde reacted as if his eyes were on the back of his head. He quickly shifted his body. Charlie missed. I saw a blur of movement, followed by a dull thud, and Charlie collapsed.

Hyde turned back to me. He leaned closer, so his teeth were a few inches from my face. A hoarse, guttural sound crackled up from his throat. He might have been speaking, but I couldn't make sense of the words. Then he hissed and slammed me up against the elevator wall a second time. I couldn't breathe. Or cry for help. I glanced down toward Charlie to see if he was all right, if he could do something to help me, but I couldn't angle my head properly. The Beast tightened his grip and my eyes started to go spotty. He started to speak to me again, but I still couldn't tell what he was saying. His teeth gnashed together and his head turned sideways so I could see straight into one of his yellow eyes. He loosened his grip and tried to speak a third time.

I answered with the knife.

While he was slowly strangling me, I'd been working it free of the sheath. I was blacking out as I swung. He blocked the stroke, but the blade must have cut through his skin because his body stiffened. The only explanation I could think of was the poison my uncle had smeared on the blade. It must have been as lethal as he said, to work so quickly. Then I noticed something around Hyde's neck—a nylon rope, white and red threaded together like a candy cane. My eyes followed it up through the darkness to the top of the elevator. Mr. Entwistle was leaning in from the hole above. He held the rope tightly in both hands like a garrote. He'd slipped it over Hyde's head and was trying to tighten it, so that the Beast's face was red and the veins of his neck bulged. That explained why Hyde had stopped moving. He was suffocating. This should have brought me some relief, but I was still suffocating myself. It was hard to feel anything but panic.

"Quickly, boys," Mr. Entwistle shouted. "Get out."

Get out. Happily. But I still couldn't breathe, let alone move. And I thought Charlie was unconscious.

Hyde's fingers dug into my throat. The knife clattered to the floor and my eyes started to go spotty again. I clawed at his hand, but it was no use. I couldn't pry it loose. Then he let go. I dropped to the floor and took a desperate gasp of air. By the time I could see clearly, the candy-cane rope was in pieces beside me. Hyde was snarling and staring upward. Just past his shoulder I caught a glimpse of Mr. Entwistle's overcoat disappearing into the shadows above. As my eyes improved their focus, I could see the old vampire retreating up a set of rungs set in the elevator shaft.

In an instant, Hyde was in pursuit. He pulled himself up through the hole, then launched himself into the air. Using the cables and the wall, he scrambled upward with a strength and speed that were dizzying. It was both awesome and terrifying. My whole body started shaking. How had Mr. Entwistle faced this thing down so many times? All I could do was cough and sputter.

I rose, still trembling, on legs that felt hollow, and moved over to where Charlie was lying in a heap on the ground. His arm was twisted awkwardly underneath him, and his eyes were glazed. One of his feet was twitching, and a huge welt was on the corner of his forehead. I straightened him out, then checked to make sure he was breathing. His heartbeat was strong. His eyelids started to flutter and his head shook slightly as he came to. Then a quiet moan escaped his lips.

"Don't . . ."

I wasn't actually doing anything. He must have been worried that I might move him. I stood up to give him some breathing room and stared through the hole in the top of the elevator. I could see the entrance to the next floor—sliding doors that led to the hall above. They had been torn back. Light from the upper corridor spilled into the dark space, illuminating the claw marks Hyde had scratched into the steel and concrete. I listened for sounds of a scuffle, but all I could hear was the pop and crackle of the still-burning wires that sparked around us, filling the small space with a nauseating odor. I felt weak, and my ankle was burning. I wondered if I'd landed on it funny when I'd fallen to the floor. I looked down and spied the knife lying beside my foot. I picked it up. Blood was on the blade. Perhaps I'd cut him after all.

Don't celebrate yet, my mind told me. *Get moving.*

I looked at the mess above, uncertain. I didn't know what to do. Mr. Entwistle was up there by himself. If I jumped and grabbed a cable, I could shimmy up to the floor above, but it meant I'd have to leave Charlie behind.

The floor tilted and I lost my balance. My ankle was definitely burning. Something was wrong. I heard the sound of steel grinding, and the elevator jumped down a foot. Then another. My first thought was that it was going to drop. Then I heard a loud bang beside me and the doors shifted apart. A slender ribbon of light appeared between them. I could see a shadow moving beyond. Someone was prying the doors open. Whoever it was, he was snarling through clenched teeth. I raised the knife in my right hand and got ready to move quickly. My head was surprisingly dizzy. A fire was spreading up my calf. I fell into the doors. The end of a small crowbar appeared between them and the ribbon of light widened. Then the smell of wine and lighter fluid mixed with smoke and Mr. Entwistle stuck his head through.

"Going down?" he asked.

He was standing below me. He'd somehow pulled the elevator closer to the floor he was on, but it wasn't quite level.

"Here, let me just"—he put his back against one door and pushed so the gap was almost shoulder width—"finish this. . . . There!" He dusted off his hands, then reached for his backpack.

My heart was frantically beating. I started forward in a daze. The burn in my calf was spreading up my leg. My whole body began to sweat.

"What is it? Did he bite you?" Mr. Entwistle was looking up through the hole Hyde had made in the ceiling. "He doesn't mess around, does he?"

I fell past him into the hall, then slipped to a knee. My balance was off.

"Watch that!" he said.

I felt him pry the knife out of my hand, then I reached forward and tumbled to the floor. Standing was impossible. It was easier to roll onto my back. Not as dizzy that way.

Mr. Entwistle was standing over me. The knife was under his nose. His face twisted in revulsion, then he crouched and set the blade on the floor. In a blink the backpack was off his shoulder and he was sifting through it, his hands a blur.

"Did you get cut? Did he cut you with the knife?"

I was having trouble speaking. The liquid fire was spreading to my chest, making it hard to breathe. Pins jabbed inside my lungs and ribs. I looked down at my leg. A small cut was on the side of my ankle. It must have happened when the knife dropped. That explained the burn. There was poison in my body. *Sixty thousand times stronger than cyanide.*

Mr. Entwistle pulled out a hatchet. My tongue was paralyzed, but I turned enough so that I could see the cut on my ankle. The edges of it were black.

"Dammit!" he snapped.

He grabbed the end of my shoe in one hand and pulled it down so that my toes were pointed. Then he put his knee on my shin and raised the hatchet. "Don't move."

Was he crazy? He was about to cut off my foot. I wanted it left where it was, thank you very much. I shifted as he swung. The head of the hatchet sparked and a chunk of tile popped out from the floor.

Mr. Entwistle swore again. "Stop squirming." He was glaring at me. Then his head started shaking back and forth. "No, no, no, no, no." He repeated it over and over. The ax clattered to the floor. His hands slid under my legs and shoulders. "No. No, you don't. Don't you dare . . ."

I wasn't about to do anything. I could barely breathe.

He stood with me in his arms and started running. I felt myself shaking. Burning. Pain froze the air in my chest. *Don't leave Charlie behind,* I wanted to say. *He's helpless.* But I couldn't talk.

Mr. Entwistle stopped. I shifted in his arms, then heard a loud bang as he kicked open a door. He turned sideways and stepped through. Then he was airborne. He didn't go down the stairs, he dropped from landing to landing. Each one rattled the air from my chest. I was suffocating. Then he stopped again. I could sense something was wrong even before he set me down. It might have been in his body language. The way his eyes widened when he looked up. It might have been the smell of fear. And something else. Something feral.

Hyde was waiting for us. I sensed him before I heard him. Another growl echoed up and down the staircase. I was lying on my back. Burning. I raised my head to take a look around. All I could see was darkness. Then suddenly, everything was on fire. My body must have been playing tricks on me. The walls, the floor, the ceiling, the stairs. And me. All of it in flames. I started to convulse. Orange, red, and yellow blurred into a smear of light. Then it got quiet. At least inside. Outside it was noisy. Like two dogs fighting over a bone. But that quickly faded. I listened, knowing I should have been able to hear something. Anything. The sound of the fight. Of air leaving my chest. My heartbeat. But they were gone. So was the burning. It had faded, too. Only the light remained. It was far off, down a long tunnel, but I knew if I was patient, I would reach it. That it would welcome me back. So I left the vanishing world of sound and fire and sped toward it.

REUNION

People generally regard dying as a downer. I assume it's because they've never tried it. Of all earthly phenomena, death is probably the most underrated. Imagine not having to worry about anything. How do I look? Where did I leave my wallet? Why do I get so many pimples? All that vanishes in a snap. So does your pain. Aches and bruises and burns. They all disappear. In the end, there is only the light. And the light is full of hope and love and all things good. And it was receding. A terrible sense of isolation came over me as I slipped away. As if I was being disconnected from something much greater than myself. I reached out so I wouldn't get separated, but it was too late. The light was gone.

I heard a faint voice. It was familiar. The person was right beside me, but he sounded light-years away. *"Clear."*

A shock went through my body. It made me want to scream. My mouth was too dry. I needed more air.

"Did it work?" asked another voice. It was also familiar. The words were packed anxiously together.

"Not yet. . . . *Clear."*

It happened again. A powerful jolt. My eyes opened. The light was blinding, with no warmth in it. I sucked in an icy breath. It stung.

"It's working. His pulse has steadied. That's all we need."

I felt a sting in my elbow. Nothing happened, then a warm rush crept up my arm. A feeling of heaviness followed. A man stepped into the light. His shadow fell over me. I saw black hair streaked with white and gray under a hat like a chimney pipe. "Get some sleep, boy. You've had a busy night."

His advice seemed reasonable, so I slept.

When I woke up, it was dark. I came out of my sleep slowly. Comfortably. My arm was a bit numb. It was tied to the metal rail of the bed I was in. I was alarmed at first. The thought of being tied up scared me, then I realized it was only surgical tubing. It was to keep my arm from moving. A machine beside the bed hummed quietly, pumping blood through a needle and into a vein near my elbow. Something brushed against my cheek. It made me jump. I heard a quiet laugh.

"Sorry. I couldn't help it."

It was her. Luna. She was crouched over my bed. "It's you," I whispered. My voice was hoarse, my throat dry.

She left her hand on my cheek and smiled. "Yes. It's me."

I felt the floor shift. Then a door opened. It made an odd metallic sound. Cool night air rushed inside the room. It smelled of concrete and wet paint. I heard city sounds. Distant feet on pavement. The hum of cars. The creak of trees nearby. Then Mr. Entwistle appeared. He had to take off his top hat to step inside. The ceiling was low. I realized why when he closed the door.

"Are we in a truck?" I asked.

"No. An ambulance," he said. "I borrowed it from the hospital."

"Borrowed?"

"Well, I'm thinking of it more as a trade-in. The hospital lost an ambulance, but the police got a pretty good aquatic car out of the deal." A stool was beside him. He handed it to Luna, then slumped down to the floor and let his head fall back against the wall, which was actually a medicine cabinet of some kind.

"Thanks." She slipped the stool beside the bed and sat down.

"How did you get here?" I asked her.

"Charlie called and said you'd been poisoned. I had my sister drive me up right away. The two of them are inside with Ophelia."

"So he's okay?"

"Charlie? Yeah. He's going to be fine. He was in here until a few minutes ago."

I felt the air rush from my chest. A breath of relief. My face stretched into a comfortable smile. Everyone was safe. And Luna was here.

"I can't believe your parents let you come." I wasn't one of their favorite people. It wasn't hard to understand why. Thanks to me, one of their daughters was a vampire and the other was in therapy.

Luna eyes flicked nervously over to where Mr. Entwistle was sitting, then she looked back at me. By the expression on her face, I would have bet a stolen ambulance that her parents had no idea where she was.

"We're just sorting that out now." Mr. Entwistle smiled, spinning his hat in his hands. I'm not sure why he found this so amusing. If Luna's parents found out that she and Suki were here, the Beast of the Apocalypse would be the least of my problems.

"They already hate me," I said.

"Who hates you?" Luna asked.

"Your parents."

"*Hate*'s a strong word, boy. They might dislike you—"

"No, they hate him." Luna was smiling now, too. I couldn't see what was so funny. "Don't sweat it. You have enough to worry about."

This was true. And lying around here wasn't going to fix anything. "Why am I not inside?"

"Ophelia didn't want to risk moving you," Mr. Entwistle explained. "And I wanted to be mobile if Agent X raised the alarm and we had to split in a hurry."

"Who is Agent X?" Luna asked.

"Someone from the Underground. He's helping with security. Zack knows him. He's walking the perimeter. I'm sure he'll want to talk to you, boy, once you're feeling better."

I was feeling better, and I said so.

Mr. Entwistle laughed. "Zack, you were clinically dead. Anything else is generally considered an improvement."

With Luna beside me, I wasn't going to argue. "How did I get here?"

"We drove," he said.

"No. I mean, how did we get out of the hospital?"

"We ran."

"Helpful, isn't he?" said Luna.

Her tone was playful, which surprised me. She couldn't have known him more than a few hours, and he looked like Jack the Ripper. If I'd seen him coming down the sidewalk, I would have crossed the street.

"My guess is, Ophelia kicked him out of the house for being a smart aleck," she added.

The old vampire smiled. "Well, at least you said *smart*." Then his smile vanished and he wiped his forehead with his sleeve. "She wasn't happy with me for dragging you out of the house last night."

I remembered the note she'd left me, advising me to stay home. I should have listened. "Was she angry?"

"Angry!" said Mr. Entwistle. "Men get angry. Women get something else. I don't think they've invented a suitable word yet. . . . But I settled her down eventually."

"What did you say?"

"That I'd made a mistake. And that I was sorry. And that we were recruiting help from Agent X—which she appreciates."

Agent X. The alias made me think of my father's journal. He always referred to people with letters. Only Maximilian and Mutada were mentioned by name. Everyone else was Dr. Q, or N, or C. I guess it was to protect people's identities.

"Aren't you going to tell me what happened?" I asked.

"At the hospital? Sure. Just let me fuel up." Mr. Entwistle took a bottle of red wine from inside his coat and downed a good mouthful. "So . . . where did I lose you?"

"You were about to chop off my foot."

"Right." He took another swig. "You would have grown it back, you know. It only takes a couple of weeks."

"How comforting."

"I didn't want the poison to reach your heart."

"Poison?"

"Yeah. From the knife. You're lucky. Not every guy is fortunate enough to stab himself in a hospital. How did you get it, by the way?"

"The cut? I think it happened in the elevator. I dropped the knife. It might have nicked me on the way down. Or maybe I fell on it."

"No," he said. "I meant the knife. Where'd you get it?"

I had to think. My memory was usually dependable, but my brain was still warming up. "It was a gift from Agent X."

Mr. Entwistle took another sip and nodded. "Should have guessed. . . . That was bad luck, getting cut like that. But that knife is our best protection right now."

"What about Mr. Hyde?" I asked. "He caught us, didn't he?"

"More like he was lying in wait for us. But, yeah, he was there." Mr. Entwistle cleared his throat, then smiled. "But he doesn't like being lit on fire. It looked a bit uncomfortable. We'll have to remember that trick. Then Charlie showed up. He had the hatchet I'd dropped. He came in swinging like a madman. Not even the walls were safe. He's got guts, that boy."

He was certainly brave in the elevator. When Mr. Entwistle carried me off, I was worried that he'd get left behind, but his was the voice I'd heard in the ambulance earlier. *Did it work?* he'd asked. Mr. Entwistle must have been the one shouting *Clear.* I'd watched enough television to know what he'd been doing—fixing my heartbeat with those paddle-size electrodes you see doctors using when a person flatlines.

"You saved my life."

Mr. Entwistle stood. He had to bend at the waist to keep his head from hitting the roof. "I'm more than just a pretty face, boy. But it was really the knife that saved you. In the end, that was what scared the fleabag away. The poison is lethal. And as you found out, it only takes a scratch. Agent X really came through with this." He tapped his waist.

"You have it?"

He nodded. "I'm going to hang on to it. At least until you're feeling better. I promised Ophelia. She's not happy we have it. Woman's intuition maybe. She was insistent I keep it as far from you as possible. *A bad feeling* is what she said."

A bad feeling. A lot of those were going around.

"What is it?" Luna asked. "Are you all right?"

I could feel that my eyes wanted to close. But this wasn't the time for sleep. "I had something important to tell you," I said to Mr. Entwistle. "It's on the tip of my tongue."

"Was it about Hyde?"

I couldn't remember. Then more questions popped into my head. Why had he wanted me to meet with my uncle? And how had the two of them met up and reconciled? But I didn't want to mention any of that with Luna right there. To her and Charlie, Maximilian was a villain.

"I'll be inside," Mr. Entwistle said. "You can tell me later." He tapped the side of the metal bed frame several times with his knuckles. "I'll give you two a minute alone, but you might want to consider making an appearance soon. We have a lot to discuss. And a few important decisions to make." He flicked the bottom of his hat in way of farewell, then opened the door and stepped out. The ambulance sank, then rose again.

Luna was looking at me, biting her bottom lip. She rested her hand on my arm. I was sure she meant to comfort me, but I could tell by the expression on her face that she was nervous about something.

"What is it?" I asked.

"I just don't know what's going to happen when my dad finds out I'm here. He's going to flip. So is Mom. But I couldn't risk staying home. If something had happened to you, I would never have forgiven myself. I needed to be here."

"I'm glad you came."

She smiled. "Me, too. I just don't want to have to turn around and go back home."

I didn't want that either, although it might have been much safer for her not to stay. "Take me with you if you go," I said.

"I'd have to sneak you in the trunk."

That sounded perfect, so long as there was room for two.

Luna stood and checked the machine at the bedside. "There's not much left."

"What's that?"

"Blood. This is the last of it. There's only about a half liter left."

She tilted her head so our faces were in line. It was dark inside, but some light from the streetlamps managed to sneak in through the tinted windows. Enough that I could see her emerald green eyes, her copper curls. She reached up and touched my fingers. Suddenly they were on fire, but in a good way.

"Do you want to go in?" she asked.

What I really wanted was to stay here with her, but if plans were being made, I didn't want her to miss out, especially if it meant she might get to stay longer. Then I remembered what I had to tell everyone—that Detective Baddon's son might be a vampire. I sat up. The room spun. Luna must have seen the look on my face.

"Better not push it." She put her hand on my chest and I flopped back down.

"Wait." I nodded toward the machine. "You can turn that off."

"Are you sure?"

"Yeah." I sat up, more slowly this time. The dizziness came back, but I toughed it out. Sleep would have to wait. "There's a faster way." I pulled the needle from my arm, snapped the surgical tubing, removed the bag of blood from the machine, and drank. It wasn't quite enough. My ankle and calf were still itchy. Some stinging remained. My head was clearing, but I didn't get the usual urge to go marathon running. "That's all we have? Is that what you said? This was it?"

Luna slipped in front of me. We stood facing each other. Like Mr. Entwistle, I had to duck to keep my head from hitting the roof. It brought our faces closer together. Enough that I could feel her breath on my cheek.

"That's the last of it," she said.

"You didn't bring any up with you?"

She shook her head. "Sorry. The last batch I got was tainted. I was hoping to find more here."

"And did you?"

She moved a bit closer. "No. But I'll be all right for a while. I didn't get poisoned last night."

"Last night? What time is it?"

"Almost midnight. You've been out for about twenty hours or so."

Asleep for twenty hours? That meant I'd been out all day. But it also meant there were a good five hours or so before sunrise. I had a pretty good idea how I wanted to spend them. Then I heard footsteps outside the door. It opened a crack and Charlie's face appeared.

"Room service." He smiled when he saw I was out of bed. "He lives." He opened the door and stepped inside. "I hate to spoil the party, but Luna's father is on the phone. He was so angry it almost blew apart. You two need to come inside."

CHAPTER 26

SECURITY

I looked at Luna. I could see she was feeling the same disappointment I was. It was probably good that I didn't have a driver's license, or I might have put the ambulance in gear and made a run for the Mexican border. Charlie was obviously worried, too. He stepped out, leaving the door open behind him.

Luna didn't move. "It's funny."

"What?"

"Just how becoming a vampire changes things so much. I don't mean the sun and food and everything like that." She was standing close to me. It made it hard to concentrate. "I mean the way you feel changes."

I didn't know what she was trying to tell me. I swallowed.

"I get upset more often now," she said. "The things people do . . . I don't know why. And I feel . . . lonely, in a way I never used to. Especially at night. I don't like it."

I understood. Vampires are complex creatures. We thrive in darkness. The setting sun awakens a deep restlessness in us. A hunger for the hunt, but also for the things that regular people want, including the company of friends. The night can be empty. Without Charlie and Ophelia, things would have been much worse for me. Luna was the only vampire in Newark, at least the only one we knew about. She was alone too often. But I was hoping to fix that.

She was still looking at me. "And some things don't change at all." Her eyes were wide. Almost luminescent. I've described them before as emerald green, but that isn't really true. Eyes are never one color. Hers had ribbons of amber in them. And olive streaks. The overall effect was shocking. And beautiful. I watched, spellbound, as her gaze fell to my necklace. She stepped closer and took the charm in her fingers. The full moon. With her other hand she took out the golden crescent that had belonged to my mother. "Some things are a perfect fit."

She looked up at me. I smiled. She smiled. We were smiling together. Again. It was nice.

"I've missed you," she said. She somehow got a bit closer. This might have been her talent.

The door was still open. Charlie leaned in. "Sometime tonight would be nice, you slowpokes. Suki's in the hot seat by herself. It's torture in there."

I backed up and stood aside while Luna slipped past. For just an instant we were side by side. Her hand slid down my arm. Her fingertips gently grazed the back of my hand as she stepped down. I held the door, then followed her out.

Charlie was looking at me funny. He had the same smile on his face when he was planning trouble.

"What?" I said.

"Nothing." But he kept smiling.

"No really. What is it?"

"It's nothing. Seriously."

I let the two of them go ahead. I didn't know exactly where to go. We were parked in a lot behind a row of three-story apartments. I had expected us to be back at Ophelia's safe house, the one we'd left to go to the hospital, but obviously, we'd had to move. I glanced back at the ambulance. It was covered, top to bottom, in a sloppy layer of black paint. That explained the smell I'd noticed earlier. It was still drying. Even the lights on top had been done. From up close, you could still see the brushstrokes. A monkey with a stick would have managed a better job.

"Who did this?" I asked.

"Me," Charlie answered.

"You missed a few spots."

"Who do I look like, Picasso? The sun was coming up. We needed to camouflage it. I was in a hurry."

I guess we wouldn't have stayed hidden for too long with a stolen ambulance in the driveway. It looked more like a hearse now.

Charlie strolled up beside me. "Come on. I don't like it out here. I got the heebs."

The breeze picked up for a second and carried away the smell of drying paint. My hackles started to rise. The same feeling had come over me at the rave the night all the trouble started. As if I was being watched.

"Do you see anything?" His eyes were busy scanning the backyards.

I didn't. Nothing unusual.

Luna opened the back door. "Come on, you guys."

Charlie started in and I followed. Then I spotted the watcher. Or rather, the man stepped out of the shadows and revealed himself.

I waited until Charlie was inside, then I hesitated on the back step and said, "Just a second." Before he could object, I closed the door and hopped the fence into the neighbor's yard.

The man waiting there was wearing a commando outfit—all black. He looked like a graduate from the school of ninja. The only difference was his headgear. To his attire he'd added some kind of tight-fitting helmet with lenses. He might have borrowed it from Cobra Commander. Even without his face showing, I could tell it was my uncle Maximilian. Agent X. Something in the way he moved, like a stone golem, gave him away.

"You feeling better?" he asked.

"Yeah. A lot. I think I just need some more sleep."

"See that you get it."

He was holding a heavy gun in his hands. The barrel was unusually large. I'm sure it could have fired a shell to Florida. He flipped it up on his shoulder just as a car turned the corner. There was just enough space between the houses that we could see it. He stepped behind a tree before the headlights could pass over him. My eyes followed the car as it rolled gently to a stop. Then the brake lights went off and it kept on moving. It was a police cruiser.

"Don't worry," he said. "I've set up motion detectors around the property. If anything larger than a cat approaches the apartment, an alarm will sound inside the house."

That was just like my uncle. One step ahead.

I glanced back over my shoulder at the apartment complex. "Do the others know you're here?"

He crossed his arm over his chest. "Not exactly. I agreed to stay out of sight, just in case. I won't be here for long. My last radiation treatment is tomorrow morning, and I'm a bit short on sleep. It's probably better if I stay out of things for now."

He didn't need to explain why. After handing us all over to the Prince of Darkness last summer, keeping his distance was probably a good idea.

"Are *you* all right?" I asked.

"As much as can be expected. I'll be fine if all goes well at the hospital." He nodded a good-bye and turned.

"Wait," I whispered. "I thought you should know a few things. After you left the room, Detective Baddon came looking for you." This led to a conversation about the detective's son and what I'd seen with Charlie in the hospital. "I think the boy might be a vampire."

"Possibly. His condition does seem very unusual. I'll look into it. If his son's infected, then we have every reason to expect Hyde will go after him, too. He'll need protection."

I agreed, and I said so. I sensed that my uncle was about to go, but I had a few questions. "When did you leave the hospital?"

"Right after I talked to you. Why?"

"Have you seen this thing?"

"No."

"But you've hunted werewolves before. Do you think that's what he is?"

He shrugged. "We shouldn't assume he is. To be honest, this thing sounds different. Faster. Stronger. More intelligent. Entwistle says it can talk. I've never heard of a shape changer that could do that. Not as a beast. But I've only seen two. Lycanthropes are very rare."

"Why?"

My uncle took a deep breath. His head tipped up, as if he was thinking. I could imagine his eyes, focused and intense, under his helmet. "They're not like vampires. They aren't immortal. Lycanthropy doesn't bring them back from death. Quite the opposite, in fact. It ages them quickly. And most werewolves kill their prey, so they don't spread whatever virus causes it. But I think the main reason is the Coven. When word of a lycanthrope gets out, they move very quickly to neutralize it."

I wondered why the Coven hadn't done anything about Hyde, but I guess I already knew the answer. They were fighting among themselves.

"We'll be all right, Zachary, if we keep our heads screwed on straight. We just can't afford to make any mistakes, that's all."

No mistakes. That sounded painfully simple. And tragically impossible.

"You need to get some more sleep," he said. "I can see it in your eyes. Your father used to get that way when he was tired and had too much to think about. You'd better get inside." He nodded a goodbye. I watched him return to the shadows, where he stopped to examine a small device staked to the ground. A motion detector, I was guessing. I heard a latch behind me and turned. Luna was waiting at the back door of the apartment. She held it open for me. She looked upset. Her eyes were watering.

I sprinted over. "What is it?"

"I'm sorry, but we have to go home."

CHAPTER 27

THE HUNT BEGINS

I felt my lungs deflate. Through the open back door I could hear Ophelia talking with Mr. Entwistle. He was ranting about the stupidity of anyone under the age of two hundred.

"Does he really think she'll be safer there?" he asked. "What protection can he offer?"

"He's still looking for a cure," someone said. "He thinks if he works hard enough, he can make her better." I didn't recognize the voice, but I figured it had to be Suki.

Luna and I walked in through the back hall, past the kitchen, and into the living room where everyone was waiting.

"I tried that route with Zachary for almost eight years," Ophelia said. "There is no cure."

I remembered this. Ointments and pills and injections and blood transfusions. Most of it just made things worse.

"It's not his speciality," Suki said, "but he thinks one of his colleagues can help. A blood specialist in Toronto. They went to school together. My dad thinks he might be close to something." She was sitting on the couch, her feet drawn up on the cushions and her knees bent so her head was resting on top of them. It seemed as if she were trying to take up as little space as possible. The change in her appearance was so dramatic, if I hadn't expected her to be sitting there, I wouldn't have recognized her. The long blond hair of last summer had been cut short and dyed black, and she had piercings above each eye. Her skin, normally bronzed, was pale as alabaster. Charlie was beside her, a foot of space between them. Last year they would have been wrapped up like two pretzels.

"Do you think we can talk him into letting you stay?" Charlie said.

Suki looked away and rolled her eyes. "Good luck."

I moved farther into the room toward the only empty chair—a La-Z-Boy across from the sofa Charlie and Suki were in. I offered it to Luna, but instead of sitting down, she pushed me into it. My body flopped back against the cushions. I could easily have fallen asleep.

Ophelia was leaning against the kitchen counter, a phone in her fist. Both she and Mr. Entwistle looked frustrated. He was standing beside the window, peeking past the blind, his face grim.

"Are you serious?" I asked Suki. She seemed a bit nervous, a far cry from the bubbly, bouncy person I'd met a year ago.

"Yeah. He wouldn't let us stay here if it was the last place on earth."

She didn't have to explain why. After what had happened last summer at the Abbott family cottage, I wasn't exactly at the top of their Christmas-card list. Dr. Abbott wouldn't want his daughters anywhere near me. It was unfortunate. With Mr. Entwistle here, this was the safest place next to the White House, but that wasn't what I'd been asking about.

"No. I mean about the cure. Is someone really close?"

Suki shrugged.

I glanced at Charlie. He was scowling. "Would you really want one?"

Would I want a cure? I wasn't sure. Of course, I could imagine being human—or at least being able to go out in the sun. But I'd been a vampire for most of my life. I didn't really know what it meant to be a normal person.

Luna sat down on the armrest of my chair. "I'm not going anywhere." Her words and tone surprised me. She wasn't normally rebellious. That was more Suki's domain. It was what made her so compatible with Charlie.

"I'm not going to shelter you here without your parents' approval," Ophelia said.

Mr. Entwistle was still holding the same wine bottle that he'd had in the ambulance. He swallowed a mouthful and frowned. He looked like an undertaker raised from the grave. "If we let Luna leave, we'll be killing her. The Coven are already sending their drones here. Hyde killed one in your driveway. When word of that gets back to head office, some higher-ups are going to send in the troops. If we don't stick together, we'll be finished."

"I'm more worried about Hyde than the Coven," Charlie said.

"You should be worried about both. But Hyde's a local problem. The Coven is global. It's just a matter of time before they're here in force. If we allow Luna to become isolated, she'll be killed." Mr. Entwistle turned and looked her square in the face. "Your father can't protect you."

"I know. I don't want to go home. No one there really understands what I'm going through."

I looked over at Suki when she said this. A hurt expression was on her face.

"When is your father coming?" I asked.

"He's leaving now. He'll be here tomorrow."

"And then what?"

Ophelia looked uncertain. "We'll see. Perhaps we can talk him out of leaving right away."

I looked at Luna, then at Suki, to see if any trace of hope was in their faces. There wasn't. No one moved. Then something beeped. It was coming from downstairs.

"What is that?" Luna asked.

"An alarm," Ophelia explained. "I'll be right back."

She disappeared downstairs. The room was as quiet as a church while she was gone. A few seconds later she returned. Her eyes were on me. "Detective Baddon just pulled into the laneway."

"What's he doing here?" I asked.

She moved past me on her way to the door. "He's here because I invited him."

"He thinks I killed Inspector Johansson."

Ophelia raised her hand to her forehead and started massaging her temples. "He doesn't think that anymore. And we need his help."

"Do you trust him?"

"Absolutely. He was Everett's best friend. They worked together in Toronto for over twenty years. The man's a saint. And he's had a very difficult year."

I wasn't sure if I should mention his son. Maybe Ophelia knew already. But I got cut off by the doorbell. She was already moving to answer it. After a brief exchange of pleasantries in the hall, she and Detective Baddon came in for a round of introductions. He obviously wasn't expecting a crowd. Ophelia noticed, too.

"You can speak plainly, Adam."

"I don't have much to tell you." He adjusted the waist of his pants. With legs the thickness of a phone pole, I was amazed they didn't stay up on their own. He looked even more exhausted than the last time I'd seen him. His eyes glanced over at me, but he didn't say anything. Then he rubbed his hand over his head, as if he needed to wake up his brain. "Do you mind if I sit?"

"No," said Ophelia. "I'll put some coffee on."

"Could you make it a decaf? I'm hoping to go to bed shortly."

Ophelia walked into the kitchen. She answered over her shoulder, "I'll see what I have. Go on. I can hear you perfectly from in here."

Officer Baddon didn't know whom to talk to. He looked around the room and settled on Mr. Entwistle. The old vampire was still standing beside the window, peeking occasionally past the blind as if he expected trouble to arrive at any moment.

"I don't have much time," the detective said. "We found some hair at the zoo, and some clothing fibers. The lab results came back. Nothing useful. The hair isn't human, so they couldn't match it to anything in the data banks. The clothing fibers are just regular jeans. Nothing special about them. But we got him on a security camera at the hospital. It picked him up on the way out."

"Do you have a copy?" asked Mr. Entwistle, his eyes still focused outside.

"Not here. But I've seen it. A blur in two frames. Seven feet at least. I'm guessing between three and four hundred pounds. Tough to tell. He's moving like a bullet." He paused. Ophelia came in from the kitchen. The detective glanced around the room. "A phone call came in to the station yesterday just before sunrise. An elderly gentleman on Gilmour. He was reporting a trespasser in his yard. A car was sent. Usual procedure. They got a description. Big and fast. It only came across my desk tonight because of the timing. So I followed up. He didn't have much more to say when I checked in, but he let me see his backyard. The tracks there speak volumes. Same as the zoo. We have a trail. I considered putting some dogs on it, but it was sixteen hours old. I figured it was too cold. At the speed that thing moves, I'm not sure if it even leaves a scent."

Mr. Entwistle rubbed at his stubble. "We can start there. If it goes nowhere, we're no worse off."

He actually wanted to go after this thing. I didn't want to run into Mr. Hyde again unless I was flying in an F-15.

Detective Baddon placed his hands on his knees and started to rise. "Well . . . I need to check in at the hospital and get home for some sleep. I'll call in the morning if anything comes up with the night crew. Please let me know if you find anything tonight. And try to keep it quiet. People are asking questions, and I don't have answers. At least none that any sane person would believe."

"Are you sure you won't have some coffee first?" Ophelia asked.

"One for the road, if you don't mind."

While Ophelia got his coffee ready, the room quieted again. I felt as if I were standing in a funeral parlor. No one spoke until she got back.

"Is there anything else you can tell us?" she asked.

Detective Baddon accepted a mug of coffee, then turned to me. "I'd like to have a word with you outside, if you don't mind." He took a sip, nodded his thanks, then turned for the door.

I looked at Ophelia.

"It will be fine," she whispered.

The words were for me only, although I don't doubt Charlie, Luna, and Mr. Entwistle heard them, too. I gulped. Then I felt Ophelia's hand on the small of my back directing me to the front entrance. She opened the door quietly, then closed it behind the detective and me.

We stood in the narrow hall. I'd never been in this apartment, but I'd seen ones like it. It was basically three separate units, all stacked on top of one another. Beside me were a set of stairs leading up to floors two and three. On the other side was the main door that led out to a front walk.

Detective Baddon sipped his coffee, then said, "I owe you an apology. I shouldn't have behaved that way back at the station. I can't believe this thing. What it did to that elevator."

I understood. It was hard for me to believe it, and I'd been right there.

"I shouldn't have brought you into the system. I think I was just angry. Everett was a close friend. When your prints were on that gun, and in his car, I . . . Well, I'm sorry."

"It's all right."

"Technically, you're still a fugitive. I'm supposed to arrest you on sight."

"You know I didn't kill the inspector."

"Yes, I do. But there is a small matter of a ruined jail, and some injured police officers, and a number of flattened cars."

I wasn't sure what to say. None of that was really my doing.

"I think what I'm saying is that I can't make this mess go away just because you didn't kill Everett. I need help. Off the record. And you know why."

I did know why. He couldn't afford to expose his son. Or any of us. If he was part of the Underground, silence was the rule.

"That was you at the hospital in your uncle's room, wasn't it?"

I nodded.

"Well, you need to keep a lower profile. Any police officer who sees you or John is going to try to arrest you. If you resist, they'll shoot. So be careful. No more public spectacles."

He reached into his coat pocket. I could see his automatic hanging in the holster. He pulled out a card.

"I need to talk to your uncle. My understanding is, he's the only man in this part of the world who's ever caught and killed a werewolf. Is that right?"

I accepted the card and read over Detective Baddon's contact information.

"A werewolf—is that what you think it is?"

He yawned and shook his head. "No idea. But it doesn't matter to me. Whatever it is, we have to catch it. I'm hoping your uncle can help."

"He can. He and my father caught a lycanthrope in England. They used bear traps."

The detective nodded. "That probably won't work in the city. But I've a few things to discuss with him. Sooner is better."

"Is there anything else?"

"Just help me get this thing." It might have been fatigue, but his eyes were starting to water. "We're running out of time."

He backed out the door, then turned and started down the steps. "Have your uncle call my cell," he said over his shoulder.

I wondered if I should have told him that my uncle was patrolling the grounds, and that we were calling him Agent X, but the detective seemed to be in a hurry to leave. And it didn't seem fair to Maximilian. He liked to do things on his own terms. And as selfish as this will sound, I wanted to get back to Luna. I turned and walked back to the door. Ophelia opened it for me.

"Did you hear any of that?" I asked.

Her eyebrows lifted a bit and she nodded. She was chewing the inside of her lip. "He wants to meet with your uncle?"

"You know they were both at the hospital?"

She nodded.

"He told me about the sensors he set up."

"We're trying to keep his involvement under wraps," she said. "If Charlie finds out, he might overreact."

"I thought you didn't trust my uncle."

"I didn't. But while you were in the ambulance, he was convincing. And John feels he has your best interests at heart. I think we were meant to work together. It's the only way we'll survive. War does make strange bedfellows."

This seemed a bit out of character for her. She wasn't a trusting person. "What did he say?"

She paused. Her eyes drifted up while she considered what to tell me. "We talked about the night he betrayed you to Vlad. We talked about mistakes and misconceptions. He was badly used, your uncle. And deceived." She took a deep breath. "The situation is complicated, but it's hard to say no to a dying man." She reached out and pinched my cheek. "Now if we could just get Gerald on board."

"Gerald?"

"Dr. Abbott."

"Do you think he'll let them stay?"

"I think the good doctor is seriously rattled. But we may have a chance to impress him. The alarms and security cameras will help. We almost seem like we know what we're doing. Leaving Luna in our care is certainly the best thing for her. If he's a reasonable man, he'll come around. Luna is a child vampire, just like you are, and so the threat is constant. Going back to Newark won't make it go away."

"Does he know that?"

"I don't think so. But that just means we'll have to be more convincing." She slipped her arm through mine and we walked back into the living room. Everyone stopped talking when we entered. Luna looked upset. Her eyes couldn't settle comfortably on anything. Mr. Entwistle was still looking out past the curtain. He let it fall.

"I'd like to leave as soon as possible," he said. "That trail isn't getting any warmer."

Ophelia nodded. "Can you let me get Luna and Suki settled on the top floor? I'd like to have a word with you before you go."

The old vampire nodded. Charlie helped Suki to her feet. He pulled her into a hug, then reluctantly let her go.

"You did the right thing coming here," I told her.

She smiled. Dimples formed at the sides of her mouth. For just a moment, she looked like the old Suki.

Then Luna bumped past me. She didn't look over, but I saw her lips move. Just enough breath was behind them for me to hear her words: "Meet me on the roof."

My ears started to burn. Then Ophelia led them upstairs. I listened as their footsteps faded to the second floor, then the third.

"What a ham," Charlie said. He must have meant Dr. Abbott.

"Don't underestimate Ophelia," Mr. Entwistle said. "If the doctor has an ounce of sense, she'll bring him around."

He had a point. No one I'd ever met could say no to her.

"And it's what both his daughters want," the old vampire added. "Although you two might have to sleep in the ambulance."

I didn't think that was funny. Charlie didn't, either. Mr. Entwistle was trying not to laugh. But the mention of the word *ambulance* reminded me of something I had to say. "I forgot to mention this to you before. When I was at the hospital visiting—"

"Agent X," Mr. Entwistle interrupted.

"While I was visiting Agent X, he had a visitor."

"Who's Agent X?" asked Charlie.

He seemed to have forgotten. I wondered if it was the effect of being drugged in the hospital. I wasn't sure what to say about this.

Fortunately Mr. Entwistle answered for me. "He's an old friend who's agreed to help us. He was the one that you and Zachary met at the Civic."

Charlie shot me a questioning glance. I felt myself blush.

"He shot you with a tranquilizer," I explained.

"That was my fault," Mr. Entwistle said. "I forgot to say there would be two of you. He was only expecting Zack."

"So you talked to this guy?" Charlie asked.

I nodded.

Mr. Entwistle cut in again. "He set up the alarms and cameras around this apartment. We're keeping his identity a secret, for his protection."

Charlie made a face. He'd want an explanation later. I told my brain it had better come up with something good, then I explained about Detective Baddon's son—and what Charlie and I had seen in the hospital. Ophelia entered about halfway through and asked me to back up and start over. When I did, it was clear she'd had no idea the boy was sick.

"I can't believe he never mentioned it! I wonder if Everett knew."

Mr. Entwistle removed the top hat from inside his coat and started for the door. "If Baddon's son is in danger, too, it's all the more reason for me to get going. I couldn't find a trail last night. I'm losing time. If I can follow Hyde's footprints from that house on Gilmour or pick up his scent, we might be able to figure out where he goes each morning. If I need to, I'll call in for some backup."

"Do you think leaving is the right move?" Ophelia asked.

"I won't be gone long. If anything comes near the place, you'll know. Agent X is on call. And with these two young bloods handy, you're well protected."

"I was more worried about you," Ophelia said.

Mr. Entwistle laughed. "I'll be fine. You have my cell number?"

Ophelia nodded.

I looked at Charlie. Disappointment was etched clearly in the lines around his mouth. He was restless, and with his girlfriend asleep upstairs, he clearly didn't want to spend the rest of the night indoors. My bet was, if he stayed housebound, he'd wear the carpet down to threads pacing the room.

"Why don't you take Charlie, just to be safe," I said.

Ophelia stiffened slightly, but the damage was done. With that one suggestion, I'd severed my friend's shackles.

"Sounds good," Mr. Entwistle said. "If we need you, we'll be in touch."

Charlie brightened up immediately. He gave me a shot in the shoulder on the way out. "Don't die of boredom while I'm gone."

I wasn't planning to. The hunt for Hyde could begin without me. I had a date on the roof with Luna.

CHAPTER 28

ON THE ROOFTOP

Ophelia wasn't thrilled to see Charlie go and let me know the minute he was out the door. "He's just as reckless as John. We'll be lucky if those two don't set the whole town on fire."

I thought this was a slight exaggeration. They wouldn't set it on fire so much as knock it down. "He's got a lot of restless energy," I said. "He can't work it off in here. You know how he can get?"

"One night inside won't kill him."

"No. But it might kill us."

Ophelia shot me a look, then headed for the basement. "I've some research to do. Watch your step on the roof."

She must have heard what Luna had said. Fortunately she was already at the top of the stairs, or she would have seen my face turn flammable red. A second later, she poked her head around the corner again. So much for hiding my embarrassment.

"I almost forgot. I'm setting you and Charlie up on the second floor. It's furnished, but there's no bedding. Why don't you come down and I'll get you some sheets."

I followed her downstairs to the basement. This simple living space had a laundry room near the back. A small office was on one corner, with the door open wide enough for me to see a long desk inside. It was covered in computer monitors. Every few seconds, the view through one would change. It didn't take long to recognize the street outside. These must have been where the security cameras were hubbed.

Ophelia retreated to a storage closet, then came out with several sets of linens. "They're a bit dusty. The key's hanging in the rack by the front door." She handed me the bedsheets. "Please don't do anything foolish. We're going to have enough trouble with Dr. Abbott as it is. And a bit more rest wouldn't kill you either."

I said my thanks and headed for the stairs, then stopped. "Are you going to be talking to my uncle?"

"Only if it's necessary. He has a cancer treatment tomorrow. Why?"

I handed her Detective Baddon's business card. "He wants Maximilian to call him."

Ophelia took the card and read it over. "I'll take care of it."

I scampered up the stairs. "He said to use the cell number," I said over my shoulder.

"Got it."

I made my way to the front door, grabbed the key to the second-floor apartment, and took the steps two at a time. I'd never had a place of my own. It was exciting just opening the door. I was making up one of the canopied beds when I heard a knock at the window. Luna was outside, hovering in midair. It was like a scene from *Harry Potter*. All she was missing was a broom.

"How are you doing that?" I asked.

She laughed and started flapping her arms like wings. Her body was bobbing gently from side to side. "Flying is my talent."

I couldn't believe it. And of course it wasn't true. She was standing on a fire escape. Her knees were bent and she was shifting her weight gently from foot to foot to make it look as if she were floating.

"You coming out sometime tonight, or were you planning to scrub the floors and vacuum the carpets?"

"Would it impress your father if he knew I was house-trained? Maybe you could take a picture and show him when he arrives."

"I think he'd just assume you were trying to steal the vacuum cleaner."

I walked over to the window and wound it open. I popped out the screen and stepped onto the fire escape. Luna grabbed my hand and nearly pulled my arm out of the socket hauling me up the steps. They led to a flat roof that was covered in pea gravel. Our feet made crunching noises on the stones. A chimney along the side made a perfect backrest. We sat. She still hadn't let go of my hand, not that I was complaining.

"Is there any chance your dad will let you stay?" I asked.

Luna's lips pressed together and one side of her mouth curled down. It was a perfect I-don't-know-but-probably-not face. "He might let Suki and I visit the lake while he meets with his colleague in Toronto. But he . . . well, he'll want us to steer clear of you. As far as he's concerned, you and Charlie are the real danger."

"Do you think he might be right?"

"What do you mean?"

I had to choose my words carefully. "I hate to say it because I want you to stay, but it might be safer for you to get away from us. At least until we've dealt with Hyde."

Luna let go of my hand. "That's not fair."

I didn't understand. What did fair have to do with it?

"If I were Charlie, would you want me to stay?"

"I already said I want you to stay. But I also want you to stay alive. This thing . . . I don't know what to tell you. You remember how terrifying Vlad was. Well, Hyde's a hundred times worse."

I didn't think she believed me, which wasn't at all surprising. Vlad was a live horror show. "Honestly. Until you see him, you won't understand."

She looked away, shook her head, stood up, and started pacing. When she spoke again, her hands were on her hips. "It's because I'm a girl."

I was totally confused at this point. I'd never had a problem with the essential girlness of her. In fact, I was pleased about it.

"If I were Charlie and I said I was leaving to go hide in New Jersey, you'd think I was a coward."

I hadn't thought about it that way.

"Ahhh, see. You know it's true. I can see it in your face."

I stood and dusted off my pants. "You're right. If you were Charlie, I would think badly of you if you left."

She put her hands in the air and started doing a victory dance. I had to admit, she had some pretty good moves. Definitely rave material. Then she started shadowboxing with me.

"You don't think I know how to fight?" She followed this question with a few jabs. Had she punched anything harder than shaving cream, she would have broken a wrist.

I waited for an opening, then slipped inside her guard and took her down to the roof. I twisted so she'd land on top of me, then I rolled over for the pin. It took about half a heartbeat. Just enough time for her to yelp.

"That was fast!"

"I had to move quickly. I was worried you might accidentally hit me and hurt yourself."

I rolled to the side, then let her up. She pulled me back to the chimney so we could sit side by side and look up at the stars.

"You've changed," she said.

"How?"

"You don't seem as shy. You were so funny at the cottage. So polite."

"What's wrong with that?"

"Nothing. I like polite." Her hand snuck into mine. "You seem a little . . . I don't know."

"I think it's the poison. Maybe I need more blood. And a bit more sleep, too."

She glanced at me and smiled. It made her eyes pinch shut. I remembered this from last summer—this smile. But seeing it was something else.

"That's not what I meant. You seem more confident. And don't take this the wrong way, but you're a little more like Charlie. I think he's rubbing off on you a bit."

Rubbing off? What did that mean? Was it good? I suppose I shouldn't have been surprised. I spent more time with Charlie than with anyone else. But I didn't think we were alike at all.

"Did I spoil things?" Luna's smile sagged a little and she looked up at the night sky.

"No. Not at all. It's wonderful to see you."

She was still holding my hand. For a moment we just stared at the arrangement of our fingers. Both pale. Hers slightly shorter, leaner, more delicate, but still strong. Years of weight lifting had built thick calluses on the inside of mine, and along the top of my palm. I had to use the back of a finger to feel how soft her skin was.

She looked at me and her face turned serious. "Could you show me how to do that . . . that thing that you just did."

"You mean how to fight?"

She nodded, then bit her lip and smiled again.

"I don't really know much," I said.

"Maybe you're a natural."

"Maybe."

She cleared a lock of hair away from her eyes and squeezed my hand. "It's wonderful to see you, too."

I took a deep breath and closed my eyes. I felt her lean into me. Her head fell onto my shoulder. We sat for a time saying nothing. I just enjoyed the feel of her beside me. Her hand in my hand. The pleasant smell of her. I could happily have frozen my life right there. Just stopped the clock and been in heaven forever.

"Are we going to be all right?" she asked.

I didn't want to spoil the moment by being honest. I tipped my head to the side so that it was resting gently against hers. She turned just enough so that our noses were almost touching. Then they were. I thought she might move away, but she did the exact opposite. Her breath was suddenly on my lips. Her hand came up and cupped the side of my face. In that instant, I promised myself two things. The first was that I wasn't going to let anything happen to her. That I would die first. The second was that I was going to find out how to properly kiss someone, because I never had.

My teeth started to slide down. I couldn't stop them. I glanced at her mouth. Her teeth were down, too. It pushed up her lips, made them look fuller. Her eyes were closed. Her chin rose a little, bringing her mouth closer. I understood in that moment why people said things like "these two have electricity." We weren't touching, but I could feel her getting closer. Even before her lips parted, I could sense them moving. Making my skin tingle.

"Hey! Get away from my daughter!" shouted a voice.

Luna shrieked. I jumped. Then I heard laughter.

Luna picked up a rock and tossed it hard at the fire escape. Charlie was standing on top. He barely ducked in time. When the rock flew past him, he put a hand on his stomach and started laughing even harder.

"You should have seen your faces!" He could barely get the words out as he wiped at his eyes. They actually had tears in them.

Luna reached for another rock. "You jerk!"

I was so relieved that it was Charlie and not Dr. Abbott that I didn't think to complain. Instead, I helped Luna to her feet. She pulled me close. Her lips brushed gently against my cheek.

"You make sure you pay him back," she whispered.

I wasn't going to suggest otherwise, but a part of me was grateful. In a way Charlie had just got me off the hook. If Luna knew I was a lousy kisser . . .

Charlie slapped my shoulder. He was breathing as if he'd just done a six-mile dash. "I hate to break it to you, Edward, but you aren't in Forks anymore. The love-in is over. We're going after Mr. Hyde."

CHAPTER 29

OF VILLAINS AND VAMPIRES

Charlie disappeared down the fire escape. It was a prudent move. Luna looked angry enough to stone him to death. Since nothing but pea-size gravel was on the roof, it would have taken her a while.

"I'd better see what this is about," I said.

We both started down the stairs. Luna stopped outside her window.

"Is it a good idea to have this here?" She shook the railing of the fire escape. "Couldn't that thing climb up?"

"It wouldn't make a difference. If he wants to get inside, he'll just plow through the wall."

Her eyes widened. "Are you serious?"

"From time to time."

We stood there for a few moments just looking at one another. Then Charlie called. I really didn't want to go.

"I should come with you."

I shook my head. "I don't like the idea of leaving Ophelia and your sister here by themselves. Will you be awake later?"

She nodded.

I turned and started down. I didn't get far. She took hold of my shirt and spun me around.

"Don't be too long," she whispered. "You still owe me a kiss."

When I heard that word, *kiss*, my brain stopped working properly. Instead of formulating a witty response, all it could do was change my face from pale to crimson. It might have been a survival thing. If I was blushing enough to produce my own light, I'd be less likely to trip on the stairs and fall to my death.

"Be careful," she added.

I nodded, then got myself turned around and slipped down to the driveway. Charlie had circled around the corner of the building. When I caught up, he was waiting with Mr. Entwistle, who was talking on his cell.

"How did things go at the house on Gilmour?" I asked. "You weren't gone very long. Did you find a trail?"

Charlie shook his head. "The owner cut the grass today. The tracks were gone and all we could smell was chlorophyll."

"Where does that leave us?"

Charlie was about to answer, but he was cut off by Mr. Entwistle, who snapped his phone closed and announced we were leaving. "Ophelia just got off the phone with Baddon. Hyde was at his house." Mr. Entwistle pulled off his hat, ran his fingers through his hair, then turned and started moving down the street.

"What about the others?" I didn't want to leave them by themselves.

"Ophelia isn't worried. It was her suggestion we go. I think she wants some time alone with the girls." He put his top hat back on and nodded to Charlie, who smiled and fell in step.

I shuffled after slowly. I wasn't sure I should be going. "I still feel awful. I think I'll only slow you down."

Mr. Entwistle laughed. "That's why I wanted you to join us. You might still have some traces of poison left in your system. This will flush it out. The best thing for you. A good run."

He sped up more. We turned a corner and started east on Sherbrooke. We were heading downtown.

"Here. Off the streets." He led us over a fence and into a backyard. He moved like a character from *The Matrix*. I kept looking above him to see where the strings were attached.

"What do we do if we find him?" I whispered.

Mr. Entwistle jumped off a tree and landed in the next yard.

"Hyde? We don't really want to find him. We want to follow him. And hope he really is a werewolf."

His words dislodged something from my tired brain. Baoh had said something similar. It didn't make sense to me at the time, and it still didn't.

"What do you mean *hope he's a werewolf*?" I asked.

Mr. Entwistle hopped another fence and stopped. He was in a crouch. I was reminded again of how wolflike his movements were. Steady, smooth, dangerous.

"Well, we don't have a lot of choices. He's one of us, or he's a lycanthrope."

"What difference does it make?" Charlie asked.

"All the difference in the world. You've seen the movies, read the stories. Every kid has." Mr. Entwistle pointed down the block. "That way's a shortcut." We took off again and he continued, "Vampires of ancient lore are creatures of pure evil. Very human, but stronger. Implacable. Almost indestructible. And in my case, uncommonly handsome."

"We're not evil," said Charlie.

"You aren't a vampire. Not in the traditional sense." Mr. Entwistle slipped through a cedar hedge. We followed, the smell of the evergreen thick in our noses. "No, boy, a vampire is an archetype for a villain. In real life, they don't exist."

"What do you mean in real life we don't exist? This is real life." Charlie gave a me look. *This guy's a nut,* he seemed to be saying.

"No, Charlie. I mean villains don't exist. In real life, everyone is both good and bad. Everyone. Whether someone is a villain or not just depends on whether they're for you or against you."

"Are you saying Hyde's not a villain?"

Mr. Entwistle didn't answer. He stepped off a lawn chair, shot up onto the roof of a shed, ran silently across the top, then launched himself into the next yard.

"Wow, he's smooth," Charlie whispered. Mr. Entwistle was already over the next fence. We hurried to catch up.

"Hyde is a villain, Charlie, but only to us," Mr. Entwistle said. "From his point of view, we're probably the bad guys. That's what I mean. Villainy is about perspective. Always has been."

We ran past a pool, crossed Momaghan Road, turned north, and started along another row of backyards.

"You still haven't explained what you meant," I said. "About wanting him to be a werewolf."

He hurdled a hedge, then stopped. Charlie and I pulled up beside him. All three of us were breathing heavily.

"Right . . . a werewolf. Well, lycanthropes are like vampires, Zack. They're blood drinkers. But they have two personae. Two aspects. One good. One bad. Like the movies. There's a guy with a normal life, then a full moon comes around, and presto! We've got a hairy-faced monster with an appetite for destruction. We want Hyde to be a werewolf, a creature that changes. That way, we don't have to deal with the Beast. He'll rip us into atoms."

I understood. If Hyde was like a vampire, if he never changed, then he was never vulnerable.

"So we're really looking for a man?"

"Not necessarily. We can't assume Hyde is a lycanthrope just because he looks different than we do. But to deal with a man would be much easier, assuming there's anyone around who fits."

"What does that mean—*fit*?" Charlie asked.

"Well, there's no getting around the laws of physics. Matter cannot be created or destroyed, only transformed. Whoever Hyde turns into, he has to be huge. Someone who would tower over us. Three to four hundred pounds of human that becomes three to four hundred pounds of werewolf."

Charlie shook his head. "Wait a minute. I knew something about this wasn't right. It wasn't a full moon the night we were at the zoo. Or when he went after Zack in the hospital."

"True enough," said Mr. Entwistle. "But there's more than one way to trigger a transformation. That full-moon stuff might be claptrap anyway. It dates back to the fertility cults of early history. They usually performed their rites when the moon was full. The Christians demonized them. Made them out to be full-moon monsters. But many myths contain kernels of truth. A full moon might do the trick, but if memory serves, they are other things that turn a lycanthrope from human to beast."

"Like what?" I asked.

"Bright lights—like a meteor shower. Injury. I read about a werewolf who changed because he took a sip from a silver cup and the purity of the metal exposed him. Probably balderdash. Heard of a man who turned just before he was hanged at the gallows. The monster inside didn't want to die. Blood might do it, too. Bring out the inner beast. For all I know, it's different for each of them. But it doesn't have to be a full moon."

Charlie looked up at the sky. A slender crescent hung overhead. "So what makes Hyde change?"

Mr. Entwistle put a hand on Charlie's back as he walked past. "No idea. Assuming he does change. It might just be wishful thinking. We want Hyde to have an alter ego. Someone we can deal with." He took off his hat and rubbed his hands through his hair. "But it all hinges on the same questions. Is he a werewolf or not? Does he change? Is he like us and vulnerable to the sun? Or just an abomination of some kind—a Beast with his own set of rules?"

I remembered Ophelia's note from the first safe house I was taken to, where the police had arrested me. *Knowledge is your best defense,* she had written. We knew little about Hyde. Who he was. What he was. Why he wanted us dead. So our best defense had more than a few holes.

"Why have we stopped?" Charlie asked.

Mr. Entwistle slapped the hat back on his head. "That's the detective's street. His house is farther down."

"Are we supposed to wait here?"

Mr. Entwistle didn't answer. Instead, he lifted his nose slightly. The wind picked up. I could smell the same canine odor I'd noticed at the zoo. Leather and wet dog. Just a trace.

"I'm just giving you a second to catch your breath," he said. "That smell could mean trouble."

I looked at Charlie. He looked at me. This was it. I let my teeth drop. He did the same.

"You two ready?"

We nodded, Charlie, then me.

Mr. Entwistle turned, then bounded through two yards, back-to-back, crossed the street, and stopped on the far sidewalk.

"It's quiet," he whispered. He pulled out his cell, punched in a number, then waited. A second later someone picked up on the other end. "We're outside your front door," Mr. Entwistle said. Then he turned down the nearest walk. "Get your game faces on, boys. This is it."

CHAPTER 30

FAMILY PORTRAIT

Detective Baddon's house was a small, two-story dwelling. Set back under an arch was the front door. In the center near the top was a small, circular window. The detective's face appeared behind it. He pushed the door open and stood aside so we could enter.

"No need," he said to me when I bent to remove my shoes. "We're going straight out the back."

When I looked up, I could see the barrel of a pistol at his side. A large wheel gun. His hand wasn't steady. A sharp smell was in the air—one I'd noticed a lot at Charlie's when his mother had her drinking spells. When the detective led us through the living room, I saw why. A bottle of alcohol and a shot glass were on the coffee table. We passed through a kitchen to the back door. Before he opened it, he turned and looked at all of us. I thought he was going to say something, but he changed his mind and hit the latch. Mr. Entwistle stepped out and we followed.

After witnessing at the hospital and the zoo what Hyde could do, I was surprised when I saw the backyard. I'd anticipated much worse. Tracks dotted the ground. The doors on a small shed at the back were pulled open. That was it. No scorched earth or torn-up sod. No debris or nuclear fallout. The lawn furniture on the patio was still sitting right where it should have been, looking old and bored.

Mr. Entwistle bent to a knee and examined the ground. Then he started touring the yard. Every now and again he would bend down to examine the grass more closely. When he was finished, he stuck his nose inside the shed.

"What do you see?" Detective Baddon asked him.

"Nothing as dramatic as I'd expected." Mr. Entwistle pointed to a spot near his foot. "He landed here from that yard." He indicated the fence. "He went straight to the shed, got a bit rough with the doors, looked inside, walked toward the back door . . ." He grunted here and examined the flattened grass more carefully. "Looks like he changed his mind, turned, and left that way." He gazed toward the backyard behind us.

I moved over to examine the prints. They were shaped just as I remembered them. Round and deep. The nails had left long scars in the lawn at the point of takeoff. "How long ago did this happen?" I asked.

The detective was still standing on the back step. "With the exception of the ten minutes I was at your place, and a short trip to the station, I've been at the hospital all night. It could have been anytime."

"There's a second set of footprints here," Mr. Entwistle said. "I assume that was you."

"Yeah. I wanted to see what he'd taken from the shed."

"And what was it?"

"Well, that's just it. He didn't take anything—not as far as I can tell."

The old vampire closed the doors. One of the hinges was broken, so they didn't fit together properly. "So he didn't find what he was looking for?"

"It looks that way."

Mr. Entwistle returned to the back step. "So the question is, what did he want? Why come here?"

"I have a theory." The detective rubbed a hand over his eyes.

"Let's hear it."

He took a full chest of air and let it out. "Before Hyde appeared,

Everett was very worried about the Coven. Apparently they don't approve of child vampires, and the rate at which the pathogen is spreading here. Everett was worried that there'd be trouble, so he brought me into the Underground to help."

"Your timing could have been better," Charlie said.

The detective snorted a laugh. "You're not kidding. He thought he was doing me a favor. I was struggling in Toronto. We both thought a change might help." He sighed. I took it from his expression that the scene in his backyard wasn't quite what he'd had in mind. "Neither of us knew that Hyde was coming down the track. He's not just going after vampires. He's taking the whole Underground apart. So when this thing killed Everett, it put me at the top of his list."

"You think Hyde is after you?" Mr. Entwistle asked.

Detective Baddon nodded. "Yes."

"Is that why he was at the hospital?" I asked.

"Maybe. Unless he was after you. Or John. It could have been any one of us."

"That doesn't explain the shed," said Charlie. "Why bother with it?"

"I was doing some work in there yesterday. My wife never liked it when I cleaned my guns in the house. My guess is, he followed my scent there." The detective adjusted his glasses and stared at the footprints all over the grass. "I don't think there's anything else in there of interest."

He held open the back door of the house and we walked inside. Just past the kitchen was a small living space with a couch and some chairs. He took off his glasses, rubbed his eyes, led us through, and sat down. Then he started unscrewing the cap on the bottle he'd left on the coffee table.

"You want one?" he asked.

The old vampire shook his head.

"Do you mind?"

"Go ahead."

The detective filled a shot glass and drained it.

"I want to get on that trail while it's still fresh," Mr. Entwistle said. "Anything else you can tell us?"

Detective Baddon shook his head. A photo was on the coffee table. A family portrait. I recognized him and his son. The woman at his side must have been his wife. Like the boy I'd seen in the hospital, she was fair and slight. Tall as well, and happy. There was another boy, too, clearly older. He was short and thick, like his father.

Mr. Entwistle started fidgeting with his hat. I could see that he was impatient to be going. He had the same restless look in his eyes I'd often seen in Charlie's.

"Do you think this has anything to do with your son?" Mr. Entwistle asked.

The detective thought for a moment. He was spent. He sighed and tipped his head so it was resting on the back of the sofa. "I don't think so."

"Is he a vampire, like us?"

He shook his head, then reached behind his back and pulled out his gun. He set it on the coffee table beside the open bottle and photo of his family. It was a grim still life. "I wish he were a vampire like you. It would certainly solve his problems."

"What do you mean?"

"He's been in a coma for six months. He took a hit to the head that did a lot of damage. God—to think I could just give him an infusion of blood and he'd regenerate the way you three do. But it's not like that. Then he got diagnosed with leukemia, like he wasn't in enough trouble. It spread to his bones, liver, and kidneys. I thought he was going to die. The cancer's gone now, but it probably doesn't matter. I don't think he'll ever wake up."

"I'm sorry to hear that."

"So am I." The detective's eyes were on the coffee table.

"And the boy's mother?" Mr. Entwistle asked.

"She died. My older boy, too." His hand reached out and fell upon the bottle. He lifted it and started pouring another shot.

Mr. Entwistle put a hand on the detective's arm. "Why don't you stay with us at the apartment? If Hyde knows you live here, you're safer with us. You can get some rest and see your son in the morning."

"I won't get any sleep tonight. I haven't been able to string more than two hours together in the last six months."

"A change of scenery might help."

"It can't hurt." Detective Baddon stood and stepped past the old vampire, then proceeded into the kitchen. When he came back, a small box was in his hand. It rattled when he set it on the coffee table. He sat and flipped the gun open, then started sliding the bullets from the chambers in the wheel. When it was empty, he opened the box in front of him and pulled out a shell. It caught the light of the room's only lamp and lit up like a new coin.

"I ordered these the night Everett was killed. Silver." He started to reload the gun with the silver bullets. "I'm not taking any chances." When the gun was full, he snapped it closed. His hand stretched out of his sleeve just enough so that the scars on his wrist were visible.

"What happened there?" Mr. Entwistle asked.

The detective looked at his wrist, then pulled his hand back so that the row of scars disappeared under the fabric. "I was attacked."

"Can I see?"

He pulled up his sleeve. A large swath of pink scar tissue ran across the tendons just under his hand. "Ended my power-lifting career."

"What happened?"

"I don't remember exactly. But I read the report after I got out of the hospital. We walked in while someone was robbing the house. I didn't see him in time. I got my hand up though. I'm told it saved my life." He held up his arm so it was resting against his forehead. A smaller scar that I hadn't noticed was on the top of his head. It lined up perfectly with the ones on his wrist, like pieces of a grisly puzzle. "He had a bottle. When it broke, it slashed through the tendons. Knocked me out."

I could imagine a bottle breaking against his head and wrist. He lowered his hand and picked up the picture. He stared at it for a long time before he continued. "He was more thorough with my wife and son. That little guy in the hospital is all I have left . . . I don't know what I'm going to do if I lose him."

"We won't let anything happen." Mr. Entwistle spoke with such confidence, I found myself believing him. He put a hand on the detective's shoulder as he passed. "I'm going to stop this thing if it kills me."

He looked at me squarely when he said this. We both knew what he'd seen in his vision—the darkness that was coming.

"Good luck tonight. Call me and let me know what you find." The detective pushed himself up from the sofa and started to rise.

"Don't get up. We'll see ourselves out." Mr. Entwistle nodded to Charlie, who fell in step behind him.

"Wait, Zachary," Detective Baddon said. "I need another word with you, if you don't mind."

I stayed behind. Charlie held the back door, but I raised my index finger. "One minute," I whispered. He nodded and let it close.

"I know you have to go, so I'll be brief." The detective's hands were shaking. "If something happens to me and my son is still in his coma . . ."

I didn't think he was going to finish. He reached for the bottle on the table, then set it back and stood up so we were face-to-face.

"Would you consider . . ." Again he stalled.

I could smell his fear. I looked into his eyes. Saw his jaw clench. Then I realized what he was asking me.

"Would I consider infecting him to keep him alive?"

"Yes." We walked to the back door. "Just think about it."

"If I infect him, he will wake up, but the Coven will come after him. They want to kill us—Charlie, me, Luna. There aren't supposed to be child vampires."

"I know." He took a deep breath. It was a miracle he was standing. He looked like a man who'd run the Daytona 500 dragging his car.

"But the alternative . . ." Again he didn't finish, but there was no need. I understood his fear. That his son might never wake up. Well, I'd died before. It wasn't as bad as everyone thought. It might be better than waking up alone, confused, in a strange place with his family gone.

The detective reached past me and opened the door. "Be careful."

"I will." Then I stepped out to join the others.

Charlie waited for the door to close, then walked over beside me. "Everything all right?"

"Yeah."

"What did he want?"

"He just wanted to make sure we'd look after his son if something happened to him."

Charlie took a deep breath. "Man, that's heavy. His kid would be an orphan, just like you."

Not quite like me. But I understood what Charlie was saying.

Mr. Entwistle started talking into his phone. "Yeah, you need to send Agent X over here. Baddon's a mess. Trust me, I'm an expert when it comes to nervous breakdowns. I have one every few years just to stay in practice." There was a long pause. "Yes, he was here. He was looking for something." Another pause. "We don't know. Baddon thinks Hyde was looking for him. . . . We've got a trail to follow." Mr. Entwistle looked at us and held up his hand—*Stay right there,* he seemed to be saying. "It means he knows where Baddon lives. We can't let him stay here. Hyde might come back. . . . Because he might not. . . . I'm going to follow this trail. . . . No, they're safer with me. . . . Then he can meet up with us. If there's trouble, he can drive them back. . . . Sounds good." Then Mr. Entwistle said good-bye and flicked his phone closed.

"What did Ophelia want?" I asked.

"She wants you two home."

Charlie started to protest.

"Don't worry. You're with me. She's just worried that if you leave, Hyde will find you; if you stay, Hyde will find you; and if he doesn't find you, you might find him instead. But I think she knows you're better off with me. Agent X might join us later if we need him."

"Or if you need to send us back," said Charlie.

"Or that," said Mr. Entwistle. "Don't forget, Luna and Suki are back there. If Hyde pays them a visit while we're hopping backyard fences, you're going to have a disappointing homecoming."

CHAPTER 31

THE TRAIL ENDS

We followed Hyde's trail east toward the downtown.

"Do you really think Hyde was going after Baddon?" Charlie asked.

Mr. Entwistle took a few backyards to think about it. "Probably. Hyde killed those other officers. He obviously has an interest in bringing down the Underground. I just hope we're following the right trail."

I hadn't realized there were others. When I asked about it, Mr. Entwistle hurdled a doghouse, ducked a clothesline, then answered over his shoulder, "We could have followed the trail backward and seen where Hyde had come from."

I hadn't considered that. "So why did we pick this one?"

"I was worried he might be heading for the apartment."

Charlie grimaced as we turned down an alley. Neither of us was keen to see Hyde do an about-face and head back to Ophelia's. Fortunately he didn't. The trail was clear. Nothing erratic, just a straight line out of town. Either he didn't expect to be followed, or he didn't care.

"Those silver bullets Baddon was putting in his gun, do they make a difference?" Charlie asked.

Mr. Entwistle shook his head. "Would it matter if I shot *you* with silver bullets? Anything traveling over two hundred yards per second is going to hurt. I don't care if it's a lima bean."

"So why do all the werewolf movies have that in them?"

Mr. Entwistle slipped between two sections of a cedar hedge, then slowed to explain, "In ancient stories about vampires and were-wolves, all you needed to kill us was metal. Regular iron was just fine. It had to do with the mysteries of metallurgy. Most people didn't really understand how iron was forged. To the average person, it was a mystical process, and it represented a kind of triumph. Man rising above nature. And above the supernatural. I remember ghost stories as a boy about men who killed restless spirits with iron knives. Then when metal was more common, and less mysterious, silver became the new iron. At least in the stories."

"Why?" Charlie asked.

Mr. Entwistle took a detour around a patio party. Someone had a stereo blasting, so Charlie had to repeat his question.

"Silver doesn't corrode like other metals. It gives it an aura of purity. It's all poppycock, of course. If I shoot you with silver, steel, lead, or Botox, it's going to do some damage."

In the next backyard he stopped. A large addition to a two-story house was in front of us. He took off his top hat, flattened it to pancake dimensions, and stuck it inside his coat. His hair looked fresh from a Jell-O mold. He rubbed his fingers through it, then wiped his forehead on the sleeve of his coat. He started scowling and his head swung back and forth in disbelief.

"What is it?" I asked.

He was looking down at the ground. I could see a deep footprint. Then he nodded toward the roof of the house. "I think he must have taken this in one stride."

"What do you mean?"

"I mean he jumped straight up onto the roof." He looked at me with his eyebrows high on his head, as if I ought to be impressed.

I was. "You having second thoughts?"

"No. I'm way past that. More like tenth or eleventh?"

Charlie looked at me. He was incredulous. All of us were.

"Think happy thoughts," said Mr. Entwistle, then he started up again.

"Happy thoughts," Charlie repeated, shaking his head. "Where did you find this guy?"

I hadn't found him. He'd found me—in a mental institution. That was before Hyde. Before Vlad. Before *that night*. Those years at the Nicholls Ward were starting to look like the glory days.

We were moving east down Parkhill Road by this time, away from the city and into an area with lots of farms. Mr. Entwistle picked up the pace. With no cars on the road, we really dropped the hammer. I bet we broke the speed limit. I spent the whole time thinking about Luna and what she would think if she could see me. I looked like the Michelin Man. My shirt was puffed up like an air balloon. It was the only thing that kept it from catching fire. We were that fast. After a few miles, Mr. Entwistle slowed. We were far out of town. I couldn't smell the Quaker Oats factory anymore.

"Why are we stopping again?" Charlie asked.

Mr. Entwistle was bent at the waist. His breathing was heavy. I was panting, too, and I wasn't running in body armor. He was so smooth and fast, I often forgot he had it on under his overcoat. It was a wonder he hadn't melted.

"Why? Because if we catch up to Hyde panting like overweight geriatric patients, he's going to slice us into small pieces." Mr. Entwistle was looking at the ground. "And because he stopped here himself." The old vampire started hopping from foot to foot. He looked like a drunk sailor trying to master an awkward version of hip-hop. Then I realized he was putting his feet in Hyde's footprints.

"What is it?" Charlie asked.

"He left the road here," Mr. Entwistle said.

I wondered why. "To avoid a car maybe?"

"Maybe."

We followed the trail off the road and into a pasture. There we found another set of tracks. These ones led back into town. Mr. Entwistle bent down to inspect them. His nostrils flared. "The ones heading back in are fresher. The scent on them is stronger."

"Did he turn around here?" Charlie asked.

Mr. Entwistle shook his head. "No. He continued that way." He pointed in the direction we'd been running—out of town. "He must have done an about-face somewhere ahead."

"So what do we do?" I asked.

Mr. Entwistle peered skyward. A few hours of night remained. He paused for a moment to think. "If we follow the first trail, we might find his lair. Or at least where he turned around. But, obviously, if we're out here, and he's back in town . . ."

"We need to find out where he lives. Where he hides," said Charlie.

"Yes, we do. Eventually. But these tracks won't disappear overnight. We can follow the first set again if we have to and see where they lead."

Charlie nudged me on the shoulder. "What are you thinking, boy genius? I can see the gears grinding."

I was thinking that Hyde knew he was faster than us. Maybe he planned for us to follow him out here. Then he could double back and do whatever he wanted in town because we were wasting our time chasing shadows. I looked at Charlie, then at Mr. Entwistle. The old vampire seemed to know what I was thinking. I heard his teeth grind. So we turned and took off in the direction of home.

"Do you think the others are all right?" Charlie asked.

"I'd better call." Mr. Entwistle pulled out his cell phone. "Thank God for technology. Can you imagine how easy life would have been for the Hardy Boys if they'd had these things?"

Charlie looked at me and mouthed, *Hardy Boys?*

I shrugged. I had no idea who they were. Pioneers maybe.

The old vampire slowed to talk. I heard Ophelia's voice on the other end. "Yeah, it's John. We're turning around. We followed tracks to Douro, but found another set heading back into town. They're fresher, so we're following those. Keep your eyes open. Hyde might be heading your way. Are Agent X and Baddon there?"

I heard Ophelia say no. They were at the hospital. I remembered what my uncle had told me. That his last radiation treatment was in the morning. He must have gone in early with Baddon so the detective could be with his son.

"Call if there's trouble," Mr. Entwistle said, then hung up. "They're alone. Let's motor."

"Why did Agent X leave?" Charlie asked.

"He was taking Baddon to the hospital. My guess is, they'll both be staying there."

Charlie shook his head. We hurdled a farm fence. Mr. Entwistle sped up and we followed. I was starting to falter. I hadn't recovered from my visit to the hospital. I loved few things more than running at night, but my gas tank was down to fumes.

"I had a bad feeling about him," Charlie said.

"Who?"

"Agent X. Who did you think I meant? Did anyone else shoot me with a tranquilizer? How do you trust a guy when you don't even know his name?"

I didn't have an answer for this. I looked over at Mr. Entwistle. He was listening, his eyes busily scanning for the next footprint.

"When you get to be my age, boys," he said, "you discover there are reasons not to trust everybody. You can twist your mind into a pretzel thinking about it. Trust, I wouldn't get too hung up on it."

I was surprised to hear this. The way Ophelia made it sound, trust was one of the founding principles of the universe. Trust and order.

"You mean you don't trust anybody?" Charlie asked.

Mr. Entwistle shook his head. "It isn't about trust. It's about understanding. Should I trust you?"

"Yeah. Of course."

"Okay. Imagine this scenario. Hyde has Suki as a hostage. He asks you to betray me, or he'll kill her. Should I still trust you?"

Charlie started to answer.

Mr. Entwistle cut him off. "Think. Is your first loyalty to her or to me? Now what about Baddon? You know how he feels about his son. What do you think he might do if something happened to the boy, if the Coven took him, for example? Would the detective sell your soul to get his son back? Count on it."

The old vampire looked at us and laughed. "See what I mean? You could go nuts worrying about all the possibilities. All the reasons not to trust people. Me, Baddon, Agent X."

I was pleased he didn't add Ophelia to that list. Or Luna or Suki for that matter.

"So don't focus on trust," he told us. "Focus on understanding everyone's situation. Everyone's point of view. And what they want. Hyde. Baddon. Dr. Abbott. Agent X. When you know what people want, and how they plan to get it, you can stop thinking about trust and focus on what you need to do to help them, if it's the right thing, or how to stop them, if that's the right thing."

"What does Agent X want?" Charlie asked.

"To stay alive," said Mr. Entwistle. "He's part of the Underground, so his interests are our interests. You can count on that."

The old vampire looked up at the sky, then sped up. He definitely had more fuel to burn than me. I did my best to follow. The pace he kept made it impossible to talk. Maybe that's what he wanted. The sun would soon be up. We were running out of night.

Eventually, Hyde's trail took us around to the south side of the city.

"This is good," said Charlie.

I agreed. It meant Hyde wasn't heading for the apartment.

We entered the land of sidewalks and roads and it got more difficult to follow the trail. At Hyde's speed, he didn't leave much of an odor behind. All we had to go on were his footprints, and with all the pavement, clear ones were often half a block apart. It was slow going. Eventually, we wound up on Neal Drive. Mr. Entwistle pointed to a set of Dumpsters sitting beside a long building. It looked like a series of miniature garages sitting side by side. The sign in the driveway said Peterborough Multiple Storage. He made his way over, crouched in the shadows, and stared at the building.

"What are we doing?" Charlie whispered.

"Thinking. Now quit stealing all my oxygen."

I tried to quiet my breathing. It was just starting to settle when Mr. Entwistle stood up and crept along the back of the storage units. He stopped outside one in the center of the row, number 6.

"Is he in there?" I whispered.

Mr. Entwistle nodded. He put a finger over his mouth and quietly tested the knob. It was locked. He paused. His eyes rolled up slightly while he considered what to do. Then he drew out the knife—the one Maximilian had given me—and kicked the door in.

CHAPTER 32

MONKSHOOD

The doorframe buckled under the force of Mr. Entwistle's boot. Pieces of cinder block scattered as the housing for the dead bolt tore loose from the wall.

"Well, there goes the element of surprise," Charlie muttered.

The old vampire laughed. "The way you two breathe, he could hear you through six feet of concrete." He stuck his head in the doorway. "Honey, I'm home." His voice was remarkably steady.

I listened, but heard nothing but the sound of dust settling on cardboard. The room was full of packing boxes and not much else.

"Well, let's see what Old Yeller was up to." Mr. Entwistle moved carefully into the room.

I stopped in the doorway. There was nowhere else to go. The room had cardboard boxes piled floor to ceiling along each wall. The only place to walk was a path down the center that ended at the far side.

"You sure he's gone?" Charlie asked.

"Unless he taped himself inside a box," Mr. Entwistle replied.

I started forward. He stopped me with his hand. He was inspecting the floor. Then he turned his attention to the labels on the boxes.

"Sorry. You can come in. I just didn't want you walking all over his footprints until I had a chance to check them out." Mr. Entwistle reached up and pulled a box down. It said CLOTHES on it. He started picking at the tape. Then he shook his head. "Here. Let's get those ones down."

"What are we doing?" I asked. I thought if Hyde was gone, we should be hightailing it. He might have been anywhere in town by now, including the apartment.

"I want to know what he came here for."

"Is all of this his?" Charlie asked.

"Not unless his name is Nancy." Mr. Entwistle pointed to a box. "That's our winner, right there." On one side the words NANCY—COSMETICS were written in black marker. The tape wasn't sticking to the cardboard properly, as if it had recently been pulled loose. Mr. Entwistle lifted the box down and opened the top, then he whistled as if he'd struck gold. Charlie and I stuck our heads closer to see inside. It was packed with makeup cases, lipstick rolls, mascara, perfumes. Enough to keep Kiss in costume for a decade. Sitting on top were a bunch of yellow flowers. They'd dried somewhat, but were still fragrant. Mr. Entwistle was staring at them.

"What are they?" I asked.

"Monkshood," he said.

The name fit. The flowers looked like tiny hoods.

"Why would he want these?" Charlie reached in.

Mr. Entwistle stopped him. "You mean you've never heard of monkshood?"

"What, like I work for FTD?"

"A simple *no* will suffice."

"Well then, *no,*" Charlie said. "I've never heard of monkshood."

"It has another name. Wolfsbane. You heard of that?"

Wolfsbane. I had heard of it. Charlie and I used to play Dungeons & Dragons. I wasn't sure if I should admit to this or not. But poisons were part of the game. Wolfsbane was right up there with hemlock and belladonna.

"You mean you never played D & D as a kid?" Mr. Entwistle asked. "Too bad. Great game. I guess you two didn't hang out with the cool kids in the neighborhood. If you had, you'd know that wolfsbane is lethal. Back when I was your age, people nailed it to their doors to keep wolves and lycanthropes away. It's deadly stuff."

"I'll try to remember that when I roll up my next half-orc assassin," Charlie said.

"I prefer human wizards, myself." Mr. Entwistle stared down inside the box, then started humming to himself and scratching at the whiskers on his chin.

"What is it?" I asked.

"More questions . . . What is this stuff doing here? What does Hyde want it for? Whose storage unit is this?" Mr. Entwistle glanced around at the other boxes. "We should call in the morning and see if we can find out. I wonder . . ."

"You wonder what?" Charlie asked.

"Well, if this is registered to a man, it might be his alter ego."

"The man he turns into?" I said.

"Yeah, his Dr. Jekyll."

"What do you mean, Dr. Jekyll? Like the guy from that horror movie?" Charlie asked.

"It was a book first. Great werewolf."

"He wasn't a werewolf!"

"Not literally," Mr. Entwistle explained. "Weren't you listening earlier? I'm speaking figuratively. In the archetypical sense, Dr. Jekyll was the good persona, Mr. Hyde was the evil one. Why do you think I picked that name?"

Charlie shrugged. "Body hair? *Hide*—you know. A hairy hide."

Mr. Entwistle looked at him, then at me.

I had thought Mr. Entwistle picked the name because we couldn't ever find him, and that his secrets were hidden, but I was too embarrassed to say.

The old vampire shook his head. "How did you two nincompoops get out of elementary school?"

"I stopped going to school in grade two," I said.

"And I think I got promoted so my teachers wouldn't have to see me again," said Charlie.

I didn't think he was joking, but Mr. Entwistle laughed anyway. "Right. Well, I think we can leave now. With any luck, we can find out who rents this unit. Hyde must have used a key. He got in without breaking the door. That's a good sign."

He started to fold the box closed.

"Don't we want to take that with us?" Charlie said.

"Charlie, that would be stealing! Zack, what kind of company are you keeping?"

All of this from a guy who'd stolen a motorcycle and a Ford Mustang from the police, and an ambulance from the hospital. I checked his face for signs that he was joking. It was like reading a cement wall. He would have been deadly in a game of Texas Hold'em.

"Do you think the Almighty would forgive us if we just borrowed a sprig or two?" the old vampire asked. "You can give some to Luna and Suki."

Yes, he was definitely joking.

"I'd rather give some to Hyde," Charlie said.

"Only if we have to. Now how should we carry it? Just one scratch and it's game over."

"It's that strong?" I asked.

"Yup."

"The box is full of makeup bags," Charlie said. "Can't we just put some in one of those?"

"And to think I called you a nincompoop. Grow a few more brain cells, Charlie, and I'll upgrade you to genius." Mr. Entwistle looked at me and smiled, then reached into the box and pulled out a purse. The outside was covered with grotesque floral patterns. He tipped it upside down and the stash of makeup thingamabobs spilled out. Then he folded the bag over the bouquet of monkshood. He was careful not to touch any. Once it was zipped shut, he handed the bag to Charlie and pushed him toward the door.

"Why do I have to carry this thing?"

"It's part of that boyish charm that got you through school. And it matches your eyes." The old vampire herded us out the door, then did his best to close it behind us. It was bent and the housing for the dead bolt had torn free from the cinder-block wall. "If only we had some duct tape," he muttered. Then he reached into his coat, pulled out a plastic bag, and jammed it under the door so that it was wedged closed. "Plastic bags—a million and one uses. Now, a million and two."

I smiled. Charlie was still trying to figure out what to do with the handbag.

"Quit fussing," Mr. Entwistle said. "Look on the bright side. If Hyde tries to kill us on the way home, you can fend him off with your purse."

"Yeah. Great. If only my friends could see me."

"Be careful what you wish for." Mr. Entwistle fished into his pocket and came out with his cell phone. "Cheese!" He snapped a photo, then started out across the lot at a slow jog. "Yeah, I'm definitely tagging you on my Facebook page."

Charlie was still staring at the handbag. "Where's a good half-orc assassin when you need one?"

"I heard that," the old vampire said. "Let's go."

"Where?"

"Good question. Can you find the trail?"

Charlie and I tested the air. All I could smell was garbage and dust and cooling asphalt. I checked the ground for prints, but saw nothing. "Where did he go?"

Mr. Entwistle snorted. "No idea. But we're out of time. The sun will be up in an hour, and I forgot to bring my stolen ambulance with me. We'd better get back. You two ready?"

"Yeah."

So we headed for home.

CHAPTER 33

INFIGHTING

Hope is a funny thing. It can be totally unreasonable—bone dumb, in fact—and a part of it still clings to your brain. I remember as a kid hoping to find a light saber in my Christmas stocking. After reading my first *Marvel Tales* comic, I hoped that I might get bitten by a radioactive bug and receive the full range of superpowers you'd expect from such a miracle. You can bet all that hope came to nothing. But other times hope is dead-on. Like when you hope the winter will soon be over and it's already late April. That's the kind of hope you want to have. It's less disappointing.

All the way home, I was thinking of Luna. I was hoping she'd be awake and that I could see her. And I was hoping that my hope wasn't too unreasonable. When we reached the apartments, my first thought was to find her and head up the fire escape. Sadly, fate had other plans. The trouble started with our greeting in the backyard. My uncle was there in his ninja garb, Cobra Commander helmet and all. Mr. Entwistle clearly wasn't expecting to see him.

"I thought you were at the hospital with Baddon?"

"I was. But I thought the greater threat was here, so I came back. I also wanted to know if you'd found Hyde." Maximilian glanced over at us. If he noticed the purse Charlie was carrying, he said nothing. I was about to make a wisecrack about our failure to find my friend a decent set of matching high heels, but the look on his face told me it was best to shut up. He was looking at Maximilian intently, his pupils wide and his nostrils slowly flaring.

In some ways, vampires are closer to dogs than humans. Humans trust their eyes more than anything else. If I showed you a chunk of hot fudge, you'd think it was hot fudge, even if it smelled like strawberries. A dog wouldn't be fooled. A strawberry is a strawberry because it smells like a strawberry. Charlie was sniffing the air as if he smelled a rat. You can bet that raised my blood pressure. He had good reason to despise my uncle—and if he figured out that Agent X was Maximilian, well then, I was sure episode one of *Charlie Goes Homicidal* was going to happen right there in the yard. I took a deep breath through my nose. The faint odor of hospital cleanser still clung to my uncle's skin and clothes. No surprises there. He'd just delivered Detective Baddon to see his son. I casually walked past my friend and took hold of his elbow, spinning him toward the door. If it sounds like an aggressive move, it wasn't. I was just trying to get him focused on something other than Maximilian.

"Come on, Charlie," I said. "The sun will be up soon. Let's get inside. Maybe the lovely Suki Abbott is awake."

Charlie fell in step beside me, but kept his head turned and his eyes on my uncle. Mr. Entwistle was giving him a play-by-play of our evening.

"We'll be inside if you need us," I said.

The old vampire nodded, then continued his narrative. Charlie and I navigated the front hall, then stopped outside of Ophelia's first-floor apartment.

"Something about that guy isn't right," Charlie said. "I don't care what Entwistle says about trust. There was no reason for him to shoot me."

I didn't know the best response for this. Any answer would have prolonged a conversation I didn't want to have, so I said nothing. I wanted to see Luna, and the sooner I checked in with Ophelia to make sure she knew we were safe, the sooner I could go knock on Luna's window.

"You know," Charlie said, "I've been thinking. If Hyde is a

werewolf, and Mr. Entwistle is right, he needs to turn into someone huge."

I wondered where Charlie was going with this.

"So. Look at Agent X. He's could be a WWE wrestler."

I must have looked incredulous. I'd never for a second considered it.

"And he was at the hospital, then left, just before Hyde showed
up. And now he's snooping around here and he's supposed to be
with Baddon."

Could this be true - that my uncle was Mr. Hyde? I was dumbstruck. And Charlie didn't know the half of it. Maximilian had been
hunting a werewolf earlier this year. He might easily have been bitten. It would explain why he'd never seen Hyde. Why they were
never around together.

Why hadn't this occurred to me? I had to warn Mr. Entwistle.
But how? He and my uncle were talking outside.

Charlie nudged me in the ribs. "What's going on in that steel
trap you call a brain?"

My steel trap was undecided. Was it really possible that my
uncle could be trying to help us as a man and kill us as a monster?
I tried to remember what I could from the movies. It seemed to me
that the man rarely knew about the beast he turned into. Even if he
did know, he could never remember what he'd done when he wasn't
human.

"Earth to Zack. You okay? You look like you just got tagged on
the chin."

I needed more time to think this through. "Maybe we should
mention it to Ophelia."

Charlie nodded, then we entered the first-floor apartment. Ophelia was pacing the room. She looked pale. I couldn't tell if she was
worried or furious.

"What is it?" I asked.

"Did you know anything about this?" Her voice was stern.

"About what?"

I looked at Charlie. His expression changed. It might have been guilt. It might have been nervousness. I couldn't tell. I looked back at Ophelia, but had no idea what to say.

"Charlie?" she said.

"Hey, don't look at me."

"What are you talking about?" I asked.

"The girls are gone." I sensed Ophelia was about to start a barrage of questions, but she didn't say any more because Mr. Entwistle and Maximilian were coming through the front door, laughing. Her attention shifted to them.

Mr. Entwistle's nose must have told him something was wrong because the humor disappeared from his face before he looked over. "What is it?"

"The girls have left," Ophelia said. "I was in the basement. I heard them on the fire escape. By the time I realized they were leaving and got to the door, they were already taking off in their car. I had hoped they'd be back by now."

Mr. Entwistle looked at me, then at Charlie. His pale blue eyes probed my friend's face. "Tell us what you know."

Charlie glanced at me. I expected him to look nervous. The old vampire was still staring at him. So was Ophelia. I would have melted under their gaze. But Charlie was used to being in trouble. He was simply irritated.

"Neither of them wants to go home," he said. "They won't be coming back here."

I thought for a second Ophelia was going to attack him. "Charlie, you have no idea how thoughtless this is."

"There wouldn't be a problem if you hadn't called Dr. Abbott."

I hadn't realized that Ophelia had placed the call. But looking back, it was the only thing that made sense. Luna was with me, and Suki wouldn't have called her father, knowing he'd get angry.

"Every parent has the right to know their children are safe."

My uncle stepped between them. "Where have they gone?"

As soon as he spoke, Charlie glared at him. I felt myself cringe.

I'd once compared Maximilian's movements to those of a stone golem. Strength and purpose were in everything he did. He was still carrying his gun, the one that looked as if it had been stolen from a Klingon war chief. I wondered if Charlie was right. If my uncle was Hyde. He swung the gun up so that it was resting on his shoulder. His other arm was folded across his chest in a familiar pose.

"My guess is, they've gone to their cottage," Ophelia said.

"They sold the cottage," I told her. "They don't own it anymore." She turned to Charlie. "Where are they?"

He wasn't going to answer. I could see his pupils getting wider. His eyebrows knotted.

"Charlie," Mr. Entwistle said, "we can deal with Dr. Abbott. We can't deal with Hyde. Neither can the girls. We have to get them back. The sun will be up soon. There's not much time."

Charlie looked at the ground, then at me. I wish he'd told me Suki was planning to go. I could have asked Luna to talk her out of it. Perhaps she'd tried.

"They're going to the lake."

He must have meant Stony Lake, where Charlie's cottage was.

"Where exactly?" Mr. Entwistle said.

"The camp."

"You mean Camp Kawartha?" my uncle asked.

Charlie glanced at me, then said yes.

Ophelia had assumed her headache pose—fingers and thumb rubbing opposite sides of her forehead. She looked at Mr. Entwistle. "Can you go now? Is there time?"

He didn't have an answer.

"I know the place," Maximilian said. "I can't go. I'm due at the hospital first thing, but you can take my car."

At the sound of the word *car*, something happened in Charlie's brain. You could see it. His face went from thoughtful, to certain, then to rage.

"This is crazy," Mr. Entwistle said. The word *crazy* hung in the air like a challenge. Then Charlie attacked my uncle. I can only assume that he figured out who Agent X really was. Perhaps it was his tone of voice. Something in the way he moved. Or dressed. Or the mention of the word *car*. My uncle had a rocket on wheels. Last year, he'd taken Charlie and Luna hostage and driven them to Montreal in the trunk while I'd sat in the cockpit, totally oblivious.

Maximilian was caught completely by surprise. He turned just in time to have Charlie knock his gun away and slam him up against the far wall. I was already moving. I threw myself at Charlie, shoulder first, in what would have been a textbook tackle if he hadn't ducked. I slipped over the top of him and hit the side of his head with my knee. To Charlie's credit, he rolled with it and came up swinging. He was actually so angry, he'd forgotten about my uncle and was attacking me. I had to play the Artful Dodger for a few seconds until Mr. Entwistle jumped over and tied him up in a bear hug.

Charlie shouted the entire time. "I knew there was something about him. I knew it. I knew it!" He mixed a few swear words in for effect. His eyes were like two black pearls. Hell hath no fury like a demented vampire. I'm sure Shakespeare said that somewhere.

My uncle rose to his feet and pulled out a stun gun.

"There's no need for that." Ophelia was right beside him, her hand on his arm.

I felt like a lost tourist in a haunted house. My friend had finally snapped. Luna was gone. Hyde was still out there, and now we were fighting among ourselves.

My uncle started coughing. His helmet had been knocked loose, and he was spitting up blood.

"You okay?" I asked. "Can you breathe?"

He nodded, then started looking around. His eyes fell to the floor. Then he stumbled over to where his gun was lying and picked it up.

By this time, Mr. Entwistle had taken Charlie to the floor. "Control . . . deep breaths," the old vampire was saying.

I don't know if Charlie was listening, but it was hard to go ballistic with a 650-year-old vampire slowly choking you in a sleeper hold.

"What are you thinking?" Ophelia snapped. Her voice was school-teacher angry.

Charlie couldn't answer. It took most of his effort just to breathe. Mr. Entwistle slowly let go. My friend sucked in a few deep breaths and started rubbing at his neck. Then another cascade of profanity tumbled out of his mouth. He described my uncle's character, his behavior, what he wanted to do to him, and just about anything else you could slap between two swear words. Or two hundred. If it had aired on the radio, it would have been one continuous beep. Then Charlie looked at me.

"You knew. You knew! It's why he shot me in the hospital. You knew he was here the whole time and you didn't say anything. If Luna was here, she'd murder you."

He might have been right. I knew she blamed my uncle for *that night*. For what happened to her. And to her sister. I didn't know what to say to Charlie. This was a disaster.

"Let go of me," Charlie said. "You may trust this bozo, but I don't. He's a backstabbing turncoat. He betrayed all of us."

"Actually, he's more of a front stabber," said Mr. Entwistle. "And if I can forgive him for blowing me up, you should be able to for-give him for trying to keep you alive."

"That's a bunch of baloney," said Charlie. "He drugged us and turned us over to that freak. We should be dead. All of us."

"It wasn't supposed to be that way," Maximilian said. "Vlad said he would accept you in the Underground. Swear you to secrecy. That way, you wouldn't be killed for knowing about Zachary and his condition. Instead, you'd have the protection of the Coven, which Zachary and I were to join."

My uncle turned to me, his face sad. And frustrated. "Vlad wanted to talk to you first, to see if you were ready to assume such an enormous responsibility. That was the arrangement I made with him. So you wouldn't lose your only friends. But Vlad broke his word. I had no idea he'd try to kill anyone."

"I don't believe you," said Charlie.

"That changes nothing. Not the present. Not the past. Nothing." My uncle lowered his gun and looked around at all of us. His eyes settled on Mr. Entwistle. "I have to go to the hospital shortly. If you are serious and really want to get the girls, you can take my car."

Blood was still at the sides of my uncle's mouth. He suddenly looked gray. A kind of exhaustion had settled over his features. I'd never seen him this way. Vulnerable. Corpselike. He did things with such self-assurance, it was easy to forget he was dying of cancer.

"It's all right," Mr. Entwistle said. "There isn't time. I'll take the ambulance once the sun goes down."

My uncle nodded. "I'm sorry about what happened. My loyalty is to my nephew. I have always kept his interests at heart."

"And your own," Charlie hissed.

"Believe that if it helps you. But I'm no good to anyone if I'm dead. Dealing with Vlad and joining the Coven—it seemed the best way at the time." Maximilian's eyes passed over all of us, then he turned to go.

"That's it? After all he's done, you're just letting him go?" Charlie shouted at us.

My uncle stopped in the doorway. For a man who'd been attacked and vilified, he had remarkable composure. "What reason would I have for hurting you?"

We all waited.

Charlie stared at him. His mouth started to move, but nothing came out. A voice in my head told me I should write this down. It was the first time in my life I'd ever seen him speechless.

"You're a one-man soap opera, Charlie," Maximilian said, reaching for the door. "You're lucky your friends are so patient."

A second later the door closed.

"We can't let him go," Charlie said.

"Why not?" Ophelia asked.

"I think he's Hyde," Charlie said. "I think he's the one we've been looking for."

Mr. Entwistle looked at Ophelia. I could tell they both thought Charlie was right out to lunch. I understood his anger. He didn't want Suki to go back to Newark. He wanted to make her a vampire so she could be one of us. That couldn't happen if her father took her away. I felt so bad for him, I started talking and didn't stop until I'd mentioned all the reasons my uncle might have been the Beast. His size. The year he'd spent hunting a werewolf. His sudden appearance in our lives—timed perfectly with Hyde's. The fact that he'd never seen Hyde, and we never actually knew his whereabouts when Hyde was around. In the end, I'd convinced everyone, even myself.

Mr. Entwistle moved to the window and started peeking from under the blind. Ophelia sat down.

"Do you really think it's possible?" she asked.

I didn't know. But if it was true, it meant he knew where we were. He knew our defenses and how to get past them. And he knew Luna was unprotected at the camp.

Charlie rose to leave.

"Where are you going?" I asked.

"I'm going to bed, *buddy*." He said the last word like a curse.

I guess, like me, he just wanted this night to be over. I opened my mouth to say sorry but he cut me off.

"Don't bother."

Then he walked out the door and slammed it shut behind him.

PARTING WAYS

Mr. Entwistle looked at me. The muscles in his jaws twitched as his teeth ground together. "This is bad," he said.

"Tell me about it."

"There's more at stake here than a summer romance, boy."

I knew this already.

Mr. Entwistle's face relaxed. He took a deep breath, apologized for losing his temper, and headed for the back door.

"Are you leaving?" I asked.

"No. Just checking on your uncle."

I'd just assumed he'd left. When I said so, Mr. Entwistle shook his head. "If I know Maximilian, he'll walk the perimeter once more just to make certain the motion detectors are working. He wasn't lying when he said he has your best interests at heart."

The old vampire slipped out the door, leaving me with Ophelia, who was chewing her cheek, her eyes lost. A few seconds later, I heard the sound of an engine starting. It was the painted ambulance in the driveway. Did that mean Mr. Entwistle was leaving?

"I'll be right back," I said.

I slipped out the back door. Mr. Entwistle was pulling out of the drive. I wondered if he'd been lying. If he hadn't been talking to my uncle at all, but was really leaving to go after Hyde. He'd said he would have to face Hyde alone. But it was so close to dawn. And he hadn't even said good-bye.

Then the garage door started to open. Two headlights lit up the apartment. It was suddenly brighter than Broadway. I heard a sound like a jet engine, and my uncle slowly pulled forward in his car. I slipped to the side of the driveway and he stopped beside me. Although I'd seen it before and had even ridden in the front, the sight of his car was still shocking. Jedi knights didn't get to drive in things this cool. It was half bat mobile, half spaceship, with doors that opened upward and a spoiler like a whale tail. The window slid down.

"Is he leaving?" I gazed at the ambulance, which was backing out onto the street.

My uncle shook his head. "No, just moving so I can get out."

I suddenly felt foolish. But life is like that sometimes. You get so used to bad news, you just expect more.

"Are you okay?" I asked my uncle.

"Tired . . . I got sloppy. I shouldn't have pushed my luck—coming in the house like that. Thoughtless . . ." Pain was in his voice. He let his head fall back against the seat rest.

"I'm sorry." It sounded lame, but I meant it.

"Don't apologize. I had that coming." He took a moment to adjust his seat belt, a double-shoulder harness.

"Your father had a belief that we should put the job ahead of everything. I put myself first. And I lied to myself. I said I was doing it for you. That if I died, I couldn't protect you from the Coven, couldn't continue your father's work—our work. So I negotiated with Vlad. It was foolish. . . . And I have paid. We all have."

He started coughing. I could smell the blood in his mouth.

"You're dying."

He nodded. "Yes. Nothing is working. I've one last option."

"What is that?"

"Biotherapeutics."

I had no idea what that meant.

"You take a nonlethal virus and use it to kill the cancer cells in your body," my uncle explained. "But I still have one more radiation treatment. I'm afraid I won't be much use for the next little while. I've never been this exhausted." His eyes drifted up to the eastern horizon. It was growing lighter. "You should go. Make sure Charlie's okay. I know he's angry with you, but this will pass. He'll come around. Just give him time." The words tumbled out slowly. He sounded tired, but sincere.

I thanked him and he slowly pulled away. The car engine whined. I could feel the power of it resonate in my stomach. A second later Mr. Entwistle pulled the ambulance back in. I didn't wait for him. The light was faint, but it still made me uncomfortable, and I was worried about Charlie.

When I came in, Ophelia was in the kitchen returning the phone to its cradle. She had the ugly purse with the wolfsbane in her other hand.

Mr. Entwistle entered a second later. "Where is he?" I guessed he meant Charlie.

"He's on the roof," Ophelia answered. "I heard him go up while you were outside."

Mr. Entwistle nodded and headed for the stairs.

"What are we going to say to Dr. Abbott when he gets here?" I asked.

"I'll call him now and tell him where his children are. He'll probably be relieved. It means he won't have to come here and talk to any of us."

This was true.

"I had no idea they were going to leave."

Ophelia nodded. "I could tell." Then she held up the purse. "Why did you bring this awful thing into the house?"

I quickly explained about the storage unit and the monkshood. I was expecting her to be impressed. We'd acquired a new poison, perhaps one that might prove useful against Hyde, but if anything, the mention of it just made her nervous. "What's wrong?" I asked.

"Wolfsbane is lethal to vampires, Zachary. And to people. If Hyde has this, it only makes him more dangerous."

I don't know why this hadn't occurred to me. I guess it indicated how poorly my mind was working.

"I'll have to call Detective Baddon," she said, "and see if he can find out who that storage unit belongs to."

"Do you think Maximilian might be Hyde?"

She sighed and zipped open the purse, then carefully examined the tiny hooded flowers inside. "I hope not. I was counting on his help. But if it is him, at least he knows us as a man and trusts us. Perhaps we could find a way to help him."

I looked away and nodded. I didn't want it to be true. I didn't want my uncle to be that thing.

"You should get some sleep. You look beat."

She was right. It had been a long and tiring night. I said good-night and made my way up to the second-floor apartment, sealed the window shutters in my room, pulled the blind closed, and shut the curtains. Then I settled on the bed and listened for Charlie.

It wasn't my intention to doze off, but it happened anyway. I woke up to the sound of someone knocking at the door. I hoped it would be him, but when I said "come in," Mr. Entwistle entered.

"You're not asleep yet. Good."

I sat up and asked if Charlie was okay.

"He's fine. Just talking to Ophelia now. They're in the apartment upstairs."

"Is something wrong?"

"He'll be fine. I just needed to explain to him why it was so important that your uncle be involved. And that he be forgiving. Are you all right?"

"Yeah. You?"

His movements were restless, his eyes busy. He strayed into the doorway, his hat tucked under his arm. The hall light was behind him, so his body was like a tall shadow. "As good as can be expected. I wanted to speak to you about a few things, but I . . ." He waved his hand through the air as if it wasn't really that important.

"No, tell me. What is it?"

He hesitated. "I just wanted to . . ." A few quiet seconds followed. "I've been trying to find a solution to this Hyde dilemma."

"Do you think Charlie's right? That his alter ego might be Maximilian?"

He started shaking his head. "I'm not convinced. It just doesn't fit."

I didn't know what he was talking about. It seemed to fit perfectly to me. But he didn't say anything else about it. He just sat down on the bed and looked at me over his shoulder.

"I believe he's a lycanthrope, Zack. Hyde, I mean. Not your uncle. But no matter how I reason it out, I can't get past the reality of the Beast, and that I have to face him. I've seen it too many times. . . ."

I realized as he spoke, as I watched his eyes move around the room, that he was terrified. I understood. Hyde terrified me, too.

"You don't think you can beat him?"

He took his hat off. It trembled in his hands. "I can't."

"Are you afraid of dying?"

He looked at me. His clear blue eyes were piercing. His forehead knotted. He looked offended. "Of dying? Me? Heavens no. I've never been afraid of that." He stood up as though I'd somehow restored his confidence. Then he seemed to sag. His face. His shoulders. It was subtle, but I didn't miss it. "But when I die, who will deal with him?"

Is that what scared him? That he would die and leave us helpless?

"I can't beat him. I've faced him several times now, and John Entwistle is no match for this thing. I can't. John Entwistle can't . . ."

When he said his name that way, I suddenly understood his fear. The air of defeat around him. He wasn't afraid of Hyde or of dying. He was afraid of himself.

"John Entwistle can't beat him," he continued, "but the Butcher can. The Butcher can kill anything."

So that was it. I was right. He was afraid he would become John Tiptoft, the Butcher of England. The man he used to be.

"I don't think you're meant to be that person," I said.

"I can't see any other way. I keep asking myself, *How can we survive?* There is no cure for lycanthropy. Only death stops the curse.

To atone for the sins of John Tiptoft I must face the Beast. I know that. But how can I atone for my sins by committing murder? How can I atone by becoming a monster myself?"

There was only one answer. He couldn't. I suddenly understood why he wanted to face Hyde alone. He didn't want us to see him becoming the thing he most feared—the Butcher. He wasn't just trying to protect us from Hyde, but from himself.

He sighed, turned, and opened the door. "You're a good kid, Zack." His voice sounded sad. It dropped to a whisper. "I had a son once . . . little boy . . . died of plague. . . . Had he grown up, I would have wanted him to be like you . . . would have been proud of that."

He put his hat on his head and closed the door. I listened to his footsteps. A great swell of pity rose up in my throat. I wondered how he could have been anyone but Mr. Entwistle. And I wondered how Luna was. And Charlie. I decided to wait up so I could ask him, but when I put my head down, I fell into a deep and dreamless sleep. Some days are like that.

I awoke at dusk to the sound of gentle knocking. It was coming from the window. I got up, drew the curtains, raised the blinds, and pulled back the shutters. A faint strip of yellow light was fading on the western horizon. The sun was gone, but I still had to squint to see.

Charlie was standing on the fire escape. A pack hung loosely over his shoulder. He looked at me. I knew what he would ask before he opened his mouth. *Are you coming?*

"Where?" I asked.

"Stony Lake."

"You mean the camp?"

He nodded.

I started looking for my shoes. Once I'd slipped them on, I climbed out onto the landing. Charlie hadn't moved.

"You should have told me," he said.

He must have been talking about my uncle—that Maximilian was Agent X.

"Yeah. I know. I'm sorry. I kept thinking there would be a good time, but stuff kept happening. . . . Are we good?"

Charlie turned and started down the steps. "Yeah. But still—you should have told me."

I closed the window and followed him to the street. "You know they'll see us leave. And it won't take a brain scientist to figure out where we're going."

He nodded. "Ophelia said the same thing last night. She wanted me to know that if I left, she'd notice. But I don't care."

We started off down the street. Then my mind started wandering. What if we ran into Hyde? Or worse. What if he followed us to the camp? I slowed. Then stopped.

"Don't tell me you're bailing already?"

"We need to go back."

Charlie looked as if he were ready to bite me. His voice was angry. And disappointed. "You want to go back to the apartment?"

"No. I want to go to Ophelia's safe house on Burnham. The one with the antiques—the weapons. If Hyde shows up, I want to be armed with more than just running shoes."

Charlie smiled, exposing his long incisors. "Now you're talkin'!"

CHAPTER 35

THE VAMPIRE'S KISS

The trip to Stony Lake was exhausting. Running with a two-handed sword isn't as easy as it looks. Video games can be deceiving that way. The thing was five feet long and weighed forty pounds. I was flushed and famished by the time I arrived. Charlie was, too.

We approached the camp from the road. Because it was just down the channel from Charlie's cottage, I'd assumed it was on Stony Lake, but he explained on the way in that it was actually on another one, Clear Lake, though the boundary wasn't really clear at all. It looked like one large body of water. It was around ten by this time, and the place was settling down.

I'd never been to a summer camp or even seen one before, so I was a bit surprised by the number of buildings scattered through the woods and along the shore. There were playing fields for football and soccer. And even a rope course.

"This place is awesome," I whispered.

Charlie laughed. "Aren't you a bit old for camp?"

Obviously not. It looked like paradise to me. We passed a rock-climbing wall, then a basketball court. You'd never get bored at a place like this. It was like Disneyland, but without the threat of anyone spontaneously bursting into a corny song.

"Where do you think the girls are?" I asked.

"My bet is, they're at the docks. Just one second." He pulled out his cell.

One text message later we were heading for the waterfront. There, on the docks, Luna and Suki were sitting side by side, their feet dangling in the water.

Charlie and I crouched in the shadows of a boathouse. We didn't want to brave the lights. Several were illuminating the shoreline. A swirling cloud of moths hovered around each lamp. From time to time, the familiar shape of a bat darted through.

Charlie raised his chin and whispered into the wind, "Hey, Luna. The president of your fan club is here."

As soon as he spoke, she turned, then smiled and tapped Suki on the shoulder. A second later they were walking toward our hiding place. Luna's expression changed from pleasure to alarm when she saw the weapons we were carrying. My sword was almost as tall as she was, and Charlie had a voulge on his back—a pole arm with a head like a halberd's, a combination of spear and cleaver with a few extra barbs and hooks thrown in for good measure. It was over seven feet long.

"What are those?" she asked.

"Security," answered Charlie. He was watching Suki. She seemed sedate and uncertain. I could smell it on her skin and see it in the anxious movement of her eyes.

"Are you expecting trouble?" she asked.

Charlie reached out and took her hand, then raised it to his mouth and kissed it. "Only the trouble I plan to make."

She smiled, then tugged at his arm and started to pull him away from the boathouse toward a trail that led through the woods. He resisted, his eyes staring out over the lake. He lifted her hand then kissed it again.

"I miss the water," he said. "Is there somewhere we can go without spotlights? I'd love to get my feet wet."

"There's a beach this way," Luna said. "Let's get out of here before someone sees you guys. You look like a pair of assassins."

"Wait. I've a better idea." Charlie tipped his head toward the boathouse. "There's got to be some canoes in here. Why don't we take one out?"

Suki shrugged, then smiled. A mischievous spark was in her eyes. A trademark of the old Suki. "I'd love to go for a midnight paddle."

Charlie laughed, then pulled her closer, which made her giggle. Then he saw the look on my face and laughed even harder. He knew I didn't like the water. I felt his hand slap the center of my back.

"Don't worry, Captain Nemo. Hyde hates the water, too, remember? It's what saved Entwistle. So at least you'll be safe for a few hours." Then Charlie looked at Luna. "Well, safe from him, at least."

A canoe is a tricky beast. It looks stable until you get in, then, just when you relax, it tries to throw you overboard. The secret, I've learned, is to stay low and let the other person do most of the work. I had never paddled before, so Luna had me sit in the bottom with my back against the piece of wood across the middle. She told me it was called the thwart, which was a perfect name, since it thwarted me from getting anywhere near her. In the end, I crawled to the front and sat facing backward so I could look at her without having to peer over my shoulder.

"Why didn't you tell me you were leaving the apartment?" I asked.

Luna raised her paddle as if she were going to hit me with it. "I didn't know anything about it. It was Suki's idea. I couldn't talk her out of it. I didn't really want to go, but the thought of going home with my dad was too depressing."

"What's going to happen when he shows up here?"

"What do you mean *when* he shows up? He showed up this afternoon and flipped out."

"What happened?"

Luna shrugged. "Suki's words, not mine. I was asleep in the trunk of the car."

Those didn't sound like the best sleeping arrangements. When I mentioned it, Luna shrugged it off. "Better than the alternative."

She took another stroke. I noticed that she turned her thumb down each time. It made the blade twist in the water so it acted like a rudder.

"I thought your dad wanted to take you home," I said.

"He does. But he wants me to see a blood specialist in Toronto first."

"Where is he now?"

"Who? Dad? He's asleep in the infirmary. The camp doctor is an old friend of his. After driving most of the night and morning, he's exhausted."

"So how long will you be here?"

She shrugged. "We'll drive to Toronto tomorrow night—that would be my guess."

For a time, neither of us spoke. I just watched the muscles in her arms and shoulders at work as she paddled us down the shore.

"Does anyone know you're here?" she asked.

I shrugged. "It won't take a rocket surgeon to figure it out."

"And then what?"

"Who knows? I don't want to think about it. I can't believe you're leaving."

Her eyes softened and she smiled sadly. "We have tonight. . . ."

I glanced over my shoulder. Charlie and Suki had already paddled farther down the shore. I think they were planning to go to his family's cottage. It was on an island down the channel.

"You look much better," Luna said.

I didn't feel much better. I needed more sleep, and another dose of blood. But mostly I just needed to hear some good news.

"Have you talked to your sister about Charlie?"

"What do you mean?"

I let my hand fall into the cool water, where it left a long V-shaped trail across the surface. "About turning. Becoming one of us?"

"A bit. I think she wants to. But she's afraid. Now might not be the best time. Why? Has Charlie said something?"

"Not lately. Not to me. But things have been crazy. I'm sure he wants to."

"Yeah, like we aren't in enough trouble." She put the paddle down across the gunnels and started sliding forward. "Don't move for a second."

I wasn't going to move if a whale breached under us. I wasn't wearing a life jacket, which for me was like skydiving without a parachute. As soon as she started toward me, I gripped the gunnels so hard I felt the wood begin to creak. Luna stopped when she crossed the thwart, then turned and backed up so that she was leaning against me.

"You seem nervous," she said. She took my arms and wrapped them around her waist, then let her head fall onto my chest.

We looked up at the moon. At the clouds. It was a perfect night. She nestled in a little closer. Then she turned so that her face was right in front of mine.

"You still owe me a kiss," she said.

My brain was starting to sizzle. The smell of her hair. The closeness of her. I'd read about moments like this. Seen them in movies. The kiss that would make some patients at the Nicholls Ward roll their eyes and others sit up in their seats. A part of me, my heart I guess, was screaming, *Yes, yes, yes, yes, yesssssssssss.* But another part of me was saying, *No, no, no, no, noooooooooo,* because my teeth were up to their usual tricks and wanted to get busy. My whole body started to buzz. And my eyes—they kept straying to that part of Luna's neck right under her ear where her muscles formed a perfect contour. It was inviting all kinds of mischief. I couldn't figure this out. I knew I wasn't supposed to bite another vampire. Her blood might be fatal. So why did I want to so badly?

Her eyes closed. Her chin rose. A quiet breath leaked past her open mouth. I should have just kissed her, but I didn't want to mess it up.

"Don't be afraid," she said.

"I'm not afraid."

"You're shaking."

"I'm not shaking." I'm not sure why I said this. It wasn't true.

"What are you waiting for?"

I wasn't sure. I just didn't know what I was doing. Her teeth were down like mine. One started to tease the front of her bottom lip. It made a gentle indentation against her skin. I was going crazy. I wondered if she felt the same.

"You think too much," she said.

Her face was close enough to me now that I could feel the warmth of her. One of her hands strayed to my chest. She turned and her other hand slipped around my neck. She tightened her grip. It surprised me. She was a vampire now, much stronger than the first time we'd been like this—last year, at her cottage. Almost kissing.

"Don't think," she said. Her eyes closed again. Her head tipped back. Mine tipped forward. "Just do what comes naturally."

So I bit her.

I took it from her yelp that this wasn't exactly what she'd been expecting. Fortunately she wasn't loud, or the whole shoreline would have woken. I'd finally get to meet an angry mob, or at least the summer-camp version. The rush I got from the taste of her blood sent shock waves through my body.

Luna gasped. Then she tightened her grip and drew me in closer. I felt her head shift. Pain jabbed my neck like two hot nails. The skin burned. Then an airy feeling filled my head. I couldn't think of anything but the rush. It was thrilling. And horrifying. She was drinking from me, and I from her. I was getting weaker. We both were. My vision went blurry. My hand was on the back of her head, my fingers massaging her warm skin. I could feel her pulse. It was quickening. My head fell back and the stars overhead started to swim. I had no strength left. I had to lie down. Somehow we managed it together so we were resting in the canoe. I closed my eyes and felt her body lying against mine. Her breathing was like my breathing. Slower now. Her heartbeat was more settled, but still strong. One hand remained on my chest, and her head nestled in the space between my arm and shoulder.

"What just happened?"

She hummed a soft sigh. "I don't know." Then her eyes opened. They were warm. Glowing. "But we have to do it again sometime." Her teeth were still down. The same one as before had strayed outside her lip and was pressing against the front of it.

"I think I need a minute," I said, and looked up at the stars. They were back in their usual arrangement. I took a deep breath and smiled. The rush was passing, but with no feeling of disappointment, of ending. Instead there was only deep contentment. A warm restfulness. Not even dying felt this good.

"You mean that?" Luna asked. She nestled her head a little deeper into my shoulder. I kissed the top of it.

"Do I mean what?"

"That this is better than dying?"

I must have been thoroughly exhausted. I was certain that I hadn't spoken a word.

"I heard you," she said.

An honest mistake. I was zonked.

"That's a funny word," she said.

I knew I hadn't spoken that time. This was odd.

I felt her hand pinch me. "What's so odd about it?"

She raised her head so that her chin sat gently against my chest. I smiled. Nothing about this was odd. It was perfect. She was perfect. I saw her smile. It was beautiful. Just for me. Then her eyes popped to full width, then somehow got bigger.

"I can hear you," she whispered.

Unbelievable!

Her head shook back and forth. Her mouth started to move as if she were going to say something, but nothing came out. Her hands were touching me. I could almost feel what she was thinking. Surprise. Wonder. Then fear. *She could hear my thoughts.*

I was stunned. Then embarrassed. Her beautiful neck was still in front of me. The two puncture wounds I'd put there were healing. To see them, and smell her blood, made me ravenous. I knew it was wrong, but I couldn't help it. Nor could I hide it. She could read my mind. I felt my face heating up. A smile crept back onto her lips. Her eyes sparkled. Beautiful shades of olive and pale emerald. They were moist and happy. Then mischievous.

That's nothing to worry about.

"I'm not worried." I realized as the words left my mouth that she hadn't spoken out loud.

I didn't.

The thought was as clear as the sound of my own heartbeat. I wasn't imagining this. It was real. I could hear her thoughts, too. I looked at her face and pulled my hand through her long, beautiful hair. This was really happening.

Yes, it really is, she thought.

She smiled, and my senses were suddenly flooded. Her hands found my sides. She squeezed me. I couldn't imagine it was possible to feel more complete than I did at that moment.

I love you, she thought. And I thought the same. And she held me tighter.

CHAPTER 36

MISSING IN ACTION

I think I must have slept, although I'm not sure, because I didn't dream. I just thought of Luna. We didn't speak. There was no need. But a kind of physical paralysis had come over me. I wasn't aware of it until I felt Luna's breath on my neck again.

You still owe me a kiss, she thought.

I wasn't sure that I could pull it off.

Why? she asked.

I thought of my answer before I had a chance to stop myself.

You've never kissed anyone? She paused. Her smile was electric. "Oh, that's so cute."

Cute. I had nothing against the word, but it had never been an ambition of mine to be described that way.

You'll get over it, she thought. Then she leaned in and kissed me.

I'm not going to say it wasn't pleasant. The whole lip-smushing experience was quite exciting. It didn't compare to the thrill of our vampires' kiss, but I soon discovered that kisses of the normal kind had an addictive quality all of their own. After one, I found I needed another. And another. I was beginning to feel as if the canoe were just about the best invention since God made air. I could have spent weeks like this. The whole time we shared thoughts. Well, one thought, over and over. But that was all right. It was a good thought. We were in love. It was nice to say it, and better to hear it, and better still to feel that it was true.

Just before midnight, we were interrupted by the sound of our canoe banging against something solid.

Luna sat up.

"What is it?" I asked. I peeked over the gunnels. The water had pushed us into a dock down from the camp. We were bumping up against a large powerboat.

"I'd better get us back," she said.

I let her go, thinking how terrible it was that some moments had to end.

"That's very romantic," she said. Then she climbed into the back of the canoe and started paddling.

Do you want to try?

I didn't, and I let her know.

This is going to take some getting used to.

You're tellin' me. I wonder how long it will last.

I have no idea, Luna thought. *But I like it.*

I did, too.

She smiled, then paddled us back to camp.

Charlie and Suki were on the farthest dock along the shore. I could see a huge waterslide beside them. It looked like fun, except that it involved landing in the water.

You just need more practice swimming, Luna thought.

This was true. I needed practice with lots of things.

"Not as much as you think," she said. "Not that we won't practice more anyway, but we should check in with those two first and see what's up."

I glanced down toward Charlie and Suki. They were sitting together, holding hands, their feet dangling in the water. I wondered if he'd bitten her.

I hope not.

As we got closer, I could hear Charlie whispering. "Man, I miss this . . ."

I felt a pang of guilt. And then sympathy. This had come from Luna.

Charlie saw us coming and put his hand in the water, then scooped a handful and splashed it our way. "I was starting to think you two lovebirds were going to float down to Burleigh Falls."

Should we tell him? Luna asked.

No, I thought. I didn't want him to know about this. Not until I was sure that things with him and Suki were solid. I was worried that he might get jealous. It was bad enough that his girlfriend was struggling and wasn't one of us. If we told him about this connection, it would just be one more thing that Luna and I shared that Suki and he couldn't.

"How were things at your cottage?" Luna asked.

"We didn't stop in," Charlie said. "But I gotta tell ya, it would be a perfect place to hide from Hyde."

"But?"

"But Dan is there with his family."

Dan was one of Charlie's older brothers. He had a gaggle of kids. I doubt he would have wanted us showing up to make things even more chaotic.

"So what happens now?" I asked.

Charlie shrugged, then he saw the marks on my neck. And on Luna's.

"You didn't! Isn't that supposed to kill you?"

"It hasn't yet," I said.

"Let's hope Daddy Abbott doesn't notice."

My stomach wasn't thrilled with the idea. Fortunately Charlie got the conversation rolling in another direction.

"I think we should call," he said.

I assumed he meant Ophelia.

"We should get back to the apartment," he added.

"Who? All of us?" I glanced at Suki, then at Luna.

Charlie looked as me like I'd just won the village idiot award. "Well, I didn't come here to work on my tan."

Are you cool with this? I asked Luna.

What? With leaving? You bet! I don't want that thing showing up here. We need to stick together, and get someplace safe.

I agreed, and pulled my cell phone from my pocket, but I couldn't get a signal.

"What is it?" Charlie asked. "Is the battery dead?"

"No. I'm not getting any coverage."

I felt Luna's hand come to rest on my arm. "I could have told you that."

I guess it explained why I hadn't heard from Ophelia. I felt a twinge of guilt in my stomach. She must have been worried sick.

"So what do we do?" Suki asked.

"Do you feel up for a drive?" Luna asked her.

A drive?

How do you think we got here? We'll just take our car.

What do we tell your father? If we just leave, he'll murder us!

No, thought Luna, *he'll murder you.*

Suki was the only one with a license, which meant Luna and I were crammed into the back of the car. It was a BMW—90 percent engine and 10 percent tire. The backseat was like an afterthought, small, cramped, with just enough leg room for a small house cat, but that was okay, it kept us close. There was a lot of nervous energy in the car. No wonder Charlie broke the rules so often at school. It was fun.

Until the phone rang. Everyone but Luna checked their pockets.

"That's me." I scanned the display. Ophelia was calling.

Are you going to answer?

I hit the button with the green phone on it and said hello.

"Oh, Zachary, thank heavens. Why did you turn your phone off?"

"I didn't. We came up to the lake to get the girls. There's no reception up here."

"So Charlie's with you? And Luna?"

"And Suki."

"I suspected as much. Is everyone all right?"

I said yes.

A wave of relief poured through the speaker of my phone. "I need to speak to John."

John? I thought for a second Ophelia must have meant Luna's father, then I remembered his name was Gerald. "You mean Mr. Entwistle?"

"Yes. I need to speak with him."

Luna was listening. So was Charlie. I looked at both of them. Charlie shrugged. Luna didn't. She was wondering what I was wondering. Why would Ophelia think Mr. Entwistle was with us?

"He's not here," I said.

There was a short pause. "So who's driving?"

"Suki."

Smart money would have bet she was in her headache pose right now.

"So is John following you? He's not answering his phone."

"No. We haven't seen him all night."

This time the pause was longer. "I beg your pardon."

"We haven't seen him all night."

It might have been static, but I could have sworn I heard a faint "Oh, no."

"What is it?" I asked. "What's going on?"

"I don't know. John left to get you just after sunset. He took the ambulance. That was hours ago."

I looked at Charlie. I heard Luna's thoughts running parallel with mine. Mr. Entwistle had left for the camp to get us and hadn't arrived. There could only be one reason. And I knew what it was.

CHAPTER 37

HOMECOMING

G et home right away," Ophelia said. "I mean here—to the apartment."

I said we would. Then she hung up. I felt another surge of sympathy from Luna as I put my phone away. And fear. She didn't know Mr. Entwistle well, but she could feel my distress and was worried.

Charlie was watching me closely. "He knew where we were going, didn't he?"

Probably.

"So Hyde got him."

I didn't think so. My guess was, he had told Ophelia he was coming to find us, but instead went after Hyde knowing we wouldn't be able to follow. It would have explained his odd behavior and the things he'd said when he came to see me that morning. It was his way of saying good-bye.

Do you think so?

I do.

Luna squeezed my hand. "Step on it," she said to her sister.

Suki didn't disappoint. The engine roared. What would have taken Charlie and me almost an hour on the Shoe-Leather Express she covered in about twenty minutes. The only thing that slowed us down were all the fire trucks on Clonsilla as we approached the apartment. Police cars and ambulances were gathering, too.

"That's smoke," said Charlie.

It was. It got thicker as we got closer to home.

"Hurry," he said.

"I can't," Suki exclaimed. "There's police everywhere. You want to get pulled over and spend the next few hours explaining why we have a car full of medieval weapons?"

She had a point. The two-handed sword and voulge were tucked along one side of the car. They were too long to lie flat against the floor, so the handles of both would be obvious to anyone who looked in.

As we rounded the corner near Gordon Avenue, I could see the apartment. It was being consumed in a pillar of fire. Gouts of flame burst from the windows, and a thick, billowing cloud of black smoke poured from the roof. The fire trucks were setting up. Men scrambled with ladders and hoses. The police were there. Someone in a paramedics uniform was waving for us to turn down Victory Crescent instead of driving past the building.

"What do I do?" asked Suki.

"Pull over up there," said Charlie.

We turned off of Clonsilla and Suki slid in along the curb. Charlie had to get out first so I could climb past his seat. I heard Luna's voice in my head: *Call her.* I dug out my phone. Found Ophelia's number. There was no answer. I started running. Several officers tried to stop me, but I was moving too quickly. Then I reached the front walk. The heat from the building was so intense, I couldn't get near the door. I felt someone take hold of my arm, a firefighter. He started talking to me.

"It's my house," I said. "My mother is inside."

I don't know if he answered me, but he let go. I guess he knew I wouldn't be able to get any closer. I just stared at the inferno. If Ophelia was in there, it was going to take a time machine to save her.

Charlie caught up a moment later. Luna was with him. *Listen!* she thought.

I looked at her, then realized Charlie was talking to me.

". . . be around."

"What was that?"

"If Hyde did this, he might still be around. We need to get out of here."

"What about Ophelia?" I couldn't leave until I knew if she'd made it out okay.

Luna took hold of my arm. *She would want you to get somewhere safe.*

That was true.

Luna started pulling me away from the crowd that was gathering on the sidewalk to watch. I didn't resist. Men and women in uniform were trying to move everyone to the other side of the street.

Then my phone rang. I checked the display. Iron Spike Enterprises. It was my uncle. He would know what to do. I picked up and said hello.

"Zack. What a relief! Everything okay?"

"No."

"Are you here—at the hospital?"

It was just up the hill. "I'm down the street at the apartment."

"What's going on? It sounds like a circus."

I told him about the fire. He swore. "I'm still at the Civic. It's crazy here, as well." I could hear him stumbling around. "Wait. I can see it from the window. Did Ophelia make it out?"

I couldn't answer. He repeated the question. Luna moved her mouth closer to my ear and told him we didn't know.

"Zachary, listen. This is important," he said. "Hyde was just here. He's taken Baddon's son."

I thought of the small, frail child and a part of my mind snapped awake. It was angry. "Is he still there?"

"Who? Hyde? I don't think so. I can't get near the room. Security has it cordoned off. I was asleep when he broke in and didn't get down the hall in time. Dammit, I can hardly move."

"Are you hurt?"

"No. It's the radiation treatment. Burns your insides. . . . Poor Adam. I think he might be dead."

Who's Adam? Luna asked.

Detective Baddon.

For a few seconds all I could hear was static and the sound of sirens and chaos.

"Get somewhere safe," my uncle said. "I'll find you. Just get out of sight."

Somewhere safe? Unless he had a spaceship and could ferry us to Mars, we weren't going to be safe anywhere. And I had to look for Ophelia. She had to be somewhere. My uncle started talking again. I couldn't really hear him. The hand I was using to hold the phone had dropped to my side, and the sirens were making a lot of noise.

"Zack. Zack, are you still there?"

Luna took the phone. "We're here. We'll call you once we're clear."

My uncle said something to her, then she hung up and handed the phone back to me. I felt Charlie's hand on my back. He'd opened the door to the car and was guiding me in.

"What's going on?" Suki asked.

She and Luna and Charlie started talking. I didn't follow their conversation. My mind was too busy trying to figure out how to find Ophelia. If she'd made it out, where would she go? Would she stay here knowing we'd be back? Did she have another safe house I didn't know about? Would she try to find Mr. Entwistle or go to the hospital to get my uncle?

Suki pulled out of the parking spot and Charlie fed her instructions. I didn't pay attention. Not until the car stopped.

We were outside of town on Highway 4. A familiar pasture was beside us. It was where Mr. Entwistle, Charlie, and I had followed Hyde's trail the night before. Charlie got out. So did Suki. I felt Luna nudge me gently. I climbed outside and she followed.

Where is this? she asked.

I told her.

What is Charlie thinking?

That we have something to take care of. I turned to face my friend. He was talking to Suki.

"Then we followed him out here. His trail is just off the road."

He reached into the car along the side of the seat to where he'd stashed our weapons. He handed me the sword, then pulled out the long-handled voulge.

"What are we doing?" I asked, although I already knew the answer.

Charlie looked at me. His pupils were widening. I saw his tongue flick up against his gums, a sure sign his teeth were dropping.

"We're going to follow Hyde's tracks," he said. "You and I. We're going to find his lair and wait for him there. Then when he comes back, we're going to kill him."

— CHAPTER 38

SCORCHED EARTH

My thoughts seemed to be stuck in slow motion. Luna's were racing. There was fear. Uncertainty. Questions. About me. About Mr. Entwistle. About Ophelia. About Hyde and the stupidity of two young boys who thought they could deal with him using weapons that were out-of-date three centuries ago. I didn't have answers. I only knew Charlie was right—we had to kill him.

I hadn't spoken to him much about the prophecies—about the son of the hunter, the messiah. The End of Days. Not after we'd read the letter together. But Luna and I had covered them thoroughly when we'd met on the Dream Road. Since then, I'd spoken to Ophelia, to the prophet Baoh, and to Mr. Entwistle. It came down to this. None of it mattered. Not one pinch. Was I special? Well, sure. Isn't everyone? We're all the heroes of our own life stories. We try to be good. To do what is right. And we have to live with ourselves. With what we do. And what we don't do.

Hyde had stolen a man's son. The boy was finished if we didn't find him. I didn't even know his name. But if Maximilian's hunch was right, his father, Detective Baddon, was dead. I thought of all that had happened in the last few nights. I heard Baoh's voice in my head. *Be righteous. And do not do to others that which is harmful to yourself.* What could be more harmful to a person than being left in the hands of a beast like Hyde? In my mind's eye, I could still see the boy as he'd appeared in that hospital bed. He reminded me of myself. I was his age when Vlad had infected me. It was just after my father died. I'd spent weeks in a coma. But I hadn't been alone. Ophelia had saved me. But she was gone now. So was Mr. Entwistle. My uncle was a walking corpse, a man just waiting for his cancer to kill him. That left only me. And Charlie. And Luna. She moved closer to me. I could feel the nervous energy in her.

Are you sure about this?

I was. And I wasn't. Our chances weren't good. The words *snowball in hell* came to mind. But maybe two snowballs have a better chance than one, and a kind of certainty comes from having a purpose, even if the odds aren't good that you'll make it to the finish line. I knew that if I balked—if I ran and hid—then every bad thing that Hyde did would, in some way, be my fault.

You aren't to blame for any of this.

No, I thought. *I'm not to blame. Unless I do nothing.*

"You girls better get going," Charlie said.

Luna looked at me. Her eyes were burning. *I'm coming with you.*

I shook my head. I remembered what she'd said on the roof. That if she were Charlie, I'd have different expectations. That was true, but what could I say? I had a double standard.

Charlie was saying good-bye to Suki. He had his arms around her. Her head was tucked under his chin. He kissed her once, then let her go and walked over to the two of us.

"Get her someplace safe," he said to Luna. "Don't let anything happen."

"She'll be fine on her own," Luna said. "I'm coming with you guys."

Charlie looked stunned. He glanced at me.

I shook my head. "No, you're not."

"Try to stop me."

"I don't have to," I said. "I'll just outrun you."

I thought she was going to hit me.

That's not fair.

Is it fair to Suki if she loses her boyfriend and sister in one night? You haven't seen this thing. We have no chance.

You have a better chance if I come with you.

I didn't think so. But she quickly reminded me of what had just happened back at the apartment.

You had a brain freeze. What if that happens again?

I grasped the handle of my two-handled sword and felt the leather grip twist and creak beneath my fingers. I understood what she was thinking—that my mind often strayed, so I wasn't always in the moment. Well—that wasn't going to happen again.

I thought back to our meeting on the roof, when she'd asked me to teach her how to fight. I didn't have anything to teach her. Fighting wasn't my forte, and it certainly wasn't hers. But I was the fastest and the strongest, so I had the best chance. And if I was going to be some kind of messiah—didn't I have to earn it?

Not by getting yourself killed!

Getting killed wasn't the plan. I wanted to find Detective Baddon's son and bolt. But if Luna came, and she got into trouble, I wouldn't be able to run. I'd have to stay and fight a losing battle. Did she understand? I could see her following my thoughts, but her mind was suddenly closed. I didn't know how she'd done it, but I couldn't hear her anymore.

I handed Charlie my sword. He shot me a puzzled glance. Then I reached up and undid the clasp of my necklace. In nine years, I'd only had it off twice, once to show Luna and once when Vlad took it from me. I slipped the two ends of the chain from around my neck, then took hold of Luna's hand.

Don't you dare give that to me! The sudden eruption from her mind was painful. She tried to pull her hand away.

I grimaced but didn't let go. Instead I put the necklace in her palm and folded her fingers around it. *Give this back to me tomorrow.*

Her eyes closed. A deep breath followed. *Just get the boy and get out. Don't try to fight with Hyde. Promise me you won't.*

I couldn't promise her anything. I had no idea what might happen. I looked at Charlie. He handed back my sword, then nodded that he was ready. It was time to go.

I love you, she thought, and I thought the same.

As she looked up at me, I studied at her face. Her chin, her mouth, her eyes. Every line. Every contour. Just so I wouldn't forget.

She turned and got in the car. Her mind was closed again. A few moments later, she pulled away.

"You didn't even say good-bye," said Charlie. "If I did that, Suki would kill me."

He jumped the ditch at the side of the road and started across the field.

"Come on. We're losing time."

I watched the car disappear down the highway, then followed him. We quickly found Hyde's tracks. They led farther out of town. We ran like two wild wolves. Never had I set such a fierce pace and maintained it for so long. In the city, we were always having to slow down, but now we were in the darkness, with nothing around us but farms and fences and the cool night air. So we reached our destination with a few good hours to spare before sunrise.

"I should have known," Charlie said. "Where else would Hyde go?"

Field had given way to forest. We crossed a road, then came to a parking lot. The sign at the entrance said WARSAW CAVES. I remembered what Mr. Entwistle had said about darkness. For a vampire, it is never total. The moon and stars are too bright. But the deep earth would be different. Dark like the grave.

Charlie pulled up beside me, then reached out and slapped my arm gently with the back of his hand. I looked up. He was pointing to a black van. It was streaked. Poorly painted. The ambulance Mr. Entwistle had stolen from the hospital.

"He's here," Charlie said.

We rushed over. The parking lot wasn't paved. I could see the marks of Mr. Entwistle's boots where he'd stepped out onto the stone dust.

"You smell that?" Charlie asked.

I could. The faint trace of wine and sweat that clung to Mr. Entwistle's body armor.

Charlie looked at the ground carefully. "Do we follow Hyde or Entwistle?"

Did it matter? They would probably take us to the same place. "Mr. Entwistle," I said. "He might still be alive."

Charlie looked doubtful. He took the voulge from his back. I followed his lead and drew my sword. The metal, dark and scarred, made an odd rasping noise, like an angry serpent, when it rubbed against the leather sheath.

"I'll go first," I said.

Charlie nodded, then followed me into the woods.

We weren't running long before Hyde's tracks and Mr. Entwistle's overlapped. And soon after that we caught the smell of blood. The first splattering was across the rocks under our feet. More showed up on the trunk of an oak. Then on the soil and the carpet of needles underfoot. On low-hanging leaves and needles, and the long grasses that grew in clumps where it was too rocky for trees to take root.

"They must have fought for hours," said Charlie.

It was impossible to know. The ground was torn up. Small trees had been uprooted or snapped at the trunk. Rocks were overturned. The bark of the tall pines was scarred. Lichen and moss were shorn loose. Every aspect of the landscape had been altered in some way.

"Have you ever seen so much blood?"

Only in a nightmare.

We followed the smell, and their footprints. We looped back again and again. Soon our own tracks were everywhere.

"We're going in circles," Charlie said.

He was panting heavily. So was I. Neither of us had expected to do so much running. I would happily have traded my sword for an inhaler.

"We must have missed something," I said.

"Yeah. The fight of the century."

We slowed and tried to follow their footprints more carefully. Still, we wound up back at the same rocky clearing.

Charlie shook his head. "We need to do something. If we take much longer to find them, there won't be time to get back before the sun rises."

I took out my phone.

"Who are you calling?"

I scrolled until I found Mr. Entwistle's number, then I hit send. Ophelia had said he wasn't answering his cell. It didn't mean it wouldn't ring.

"What are you doing?"

"Just listen." I tucked my cell into my pocket to muffle the noise. I didn't hear anything. Neither did Charlie. So I started running. After a few moments, I pulled out my cell phone, hit redial, then started moving again. Charlie followed. I listened. A far-off river gurgled gently. The wind swished through pine and oak, cedar and maple. Crickets buzzed, quieting only when our footsteps drew close. I could hear Charlie's breathing, and mine. Our footfalls. Then I heard it. Electronic notes. *Hallelujah.*

Charlie tapped my shoulder. "It's coming from behind that rock."

We were in a clearing. Just one of the many areas where the rock was exposed. We'd passed this way several times already. A large lip of limestone rose up beside us, walling off the clearing from whatever lay behind. No prints led in that direction, but a leap would have taken Mr. Entwistle over the top. Or he might have been thrown. . . .

Charlie zipped past and scampered up the rock face. It was about twelve feet high. Once he cleared the top, he looked back. "Call again."

I did, then bounded up after him. The ringing started again. We followed it down a tree-covered slope to the edges of the Indian River. And there, on the bank, chained to a huge stone, was the body of Mr. Entwistle, lifeless and bloodied, just waiting for the sun.

CHAPTER 39

HYDE'S LAIR

I stuck my sword into the soft earth of the riverbank, then bent to examine Mr. Entwistle. He was chained to the rock so that his hands were stretched out to the sides—as if he'd been crucified. The stone behind him was scorched. Ashes were all over the ground underneath him. His coat was torn in a dozen places. Blood was caked on his face and in his hair. The knife I'd been given by my uncle, the one with the dioxin, was buried right up to the hilt just below his chest. Teeth marks scarred his neck. Were they from Hyde? Mr. Entwistle's words came back to me. That werewolves were blood drinkers, too.

"He's dead, isn't he," Charlie said.

I nodded. The eyes were dull. Dry. Lifeless. I wondered who had actually died here—Mr. Entwistle or the Butcher.

Charlie handed me something: Mr. Entwistle's lucky top hat. Bloodstained, torn, crumpled. Its luck was spent.

"He'll go up like a Roman candle when the sun comes up."

"Unless we can move him in time." To the east, the sky was still dark, but I could tell by the stars that dawn was only an hour or so away. By the look of things, more than a few vampires had been chained here. The rocks on the ground were stained black, the bushes nearby burnt. I reached out and took the pole-arm from Charlie's hand. Then I set about breaking the chains. It was noisy work. And time-consuming. But I was furious, and hammered steel, even the old stuff, is tougher than poured iron, so the links gave way under my assault.

"We'll never get him back to town before the sun comes up."

I agreed. "We'll have to find a cave and wait it out." I handed him the voulge. The blade looked as if I'd taken a can opener to it. Somewhere in Western Europe, a medieval blacksmith was rolling over in his grave.

"This was an antique," said Charlie.

"It still is." I lifted one of Mr. Entwistle's arms and drew it over my shoulder, then picked him up. "You still feeling confident about your plan?"

Charlie shook his head. "Not really. I wasn't counting on the mess of tracks back there. I felt like a mouse in a maze. It really slowed us down. And you just made more noise than a five-man electrical band. Unless Hyde's got six inches of wax in each ear, he'll know we're here."

I figured as much. But the sun was certain death, so we had to get underground. "Don't forget my sword," I said. The tip of the blade was still stuck in the earth. It made the arms and the pommel of the hilt look like a cross. More like a grave marker than a weapon.

Charlie pulled it out and wiped the blade clean in the long grass by the water. "Okay," he said. "Let's see if we can find that boy and scram."

The area around the river was dotted everywhere with caves. It didn't take long for Charlie to find one.

"What do you see?" I asked.

He was peering down a hole that looked wide enough for us to hide in. "Ice." Then he got on his stomach, slid the weapons down in front of him, and crawled into the darkness.

It wasn't at all what I'd expected. I'd only seen caves on television. It turns out Bruce Wayne's Batcave was the Hilton compared to the dump we found ourselves in. It was cold. Moldy. Wet. The ceiling was three feet high, so it was impossible to stand. White ice covered the floor. Within seconds of crawling in, I was soaked.

"Should we leave him here?" Charlie said.

I nodded. Without a system of mirrors, the sunlight wasn't going to get in. And I didn't want to move him farther underground. It would have been too difficult in such a cramped space.

"These weapons are going to be useless in here."

True enough. There wasn't enough space to swing a flashlight, let alone a five-foot sword.

Charlie was eyeing the knife still protruding from Mr. Entwistle's chest. "We should take that."

I felt a bit squeamish about removing it, but he was right, so we worked the blade free. It was wedged between two plates in Mr. Entwistle's armor. I examined the blade. No trace of the dioxin was on it.

Charlie stared the slender wound the knife had left. "You know, you're about the same height as him. A little shorter, maybe, but I bet that armor would fit."

I hadn't considered it. It seemed wrong to take the clothes from a dead man.

"He'd want you to have it."

I nodded. "Yeah, he would."

It wasn't easy stripping down on an icy floor with a roof three feet overhead. And the armor was a bit tight. It amazed me that Mr. Entwistle could move so smoothly with it on. By the time I was finished, my fingers were frozen. Not a good sign. It meant I was tired.

"I've never had more sympathy for penguins than I do right now," said Charlie. He was shivering, "What happens now?"

We had to find the detective's son. We couldn't look outside; the daylight was arriving. That left only one option.

"Let's move," I said. "Maybe we'll find a clue down here."

So we began to crawl. Eventually, we hit a dead end. Charlie started swearing. It poured out of him like gangster rap. I didn't recognize half of the words he used.

"Did we miss something?" he asked.

It was too tight in the cave to turn around, so we had to creep our way backward. It was a good thing neither of us was claustrophobic. There was barely enough room for a mole rat.

"This is worse than a coffin," Charlie said.

Then he found what we had missed. There was a scrape along the rocky floor where an enormous stone had been moved. I would have needed Yoda's help just to lift it. A faint odour of wet fur clung to its surface. Judging by the smell, Hyde had dragged the rock away some time ago, perhaps several days. It exposed an opening barely large enough for us to snake through. The way the wall was angled, the hole was hard to spot when you were approaching from the front.

Charlie looked at me, then down into the shadows below. I knew what he was thinking. We were wet, cold, tired, and underarmed. Anyone with a lick of sense would have stayed put.

"Do you think that boy's still alive?" he asked.

I didn't know. But it didn't matter. If there was even a chance, we had to keep going.

"I'll go first," I said. But Charlie was already ahead of me.

We squeezed through the hole and emerged in a cavern. It was long, as if a giant worm had plowed its way through the solid rock. At least now we could comfortably stand.

"This is more like it," Charlie said. A trickle of water ran along a groove in the rock floor down the center of the tunnel. He put his hand in it, then shook the droplets from his fingers. "Freezing." Then he looked around. "Must have been bigger at one time."

"What do you mean?"

"This little stream. It must have been a full-blown river at one time to have carved this out."

I nodded.

"Can you smell that?"

I could. Like leather and wet dog. It was much stronger here.

"I think it's coming from that way." The tunnel led in two directions. Up to the right or down to the left. He was pointing down.

"Are you ready?" I asked.

He held up the knife. The blade looked purple against the black cave walls. "Yeah," he whispered.

The patter of padded feet echoed up the tunnel. Long strides. Hyde was coming.

I swallowed. "Is it too late to discuss strategies?"

"How about you attack him, and I slip out the back?"

"That's not funny."

"Or you could distract him somehow. Why don't you try dancing? You might as well do it once before you die. Or—die again."

I shook my head. This was no time for jokes. I needed Charlie to put his gladiator face on.

"I think you should try to get around him," I said. "See if you can find the detective's son. I've got the armor. I'll do my best to keep Hyde off your back."

Charlie nodded, then turned to look me squarely in the eyes. His teeth were dropping. "Zack." He didn't bother keeping his voice down. "You can't make him good."

"What do you mean?"

"I know you. You want to make everyone good. You can't. Do you understand? This thing is going to kill us unless we kill it first. All that talk of Entwistle's about villains and evil. I don't care about that stuff. This is about Hyde and us. You can't hesitate. You can't wonder if you're doing the right thing. Attack, attack, attack. Like a berserker. Like Alexander."

I nodded. We were both big on Alexander the Great. Attack, he believed, even in defense. It seemed reasonable. But I'd only been in two fights before. In one I got trounced. In the other I died. Not a great track record. And I remembered clearly what Baoh had told me: *Do not do to others that which is harmful to yourself.* It didn't seem like the best fight strategy. But I had no more time to consider it.

Hyde had arrived.

CHAPTER 40

HELL HATH NO FURY...

The darkness around us was complete. There is no light underground. Not unless you burrow right through the crust to the molten rock below. Hyde was a shadow. A black shape against a black background. But Charlie and I could see him. Our eyes were built for it. He stood to his full height and stepped forward. He looked like a demon. Huge. Taloned. Emanating anger. One eye was swollen shut. The other looked like a hollow pit. A tooth was chipped, and he walked with a slight limp. Mr. Entwistle had done some damage. But for all this, Hyde still smiled. I heard his throat rumble—it might have been a laugh. Then he spoke. This time, the word came out like a raspy gargle. I understood clearly.

Welcome. . . .

Charlie shifted beside me. We were shoulder to shoulder. I understood his strategy. Be like a berserker, those Viking warriors who charged fearlessly into battle. No thoughts of self-preservation. No hesitation. Just relentless assault. Well, that wasn't me. I had no idea who Hyde was. What he wanted. Why he'd done the things he'd done. A part of my mind insisted on understanding.

"Where is the boy?" I asked.

Hyde stopped. His head snaked forward, his good eye narrowed. He squinted at me, then at Charlie. He must have seen something he didn't like. He attacked. I expected a lunge. A charge. Something similar to what Charlie and I had witnessed that first night at the zoo, when he'd ambushed Mr. Entwistle. But Hyde must have understood the value of unpredictability because he did the last thing I'd expected him to do. He jumped straight up. His arm snaked out and he smashed off a stalactite, one of those cone-shaped rocks that was hanging from the top of the tunnel. Then he wound up and hurled it at me.

I twisted and the chunk of rock shot past. It was moving with the speed of a bullet. In the meantime, he closed the space between us. After watching him limp down the tunnel, I hadn't expected him to move so quickly. He pushed Charlie aside, then hit me flush on the chest with his fist. The punch lifted me cleanly off my feet. An instant later, I smashed headfirst into the rock wall behind me. I felt a shock wave run down through my spine. Pain followed, and the kind of paralysis you feel when your nerves are on fire. My eyes swam. I was on my back. A few seconds passed before I could move. I rolled over and pushed myself slowly up to my knees.

I could see Charlie. He was attacking Hyde with reckless abandon. Like a berserker. No thoughts of self-defense. The knife swung back and forth in wild arcs. Had it still been poisoned with dioxin, he might have had a chance. But his opponent was stronger. Faster. And patient.

Hyde backed up, circled, waited. Charlie swung again and again. Then he overextended himself. Hyde shot forward, caught my friend around the wrist with his long fingers, twisted the knife loose, then slammed him against the wall. Bones snapped and Charlie sagged to the ground.

I rose awkwardly to my feet. The back of my head was burning. I could feel blood running down through my hair and along the skin on the back of my neck. My legs were unsteady.

Hyde picked up the knife and came toward me. The sight of him was terrifying. There was death in his eyes. It made my whole body shake.

Get around him, a voice in my head told me. *Stick to the plan. Get the boy.*

It was Luna. She must have come back. The sound of her voice was like a jolt of electricity. I snapped to attention.

Hyde was only a few steps away, limping. It gave me an opening. I ran for the near wall, jumped up off the rocks, and soared past him. It almost worked, but I jumped too high. I'd expected Mr. Entwistle's armor to weigh me down more than it did. My shoulder scraped against the top of the tunnel. It slowed me enough that Hyde was able to spin, reach up, and get a hand around my ankle. Then he introduced me to the floor. My eyes sparked. Spots dotted the darkness. I rolled over onto my back and gasped from the pain.

A new shadow flitted across my vision. Darkness within the darkness. In that instant, I had an epiphany, more sudden than a spark. First, Mr. Entwistle's words came back to me. *Be a saint,* he'd said. Then Baoh's eyeless face drifted through my mind. *Do not do to others that which is harmful to yourself.* Just like that, I knew exactly what to do.

Hyde stood over me. I rose and started shouting as if my pants were on fire. I knew I'd never beat him, but I might have been able to outrun him. He was hurt. It gave me a small edge. But that would mean leaving Charlie and the detective's son if he was here somewhere. That wasn't what saints did. Instead, I kept my eyes on the knife. The handle, too small for his large fingers. The blade—slightly curved, like a half moon that angled to a point. He swung. I stepped back. The knife whistled past. He punched out with his other hand and knocked me flat. I stayed down. It would make things easier. An instant later his fingers closed around my throat. I flailed. I kicked. I pushed and squirmed. It didn't matter. Escape was impossible. But escape was not my plan.

Hyde drew the knife back a fraction of an inch, then his whole body exploded toward me. He aimed for my heart. I managed to deflect his hand low. The point of the blade hit an armor plate and stopped. I kept struggling. He aimed a second time. The knife sparked, but stopped again. Then he got wise and worked the tip of the knife to an area between the platinum plates. He must have done this before in his fight with Mr. Entwistle. An instant later he rammed the blade through. I had just fractions of a second before the pain arrived. Fortunately I'd told my hands what to do ahead of time, so they were already on the move. I grabbed his wrist and hung on. He wasn't going to get the knife free. Not in time. Then the pain paralyzed me. Locked my fingers in place. I squeezed as hard as I could and prayed it was enough. And I kept shouting.

Hyde twisted the knife. My shout became a scream. He pulled. My hands were too weak to stop him. The blade slipped out slowly. Metal on metal. I ran out of air. For an instant, I felt despair. And the fear of failure. I needed to make more noise and couldn't. But I'd held on long enough, and I'd filled his ears with my screams. Mr. Entwistle would have been proud. I had martyred myself—like a saint.

The shadow I'd seen earlier was now beside us. I heard a hiss like that of an aerosol can. Then Hyde jumped back. His hands were over his eyes and face. He snarled. Then I felt Ophelia's hand on my chest.

"Don't budge," she whispered.

I couldn't have moved with a team of oxen helping me. My stomach had a hole in it. I was in pain from head to toe.

Hyde stood. Whatever Ophelia had sprayed in his face was working. His eyes were horrid. Bloodstained yellow. Furious. Then he fell to his knees. His hands rose up to the sides of his head and he let out a howl. He started to change. His arms shortened. Thickened. His fingers, too—from long and clawed to thick sausages. His teeth receded. Hair disappeared. Not just from his body, but from his face. Even the top of his head. But the greatest change was in his legs. They went from long and lean, feet stretched up at the arches, to something that looked like a pair of tree trunks. And there lying on the ground beside us was Detective Baddon.

CHAPTER 41

THE WEREWOLF

Ophelia stared at the detective, unspeaking. I tried to sit up. Her hand was still on my chest.

"Just lie still," she said. "I know it hurts, but it won't be fatal."

"Where's Luna?" I asked.

Ophelia looked surprised for a moment, then glanced over her shoulder. "She's not with me."

"She was here. She must have been. . . ."

Ophelia shook her head.

Had I imagined it? I was certain I'd heard her voice.

Beside us, Detective Baddon moaned.

"What did you do to him?" I asked.

"I used the wolfsbane."

"Will it kill him?"

She shook her head. "No. Wolfsbane is lethal, but not to werewolves. It doesn't kill them. It transforms them. There were teeth marks on the flowers Charlie brought me. I think Hyde chewed it when he needed to turn back into Adam."

Amazing! And more impressive, Ophelia was able to turn this knowledge to our advantage. I guess it was true—knowledge was our best defense. Or in this case, our best offense.

"Did you know it was him?" I asked.

"I wasn't positive, but you never can be." She turned to face the unconscious detective. "But I suspected it was him when his son was taken from the hospital. The boy isn't a vampire, so why would

Hyde care about him? And Adam was nowhere to be found. He would have called or at least put up a fight."

My mind started putting the pieces of the detective's story together. It started by answering the most obvious question. How was this possible? Only one explanation fit with what I knew. The day he'd been attacked in his house, back when he lived in Toronto, it hadn't been a robber with a bottle. The police must have fabricated the story. If they were part of the Underground, they wouldn't have wanted him to know the truth. That he'd been attacked by a werewolf. Perhaps the same one that Maximilian had been hunting. The boy must have been infected, too. It explained his illness. Like his father, he must have been a lycanthrope.

Beside us, Detective Baddon began to stir. He had his hands on his head. As soon as he came to, he started groping around as if looking for something. "Where are my glasses?" he muttered. He was totally confused.

"Are you all right?" Ophelia asked.

At the sound of her voice, the detective jumped as if someone had kicked him. He couldn't see. "Who's there? Where am I?"

"It's Ophelia. And you're underground. You won't be able to see. There's no light."

I heard him take a deep breath. "My leg is killing me. Was I sleepwalking again?"

"Not exactly."

He was on his hands and knees. He stood and started to wobble. Ophelia reached out, took his arm and helped him to sit again.

"Where is my son?"

Ophelia wasn't certain.

"He might be farther down that way." I pointed in the direction Hyde had come.

"Who was that? Is that Charlie?" asked the detective.

"No." Ophelia still had a hand on his shoulder. "No. It's Zack. He's hurt. It would probably be best if you two stay here and let me go ahead."

I hoped she was kidding. I didn't want her to leave me alone with Detective Baddon. What if he changed back? With Charlie lying nearby helpless, and me with a hole where no hole should be, Hyde would find himself with a handy meal right at his feet. Ophelia was obviously thinking the same. She stepped over to me, then bent down and put her mouth next to my ear.

"I'm leaving these with you," she whispered. "Just in case." She put a small aerosol can into my hand. It was the wolfsbane. She must have made a serum of some kind from the monkshood we'd brought home. In my other hand she placed the knife, the one Hyde had rammed into my stomach. Then she stood and started up the tunnel. She stopped when she saw Charlie lying across the small rivulet of water.

"Dear Lord . . ."

I could hear her shifting him carefully. "Is he dead?" I asked.

"No, he's breathing. But the base of his spine has been shattered. . . . Don't worry. We can fix it."

"What about Mr. Entwistle?"

"Did you find him?" she asked.

"Yes. We dragged him into a cave. It's right above us."

"Is he dead?"

"Yes."

"It doesn't matter. We can heal all of you. We just need to get you out of here. Give me a moment. I'll be right back." Then she took off in search of Detective Baddon's missing son.

I clenched my teeth. It was getting harder to hold my stomach together. As the pain intensified, the feeling of weakness in my limbs grew. I was starting to feel cold. This was definitely spoiling my first visit to the Warsaw Caves.

"Is it bad?" Detective Baddon asked.

"No, it just hurts."

"Stomach?"

"Yeah."

He nodded. "I've heard it's the worst place to get shot."

I could imagine at least one place that would top it, but I kept that to myself. Still, there had to be something to what he'd said. Whenever a samurai committed suicide, he sliced his belly open because the pain was off the charts. It was the only way to restore lost honor. I guess that was more or less what I'd done. Committed a kind of suicide. But Ophelia had arrived just in time.

The detective was still rubbing his neck. Funny how wrong I'd been about him. About Hyde's alter ego. I'd imagined someone ten feet tall. But Detective Baddon was probably three hundred pounds of solid muscle, most of it in his legs. We hadn't considered that he might be Hyde. He probably hadn't considered it himself.

"How did I get here?" he asked.

I took a few breaths to ready my body for speech. "You ran."

The detective didn't understand. He rubbed a hand over his head. "So I *was* sleepwalking."

I shook my head. Pain ran down my neck and back.

"Where did you say Mr. Entwistle was?" he asked.

I didn't get to answer. Detective Baddon started coughing. I heard him muttering something about the air not being right. His voice was off. I turned. He was standing. Stumbling. His hands were pressed against the sides of his head. Then he started to change. His eyes got bigger. Blacker at the center. They yellowed, then focused on the canister in my hand.

There's more than one way to trigger a transformation, Mr. Entwistle had said. Obviously, whatever it was that made Detective Baddon turn, it was in this tunnel. As I watched, he lengthened. Thinned. His teeth descended. Hair rose on his head and arms and face. He looked over to where Charlie was lying beside him. He smiled, then he stepped toward me.

I raised the can and pointed it at his face, but before I could press the nozzle, he turned and fled. I took a deep breath. Would it be an overstatement to say I'd just dodged a bullet? Maybe—but that same bullet was heading straight for Ophelia.

I rolled over onto my side. Blood from the wound in my stomach mixed with the thin stream of water on the tunnel floor. It must have been worse than Ophelia thought. I was weak. Too weak to stand. I started crawling.

"Ophelia . . . Ophelia!" I shouted her name as loudly as I could. The effort caused me to black out. Like a sleeper who nods and wakes up, I came to as my head sank. It happened twice more. "Ophelia!"

She'd be trapped with Hyde by herself. Her only defense was the canister of wolfsbane in my hand.

I reached Charlie. Ophelia had straightened his body so it lay flat and straight on the ground. His breathing came in shallow fits. My movement and shouting must have roused him from unconsciousness. His eyes fluttered open. He saw me and groaned.

"How did we do?" he gasped. The words were hard to make out.

"Not well."

"I feel cold . . . I can't move."

"Your back is broken."

He seemed to take this news remarkably well. "Hyde?"

"He's going after Ophelia."

His eyes started to water. He must have known we were finished. "Any more good news?"

I laughed, then coughed up a mouthful of blood. "Yeah. I'm afraid I'm going to have to kill you."

His head moved just a little. "What are friends for?"

My teeth were down. One of them was broken. I rolled up Charlie's sleeve.

"Wait," he said. "Are you sure this won't kill you?"

It hadn't with Luna. I still didn't understand why. But what did I have to lose?

Charlie started sputtering. Tears were spilling out of his eyes. They were crimson. "Don't hesitate this time. Do what you have to do."

I wasn't going to argue. Instead, I drank. Charlie gasped. I took what I needed and left him with a slow pulse. I told myself this was necessary. That one of us had to be strong or Hyde would finish us all. Permanently. It didn't change the feeling of wrongness about it.

But what choice did I have? My stomach was in knots. Actually, it was in sliced-up knots. They started to twist and burn. The pain in my chest and limbs disappeared. So did my doubt—the feeling that this was a mistake. Ophelia was alone with that thing. Was he evil? Did he deserve to die? It didn't matter now. Not to me. So I picked up the can and knife and sprinted down the tunnel.

CHAPTER 42

CAVE-IN

I ran down a steep slope and around a corner. I could have tracked Hyde by his scent but it wasn't necessary. He was shouting. The sound was ferocious.

Where is my son?

His voice was coming from a smaller enclave that branched from the main tunnel. I ducked inside. The entrance was low and braced with thick logs. So were the walls. It looked like a cave-in that hadn't finished collapsing.

Hyde was holding Ophelia off the ground. He had one hand around her neck. In the other was a hospital blanket.

Where is he?

His voice was quiet now, but still terrifying. He could easily have killed her, and she must have known it.

What are you waiting for? Tell him where his son is, I thought.

But she didn't know.

Hyde turned my way. He saw the canister in my hand.

Drop that.

"No." I ran straight for him.

I was a terrible poker player. I couldn't bluff. Some people can hide what they think and feel. I can't. So the only way I could bluff was to not bluff. If he snapped Ophelia's neck, she'd die. But I could bring her back. And if he did that, I'd blast him with the wolfsbane and turn him back into his human self. He couldn't allow that. As Hyde he was invincible. As Adam Baddon, he wasn't.

He thought Ophelia knew where his son was. He knew I didn't. That made me expendable. So he did what I expected him to do. He attacked me.

I assumed he'd drop his son's blanket. It was useless to him, or so I thought. But instead, he flicked it at my face, the way a kid flicks a towel. It snapped like a whip over my eye. It didn't slow me down, but instinctively I turned my head, so I didn't see him kick out with his leg until it was too late. I was raising my hand so I could depress the nozzle of the canister when his foot hit my chest. It knocked me back toward the cave entrance. The canister flew from my hand. It hit the rock wall and ripped open with a loud pop. The poison leaked out onto the floor. It was useless now.

Hyde growled. Then he turned back to Ophelia.

Where is my son? Where?

My nose and ears told me the answer. I smelled disinfectant. And I heard the careful steps of heavy boots. I should have guessed. I rose to my feet as noisily as I could, coughing and scuffing my shoes against the stone floor. I even pretended to slip, scattering loose pebbles across the ground. It was loud enough that Hyde didn't hear my uncle until he'd ducked inside the room. Maximillian smelled the way he always did when he got back from the hospital—like cleanser. He'd traded in his gray skin for white. His face was so drawn and pale it practically glowed in the dark. But his eyes were alert and intense, his pupils wide. And his timing was perfect—as always. He had Hyde's son cradled in one arm. The boy was unconscious, his breathing irregular. Shallow. Strained. In Maximilian's other hand was a gun. It was pointing at the boy's head, right at the base of his skull. Before anyone could blink, he cocked the gun. The trigger was already pulled back all the way. If anyone breathed on him too heavily, his thumb would slip, the hammer would slam into the cap of the next bullet, and the boy would die.

"Put her down and step back." my uncle said.

Hyde stood to his full height. His eyes moved between his son and the man who was about to shoot him. He roared.

Maximilian kept his face expressionless, his eyes level. He pushed the tip of the gun barrel more firmly against the back of the boy's head. "Whether he lives or dies is up to you. Now put her down and move back."

Was this a bluff? My uncle knew the stakes. He was a cunning man. Obviously smart enough to figure out that Detective Baddon was also Hyde—that they were two halves of a single person. Like Ophelia, he must have figured things out at the hospital.

"My friends and I are walking out of here," my uncle said. "I'll take your boy back to the hospital. You can visit him there, as Adam. I won't deal with you."

Hyde growled.

Baddon is weak. How can he protect the boy from others like you?

Maximilian stared at Hyde's face. What was he looking for? Some sign of reason or compassion?

"Is he in there?" my uncle asked. "Can Adam hear this? Does he know about you?"

Hyde didn't answer. He probably didn't know. But I'd seen Detective Baddon's face and heard his confusion after his transformation back in the tunnel. It was genuine. He didn't know about this—that he was Hyde. A beast that hunted vampires.

Leave my son and I'll let you go.

"I won't turn him over to you. I'll turn him over to Adam. That's the best offer you're going to get."

Hyde glared at him. Seconds passed. It felt like forever. Then he snarled and let Ophelia drop to the floor. Once her feet were set, he turned her toward the entrance. I couldn't believe it. That he was agreeing to this. But he wasn't. It was just a distraction. As soon as she moved in front of him, he pushed her hard at my uncle. Then he lunged. It was a bold move, but it made sense. My uncle wouldn't kill an innocent child, and Hyde must have known it.

But people always underestimated Maximilian. Was it because he was human? Because he had one foot in the grave? We were all wrong about that. He had both feet in the grave. I don't know if it was because of my fear, or the desperation of our situation, but my mind wasn't asking itself the questions it should have about him. Where did his confidence come from? The guy was underground with a bunch of vampires strong enough to knock his teeth out through his ears, and he wasn't a bit intimidated. Most humans were afraid of the dark. How could Maximilian even see?

I got my answer as soon as Hyde attacked him. Maximilian dropped the boy and fired a round that grazed Hyde's shoulder. In the next instant, his gun got knocked away and he was pushed back through the entrance of the lair. Even though Hyde was faster, Maximilian's movements had changed. Nothing like a stone golem. He was fluid. Perfectly balanced. Like a vampire. Don't ask me how he'd done it, but he was one of us now. I should have guessed that he'd do this. Mr. Entwistle had given me the first clue when he'd told me and Charlie to focus on what a person wanted. Maximilian wanted to live. To hunt vampires. This was the only way. Biotherapeutics, he'd said. Killing cancer cells with a virus. Well, he'd used the heavyweight champion of contagions. My guess was he'd taken my blood—in the hospital maybe. But I suppose it didn't matter how he'd done it. What mattered was that he'd dropped Hyde's son, and so we'd lost our leverage.

But my uncle always had a plan B. He put it into action as he stumbled back into the main tunnel, still reeling from Hyde's assault. Not a bad bit of multitasking. He was a talented hunter. Always prepared. And he loved his toys. Guns and Tasers and things that go bang in the night. I shouldn't have been surprised to see the detonator appear in his hand. He'd used one just like it to stop Vlad. A year ago, he'd blown out some windows and let a little sunlight into our lives. This time, when he pressed the magic button, the wooden supports around us exploded. He must have done a quick wiring job while the rest of us were out in the tunnel, fighting and talking and stumbling around.

Without the wooden timbers in place, gravity went to work. A huge column of broken stone started to slide down. I leapt for the opening. So did Ophelia. We were close enough to make it easily, and my uncle would have known that. But as always, Hyde was fastest. He grabbed us both, hurled us back, and used the momentum to throw himself into the entrance. It put him directly in the path of the largest chunk of falling rock. The weight of it was unimaginable. It would have flattened Superman. But Hyde stopped it. Or slowed it. He was forced to his knees. He had his arms straight over his head, but the immensity of the stone forced him to lower it across the back of his shoulders. He crouched across the doorway, his son on the ground in front of him. The two were blocking the exit.

Then Hyde started to change. It started in his arms and legs. His hair began to vanish. It was the wolfsbane. The shattered canister was right beside him, the air around it fragrant with the smell of monkshood, the flowers Ophelia had used to make the poison. If Hyde became human, we'd be doomed. Buried in a grave of stone and dust. The rock column forced him onto his hands and knees. His son was trapped underneath him. He was like a bridge. And he was breaking.

Hurry . . . your knife. Hurry!

He was looking more like Detective Baddon with each passing moment.

I still had the blade in my hand. It was well-balanced with a keen edge, but was about as useful for stopping a rockslide as a handful of pudding.

Cut yourself. Hurry.

Was he serious? Before I could come up with an answer, Ophelia snatched the knife, dragged it over the palm of her hand, and stuck it under Hyde's nose. He started to change back.

Blood might do it, too. Bring out the inner beast. For all I know, it's different for each of them. But it doesn't have to be a full moon.

Mr. Entwistle had said this to Charlie and me. Vampire blood was Hyde's trigger. That must have been why Detective Baddon said the air in the tunnel wasn't right. And why he had changed in the hospital. I'd cut my wrist on a piece of metal above the ceiling as I was leaving his son's room.

Hyde growled. The rock was crushing him. He raised one hand. I assumed he was trying to get out of the way, but he grabbed Ophelia by the arm instead.

My boy . . . get him out.

The words were scarcely louder than his breath. He could barely get them out. The strain of holding up the stone avalanche had every vein in his neck bulging. He couldn't even raise his head. His eyes were glued on his son.

Not his fault . . .

Ophelia nodded. Sympathy was one of her strong points. It made her the perfect person to ask.

Hyde let her go. She crouched and slipped past. Then she turned and pulled his son free. I wondered if this was going to be my tomb. If he'd let me leave as well.

Get out.

I couldn't believe what I was hearing.

Adam chose you. . . . Now go.

Adam chose you. What was that about? That he'd asked me to look after his son—to infect him? There wasn't time to ask. I dove for the opening. My head was barely out in the tunnel when I felt Ophelia's hands pulling at my arms. She helped me to my feet. The boy was lying on the ground beside her.

I looked around for my uncle. He was gone. A thick cloud of dust obscured my view ahead. I heard a loud crack above. The cave roof was shifting.

"Come on," Ophelia said.

She bent and scooped Hyde's son off the ground. As she straightened back up, I slid my hands underneath him so he was draped across my arms. I nodded, and we raced back up the tunnel.

CHAPTER 43

THE PROPHECY REVISITED

Ophelia and I didn't get far. As we rounded the corner, we could see my uncle ahead. He was supporting Charlie with one hand and had a bag of blood in the other. Luna was crouched beside them.

"Come on!" Maximilian said. "Or we're going to spend the next hundred years digging up your friends."

The air was charged with panic. Charlie was unconscious and most of the blood was dribbling out of his mouth. As Ophelia and I approached, my uncle glanced over.

"We're okay," I said.

Luna stood. *Thank God.*

You can say that again.

She slipped over beside me. I set the detective's son on the ground and Luna and I sort of melted into one another.

I was sure I'd heard you. That you were here somewhere.

She looked at me and smiled. *Did you think an army of werewolves could have kept me away?*

I should have known better than to underestimate her resolve. *How did you find us?*

I drove back and followed the trail. Why did you guys run in circles for so long?

I wasn't sure how to answer that. We certainly hadn't meant to.

I was climbing over that pile of rocks when I heard your voice in my mind. You were talking to Charlie. You must have been moving away from me because your thoughts faded almost right away. But it led me to that cave.

She thought of Mr. Entwhistle and a wave of pity spilled out of her. But it was all right—we were going to make it out now. All we'd need was more blood, then we could restore his ruined body. Charlie's, too.

I heard your voice, I told her. *I wasn't sure if I'd imagined it because I didn't hear you again.*

I don't really understand any of this, she thought. *When I got closer to you, I could feel your panic. I was above, and tried to reach out—to keep you moving, but I wasn't sure if you could hear me. After that, once you got slammed to the ground, I couldn't get through. And it took me a while to find the hole that led down here.*

She was standing beside me, with her arms wrapped around my waist. She pulled me a bit closer. *I'm sorry it took so long.*

I thought of what had happened with Hyde. How he had closed in on me with the knife—his mind bent on murder. I'd frozen.

Your timing was perfect, I told her.

She looked away. *I know you're exaggerating, but I appreciate it.*

I wasn't exaggerating. If she hadn't restored my focus at the moment Hyde attacked me, things might have turned out differently. But it looked as if we were all going to be okay. I had Ophelia and my uncle to thank, as well. She was hovering over the detective's son. Maximilian was trying to get Charlie to swallow more blood.

"How did you know where we were?" I asked him.

Maximilian lay Charlie flat. "The transponder."

Transponder? Then I remembered. I reached back and felt a small bump on the top of my shoulder blade. My uncle had put it there with his Teletoon gun during our conversation in the hospital.

He looked up at me. Relief washed over his face. Deep lines of worry around his eyes and mouth disappeared. "I expected you to come out right behind me. When you didn't, I nearly had a heart attack. I came back here to get reinforcements."

"It was Hyde," Ophelia said. "He stopped us."

"How is the boy?" Maximilian asked.

"He's alive," Ophelia said. "But weak."

"How did you get him out?"

"Hyde held the door."

My uncle looked surprised. He was about to ask another question, but was interrupted by Charlie. He started to hack and cough. A fine mist of air and blood exploded from his mouth. Then he began to convulse.

"Get your hands on his shoulders," Maximilian shouted.

Ophelia and Luna took his arms and pinned him to the rock. I steadied one of his legs, my uncle took the other. Then my friend's eyes popped open. His teeth were down. He looked around at all of us.

"What are you doing to me?"

He seemed to be past the worst of it, so the others rose to give him space. He wiped blood from around his mouth. The bruises on his face were clearing. A second later they were entirely gone. He reached for my hand so I could pull him to a sitting position. "What happened?"

I started to answer but he waved for me to stop. "I need more blood."

"I have more in my car," Maximilian said.

"Where did you get it?" I asked.

"I stole it."

I thought about what Inspector Johansson had said. That shipments of blood had disappeared from the Underground. I'd assumed this was Hyde's doing, but my uncle must have been behind it. I guess it was a good thing. I was going to need a few gallons myself.

I felt Luna's hand on my arm. *I have something to give you first.* She took out the necklace. The two parts were attached, the chains woven together. She gently separated her crescent from my silver moon, then slipped the chains apart. I bowed my head and she clasped the necklace into place. I felt her hand on my chest. She was beaming.

Now everything is as it should be.

Not quite, I thought. I looked down at the boy. He was still un-well. His breathing was shallow. And Mr. Entwistle was still in the cave above.

My uncle moved over beside us, then pointed down the tunnel.

"I came in another way. That direction. It would be faster, unless the path is blocked."

I looked back the way we'd come, but there was so much dust in the air, I couldn't see far.

"I'm sorry about what happened in there," he added. "One thing your father and I learned the hard way—nothing ever goes according to plan."

"We would have made it out if he hadn't taken hold of us so quickly," Ophelia said. "I've never seen anything so fast. I was certain that cave was going to be our tomb."

"Well, you wouldn't have been buried long," my uncle replied. He was looking at her intently. Something was wrong. I'd been so focused on Charlie, I hadn't noticed, but I could see it now in her eyes.

"What is it?" I asked her.

"Can you go back and get Hyde? He might still be alive."

"Where is he?" Charlie asked. He started to cough again. He tried to stand up but couldn't manage it.

My uncle offered him a hand. Charlie paused, then he took it and rose unsteadily to his feet. I couldn't help but smile. My uncle and Charlie. Both vampires.

Hyde's son stirred. His breathing was still ragged. He looked awful. Pale. Emaciated.

"Do you know what's wrong with him?" I asked.

"Later," said Ophelia. "You have to save Adam. Quickly."

"Are you certain that's what we want to do?" my uncle asked. "I know Adam was a good man."

Charlie turned and nearly fell over. "Adam? You mean Detective Baddon? What are you talking about? What is he doing here?"

"Detective Baddon was Hyde," I explained.

Charlie looked at all of us. Then at Maximilian. "I'll be

damned . . ." Charlie's surprise quickly turned to alarm. He looked at the dying boy lying on the tunnel floor. "That means he's Hyde's son."

As soon as he said this, I had my second epiphany of the night. A personal best. I looked at Ophelia. She understood, too. She was crouched over the boy, her finger gently touching his neck. She was taking his pulse.

"Go," she said.

I turned and started running.

"The whole tunnel is unstable," my uncle said.

"Then hurry," I shouted back. We had to save Adam. I started sprinting.

My uncle was right on my heels. "This makes no sense."

It made perfect sense to me. But I knew the prophecy. And I knew that I wasn't the messiah all the proselytizing vampires were waiting for.

As a kid, I never knew my father was a vampire hunter. To me, he was just Dad. The man who read me bedtime stories, who took me on archaeological digs, who made popcorn for *Saturday Night at the Movies* and did all the other things good fathers do. He was patient. Gentle. Kind. He only yelled at me once in my life—for going into the closet where he kept his gun. But he must have had another side because he was lethal. As a man, and as a vampire hunter, people praised him to the skies, and I never got tired of hearing it. But despite what was said, he couldn't have been the greatest vampire hunter ever. That honor went to Hyde. And his son was a blood drinker, a werewolf. If *he* became an orphan, he would be the one the prophecies spoke of, not me. And if he inherited his father's habit of killing vampires, of feeding on them, we might soon find ourselves on an endangered species list.

A shepherd or a scourge. A saint or a demon. The messiah would be one of these things. I couldn't let him become an orphan.

I rounded the corner with my uncle beside me. The air was thick with dust, the tunnel floor treacherous from all the fallen rocks. We scrambled to the entrance of Hyde's cave. He was still there, but the rock had slipped farther and forced one of his shoulders to the ground. His knees were underneath him. The rock seemed to have settled. I had no idea how we would get him out.

"Quickly, that rock over there," my uncle shouted. "Help me move it."

A large chunk of stone had collapsed from the ceiling outside the chamber. It wasn't in the way. I didn't understand why we should bother with it. I heard more cracking above and the roof fell down a few more inches.

"We'll set it beside him to hold up the stone, then try to slide him out."

That made sense. I nodded, then put my hands under it to test its weight. I wouldn't have been able to move it on my own, but with my uncle's help, we slid it into place beside Hyde. A few seconds later Luna arrived.

Hyde watched us. He was nearly pinned to the floor. Blood was dripping from his mouth and nose and ears. We were almost there. Then Luna took hold of my arm and yanked me backward. I wasn't expecting it, so I stumbled, arms flailing. Our feet got tangled up and I hit the ground on my back. Air shot from my lungs. Luna landed right beside me, but I didn't hear her. All sound was drowned out by a crack so loud, I'm sure it echoed right down to the earth's core. Then the roof of the tunnel at the entrance to Hyde's den plummeted to the floor.

CHAPTER 44

BLOOD DEBT

A cloud of dust shot past Luna and me. Tons of rock continued to fall. She took hold of my arm. She was shouting in my ear. The shock and noise had turned my eardrums into sirens. Nothing could get past their shrill ringing. But her thoughts were clear.

Get moving!

I stood, stunned. We'd come so close. I just assumed we'd get everyone out. That the story would have a happy ending. But that wasn't going to happen. Now my uncle and Hyde were buried together under a mountain of stone.

Luna started hauling me up the passage. *I don't want you to join them!*

I kept looking back over my shoulder through the hail of rock and dust and small stones, hoping I might see my uncle emerge, but it didn't happen. There was nothing I could do. We stumbled awkwardly, side by side, while the earth shook and the caves collapsed. We didn't stop until we reached the others. Then Ophelia took the lead. I carried Detective Baddon's son. Luna helped Charlie. The ground lurched. The rock above us cracked. It was as if the world were falling apart.

We hadn't run far up when Charlie stopped. "Entwistle's still up there," he shouted.

The tunnel roof lurched and fell. We barely got out of the way. I started to turn back, but Ophelia took hold of my arm and dragged me away. Her grip was iron. So was her voice: "I'm not losing you."

Eventually we reached a more stable section. The noise was far behind us. Then the tunnel roof began to slope downward, forcing us to crouch. We came to a fork. Ophelia reached up and touched the rock, then pointed to the right, where the ceiling hung even lower. She and the others dropped to their hands and knees. I had to do a crab walk with the boy balanced on my chest. I would have scraped my back raw if it hadn't been for Mr. Entwistle's body armor. Then the air grew fresher, and over our ragged breathing I could hear the babble of water. Not a trickle, but the Indian River. A few minutes later, we approached a cave dimly lit with morning light. Everyone stopped.

"Where are we?" Luna asked.

I'm not sure if anyone answered. I was squinting ahead, wondering where we would go. Ahead was daylight. And the river. A bulletproof aquatic car would have been handy.

"I guess we'll have to wait things out down here," Ophelia said. She retreated to a darker corner. We all followed. I lay down and practically sank into the cold stone. Relief calmed every nerve. Then I felt a warm presence beside me—Luna.

We made it.

We had. But others hadn't. Mr. Entwistle. My uncle. I wondered if there was some way we could dig them out. Heal them. But not Hyde. He was finished. A few days ago, this would have been cause for celebration. Music. Fireworks. Dancing in the streets. But his death seemed more like a tragedy now. Adam Baddon was a good man who loved his son. Now his boy was an orphan. *Perhaps the orphan.* The one who would control the future of our kind.

"What are we going to do?" I asked.

Ophelia was sitting up against the cave wall, staring at me. At the boy in my arms. "We're going to survive," she said.

Adam's son stirred again. His breathing came in short gasps.

"Do we even know his name?" Charlie asked.

Luna shook her head. "He doesn't sound so good."

I glanced at Ophelia. Her eyes were intense. Nervous.

"Can you help him?" I asked.

"I don't know." Something in her voice was off.

The words were barely out of her mouth when the boy stopped breathing.

I looked around at everyone. "What do we do?"

No one answered.

I grabbed his wrist. I'd seen doctors do this on television. I searched for a pulse, but couldn't find one, so I put my head on his chest. His heartbeat was weak. Irregular. It sped up to a frantic pace. Then it stopped.

"Is he dead?" Charlie asked.

I wasn't sure.

Luna was right beside me.

Do something!

But she didn't know what to do. Neither did I. I looked over at Ophelia. She hadn't moved. Her face was a blank mask. I stared into her eyes. They were out of focus.

"What do we do?" I asked.

She didn't respond.

"What do we do?"

My voice brought her out of it. She looked at me. Her face was uncertain. Scared.

"He's just a boy," I said.

"He's more than that," Ophelia replied. "We'll pay for this."

We'd already paid. Three lives had just been lost. And we had promised Hyde we'd look after his son. It was the price of our freedom.

Ophelia handed me the knife. She'd had a bad feeling about it. No wonder. It had killed Mr. Entwistle. It had almost killed me.

"It's fitting that it would be you," she said.

I steadied my hands and pulled the blade across my open palm. I gasped and made a fist, then moved my hand until it was overtop of the boy's mouth. Beads of scarlet blood dripped down inside.

"Don't touch him," Ophelia warned. "If he bites you, or infects you, you'll die."

After a few seconds, she put her hands over his heart and compressed his chest. She did this several times, then moved my hand away from his mouth and started pressing on his diaphragm.

"You need to breathe into his mouth," Luna said.

I agreed. I'd seen CPR on TV before. That was always what they did—blew oxygen straight into the patient's lungs.

"Don't go near his mouth," Ophelia snapped.

She continued to press down on his trunk, forcing the air out of his chest. Then she went back to compressing his heart. While she did this, I dribbled more of my blood into his mouth. While I watched and bled, his teeth lengthened. Then he tried to bite me. His movements were so sudden, Luna shrieked. I jerked my hand away. The boy was still unconscious. He'd done it in his sleep.

Ophelia moved back. I kept my eyes on the boy. His breathing strengthened. His face started to change. His blond hair lengthened. His forehead stretched back. His ears sloped to two sharp points. He looked almost elflike. Tiny, with fine features. A few breaths later, he started to change back.

"What is happening?"

Ophelia shook her head. "I don't know."

"Was he dead?" Luna asked. "Did he just die and come back?"

I nodded. He had. Just like me. Like the messiah. *A saint or a scourge . . .*

Charlie stumbled over. He was still unsteady on his feet. "Your blood did that? Does this mean he feeds on vampires, like his father—like Hyde?"

It appeared that way.

My best friend was incredulous. "Why did you save him?"

What could I say? For lots of reasons. Because he was an orphan, like me. Because I had failed to save his father, Adam. But mostly because Hyde was right, none of this was the boy's fault. I put my hand near the side of his neck and felt his pulse with the back of my fingers. It was strong now. Steady.

What does this mean? Luna asked me.

I thought about it—what the boy might become if we weren't careful.

It means when he wakes up, we'd better be really, really nice to him.

CHAPTER 45

IRON SPIKE ENTERPRISES—ONE MONTH LATER

We stood in the room, the four of us, shoulder to shoulder, not speaking. Even Charlie was dumbstruck. It lasted about ten seconds. That might have been his personal best.

"Sick!" he said. "Did you know about all of this?"

Not exactly.

Luna nudged me. *Out loud,* she reminded me.

"No," I said. "But I probably should have known it would be here. He had to keep this stuff someplace."

We were in Montreal, at Iron Spike Enterprises, my uncle's business headquarters. The building was practically a skyscraper. Every floor had its hidden secrets, but this room was pay dirt.

"So all of this is yours now?" Suki asked. She and Charlie were standing side by side, his arm over her shoulder, her arm around his waist. With each passing day she was more like the Suki of old. Confident. Bubbly. Fun. Spending time with Charlie had done her wonders. It might have been the one reason Dr. Abbott let her stay with us. Love cures all ills, as they say. It had done wonders for Charlie, too. I hadn't seen him this happy since last summer.

"Technically, the whole inheritance is in a trust," I told Suki. "But we can use whatever we need."

I looked around the room. We'd been doing a tour with Ophelia, floor by floor, room by room. It had ended here, in a weapons depot. All of my uncle's military equipment guns and grenades were here.

"Do you know what all of this stuff does?" Luna was staring at a rack of weighted nets that looked like spiderwebs.

Not all of it. Not yet.

She nudged me again.

I cleared my throat. "It looks like some kind of electrified netting."

I heard a quiet "Wow!" leak from Charlie's mouth.

If he thought this was impressive, the numbers in my uncle's bank account would have floored him.

Luna was playing with the charm on her necklace. She looked at me and winked. *A rich vampire messiah. Do I know how to pick 'em, or what?*

I laughed. But I wasn't rich yet. I'd get my inheritance when I turned eighteen. If I lived that long . . .

Don't be such a pessimist, she chided. *You have some pretty good help here.*

Pretty and good, I thought.

"Where did Ophelia go?" Suki asked. She was rubbing her neck. I half expected to see some teeth marks there, but both she and Charlie seemed to have agreed that it would be better to wait than risk infecting her now. Hyde was gone, but the danger of the Coven hadn't passed.

"She went to check on Vincent," Luna said.

Vincent was the detective's son. He was still in a coma. We'd moved him to the second floor of the building. My uncle had a full medical lab there, so he was wired up to an IV and a slew of machines that monitored his heart rate, blood sugar, and oxygen levels. The situation was stable, at least medically, but the rest was a bit messy. Issues surrounded the inheritance of his father's house and belongings, including the contents of the storage shed we'd broken into— the place where we'd found the wolfsbane. And Vincent still had family. Aunts, uncles, cousins, grandparents. Eventually they would have to be informed about his condition, but we thought it best to keep him hidden until we had a better understanding of whether he would be a danger to them. Or to us. He was in for some bad news when he awoke, and we all dreaded having to tell him. Ophelia was particularly troubled.

"Why the long face, Romeo?" Charlie asked. He'd wandered over to a rack that housed a number of impressive-looking assault rifles, and something that might have belonged on the top of a tank.

Why the long face? I didn't want to answer this question. We'd just done a tour of my uncle's garage. He had a collection of street racers and a number of motorcycles. And older prototypes of the rocket car that was now our main form of transportation. But I hadn't seen what I'd hoped to find—some construction equipment.

As soon as this thought passed through my head, I felt Luna close herself off. It kept me from hearing her thoughts. Our abilities were evolving. We could still communicate without speaking, but over the last month we'd learned to control what the other could hear. Whatever she was thinking now, she wanted to keep to herself. I understood. She thought I was in denial. They all did. Even Ophelia. I told myself that staying hopeful was better than grieving, but I'm not sure I really had a choice. My heart was just being stubborn. It couldn't accept that Mr. Entwistle and my uncle were really gone. They were vampires. All we needed to do was move a few million tons of rock from a very public provincial park, then give them some of the blood my uncle had pilfered from the Underground. There was enough to fill a swimming pool.

Charlie must have sensed what was on my mind. He looked away. Like the others, he expected me to be sad and thought it was odd that I wasn't, but I still wanted my happy ending.

"Is the body armor ready?" he asked.

I shook my head. "Not yet. A few more weeks."

"I thought Entwistle's stash was impressive, but this is the mother lode."

I had to agree. In the days before we came here, the five of us had toured Mr. Entwistle's safe houses in Peterborough. He'd kept extensive files, which included a contact that made specialized military equipment. We'd ordered suits for everyone. We also found blue-prints for an Abrams tank he'd customized. But it was located in a hidden garage we hadn't yet discovered.

"You never answered my question," Charlie said. "Why the long face?"

I had a lot on my mind.

Luna smiled and slipped her hand into mine.

"Just thinking," I said.

"Thinking or worrying?"

"A bit of both."

Charlie surveyed the room. There was enough equipment here to outfit the Rebel Alliance. "How are we going to learn how to use all this stuff?"

"There's a shooting range on the third floor," Suki said. "You guys were in the gym when we found it. We could practice there."

I couldn't believe it. A shooting range. Charlie and I had missed that part of the tour. The exercise equipment in my uncle's fitness room was so impressive, we'd stayed behind to try it out when the girls went ahead. This place was like a spy school. The only things missing were the students.

Luna laughed. *Not anymore.*

"What is it with you two?" Charlie asked. "Always laughing to yourselves like that."

Luna raised her hands as if it were nothing. I didn't know what to say.

"All right, keep your secrets." Charlie wandered over to the far wall. A piece of equipment that might have fallen from space was hanging from the ceiling. "What is this thing? Some kind of pho-ton torpedo?"

It looked more like a futuristic coffin to me, but I had no idea. "The equipment lists and operation manuals are all in the library," I said.

We'd hit that earlier in the tour. I was anxious to get back. I had noticed among the shelves some notebooks that might have been journals. If my uncle kept a log like my father, it might have some information about the Coven of the Dragon. It was time to find out how much trouble we were in.

"Well, let's go," said Suki. "This place freaks me out. I'm afraid to breathe too hard. Something might blow up." She cozied up beside Charlie and took hold of his hand.

"Where to?" Charlie asked. "There's a home theater on the fourth floor. I wonder what's playing."

"I was leaning toward a swim," she answered. "Ophelia says there's a pool on the roof beside a penthouse apartment."

"I think we should go back to the library," I said. "Check the catalogs and see what all this stuff does."

Charlie looked at me in disbelief. "Zack, it will take weeks to read through all that."

"Yeah, so we'd better get started."

As soon as I said this, my mind drifted back to the safe house where Charlie and I had been caught by the police. Where we'd found the letter with the prophecies, and the handwritten notes—that the End of Days was coming and that knowledge was our best defense.

Charlie looked at me. He seemed to know what I was thinking. He glanced around the room, then pulled a canister from a crate beside him. It was a thermite bomb. A smile creased his face.

"Knowledge is your best defense, huh? Well, not anymore."